I0645938

THE
UNCLE ABNER
MYSTERIES

THE UNCLE ABNER MYSTERIES

MELVILLE DAVISSON POST

COACHWHIP PUBLICATIONS

Landisville, Pennsylvania

The Uncle Abner Mysteries, by Melville Davisson Post.
Copyright © 2010 Coachwhip Publications

Uncle Abner, Master of Mysteries first published 1918.
"The Devil's Track" first published in *Country Gentleman* in 1927.
"The God of the Hills" first published in *Country Gentleman* in 1927.
"The Dark Night" first published in *Country Gentleman* in 1927.
"The Mystery at Hillhouse" first published in *Country Gentleman* in 1928.

ISBN 1-61646-016-4
ISBN-13 978-1-61646-016-7

Cover Image: Fog on Split Rail Fence © Judy Kennamer

CoachwhipBooks.com

All Rights Reserved. No part of this publication may be reproduced, stored in a retrieval system or transmitted in any form or by any means—electronic, mechanical, photocopy, recording or any other—except for brief quotations in printed reviews, without the prior permission of the author or publisher.

CONTENTS

1

The Doomdorf Mystery

The pioneer was not the only man in the great mountains behind Virginia. Strange aliens drifted in after the Colonial wars. All foreign armies are sprinkled with a cockle of adventurers that take root and remain. They were with Braddock and La Salle, and they rode north out of Mexico after her many empires went to pieces.

I think Doomdorf crossed the seas with Iturbide when that ill-starred adventurer returned to be shot against a wall; but there was no Southern blood in him. He came from some European race remote and barbaric. The evidences were all about him. He was a huge figure of a man, with a black spade beard, broad, thick hands, and square, flat fingers.

He had found a wedge of land between the Crown's grant to Daniel Davisson and a Washington survey. It was an uncovered triangle not worth the running of the lines; and so, no doubt, was left out, a sheer rock standing up out of the river for a base, and a peak of the mountain rising northward behind it for an apex.

Doomdorf squatted on the rock. He must have brought a belt of gold pieces when he took to his horse, for he hired old Robert Steuart's slaves and built a stone house on the rock, and he brought the furnishings overland from a frigate in the Chesapeake; and then in the handfuls of earth, wherever a root would hold, he planted the mountain behind his house with peach trees. The gold gave out; but the devil is fertile in resources. Doomdorf built a log still and turned the first fruits of the garden into a hell-brew. The idle and the vicious came with their stone jugs, and violence and riot flowed out.

The government of Virginia was remote and its arm short and feeble; but the men who held the lands west of the mountains against the savages under grants from George, and after that held them against George himself, were efficient and expeditious. They had long patience, but when that failed they went up from their fields and drove the thing before them out of the land, like a scourge of God.

There came a day, then, when my Uncle Abner and Squire Randolph rode through the gap of the mountains to have the thing out with Doomdorf. The work of this brew, which had the odors of Eden and the impulses of the devil in it, could be borne no longer. The drunken negroes had shot old Duncan's cattle and burned his haystacks, and the land was on its feet.

They rode alone, but they were worth an army of little men. Randolph was vain and pompous and given over to extravagance of words, but he was a gentleman beneath it, and fear was an alien and a stranger to him. And Abner was the right hand of the land.

It was a day in early summer and the sun lay hot. They crossed through the broken spine of the mountains and trailed along the river in the shade of the great chestnut trees. The road was only a path and the horses went one before the other. It left the river when the rock began to rise and, making a detour through the grove of peach trees, reached the house on the mountain side. Randolph and Abner got down, unsaddled their horses and turned them out to graze, for their business with Doomdorf would not be over in an hour. Then they took a steep path that brought them out on the mountain side of the house.

A man sat on a big red-roan horse in the paved court before the door. He was a gaunt old man. He sat bare-headed, the palms of his hands resting on the pommel of his saddle, his chin sunk in his black stock, his face in retrospection, the wind moving gently his great shock of voluminous white hair. Under him the huge red horse stood with his legs spread out like a horse of stone.

There was no sound. The door to the house was closed; insects moved in the sun; a shadow crept out from the motionless figure, and swarms of yellow butterflies maneuvered like an army.

Abner and Randolph stopped. They knew the tragic figure—a circuit rider of the hills who preached the invective of Isaiah as though he were the mouthpiece of a militant and avenging overlord; as though the government of Virginia were the awful theocracy of the Book of Kings. The horse was dripping with sweat and the man bore the dust and the evidences of a journey on him.

"Bronson," said Abner, "where is Doomdorf?"

The old man lifted his head and looked down at Abner over the pommel of the saddle.

"'Surely,'" he said, "'he covereth his feet in his summer chamber.'"

Abner went over and knocked on the closed door, and presently the white, frightened face of a woman looked out at him. She was a little, faded woman, with fair hair, a broad foreign face, but with the delicate evidences of gentle blood.

Abner repeated his question.

"Where is Doomdorf?"

"Oh, sir," she answered with a queer lisping accent, "he went to lie down in his south room after his midday meal, as his custom is; and I went to the orchard to gather any fruit that might be ripened." She hesitated and her voice lisped into a whisper: "He is not come out and I cannot wake him."

The two men followed her through the hall and up the stairway to the door.

"It is always bolted," she said, "when he goes to lie down." And she knocked feebly with the tips of her fingers.

There was no answer and Randolph rattled the doorknob.

"Come out, Doomdorf!" he called in his big, bellowing voice.

There was only silence and the echoes of the words among the rafters. Then Randolph set his shoulder to the door and burst it open.

They went in. The room was flooded with sun from the tall south windows. Doomdorf lay on a couch in a little offset of the room, a great scarlet patch on his bosom and a pool of scarlet on the floor.

The woman stood for a moment staring; then she cried out:

"At last I have killed him!" And she ran like a frightened hare.

The two men closed the door and went over to the couch. Doomdorf had been shot to death. There was a great ragged hole in his waistcoat. They began to look about for the weapon with which the deed had been accomplished, and in a moment found it—a fowling piece lying in two dogwood forks against the wall. The gun had just been fired; there was a freshly exploded paper cap under the hammer.

There was little else in the room—a loom-woven rag carpet on the floor; wooden shutters flung back from the windows; a great oak table, and on it a big, round, glass water bottle, filled to its glass stopper with raw liquor from the still. The stuff was limpid and clear as spring water; and, but for its pungent odor, one would have taken it for God's brew instead of Doomdorf's. The sun lay on it and against the wall where hung the weapon that had ejected the dead man out of life.

"Abner," said Randolph, "this is murder! The woman took that gun down from the wall and shot Doomdorf while he slept."

Abner was standing by the table, his fingers round his chin.

"Randolph," he replied, "what brought Bronson here?"

"The same outrages that brought us," said Randolph. "The mad old circuit rider has been preaching a crusade against Doomdorf far and wide in the hills."

Abner answered, without taking his fingers from about his chin:

"You think this woman killed Doomdorf? Well, let us go and ask Bronson who killed him."

They closed the door, leaving the dead man on hit couch, and went down into the court.

The old circuit rider had put away his horse and got an ax. He had taken off his coat and pushed his shirtsleeves up over his long elbows. He was on his way to the still to destroy the barrels of liquor. He stopped when the two men came out, and Abner called to him.

"Bronson," he said, "who killed Doomdorf?"

"I killed him," replied the old man, and went on toward the still.

Randolph swore under his breath. "By the Almighty," he said, "everybody couldn't kill him!"

"Who can tell how many had a hand in it?" replied Abner.

"Two have confessed!" cried Randolph. "Was there perhaps a third? Did you kill him, Abner? And I too? Man, the thing is impossible!"

"The impossible," replied Abner, "looks here like the truth. Come with me, Randolph, and I will show you a thing more impossible than this."

They returned through the house and up the stairs to the room. Abner closed the door behind them.

"Look at this bolt," he said; "it is on the inside and not connected with the lock. How did the one who killed Doomdorf get into this room, since the door was bolted?"

"Through the windows," replied Randolph.

There were but two windows, facing the south, through which the sun entered. Abner led Randolph to them.

"Look!" he said. "The wall of the house is plumb with the sheer face of the rock. It is a hundred feet to the river and the rock is as smooth as a sheet of glass. But that is not all. Look at these window frames; they are cemented into their casement with dust and they are bound along their edges with cobwebs. These windows have not been opened. How did the assassin enter?"

"The answer is evident," said Randolph: "The one who killed Doomdorf hid in the room until he was asleep; then he shot him and went out."

"The explanation is excellent but for one thing," replied Abner: "How did the assassin bolt the door behind him on the inside of this room after he had gone out?"

Randolph flung out his arms with a hopeless gesture.

"Who knows?" he cried. "Maybe Doomdorf killed himself."

Abner laughed.

"And after firing a handful of shot into his heart he got up and put the gun back carefully into the forks against the wall!"

"Well," cried Randolph, "there is one open road out of this mystery. Bronson and this woman say they killed Doomdorf, and if they killed him they surely know how they did it. Let us go down and ask them."

"In the law court," replied Abner, "that procedure would be considered sound sense; but we are in God's court and things are managed there in a somewhat stranger way. Before we go let us find out, if we can, at what hour it was that Doomdorf died."

He went over and took a big silver watch out of the dead man's pocket. It was broken by a shot and the hands lay at one hour after noon. He stood for a moment fingering his chin.

"At one o'clock," he said. "Bronson, I think, was on the road to this place, and the woman was on the mountain among the peach trees."

Randolph threw back his shoulders.

"Why waste time in a speculation about it, Abner?" he said. "We know who did this thing. Let us go and get the story of it out of their own mouths. Doomdorf died by the hands of either Bronson or this woman."

"I could better believe it," replied Abner, "but for the running of a certain awful law."

"What law?" said Randolph. "Is it a statute of Virginia?"

"It is a statute," replied Abner, "of an authority somewhat higher. Mark the language of it: 'He that killeth with the sword must be killed with the sword.'"

He came over and took Randolph by the arm.

"Must! Randolph, did you mark particularly the word 'must'? It is a mandatory law. There is no room in it for the vicissitudes of chance or fortune. There is no way round that word. Thus, we reap what we sow and nothing else; thus, we receive what we give and nothing else. It is the weapon in our own hands that finally destroys us. You are looking at it now." And he turned him about so that the table and the weapon and the dead man were before him. "'He that killeth with the sword must be killed with the sword.' And now," he said, "let us go and try the method of the law courts. Your faith is in the wisdom of their ways."

They found the old circuit rider at work in the still, staving in Doomdorf's liquor casks, splitting the oak heads with his ax.

"Bronson," said Randolph, "how did you kill Doomdorf?"

The old man stopped and stood leaning on his ax.

"I killed him," replied the old man, "as Elijah killed the captains of Ahaziah and their fifties. But not by the hand of any man did I pray the Lord God to destroy Doomdorf, but with fire from heaven to destroy him."

He stood up and extended his arms.

"His hands were full of blood," he said. "With his abomination from these groves of Baal he stirred up the people to contention, to strife and murder. The widow and the orphan cried to heaven against him. 'I will surely hear their cry,' is the promise written in the Book. The land was weary of him; and I prayed the Lord God to destroy him with fire from heaven, as he destroyed the Princes of Gomorrah in their palaces!"

Randolph made a gesture as of one who dismisses the impossible, but Abner's face took on a deep, strange look.

"With fire from heaven!" he repeated slowly to himself. Then he asked a question. "A little while ago," he said, "when we came, I asked you where Doomdorf was, and you answered me in the language of the third chapter of the Book of Judges. Why did you answer me like that, Bronson?— 'Surely he covereth his feet in his summer chamber.'"

"The woman told me that he had not come down from the room where he had gone up to sleep," replied the old man, "and that the door was locked. And then I knew that he was dead in his summer chamber like Eglon, King of Moab."

He extended his arm toward the south.

"I came here from the Great Valley," he said, "to cut down these groves of Baal and to empty out this abomination; but I did not know that the Lord had heard my prayer and visited His wrath on Doomdorf until I was come up into these mountains to his door. When the woman spoke I knew it." And he went away to his horse, leaving the ax among the ruined barrels.

Randolph interrupted.

"Come, Abner," he said; "this is wasted time. Bronson did not kill Doomdorf."

Abner answered slowly in his deep, level voice:

"Do you realize, Randolph, how Doomdorf died?"

"Not by fire from heaven, at any rate," said Randolph.

"Randolph," replied Abner, "are you sure?"

"Abner," cried Randolph, "you are pleased to jest, but I am in deadly earnest. A crime has been done here against the state. I am an officer of justice and I propose to discover the assassin if I can."

He walked away toward the house and Abner followed, his hands behind him and his great shoulders thrown loosely forward, with a grim smile about his mouth.

"It is no use to talk with the mad old preacher," Randolph went on. "Let him empty out the liquor and ride away. I won't issue a warrant against him. Prayer may be a handy implement to do a murder with, Abner, but it is not a deadly weapon under the statutes of Virginia. Doomdorf was dead when old Bronson got here with his Scriptural jargon. This woman killed Doomdorf. I shall put her to an inquisition."

"As you like," replied Abner. "Your faith remains in the methods of the law courts."

"Do you know of any better methods?" said Randolph.

"Perhaps," replied Abner, "when you have finished."

Night had entered the valley. The two men went into the house and set about preparing the corpse for burial. They got candles, and made a coffin, and put Doomdorf in it, and straightened out his limbs, and folded his arms across his shot-out heart. Then they set the coffin on benches in the hall.

They kindled a fire in the dining room and sat down before it, with the door open and the red firelight shining through on the dead man's narrow, everlasting house. The woman had put some cold meat, a golden cheese and a loaf on the table. They did not see her, but they heard her moving about the house; and finally, on the gravel court outside, her step and the whinny of a horse. Then she came in, dressed as for a journey. Randolph sprang up.

"Where are you going?" he said.

"To the sea and a ship," replied the woman. Then she indicated the hall with a gesture. "He is dead and I am free."

There was a sudden illumination in her face. Randolph took a step toward her. His voice was big and harsh.

"Who killed Doomdorf?" he cried.

"I killed him," replied the woman. "It was fair!"

"Fair!" echoed the justice. "What do you mean by that?"

The woman shrugged her shoulders and put out her hands with a foreign gesture.

"I remember an old, old man sitting against a sunny wall, and a little girl, and one who came and talked a long time with the old man, while the little girl plucked yellow flowers out of the grass and put them into her hair. Then finally the stranger gave the old man a gold chain and took the little girl away." She flung out her hands. "Oh, it was fair to kill him!" She looked up with a queer, pathetic smile.

"The old man will be gone by now," she said; "but I shall perhaps find the wall there, with the sun on it, and the yellow flowers in the grass. And now, may I go?"

It is a law of the story-teller's art that he does not tell a story. It is the listener who tells it. The story-teller does but provide him with the stimuli.

Randolph got up and walked about the floor. He was a justice of the peace in a day when that office was filled only by the landed gentry, after the English fashion; and the obligations of the law were strong on him. If he should take liberties with the letter of it, how could the weak and the evil be made to hold it in respect? Here was this woman before him a confessed assassin. Could he let her go?

Abner sat unmoving by the hearth, his elbow on the arm of his chair, his palm propping up his jaw, his face clouded in deep lines. Randolph was consumed with vanity and the weakness of ostentation, but he shouldered his duties for himself. Presently he stopped and looked at the woman, wan, faded like some prisoner of legend escaped out of fabled dungeons into the sun.

The firelight flickered past her to the box on the benches in the hall, and the vast, inscrutable justice of heaven entered and overcame him.

"Yes," he said. "Go! There is no jury in Virginia that would hold a woman for shooting a beast like that." And he thrust out his arm, with the fingers extended toward the dead man.

The woman made a little awkward curtsy.

"I thank you, sir." Then she hesitated and lisped, "But I have not shoot him."

"Not shoot him!" cried Randolph. "Why, the man's heart is riddled!"

"Yes, sir," she said simply, like a child. "I kill him, but have not shoot him."

Randolph took two long strides toward the woman.

"Not shoot him!" he repeated. "How then, in the name of heaven, did you kill Doomdorf?" And his big voice filled the empty places of the room.

"I will show you, sir," she said.

She turned and went away into the house. Presently she returned with something folded up in a linen towel. She put it on the table between the loaf of bread and the yellow cheese.

Randolph stood over the table, and the woman's deft fingers undid the towel from round its deadly contents; and presently the thing lay there uncovered.

It was a little crude model of a human figure done in wax with a needle thrust through the bosom.

Randolph stood up with a great intake of the breath.

"Magic! By the eternal!"

"Yes, sir," the woman explained, in her voice and manner of a child. "I have try to kill him many times—oh, very many times!— with witch words which I have remember; but always they fail. Then, at last, I make him in wax, and I put a needle through his heart; and I kill him very quickly."

It was as clear as daylight, even to Randolph, that the woman was innocent. Her little harmless magic was the pathetic effort of a child to kill a dragon. He hesitated a moment before he spoke, and then he decided like the gentleman he was. If it helped the child to believe that her enchanted straw had slain the monster— well, he would let her believe it.

"And now, sir, may I go?"

Randolph looked at the woman in a sort of wonder.

"Are you not afraid," he said, "of the night and the mountains, and the long road?"

"Oh no, sir," she replied simply. "The good God will be everywhere now."

It was an awful commentary on the dead man—that this strange half-child believed that all the evil in the world had gone out with him; that now that he was dead, the sunlight of heaven would fill every nook and corner.

It was not a faith that either of the two men wished to shatter, and they let her go. It would be daylight presently and the road through the mountains to the Chesapeake was open.

Randolph came back to the fireside after he had helped her into the saddle, and sat down. He tapped on the hearth for some time idly with the iron poker; and then finally he spoke.

"This is the strangest thing that ever happened," he said. "Here's a mad old preacher who thinks that he killed Doomdorf with fire from Heaven, like Elijah the Tishbite; and here is a simple child of a woman who thinks she killed him with a piece of magic of the Middle Ages—each as innocent of his death as I am. And yet, by the eternal, the beast is dead!"

He drummed on the hearth with the poker, lifting it up and letting it drop through the hollow of his fingers.

"Somebody shot Doomdorf. But who? And how did he get into and out of that shut-up room? The assassin that killed Doomdorf must have gotten into the room to kill him. Now, how did he get in?" He spoke as to himself; but my uncle sitting across the hearth replied:

"Through the window."

"Through the window!" echoed Randolph. "Why, man, you yourself showed me that the window had not been opened, and the precipice below it a fly could hardly climb. Do you tell me now that the window was opened?"

"No," said Abner, "it was never opened."

Randolph got on his feet.

"Abner," he cried, "are you saying that the one who killed Doomdorf climbed the sheer wall and got in through a closed window, without disturbing the dust or the cobwebs on the window frame?"

My uncle looked Randolph in the face.

"The murderer of Doomdorf did even more," he said. "That assassin not only climbed the face of that precipice and got in through the closed window, but he shot Doomdorf to death and got out again through the closed window without leaving a single track or trace behind, and without disturbing a grain of dust or a thread of a cobweb."

Randolph swore a great oath.

"The thing is impossible!" he cried. "Men are not killed today in Virginia by black art or a curse of God."

"By black art, no," replied Abner; "but by the curse of God, yes. I think they are."

Randolph drove his clenched right hand into the palm of his left.

"By the eternal!" he cried. "I would like to see the assassin who could do a murder like this, whether he be an imp from the pit or an angel out of Heaven."

"Very well," replied Abner, undisturbed. "When he comes back tomorrow I will show you the assassin who killed Doomdorf."

When day broke they dug a grave and buried the dead man against the mountain among his peach trees. It was noon when that work was ended. Abner threw down his spade and looked up at the sun.

"Randolph," he said, "let us go and lay an ambush for this assassin. He is on the way here."

And it was a strange ambush that he laid. When they were come again into the chamber where Doomdorf died he bolted the door; then he loaded the fowling piece and put it carefully back on its rack against the wall. After that he did another curious thing: He took the blood-stained coat, which they had stripped off the dead man when they had prepared his body for the earth, put a pillow in it and laid it on the couch precisely where Doomdorf had slept.

And while he did these things Randolph stood in wonder and Abner talked:

"Look you, Randolph. . . . We will trick the murderer. . . . We will catch him in the act."

Then he went over and took the puzzled justice by the arm.

"Watch!" he said. "The assassin is coming along the wall!"

But Randolph heard nothing, saw nothing. Only the sun entered. Abner's hand tightened on his arm.

"It is here! Look!" And he pointed to the wall.

Randolph, following the extended finger, saw a tiny brilliant disk of light moving slowly up the wall toward the lock of the fowling piece. Abner's hand became a vise and his voice rang as over metal.

"'He that killeth with the sword must be killed with the sword.' It is the water bottle, full of Doomdorf's liquor, focusing the sun. . . . And look, Randolph, how Bronson's prayer was answered!"

The tiny disk of light traveled on the plate of the lock.

"It is fire from heaven!"

The words rang above the roar of the fowling piece, and Randolph saw the dead man's coat leap up on the couch, riddled by the shot. The gun, in its natural position on the rack, pointed to the couch standing at the end of the chamber, beyond the offset of the wall, and the focused sun had exploded the percussion cap.

Randolph made a great gesture, with his arm extended.

"It is a world," he said, "filled with the mysterious joinder of accident!"

"It is a world," replied Abner, "filled with the mysterious justice of God!"

2
THE WRONG HAND

Abner never would have taken me into that house if he could have helped it. He was on a desperate mission and a child was the last company he wished; but he had to do it. It was an evening of early winter—raw and cold. A chilling rain was beginning to fall; night was descending and I could not go on. I had been into the upcountry and had taken this short cut through the hills that lay here against the mountains. I would have been home by now, but a broken shoe had delayed me.

I did not see Abner's horse until I approached the crossroads, but I think he had seen me from a distance. His great chestnut stood in the grassplot between the roads, and Abner sat upon him like a man of stone. He had made his decision when I got to him.

The very aspect of the land was sinister. The house stood on a hill; round its base, through the sodded meadows, the river ran—dark, swift and silent; stretching westward was a forest and for background the great mountains stood into the sky. The house was very old. The high windows were of little panes of glass and on the ancient white door the paint was seamed and cracked with age.

The name of the man who lived here was a byword in the hills. He was a hunchback, who sat his great roan as though he were a spider in the saddle. He had been married more than once; but one wife had gone mad, and my Uncle Abner's drovers had found the other on a summer morning swinging to the limb of a great elm that stood before the door, a bridle-rein knotted around her throat and her bare feet scattering the yellow pollen of the ragweed.

That elm was to us a duletree. One could not ride beneath it for the swinging of this ghost.

The estate, undivided, belonged to Gaul and his brother. This brother lived beyond the mountains. He never came until he came that last time. Gaul rendered some accounting and they managed in that way. It was said the brother believed himself defrauded and had come finally to divide the lands; but this was gossip. Gaul said his brother came upon a visit and out of love for him.

One did not know where the truth lay between these stories. Why he came we could not be certain; but why he remained was beyond a doubt.

One morning Gaul came to my Uncle Abner, clinging to the pommel of his saddle while his great horse galloped, to say that he had found his brother dead, and asking Abner to go with some others and look upon the man before one touched his body—and then to get him buried.

The hunchback sniveled and cried out that his nerves were gone with grief and the terror of finding his brother's throat cut open and the blood upon him as he lay ghastly in his bed. He did not know a detail. He had looked in at the door—and fled. His brother had not got up and he had gone to call him. Why his brother had done this thing he could not imagine—he was in perfect health and he slept beneath his roof in love. The hunchback had blinked his red-lidded eyes and twisted his big, hairy hands, and presented the aspect of grief. It looked grotesque and loathsome; but—how else could a toad look in his extremity?

Abner had gone with my father and Elnathan Stone. They had found the man as Gaul said—the razor by his hand and the marks of his fingers and his struggle on him and about the bed. And the country had gone to see him buried. The hills had been afire with talk, but Abner and my father and Elnathan Stone were silent. They came silent from Gaul's house; they stood silent before the body when it was laid out for burial; and, bareheaded, they were silent when the earth received it.

A little later, however, when Gaul brought forth a will, leaving the brother's share of the estate to the hunchback, with certain loving words, and a mean allowance to the man's children, the three had met together and Abner had walked about all night.

As we turned in toward the house Abner asked me if I had got my supper. I told him "Yes"; and at the ford he stopped and sat a moment in the saddle.

"Martin," he said, "get down and drink. It is God's river and the water clean in it."

Then he extended his great arm toward the shadowy house.

"We shall go in," he said; "but we shall not eat nor drink there, for we do not come in peace."

I do not know much about that house, for I saw only one room in it; that was empty, cluttered with dust and rubbish, and pre-empted by the spider. Long double windows of little panes of glass looked out over the dark, silent river slipping past without a sound, and the rain driving into the forest and the loom of the mountains. There was a fire—the trunk of an apple tree burning, with one end in the fireplace. There were some old chairs with black hair-cloth seats, and a sofa—all very old. These the hunchback did not sit on, for the dust appeared when they were touched. He had a chair be-side the hearth, and he sat in that—a high-backed chair, made like a settee and padded,—the arms padded too; but there the padding was worn out and ragged, where his hands had plucked it.

He wore a blue coat, made with little capes to hide his hump, and he sat tapping the burning tree with his cane. There was a gold piece set into the head of this black stick. He had it put there, the gossips said, that his fingers might be always on the thing he loved. His gray hair lay along his face and the draft of the chimney moved it.

He wondered why we came, and his eyes declared how the thing disturbed him; they flared up and burned down—now gleaming in his head as he looked us over, and now dull as he considered what he saw.

The man was misshapen and doubled up, but there was strength and vigor in him. He had a great, cavernous mouth, and his voice was a sort of bellow. One has seen an oak tree, dwarfed and stunted into knots, but with the toughness and vigor of a great oak in it. Gaul was a thing like that.

He cried out when he saw Abner. He was taken by surprise; and he wished to know if we came by chance or upon some errand.

"Abner," he said, "come in. It's a devil's night—rain and the driving, wind."

"The weather," said Abner, "is in God's hand."

"God!" cried Gaul. "I would shoestrap such a God! The autumn is not half over and here is winter come, and no pasture left and the cattle to be fed."

Then he saw me, with my scared white face—and he was certain that we came by chance. He craned his thick neck and looked.

"Bub," he said, "come in and warm your fingers. I will not hurt you. I did not twist my body up like this to frighten children—it was Abner's God."

We entered and sat down by the fire. The apple tree blazed and crackled; the wind outside increased; the rain turned to a kind of sleet that rattled on the window-glass like shot. The room was lighted by two candles in tall brass candlesticks. They stood at each end of the mantelpiece, smeared with tallow. The wind whopped and spat into the chimney; and now and then a puff of wood-smoke blew out and mounted up along the blackened fireboard.

Abner and the hunchback talked of the price of cattle, of the "blackleg" among yearlings—that fatal disease that we had so much trouble with—and of the "lump-jaw."

Gaul said that if calves were kept in small lots and not all together the "blackleg" was not so apt to strike them; and he thought the "lump-jaw" was a germ. Fatten the bullock with green corn and put it in a car, he said, when the lump begins to come. The Dutch would eat it—and what poison could hurt the Dutch! But Abner said the creature should be shot.

"And lose the purchase money and a summer's grazing?" cried Gaul. "Not I! I ship the beast."

"Then," said Abner, "the inspector in the market ought to have it shot and you fined to boot."

"The inspector in the market!" And Gaul laughed. "Why, I slip him a greenback—thus!"—and he set his thumb against his palm. "And he is glad to see me. 'Gaul, bring in all you can,' said one; 'it means a little something to us both.'" And the hunchback's laugh clucked and chuckled in his throat.

And they talked of renters, and men to harvest the hay and feed the cattle in the winter. And on this topic Gaul did not laugh; he cursed. Labor was a lost art and the breed of men run out. This new set were worthless—they had hours—and his oaths filled all the rafters. Hours! Why, under his father men worked from dawn until dark and cleaned their horses by a lantern. . . . These were decadent times that we were come on. In the good days one bought a man for two hundred eagles; but now the creature was a citizen and voted at the polls—and could not be kicked. And if one took his cane and drubbed him he was straightway sued at law, in an action of trespass on the case, for damages. . . . Men had gone mad with these newfangled notions, and the earth was likely to grow up with weeds!

Abner said there was a certain truth in this—and that truth was that men were idler than their fathers. Certain preachers preached that labor was a curse and backed it up with Scripture; but he had read the Scriptures for himself and the curse was idleness. Labor and God's Book would save the world; they were two wings that a man could get his soul to Heaven on.

"They can all go to hell, for me," said Gaul, "and so I have my day's work first."

And he tapped the tree with his great stick and cried out that his workhands robbed him. He had to sit his horse and watch or they hung their scythes up; and he must put sulphur in his cattle's meal or they stole it from him; and they milked his cows to feed their scurvy babies. He would have their hides off if it were not for these tender laws.

Abner said that, while one saw to his day's work done, he must see to something more; that a man was his brother's keeper in spite of Cain's denial—and he must keep him; that the elder had his right to the day's work, but the younger had also his right to the benefits of his brother's guardianship. The fiduciary had One to settle with. It would go hard if he should shirk the trust.

"I do not recognize your trust," said Gaul. "I live here for myself."

"For yourself!" cried Abner. "And would you know what God thinks of you?"

"And would you know what I think of God?" cried Gaul.

"What do you think of Him?" said Abner.

"I think He's a scarecrow," said Gaul. "And I think, Abner, that I am a wiser bird than you are. I have not sat cawing in a tree, afraid of this thing. I have seen its wooden spine under its patched jacket, and the crosspiece peeping from the sleeves, and its dangling legs. And I have gone down into its field and taken what I liked in spite of its flapping coattails. . . . Why, Abner, this thing your God depends on is a thing called fear; and I do not have it."

Abner looked at him hard, but he did not answer. He turned, instead, to me.

"Martin," he said, "you must go to sleep, lad." And he wrapped me in his greatcoat and put me to bed on the sofa—behind him in the corner. I was snug and warm there and I could have slept like Saul, but I was curious to know what Abner came for and I peeped out through a buttonhole of the greatcoat.

Abner sat for a long time, his elbows on his knees, his hands together and his eyes looking into the fire. The hunchback watched him, his big, hairy hands moving on the padded arms of his chair and his sharp eyes twinkling like specks of glass. Finally Abner spoke—I judged he believed me now asleep.

"And so, Gaul," he said, "you think God is a scarecrow?"

"I do," said Gaul.

"And you have taken what you liked?"

"I have," said Gaul.

"Well," said Abner, "I have come to ask you to return what you have taken—and something besides, for usury."

He got a folded paper out of his pocket and handed it across the hearth to Gaul.

The hunchback took it, leaned back in his chair, unfolded it at his leisure and at his leisure read it through.

"A deed in fee," he said, "for all these lands . . . to my brother's children. The legal terms are right: 'Doth grant, with covenants of general warranty.' . . . It is well drawn, Abner; but I am not pleased to 'grant.'"

"Gaul," said Abner, "there are certain reasons that may move you."

The hunchback smiled.

"They must be very excellent to move a man to alienate his lands."

"Excellent they are," said Abner. "I shall mention the best one first."

"Do," said Gaul, and his grotesque face was merry.

"It is this," said Abner: "You have no heirs. Your brother's son is now a man; he should marry a wife and rear up children to possess these lands. And, as he is thus called upon to do what you cannot do, Gaul, he should have the things you have, to use."

"That's a very pretty reason, Abner," said the hunchback, "and it does you honor; but I know a better."

"What is it, Gaul?" said Abner.

The hunchback grinned. "Let us say, my pleasure!"

Then he struck his bootleg with his great black stick.

"And now," he cried, "who's back of this tomfoolery?"

"I am," said Abner.

The hunchback's heavy brows shot down. He was not disturbed, but he knew that Abner moved on no fool's errand.

"Abner," he said, "you have some reason for this thing. What is it?"

"I have several reasons for it," replied Abner, "and I gave you the best one first."

"Then the rest are not worth the words to say them in," cried Gaul.

"You are mistaken there," replied Abner; "I said that I would give you the best reason, not the strongest. . . . Think of the reason I have given. We do not have our possessions in fee in this world,

Gaul, but upon lease and for a certain term of service. And when we make default in that service the lease abates and a new man can take the title."

Gaul did not understand and he was wary.

"I carry out my brother's will," he said.

"But the dead," replied Abner, "cannot retain dominion over things. There can be no tenure beyond a life estate. These lands and chattels are for the uses of men as they arrive. The needs of the living overrule the devises of the dead."

Gaul was watching Abner closely. He knew that this was some digression, but he met it with equanimity. He put his big, hairy fingers together and spoke with a judicial air.

"Your argument," he said, "is without a leg to stand on. It is the dead who govern. Look you, man, how they work their will upon us! Who have made the laws? The dead! Who have made the customs that we obey and that form and shape our lives? The dead! And the titles to our lands—have not the dead devised them? . . . If a surveyor runs a line he begins at some corner that the dead set up; and if one goes to law upon a question the judge looks backward through his books until he finds out how the dead have settled it—and he follows that. And all the writers, when they would give weight and authority to their opinions, quote the dead; and the orators and all those who preach and lecture—are not their mouths filled with words that the dead have spoken? Why, man, our lives follow grooves that the dead have run out with their thumbnails!"

He got on his feet and looked at Abner.

"What my brother has written in his will I will obey," he said. "Have you seen that paper, Abner?"

"I have not," said Abner, "but I have read the copy in the county clerk's book. It bequeathed these lands to you."

The hunchback went over to an old secretary standing against the wall. He pulled it open, got out the will and a pack of letters and brought them to the fire. He laid the letters on the table beside Abner's deed and held out the will.

Abner took the testament and read it.

"Do you know my brother's writing?" said Gaul.

"I do," said Abner.

"Then you know he wrote that will."

"He did," said Abner. "It is in Enoch's hand." Then he added: "But the date is a month before your brother came here."

"Yes," said Gaul; "it was not written in this house. My brother sent it to me. See—here is the envelope that it came in, postmarked on that date."

Abner took the envelope and compared the date. "It is the very day," he said, "and the address is in Enoch's hand."

"It is," said Gaul; "when my brother had set his signature to this will he addressed that cover. He told me of it." The hunchback sucked in his cheeks and drew down his eyelids. "Ah, yes," he said, "my brother loved me!"

"He must have loved you greatly," replied Abner, "to thus disinherit his own flesh and blood."

"And am not I of his own flesh and blood too?" cried the hunchback. "The strain of blood in my brother runs pure in me; in these children it is diluted. Shall not one love his own blood first?"

"Love!" echoed Abner. "You speak the word, Gaul;—but do you understand it?"

"I do," said Gaul; "for it bound my brother to me."

"And did it bind you to him?" said Abner. I could see the hunchback's great white eyelids drooping and his lengthened face.

"We were like David and Jonathan," he said. "I would have given my right arm for Enoch and he would have died for me."

"He did!" said Abner.

I saw the hunchback start, and, to conceal the gesture, he stooped and thrust the trunk of the apple tree a little farther into the fireplace. A cloud of sparks sprang up. A gust of wind caught the loose sash in the casement behind us and shook it as one, barred out and angry, shakes a door. When the hunchback rose Abner had gone on.

"If you loved your brother like that," he said, "you will do him this service—you will sign this deed."

"But, Abner," replied Gaul, "such was not my brother's will. By the law, these children will inherit at my death. Can they not wait?"

"Did you wait?" said Abner.

The hunchback flung up his head.

"Abner," he cried, "what do you mean by that?" And he searched my uncle's face for some indicatory sign; but there was no sign there—the face was stern and quiet.

"I mean," said Abner, "that one ought not to have an interest in another's death."

"Why not?" said Gaul.

"Because," replied Abner, "one may be tempted to step in before the providence of God and do its work for it."

Gaul turned the innuendo with a cunning twist.

"You mean," he said, "that these children may come to seek my death?"

I was astonished at Abner's answer.

"Yes," he said; "that is what I mean."

"Man," cried the hunchback, "you make me laugh!"

"Laugh as you like," replied Abner; "but I am sure that these children will not look at this thing as we have looked at it."

"As who have looked at it?" said Gaul.

"As my brother Rufus and Elnathan Stone and I," said Abner.

"And so," said the hunchback, "you gentlemen have considered how to save my life. I am much obliged to you." He made a grotesque, mocking bow. "And how have you meant to save it?"

"By the signing of that deed," said Abner.

"I thank you!" cried the hunchback. "But I am not pleased to save my life that way."

I thought Abner would give some biting answer; but, instead, he spoke slowly and with a certain hesitation.

"There is no other way," he said. "We have believed that the stigma of your death and the odium on the name and all the scandal would in the end wrong these children more than the loss of this estate during the term of your natural life; but it is clear to me that they will not so regard it. And we are bound to lay it before them if you do not sign this deed. It is not for my brother Rufus and Elnathan Stone and me to decide this question."

"To decide what question?" said Gaul.

"Whether you are to live or die!" said Abner.

The hunchback's face grew stern and resolute. He sat down in his chair, put his stick between his knees and looked my uncle in the eyes.

"Abner," he said, "you are talking in some riddle. . . . Say the thing out plain. Do you think I forged that will?"

"I do not," said Abner.

"Nor could any man!" cried the hunchback. "It is in my brother's hand—every word of it; and, besides, there is neither ink nor paper in this house. I figure on a slate; and when I have a thing to say I go and tell it."

"And yet," said Abner, "the day before your brother's death you bought some sheets of foolscap of the postmaster."

"I did," said Gaul— "and for my brother. Enoch wished to make some calculations with his pencil. I have the paper with his figures on it."

He went to his desk and brought back some sheets.

"And yet," said Abner, "this will is written on a page of foolscap."

"And why not?" said Gaul. "Is it not sold in every store to Mexico?"

It was the truth—and Abner drummed on the table.

"And now," said Gaul, "we have laid one suspicion by looking it squarely in the face; let us lay the other. What did you find about my brother's death to moon over?"

"Why," said Abner, "should he take his own life in this house?"

"I do not know that," said Gaul.

"I will tell you," said Abner; "we found a bloody handprint on your brother!"

"Is that all that you found on him?"

"That is all," said Abner.

"Well," cried Gaul, "does that prove that I killed him? Let me look your ugly suspicion in the face. Were not my brother's hands covered with his blood and was not the bed covered with his finger-prints, where he had clutched about it in his death-struggle?"

"Yes," said Abner; "that is all true."

"And was there any mark or sign in that print," said Gaul, "by which you could know that it was made by any certain hand"—and he spread out his fingers;— "as, for instance, my hand?"

"No," said Abner.

There was victory in Gaul's face.

He had now learned all that Abner knew and he no longer feared him. There was no evidence against him—even I saw that.

"And now," he cried, "will you get out of my house? I will have no more words with you. Begone!"

Abner did not move. For the last five minutes he had been at work at something, but I could not see what it was, for his back was toward me. Now he turned to the table beside Gaul and I saw what he had been doing. He had been making a pen out of a goose-quill! He laid the pen down on the table and beside it a horn of ink. He opened out the deed that he had brought, put his finger on a line, dipped the quill into the ink and held it out to Gaul.

"Sign there!" he said.

The hunchback got on his feet, with an oath.

"Begone with your damned paper!" he cried.

Abner did not move.

"When you have signed," he said.

"Signed!" cried the hunchback. "I will see you and your brother Rufus, and Elnathan Stone, and all the kit and kittle of you in hell!"

"Gaul," said Abner, "you will surely see all who are to be seen in hell!"

By Abner's manner I knew that the end of the business had arrived. He seized the will and the envelope that Gaul had brought from his secretary and held them out before him.

"You tell me," he said, "that these papers were written at one sitting! Look! The hand that wrote that envelope was calm and steady, but the hand that wrote this will shook. See how the letters wave and jerk! I will explain it. You have kept that envelope from some old letter; but this paper was written in this house—in fear! And it was written on the morning that your brother died. . . . Listen! When Elnathan Stone stepped back from your brother's bed he stumbled over a piece of carpet. The under side of that carpet was smeared with ink, where a bottle had been broken. I put my finger on it and it was wet."

The hunchback began to howl and bellow like a beast penned in a corner. I crouched under Abner's coat in terror. The creature's cries filled the great, empty house. They rose a hellish crescendo on the voices of the wind; and for accompaniment the sleet played shrill notes on the windowpanes, and the loose shingles clattered a staccato, and the chimney whistled—like weird instruments under a devil's fingers.

And all the time Abner stood looking down at the man—an implacable, avenging Nemesis—and his voice, deep and level, did not change.

"But, before that, we knew that you had killed your brother! We knew it when we stood before his bed. 'Look there,' said Rufus— 'at that bloody handprint!' . . . We looked. . . . And we knew that Enoch's hand had not made that print. Do you know how we knew that, Gaul? . . . I will tell you. . . . The bloody print on your brother's right hand was the print of a right hand!"

Gaul signed the deed, and at dawn we rode away, with the hunchback's promise that he would come that afternoon before a notary and acknowledge what he had signed; but he did not come— neither on that day nor on any day after that.

When Abner went to fetch him he found him swinging from his elm tree.

3

THE ANGEL OF THE LORD

I always thought my father took a long chance, but somebody had to take it and certainly I was the one least likely to be suspected. It was a wild country. There were no banks. We had to pay for the cattle, and somebody had to carry the money. My father and my uncle were always being watched. My father was right, I think.

"Abner," he said, "I'm going to send Martin. No one will ever suppose that we would trust this money to a child."

My uncle drummed on the table and rapped his heels on the floor. He was a bachelor, stern and silent. But he could talk . . . and when he did, he began at the beginning and you heard him through; and what he said—well, he stood behind it.

"To stop Martin," my father went on, "would be only to lose the money; but to stop you would be to get somebody killed."

I knew what my father meant. He meant that no one would undertake to rob Abner until after he had shot him to death.

I ought to say a word about my Uncle Abner. He was one of those austere, deeply religious men who were the product of the Reformation. He always carried a Bible in his pocket and he read it where he pleased. Once the crowd at Roy's Tavern tried to make sport of him when he got his book out by the fire; but they never tried it again. When the fight was over Abner paid Roy eighteen silver dollars for the broken chairs and the table—and he was the only man in the tavern who could ride a horse. Abner belonged to the church militant, and his God was a war lord.

So that is how they came to send me. The money was in green-backs in packages. They wrapped it up in newspaper and put it into a pair of saddle-bags, and I set out. I was about nine years old. No, it was not as bad as you think. I could ride a horse all day when I was nine years old—most any kind of a horse. I was tough as whit'-leather, and I knew the country I was going into. You must not picture a little boy rolling a hoop in the park.

It was an afternoon in early autumn. The clay roads froze in the night; they thawed out in the day and they were a bit sticky. I was to stop at Roy's Tavern, south of the river, and go on in the morning. Now and then I passed some cattle driver, but no one overtook me on the road until almost sundown; then I heard a horse behind me and a man came up. I knew him. He was a cattleman named Dix. He had once been a shipper, but he had come in for a good deal of bad luck. His partner, Alkire, had absconded with a big sum of money due the grazers. This had ruined Dix; he had given up his land, which wasn't very much, to the grazers. After that he had gone over the mountain to his people, got together a pretty big sum of money and bought a large tract of grazing land. Foreign claimants had sued him in the courts on some old title and he had lost the whole tract and the money that he had paid for it. He had married a remote cousin of ours and he had always lived on her lands, adjoining those of my Uncle Abner.

Dix seemed surprised to see me on the road.

"So it's you, Martin," he said; "I thought Abner would be going into the upcountry."

One gets to be a pretty cunning youngster, even at this age, and I told no one what I was about.

"Father wants the cattle over the river to run a month," I returned easily, "and I'm going up there to give his orders to the grazers."

He looked me over, then he rapped the saddlebags with his knuckles. "You carry a good deal of baggage, my lad."

I laughed. "Horse feed," I said. "You know my father! A horse must be fed at dinner time, but a man can go till he gets it."

One was always glad of any company on the road, and we fell into an idle talk. Dix said he was going out into the Ten Mile country; and I have always thought that was, in fact, his intention. The road turned south about a mile our side of the tavern. I never liked Dix; he was of an apologetic manner, with a cunning, irresolute face.

A little later a man passed us at a gallop. He was a drover named Marks, who lived beyond my Uncle Abner, and he was riding hard to get in before night. He hailed us, but he did not stop; we got a shower of mud and Dix cursed him. I have never seen a more evil face. I suppose it was because Dix usually had a grin about his mouth, and when that sort of face gets twisted there's nothing like it.

After that he was silent. He rode with his head down and his fingers plucking at his jaw, like a man in some perplexity. At the crossroads he stopped and sat for some time in the saddle, looking before him. I left him there, but at the bridge he overtook me. He said he had concluded to get some supper and go on after that.

Roy's Tavern consisted of a single big room, with a loft above it for sleeping quarters. A narrow covered way connected this room with the house in which Roy and his family lived. We used to hang our saddles on wooden pegs in this covered way. I have seen that wall so hung with saddles that you could not find a place for another stirrup. But tonight Dix and I were alone in the tavern. He looked cunningly at me when I took the saddle-bags with me into the big room and when I went with them up the ladder into the loft. But he said nothing—in fact, he had scarcely spoken. It was cold; the road had begun to freeze when we got in. Roy had lighted a big fire. I left Dix before it. I did not take off my clothes, because Roy's beds were mattresses of wheat straw covered with heifer skins—good enough for summer but pretty cold on such a night, even with the heavy, hand-woven coverlet in big white and black checks.

I put the saddle-bags under my head and lay down. I went at once to sleep, but I suddenly awaked. I thought there was a candle in the loft, but it was a gleam of light from the fire below, shining through a crack in the floor. I lay and watched it, the coverlet pulled up to my chin. Then I began to wonder why the fire burned so brightly. Dix ought to be on his way some time and it was a custom for the last man to rake out the fire. There was not a sound. The light streamed steadily through the crack.

Presently it occurred to me that Dix had forgotten the fire and that I ought to go down and rake it out. Roy always warned us about the fire when he went to bed. I got up, wrapped the great coverlet around me, went over to the gleam of light and looked down through the crack in the floor. I had to lie out at full length to get my eye against the board. The hickory logs had turned to great embers and glowed like a furnace of red coals.

Before this fire stood Dix. He was holding out his hands and turning himself about as though he were cold to the marrow; but with all that chill upon him, when the man's face came into the light I saw it covered with a sprinkling of sweat.

I shall carry the memory of that face. The grin was there at the mouth, but it was pulled about; the eyelids were drawn in; the teeth were clamped together. I have seen a dog poisoned with strychnine look like that.

I lay there and watched the thing. It was as though something potent and evil dwelling within the man were in travail to re-form his face upon its image. You cannot realize how that devilish labor held me—the face worked as though it were some plastic stuff, and the sweat oozed through. And all the time the man was cold; and he was crowding into the fire and turning himself about and putting out his hands. And it was as though the heat would no more enter in and warm him than it will enter in and warm the ice.

It seemed to scorch him and leave him cold—and he was fearfully and desperately cold! I could smell the singe of the fire on him, but it had no power against this diabolic chill. I began myself to shiver, although I had the heavy coverlet wrapped around me.

The thing was a fascinating horror; I seemed to be looking down into the chamber of some abominable maternity. The room was filled with the steady red light of the fire. Not a shadow moved in it. And there was silence. The man had taken off his boots and he twisted before the fire without a sound. It was like the shuddering tales of possession or transformation by a drug. I thought the man would burn himself to death. His clothes smoked. How could he be so cold?

Then, finally, the thing was over! I did not see it for his face was in the fire. But suddenly he grew composed and stepped back into the room. I tell you I was afraid to look! I do not know what thing I expected to see there, but I did not think it would be Dix.

Well, it was Dix; but not the Dix that any of us knew. There was a certain apology, a certain indecision, a certain servility in that other Dix, and these things showed about his face. But there was none of these weaknesses in this man.

His face had been pulled into planes of firmness and decision; the slack in his features had been taken up; the furtive moving of the eye was gone. He stood now squarely on his feet and he was full of courage. But I was afraid of him as I have never been afraid of any human creature in this world! Something that had been servile in him, that had skulked behind disguises, that had worn the habiliments of subterfuge, had now come forth; and it had molded the features of the man to its abominable courage.

Presently he began to move swiftly about the room. He looked out at the window and he listened at the door; then he went softly into the covered way. I thought he was going on his journey; but then he could not be going with his boots there beside the fire. In a moment he returned with a saddle blanket in his hand and came softly across the room to the ladder.

Then I understood the thing that he intended, and I was motionless with fear. I tried to get up, but I could not. I could only lie there with my eye strained to the crack in the floor. His foot was on the ladder, and I could already feel his hand on my throat and that blanket on my face, and the suffocation of death in me, when far away on the hard road I heard a horse!

He heard it, too, for he stopped on the ladder and turned his evil face about toward the door. The horse was on the long hill beyond the bridge, and he was coming as though the devil rode in his saddle. It was a hard, dark night. The frozen road was like flint;

I could hear the iron of the shoes ring. Whoever rode that horse rode for his life or for something more than his life, or he was mad. I heard the horse strike the bridge and thunder across it. And all the while Dix hung there on the ladder by his hands and listened. Now he sprang softly down, pulled on his boots and stood up before the fire, his face—this new face—gleaming with its evil courage. The next moment the horse stopped.

I could hear him plunge under the bit, his iron shoes ripping the frozen road; then the door leaped back and my Uncle Abner was in the room. I was so glad that my heart almost choked me and for a moment I could hardly see—everything was in a sort of mist.

Abner swept the room in a glance, then he stopped.

"Thank God!" he said; "I'm in time." And he drew his hand down over his face with the fingers hard and close as though he pulled something away.

"In time for what?" said Dix.

Abner looked him over. And I could see the muscles of his big shoulders stiffen as he looked. And again he looked him over. Then he spoke and his voice was strange.

"Dix," he said, "is it you?"

"Who would it be but me?" said Dix.

"It might be the devil," said Abner. "Do you know what your face looks like?"

"No matter what it looks like!" said Dix.

"And so," said Abner, "we have got courage with this new face."

Dix threw up his head.

"Now, look here, Abner," he said, "I've had about enough of your big manner. You ride a horse to death and you come plunging in here; what the devil's wrong with you?"

"There's nothing wrong with me," replied Abner, and his voice was low. "But there's something damnably wrong with you, Dix."

"The devil take you," said Dix, and I saw him measure Abner with his eye. It was not fear that held him back; fear was gone out of the creature; I think it was a kind of prudence.

Abner's eyes kindled, but his voice remained low and steady.

"Those are big words," he said.

"Well," cried Dix, "get out of the door then and let me pass!"

"Not just yet," said Abner; "I have something to say to you."

"Say it then," cried Dix, "and get out of the door."

"Why hurry?" said Abner. "It's a long time until daylight, and I have a good deal to say."

"You'll not say it to me," said Dix. "I've got a trip to make to-night; get out of the door."

Abner did not move. "You've got a longer trip to make tonight than you think, Dix," he said; "but you're going to hear what I have to say before you set out on it."

I saw Dix rise on his toes and I knew what he wished for. He wished for a weapon; and he wished for the bulk of bone and muscle that would have a chance against Abner. But he had neither the one nor the other. And he stood there on his toes and began to curse—low, vicious, withering oaths, that were like the swish of a knife.

Abner was looking at the man with a curious interest.

"It is strange," he said, as though speaking to himself, "but it explains the thing. While one is the servant of neither, one has the courage of neither; but when he finally makes his choice he gets what his master has to give him."

Then he spoke to Dix.

"Sit down!" he said; and it was in that deep, level voice that Abner used when he was standing close behind his words. Every man in the hills knew that voice; one had only a moment to decide after he heard it. Dix knew that, and yet for one instant he hung there on his toes, his eyes shimmering like a weasel's, his mouth twisting. He was not afraid! If he had had the ghost of a chance against Abner he would have taken it. But he knew he had not, and with an oath he threw the saddle blanket into a corner and sat down by the fire.

Abner came away from the door then. He took off his great coat. He put a log on the fire and he sat down across the hearth from Dix. The new hickory sprang crackling into flames. For a good while there was silence; the two men sat at either end of the hearth without a word. Abner seemed to have fallen into a study of the man before him. Finally he spoke:

"Dix," he said, "do you believe in the providence of God?"

Dix flung up his head.

"Abner," he cried, "if you are going to talk nonsense I promise you upon my oath that I will not stay to listen."

Abner did not at once reply. He seemed to begin now at another point. "Dix," he said, "you've had a good deal of bad luck. . . . Perhaps you wish it put that way."

"Now, Abner," he cried, "you speak the truth; I have had hell's luck."

"Hell's luck you have had," replied Abner. "It is a good word. I accept it. Your partner disappeared with all the money of the grazers on the other side of the river; you lost the land in your lawsuit; and you are to-night without a dollar. That was a big tract of land to lose. Where did you get so great a sum of money?"

"I have told you a hundred times," replied Dix. "I got it from my people over the mountains. You know where I got it."

"Yes," said Abner. "I know where you got it, Dix. And I know another thing. But first I want to show you this," and he took a little penknife out of his pocket. "And I want to tell you that I believe in the providence of God, Dix."

"I don't care a fiddler's damn what you believe in," said Dix.

"But you do care what I know," replied Abner.

"What do you know?" said Dix.

"I know where your partner is," replied Abner.

I was uncertain about what Dix was going to do, but finally he answered with a sneer.

"Then you know something that nobody else knows."

"Yes," replied Abner, "there is another man who knows."

"Who?" said Dix.

"You," said Abner.

Dix leaned over in his chair and looked at Abner closely.

"Abner," he cried, "you are talking nonsense. Nobody knows where Alkire is. If I knew I'd go after him."

"Dix," Abner answered, and it was again in that deep, level voice, "if I had got here five minutes later you would have gone after him. I can promise you that, Dix.

"Now, listen! I was in the upcountry when I got your word about the partnership; and I was on my way back when at Big Run I broke a stirrup-leather. I had no knife and I went into the store and bought this one; then the storekeeper told me that Alkire had gone to see you. I didn't want to interfere with him and I turned back. . . . . . So I did not become your partner. And so I did not disappear. . . . What was it that prevented? The broken stirrup-leather? The knife? In old times, Dix, men were so blind that God had to open their eyes before they could see His angel in the way before them. . . . They are still blind, but they ought not to be that blind. . . . Well, on the night that Alkire disappeared I met him on his way to your house. It was out there at the bridge. He had broken a stirrup-leather and he was trying to fasten it with a nail. He asked me if I had a knife, and I gave him this one. It was beginning to rain and I went on, leaving him there in the road with the knife in his hand."

Abner paused; the muscles of his great iron jaw contracted.

"God forgive me," he said; "it was His angel again! I never saw Alkire after that."

"Nobody ever saw him after that," said Dix. "He got out of the hills that night."

"No," replied Abner; "it was not in the night when Alkire started on his journey; it was in the day."

"Abner," said Dix, "you talk like a fool. If Alkire had traveled the road in the day somebody would have seen him."

"Nobody could see him on the road he traveled," replied Abner.

"What road?" said Dix.

"Dix," replied Abner, "you will learn that soon enough."

Abner looked hard at the man.

"You saw Alkire when he started on his journey," he continued; "but did you see who it was that went with him?"

"Nobody went with him," replied Dix; "Alkire rode alone."

"Not alone," said Abner; "there was another."

"I didn't see him," said Dix.

"And yet," continued Abner, "you made Alkire go with him."

I saw cunning enter Dix's face. He was puzzled, but he thought Abner off the scent.

"And I made Alkire go with somebody, did I? Well, who was it? Did you see him?"

"Nobody ever saw him."

"He must be a stranger."

"No," replied Abner, "he rode the hills before we came into them."

"Indeed!" said Dix. "And what kind of a horse did he ride?"

"White!" said Abner.

Dix got some inkling of what Abner meant now, and his face grew livid.

"What are you driving at?" he cried. "You sit here beating around the bush. If you know anything, say it out; let's hear it. What is it?"

Abner put out his big sinewy hand as though to thrust Dix back into his chair.

"Listen!" he said. "Two days after that I wanted to get out into the Ten Mile country and I went through your lands; I rode a path through the narrow valley west of your house. At a point on the path where there is an apple tree something caught my eye and I stopped. Five minutes later I knew exactly what had happened under that apple tree. . . . Someone had ridden there; he had stopped under that tree; then something happened and the horse had run away—I knew that by the tracks of a horse on this path. I knew that the horse had a rider and that it had stopped under this tree, because there was a limb cut from the tree at a certain height. I knew the horse had remained there, because the small twigs of the apple limb had been pared off, and they lay in a heap on the path. I knew that something had frightened the horse and that it had run away, because the sod was torn up where it had jumped. . . . Ten minutes later I knew that the rider had not been in the saddle when the horse jumped; I knew what it was that had frightened the horse; and I knew that the thing had occurred the day before. Now, how did I know that?

"Listen! I put my horse into the tracks of that other horse under the tree and studied the ground. Immediately I saw where the weeds beside the path had been crushed, as though some animal had been lying down there, and in the very center of that bed I saw a little heap of fresh earth. That was strange, Dix, that fresh earth where the animal had been lying down! It had come there after the animal had got up, or else it would have been pressed flat. But where had it come from?

"I got off and walked around the apple tree, moving out from it in an ever-widening circle. Finally I found an ant heap, the top of which had been scraped away as though one had taken up the loose earth in his hands. Then I went back and plucked up some of the earth. The under clods of it were colored as with red paint. . . . No, it wasn't paint.

"There was a brush fence some fifty yards away. I went over to it and followed it down.

"Opposite the apple tree the weeds were again crushed as though some animal had lain there. I sat down in that place and drew a line with my eye across a log of the fence to a limb of the apple tree. Then I got on my horse and again put him in the tracks of that other horse under the tree; the imaginary line passed through the pit of my stomach! . . . I am four inches taller than Alkire."

It was then that Dix began to curse. I had seen his face work while Abner was speaking and that spray of sweat had reappeared. But he kept the courage he had got.

"Lord Almighty, man!" he cried. "How prettily you sum it up! We shall presently have Lawyer Abner with his brief. Because my renters have killed a calf; because one of their horses frightened at the blood has bolted, and because they cover the blood with earth so the other horses traveling the path may not do the like; straightway I have shot Alkire out of his saddle. . . . Man! What a mare's nest! And now, Lawyer Abner, with your neat little conclusions, what did I do with Alkire after I had killed him? Did I cause him to vanish into the air with a smell of sulphur or did I cause the earth to yawn and Alkire to descend into its bowels?"

"Dix," replied Abner, "your words move somewhat near the truth."

"Upon my soul," cried Dix, "you compliment me. If I had that trick of magic, believe me, you would be already some distance down."

Abner remained a moment silent.

"Dix," he said, "what does it mean when one finds a plot of earth resodded?"

"Is that a riddle?" cried Dix. "Well, confound me, if I don't answer it! You charge me with murder and then you fling in this neat conundrum. Now, what could be the answer to that riddle, Abner? If one had done a murder this sod would overlie a grave and Alkire would be in it in his bloody shirt. Do I give the answer?"

"You do not," replied Abner.

"No!" cried Dix. "Your sodded plot no grave, and Alkire not within it waiting for the trump of Gabriel! Why, man, where are your little damned conclusions?"

"Dix," said Abner, "you do not deceive me in the least; Alkire is not sleeping in a grave."

"Then in the air," sneered Dix, "with a smell of sulphur?"

"Nor in the air," said Abner.

"Then consumed with fire, like the priests of Baal?"

"Nor with fire," said Abner.

Dix had got back the quiet of his face; this banter had put him where he was when Abner entered. "This is all fools' talk," he said; "if I had killed Alkire, what could I have done with the body? And the horse! What could I have done with the horse? Remember, no man has ever seen Alkire's horse any more than he has seen Alkire— and for the reason that Alkire rode him out of the hills that night. Now, look here, Abner, you have asked me a good many questions. I will ask you one. Among your little conclusions do you find that I did this thing alone or with the aid of others?"

"Dix," replied Abner, "I will answer that upon my own belief you had no accomplice."

"Then," said Dix, "how could I have carried off the horse? Alkire I might carry; but his horse weighed thirteen hundred pounds!"

"Dix," said Abner, "no man helped you do this thing; but there were men who helped you to conceal it."

"And now," cried Dix, "the man is going mad! Who could I trust with such work, I ask you? Have I a renter that would not tell it when he moved on to another's land, or when he got a quart of cider in him? Where are the men who helped me?"

"Dix," said Abner, "they have been dead these fifty years."

I heard Dix laugh then, and his evil face lighted as though a candle were behind it. And, in truth, I thought he had got Abner silenced.

"In the name of Heaven!" he cried. "With such proofs it is a wonder that you did not have me hanged."

"And hanged you should have been," said Abner.

"Well," cried Dix, "go and tell the sheriff, and mind you lay before him those little, neat conclusions: How from a horse track and the place where a calf was butchered you have reasoned on Alkire's murder, and to conceal the body and the horse you have reasoned on the aid of men who were rotting in their graves when I was born; and see how he will receive you!"

Abner gave no attention to the man's flippant speech. He got his great silver watch out of his pocket, pressed the stem and looked. Then he spoke in his deep, even voice.

"Dix," he said, "it is nearly midnight; in an hour you must be on your journey, and I have something more to say. Listen! I knew this thing had been done the previous day because it had rained on the night that I met Alkire, and the earth of this ant heap had been disturbed after that. Moreover, this earth had been frozen, and that showed a night had passed since it had been placed there. And I knew the rider of that horse was Alkire because, beside the path near the severed twigs lay my knife, where it had fallen from his hand. This much I learned in some fifteen minutes; the rest took somewhat longer.

"I followed the track of the horse until it stopped in the little valley below. It was easy to follow while the horse ran, because the sod was torn; but when it ceased to run there was no track that I could follow. There was a little stream threading the valley, and I began at the wood and came slowly up to see if I could find where the horse had crossed. Finally I found a horse track and there was also a man's track, which meant that you had caught the horse and were leading it away. But where?

"On the rising ground above there was an old orchard where there had once been a house. The work about that house had been done a hundred years. It was rotted down now. You had opened this orchard into the pasture. I rode all over the face of this hill and finally I entered this orchard. There was a great, flat, moss-covered stone lying a few steps from where the house had stood. As I looked I noticed that the moss growing from it into the earth had been broken along the edges of the stone, and then I noticed that for a few feet about the stone the ground had been resodded. I got down and lifted up some of this new sod. Under it the earth had been soaked with that . . . red paint.

"It was clever of you, Dix, to resod the ground; that took only a little time and it effectually concealed the place where you had killed the horse; but it was foolish of you to forget that the broken moss around the edges of the great flat stone could not be mended."

"Abner!" cried Dix. "Stop!" And I saw that spray of sweat, and his face working like kneaded bread, and the shiver of that abominable chill on him.

Abner was silent for a moment and then he went on, but from another quarter.

"Twice," said Abner, "the Angel of the Lord stood before me and I did not know it; but the third time I knew it. It is not in the cry of the wind, nor in the voice of many waters that His presence is made known to us. That man in Israel had only the sign that the beast under him would not go on. Twice I had as good a sign, and tonight, when Marks broke a stirrup-leather before my house and called me to the door and asked me for a knife to mend it, I saw and I came!"

The log that Abner had thrown on was burned down, and the fire was again a mass of embers; the room was filled with that dull red light. Dix had got on to his feet, and he stood now twisting before the fire, his hands reaching out to it, and that cold creeping in his bones, and the smell of the fire on him.

Abner rose. And when he spoke his voice was like a thing that has dimensions and weight.

"Dix," he said, "you robbed the grazers; you shot Alkire out of his saddle; and a child you would have murdered!"

And I saw the sleeve of Abner's coat begin to move, then it stopped. He stood staring at something against the wall. I looked to see what the thing was, but I did not see it. Abner was looking beyond the wall, as though it had been moved away.

And all the time Dix had been shaking with that hellish cold, and twisting on the hearth and crowding into the fire. Then he fell back, and he was the Dix I knew—his face was slack; his eye was furtive; and he was full of terror.

It was his weak whine that awakened Abner. He put up his hand and brought the fingers hard down over his face, and then he looked at this new creature, cringing and beset with fears.

"Dix," he said, "Alkire was a just man; he sleeps as peacefully in that abandoned well under his horse as he would sleep in the churchyard. My hand has been held back; you may go. Vengeance is mine, I will repay, saith the Lord."

"But where shall I go, Abner?" the creature wailed; "I have no money and I am cold."

Abner took out his leather wallet and flung it toward the door.

"There is money," he said— "a hundred dollars—and there is my coat. Go! But if I find you in the hills to-morrow, or if I ever find you, I warn you in the name of the living God that I will stamp you out of life!"

I saw the loathsome thing writhe into Abner's coat and seize the wallet and slip out through the door; and a moment later I heard a horse. And I crept back on to Roy's heifer skin.

When I came down at daylight my Uncle Abner was reading by the fire.

4
An Act of God

It was the last day of the County Fair, and I stood beside my Uncle Abner, on the edge of the crowd, watching the performance of a mountebank.

On a raised platform, before a little house on wheels, stood a girl dressed like a gypsy, with her arms extended, while an old man out in the crowd, standing on a chair, was throwing great knives that hemmed her in with a steel hedge. The girl was very young, scarcely more than a child, and the man was old, but he was hale and powerful. He wore wooden shoes, travel-worn purple velvet trousers, a red sash, and a white blouse of a shirt open at the throat.

I was watching the man, whose marvelous skill fascinated me. He seemed to be looking always at the crowd of faces that passed between him and the wagon, and yet the great knife fell to a hair on the target, grazing the body of the girl.

But while the old man with his sheaf of knives held my attention, it was the girl that Abner looked at. He stood studying her face with a strange rapt attention. Sometimes he lifted his head and looked vacantly over the crowd with the eyelids narrowed, like one searching for a memory that eluded him, then he came back to the face in its cluster of dark ringlets, framed in knives that stood quivering in the poplar board.

It was thus that my father found us when he came up.

"Have you noticed Blackford about?" he said; "I want to see him."

"No," replied Abner, "but he should be here, I think; he is at every frolic."

48

"I sent him the money for his cattle last night," my father went on, "and I wish to know if he got it."

Abner turned upon him at that.

"You will always take a chance with that scoundrel, Rufus," he said, "and some day you will be robbed. His lands are covered with a deed of trust."

"Well," replied my father, with his hearty laugh, "I shall not be robbed this time. I have Blackford's request over his signature for the money, with the statement that the letter is to be evidence of its payment."

And he took an envelope out of his pocket and handed it to Abner.

My uncle read the letter to the end, and then his great fingers tightened on the sheet, and he read it carefully again, and yet again, with his eyes narrowed and his jaw protruding. Finally he looked my father in the face.

"Blackford did not write this letter!" he said.

"Not write it!" my father cried. "Why, man, I know the deaf mute's writing like a book. I know every line and slant of his letters, and every crook and twist of his signature."

But my uncle shook his head.

My father was annoyed.

"Nonsense!" he said. "I can call a hundred men on these fair grounds who will swear that Blackford made every stroke of the pen in that letter, even against his denial, and though he bring Moses and the prophets to support him."

Abner looked my father steadily in the face.

"That is true, Rufus," he said; "the thing is perfect. There is no letter or line or stroke or twist of the pen that varies from Blackford's hand, and every grazer in the hills, to a man, will swear upon the Bible that he wrote it. Blackford himself cannot tell this writing from his own, nor can any other living man; and yet the deaf mute did not write it."

"Well," said my father, "yonder is Blackford now; we will ask him."

But they never did.

I saw the tall deaf mute swagger up and enter the crowd before the mountebank's wagon. And then a thing happened. The chair upon which the old man stood broke under him. He fell and the great knife in his hand swerved downward and went through the deaf mute's body, as though it were a cheese. The man was dead when we picked him up; the knife blade stood out between his shoulders, and the haft was jammed against his bloody coat.

We carried him into the Agricultural Hall among the prize apples and the pumpkins, summoned Squire Randolph from the cattle pens, and brought the mountebank before him.

Randolph came in his big blustering manner and sat down as though he were the judge of all the world. He heard the evidence, and upon the word of every witness the tragedy was an accident clean through. But it was an accident that made one shudder. It came swift and deadly and unforeseen, like a vengeance of God in the Book of Kings. One passing among his fellows, in no apprehension, had been smitten out of life. There was terror in the mystery of selection that had thus claimed Blackford in this crowd for death. It brought our voices to a whisper to feel how unprotected a man was in this life, and how little we could see.

And yet the thing had the aspect of design and moved with our stern Scriptural beliefs. In the pulpit this deaf mute had been an example and a warning. His life was profligate and loose. He was a cattle shipper who knew the abominations indexed by the Psalmist. He was an Ishmaelite in more ways than his affliction. He had no wife nor child, nor any next of kin. He had been predestined to an evil end by every good housewife in the hills. He would go swiftly and by violence into hell, the preachers said; and swiftly and by violence he had gone on this autumn morning when the world was like an Eden.

He lay there among the sheaves of corn and the fruits and cereals of the earth, so fully come to the end predestined that those who had cried the prophecy the loudest were the most amazed. With all their vaporings, they could not believe that God would be so expeditious, and they spoke in whispers and crowded about on tiptoe, as though the Angel of the Lord stood at the entrance of this little festal hall, as before the threshing floor of Araunah the Jebusite.

Randolph could do nothing but find the thing an accident, and let the old man go. But he thundered from behind his table on the dangers of such a trade as this. And all the time the mountebank stood stupidly before him like a man dazed, and the little girl wept and clung to the big peasant's hand. Randolph pointed to the girl and told the old man that he would kill her some day, and with the gestures and authority of omnipotence forbade his trade. The old mountebank promised to cast his knives into the river and get at something else. Randolph spoke upon the law of accidents sententiously for some thirty minutes, quoted Lord Blackstone and Mr. Chitty, called the thing an act of God, within a certain definition of the law, and rose.

My Uncle Abner had been standing near the door, looking on with a grave, undecipherable face. He had gone through the crowd to the chair when the old man fell, had drawn the knife out of Blackford's body, but he had not helped to carry him in, and he had remained by the door, his big shoulders towering above the audience. Randolph stopped beside him as he went out, took a pinch of snuff, and trumpeted in his big, many-colored handkerchief.

"Ah, Abner," he said, "do you concur in my decision?"

"You called the thing an act of God," replied Abner, "and I concur in that."

"And so it is," said Randolph, with judicial pomp; "the writers on the law, in their disquisitions upon torts, include within that term those inscrutable injuries that no human intelligence can foresee; for instance, floods, earthquakes and tornadoes."

"Now, that is very stupid in the writers on the law," replied Abner; "I should call such injuries acts of the devil. It would not occur to me to believe that God would use the agency of the elements in order to injure the innocent."

"Well," said Randolph, "the writers upon the law have not been theologians, although Mr. Greenleaf was devout, and Chitty with a proper reverence, and my lords Coke and Blackstone and Sir

Matthew Hale in respectable submission to the established church. They have grouped and catalogued injuries with delicate and nice distinctions with respect to their being actionable at law, and they found certain injuries to be acts of God, but I do not read that they found any injury to be an act of the devil. The law does not recognize the sovereignty and dominion of the devil."

"Then," replied Abner, "with great fitness is the law represented blindfold. I have not entered any jurisdiction where his writs have failed to run."

There was a smile about the door that would have broken into laughter but for the dead man inside.

Randolph blustered, consulted his snuffbox, and turned the conversation into a neighboring channel.

"Do you think, Abner," he said, "that this old showman will give up his dangerous practice as he promised me?"

"Yes," replied Abner, "he will give it up, but not because he promised you."

And he walked away to my father, took him by the arm, and led him aside.

"Rufus," he said, "I have learned something. Your receipt is valid."

"Of course it is valid," replied my father; "it is in Blackford's hand."

"Well," said Abner, "he cannot come back to deny it, and I will not be a witness for him."

"What do you mean, Abner?" my father said. "You say that Blackford did not write this letter, and now you say that it is valid."

"I mean," replied Abner, "that when the one entitled to a debt receives it, that is enough."

Then he walked away into the crowd, his head lifted and his fingers locked behind his massive back.

The County Fair closed that evening in much gossip and many idle comments on Blackford's end. The chimney corner lawyers, riding out with the homing crowd, vapored upon Mr. Jefferson's Statute of Descents, and how Blackford's property would escheat to the state since there was no next of kin, and were met with the

information that his lands and his cattle would precisely pay his
debts, with an eagle or two beyond for a coffin. And, after the manner of lawyers, were not silenced, but laid down what the law would
be if only the facts were agreeable to their premise. And the prophets, sitting in their wagons, assembled their witnesses and established the dates at which they had been prophetically delivered.

Evening descended, and the fair grounds were mostly deserted.
Those who lived at no great distance had moved their live stock
with the crowd and had given up their pens and stalls. But my
father, who always brought a drove of prize cattle to these fairs,
gave orders that we should remain until the morning. The distance
home was too great and the roads were filled. My father's cattle
were no less sacred than the bulls of Egypt, and not to be crowded
by a wagon wheel or ridden into by a shouting drunkard.

The night fell. There was no moon, but the earth was not in
darkness. The sky was clear and sown with stars like a seeded field.
I did not go to bed in the cattle stall filled with clover hay under a
handwoven blanket, as I was intended to do. A youngster at a certain age is a sort of jackal and loves nothing in this world so much
as to prowl over the ground where a crowd of people has encamped.
Besides, I wished to know what had become of the old mountebank, and it was a thing I soon discovered.

His wagon stood on the edge of the ground among the trees
near the river, with the door closed. His horse, tethered to a wheel,
was nosing an armful of hay. The light of the stars filtered through
the treetops, filled the wheels with shadows and threw one side of
the wagon into the blackness of the pit. I went down to the fringe
of trees; there I sat squatted on the earth until I heard a footstep
and saw my Uncle Abner coming toward the wagon. He walked as
I had seen him walking in the crowd, his hands behind him and
his face lifted as though he considered something that perplexed
him. He came to the steps, knocked with his clenched hand on the
door, and when a voice replied, entered.

Curiosity overcame me. I scurried up to the dark side of the
wagon. There a piece of fortune awaited me; a gilded panel had
cracked with some jolt upon the road, and by perching myself upon

the wheel I could see inside. The old man had been seated behind a table made by letting down a board hinged to the wall. His knives were lying on the floor beside him, bound together in a sheaf with a twine string. There were some packets of old letters on the table and a candle. The little girl lay asleep in a sort of bunk at the end of the wagon. The old man stood up when my uncle entered, and his face, that had been dull and stupid before the justice of the peace, was now keen and bright.

"Monsieur does me an honor," he said. The words were an interrogation with no welcome in them.

"No honor," replied my uncle, standing with his hat on; "but possibly a service."

"That would be strange," the mountebank said dryly, "for I have received no service from any man here."

"You have a short memory," replied Abner; "the justice of the peace rendered you a great service on this day. Do you put no value on your life?"

"My life has not been in danger, monsieur," he said.

"I think it has," replied Abner.

"Then monsieur questions the decision?"

"No," said Abner; "I think it was the very wisest decision that Randolph ever made."

"Then why does monsieur say that my life was in danger?"

"Well," replied my uncle, "are not the lives of all men in danger? Is there any day or hour of a day in which they are secure, or any tract or parcel of this earth where danger is not? And can a man say when he awakes at daylight in his bed, on this day I shall go into danger, or I shall not? In the light it is, and in the darkness it is, and where one looks to find it, and where he does not. Did Blackford believe himself in danger today when he passed before you?"

"Ah, monsieur," replied the man, "that was a terrible accident!"

My uncle picked up a stool, placed it by the table and sat down. He took off his hat and set it on his knees, then he spoke, looking at the floor.

"Do you believe in God?"

I saw the old man rub his forehead with his hand and the ball of his first finger make a cross.

"Yes, monsieur," he said, "I do."

"Then," replied Abner, "you can hardly believe that things happen out of chance."

"We call it chance, monsieur," said the man, "when we do not understand it."

"Sometimes we use a better term," replied Abner. "Now, today Randolph did not understand this death of Blackford, and yet he called it an act of God."

"Who knows," said the man; "are not the ways of God past finding out?"

"Not always," replied my uncle.

He gathered his chin into his hand and sat for some time motionless, then he continued:

"I have found out something about this one."

The old mountebank moved to his stool beyond the table and sat down.

"And what is that, monsieur?" he said.

"That you are in danger of your life—for one thing."

"In what danger?"

"Do you come from the south of Europe," replied Abner, "and forget that when a man is killed there are others to threaten his assassin?"

"But this Blackford has no kin to carry a blood feud," said the mountebank.

"And so," cried Abner, "you knew that before you killed him. And yet, in spite of that precaution, there stood a man in the crowd before the justice of the peace who held your life in his hand. He had but to speak."

"And why did he not speak—this man?" said the mountebank, looking at Abner across the table.

"I will tell you that," replied Abner. "He feared that the justice of the law might contravene the justice of God. It is a fabric woven from many threads—this justice of God. I saw three of these threads today stretching into the great loom, and I feared to touch them lest I disturb the weaver at his work. I saw men see a murder and not know it. I saw a child see its father and not know it, and I saw a letter in the handwriting of a man who did not write it."

The face of the old mountebank did not whiten, but instead it grew stern and resolute, and the muscles came out in it so that it seemed a thing of cords under the tanned skin.

"The proofs," he said.

"They are all here," replied Abner.

He stooped, lifted the sheaf of knives, broke the string and spread them on the table. He selected the one from which Blackford's blood had been wiped off.

"Randolph examined this knife," he continued, "but not the others; he assumed that they are all alike. Well, they are not. The others are dull, but this one has the edge of a razor."

And he plucked a piece of paper from the table and sheared it in two. Then he put the knife down on the board and looked toward the far end of the wagon.

"And the child's face," he said— "I was not certain of that until I saw Blackford's ironed out under the hand of death, and then I knew. And the letter—"

But the old man was on his feet straining over the table, his features twitching like a taut rope.

"Hush! Hush!" he said.

There came a little gust of wind that whispered in the dry grass and blew the dead leaves against the wagon and about my face. They fluttered like a presence, these dead leaves, and pecked and clawed at the gilded panel like the nails of some feeble hand. I began to be assailed with fear as I sat there alone in the darkness looking in upon this tragedy.

My Uncle Abner sat down, and the old man remained with the palms of his hands pressed against the table. Finally he spoke.

"Monsieur," he said, "shall a man lead another into hell and escape the pit himself? Yes, she is his daughter, and her mother was mine, and I have killed him. He could not speak, but with those letters he persuaded her."

The man paused and turned over the packet of yellow envelopes tied up with faded ribbon.

"And she believed what a woman will always believe. What would you have done, monsieur? Go to the law—your English law that gives the woman a pittance and puts her out of the court-house door for the ribald to laugh at! Diable! Monsieur, that is not the law. I know the law, as my father and my father's father, and your father and your father's father knew it. I would have killed him then, when she died, but for this child. I would have followed him into these hills, day after day, like his shadow behind him, until I got a knife into him and ripped him up like a butchered pig. But I could not go to the hangman and leave this child, and so I waited."

He sat down.

"We can wait, monsieur. That is one thing we have in my country—patience. And when I was ready I killed him."

The old man paused and put out his hand, palm upward, on the table. It was a wonderful hand, like a live thing.

"You have eyes, monsieur, but the others are as blind men. Did they think that hand could have failed me? Cunning men have made machinery so accurate that you marvel at them; but there was never a machine with the accuracy of the human hand when it is trained as we train it. Monsieur, I could scratch a line on the door behind you with a needle, and with my eyes closed set a knife point into every twist and turn of it. Why, monsieur, there was a straw clinging to Blackford's coat—a straw that had fallen on him as he passed some horse stall. I marked it as he came up through the crowd, and I split it with the knife.

"And now, monsieur?"

But my uncle stopped him. "Not yet," he said. "I am concerned about the living and not the dead. If I had thought of the dead only, I should have spoken this day; but I have thought also of the living. What have you done for the child?"

There came a great tenderness into the old man's face.

"I have brought it up in love," he said, "and in honor, and I have got its inheritance for it."

He stopped and indicated the pack of letters.

"I was about to burn these when you came in, monsieur, for they have served their purpose. I thought I might need to know Blackford's hand and I set out to learn it. Not in a day, monsieur, nor a week, like your common forger, and with an untried hand— but in a year, and years—with a hand that obeys me, I went over and over every letter of every word until I could write the man's hand, not an imitation of it, monsieur, not that, but the very hand itself—the very hand that Blackford writes with his own fingers. And it was well, for I was able to get the child all that Blackford had, beyond his debts, by a letter that no man could know that Blackford did not write."

"I knew that he did not write it," said Abner.

The old man smiled.

"You jest, monsieur," he said; "Blackford himself could not tell the writing from his own. I could not, nor can any living man."

"That is true," replied Abner; "the letter is in Blackford's hand, as he would have written it with his own fingers. It is no imitation, as you say; it is the very writing of the man, and yet he did not write it, and when I saw it I knew that he did not."

The old man's face was incredulous.

"How could you know that, monsieur?" he said.

My uncle took the letter which my father had received out of his pocket and spread it out on the table.

"I will tell you," he said, "how I knew that Blackford did not write this letter, although it is in his very hand. When my brother Rufus showed me this letter, and I read it, I noticed that there were words misspelled in it. Well, that of itself was nothing for the deaf mute did not always spell correctly. It was the manner in which the words were misspelled. Under the old system, when a deaf mute was taught to write he was taught by the eye; consequently, he writes words as he remembers them to look, and not as he remembers them to sound. His mistakes, then, are mistakes of the eye and not of the ear. And in this he differs from every man who can hear; for the man who can hear, when he is uncertain about the spelling of a word, spells it as it sounds phonetically, using not a letter that looks like the correct one, but a letter that sounds like it—using 's' for 'c' and 'o' for 'u'—a thing no deaf mute would ever do in this world, because he does not know what letters sound like. Consequently, when I saw the words in this letter misspelled by sound—when I saw that the person who had written this letter remembered his word as a sound, and by the arrangement of the letters in it was endeavoring to indicate that sound—I knew he could hear."

The old man did not reply, but he rose and stood before my uncle. He stood straight and fearless, his long white hair thrown back, his bronzed throat exposed, his face lifted, and his eyes calm and level, like some ancient druid among his sacred oak trees.

And I crowded my face against the cracked panel, straining to hear what he would say.

"Monsieur," he said, "I have done an act of justice, not as men do it, but as the providence of God does it. With care and with patience I have accomplished every act, so that to the eyes of men it bore the relation and aspect of God's providence. And all who saw were content but you. You have pried and ferreted behind these things, and now you must bear the obligations of your knowledge."

He spread out his hands toward the sleeping girl.

"Shall this child grow up to honor in ignorance, or in knowledge go down to hell? Shall she know what her mother was, and what her father was, and what I am, and be fouled by the knowledge of it, and shall she be stripped of her inheritance and left not only outlawed, but paupered? And shall I go to the hangman, and she to the street? These are things for you to decide, since you would search out what was hidden and reveal what was covered! I leave it in your hands."

"And I," replied Abner, rising, "leave it in God's."

5

THE TREASURE HUNTER

I remember very well when the sailor came to Highfield. It was the return of the prodigal—a belated return. The hospitalities of the parable did not await him. Old Thorndike Madison was dead. And Charlie Madison, in possession as sole heir, was not pleased to see a lost brother land from a river boat after twenty years of silence.

The law presumes death after seven years, and for twenty Dabney Madison had been counted out of life—counted out by old Thorndike when he left his estate to pass by operation of law to the surviving son; and counted out by Charlie when he received the title.

The imagination of every lad in the Hills was fired by the romantic properties of this event. The negroes carried every detail, and they would have colored it to suit the fancy had not the thing happened in ample color.

The estate had gone to rack with Charlie drunk from dawn until midnight. Old Clayborne and Mariah kept the negro quarters, half a mile from the house. Clayborne would put Charlie to bed and then go home to his cabin. In the morning Mariah would come to get his coffee. So Charlie lived after old Thorndike, at ninety, had gone to the graveyard.

It was a witch's night when the thing happened—rain and a high wind that wailed and whooped round the pillars and chimneys of the house. The house was set on a high bank above the river, where

60

the swift water, running like a flood, made a sharp bend. It caught the full force of wind and rain. It was old and the timbers creaked.

Charlie was drunk. He cried out when he saw the lost brother and got unsteadily on his legs.

"You are not Dabney!" he said. "You are a picture out of a storybook!" And he laughed in a sort of half terror, like a child before a homemade ghost. "Look at your earrings!"

It was a good comment for a man in liquor; for if ever a character stepped out of the pages of a pirate tale, here it was.

Dabney had lifted the latch and entered without warning. He had the big frame and the hawk nose of his race. He was in sea-stained sailor clothes, his face white as plaster, a red cloth wound tightly round his head, huge half-moon rings in his ears; and he carried a seaman's chest on his shoulder.

Old Clayborne told the story.

Dabney put down his chest carefully, as though it had something precious in it. Then he spoke.

"Are you glad to see me, brother?"

Charlie was holding on to the table with both hands, his eyes bleared, his mouth gaping.

"I don't see you," he quavered. Then he turned his head, with a curious duck of the chin, toward the old negro. "I don't see anything—do I?"

Dabney came over to the table then; he took up the flask of liquor and a glass.

"Clabe," he said, "is this apple whisky?"

I have heard the ancient negro tell the story a thousand times. He gave a great shout of recognition. Those words—those five words—settled it. He used to sing this part in a long, nasal chant when he reached it in his tale: "Marse Dabney! Oh, my Lord! How many times ain't I heard 'im say dem words—jis' lak dat: 'Clabe, is dis apple whisky?' Dem outlandish clo's couldn't fool dis nigger! I'd 'a' knowed Marse Dabney after dat if he'd been 'parisoned in de garments ob Israel!"

But the old negro had Satan's time with Charlie, who held on to the table and cursed.

"You're not Dabney!" he cried. ". . . I know you! You're old Lafitte, the Pirate, who helped General Jackson thrash the British at New Orleans. Grandfather used to tell about you!"

He began to cry and blame his grandfather for so vividly impressing the figure that it came up now in his liquor to annoy him. Then he would get his courage and shake a trembling fist across the table.

"You can't frighten me, Lafitte—curse you! I've seen worse things than you over there. I've seen the devil, with a spade, digging a grave; and a horsefly, as big as a buzzard, perched on the highboy, looking at me and calling out to the devil: 'Dig it deep! We'll bury old Charlie deep'!"

Clayborne finally got him to realize that Dabney was a figure in life, in spite of the chalk face under the red headcloth.

And then Charlie went into a drunken mania of resentment. Dabney was dead—or if he was not dead he ought to be; and he started to the highboy for a dueling pistol. His fury and his drunken curses filled the house. The place belonged to him! He would not divide it.

It was the devil's night. About daybreak the ancient negro got Charlie into bed and the sailor installed in old Thorndike's room, with a fire and all the attentions of a guest.

After that Charlie was strangely quiet. He suffered the intrusion of the sailor with no word. Dabney might have been always in the house for any indication in Charlie's manner. There was peace; but one was impressed that it was a sort of armistice.

Dabney went over the old estate pretty carefully, but he did not interfere with Charlie's possession. He laid no claim that anybody heard of. Charlie seemed to watch him. He kept the drink in hand and he grew silent.

There seemed no overt reason, old Clayborne said, but presently Dabney began to act like a man in fear. He made friends with the dog, a big old bearhound. He got a fowling piece and set it up by the head of his bed, and finally took the dog into the room with him at night. He kept out of the house by day.

One could see him, with a mariner's glass, striding across the high fields above the river, or perched in the fork of a tree. He wore the sailor clothes, and the red cloth wound round his head.

I am sure my uncle Abner saw him more than once. I know of one time. He was riding home from a sitting of the county justices. Dabney was walking through the deep broom sedge in the high field beyond the old house. Abner called and he came down to the road. He had the mariner's glass, the sailor clothes and the headcloth.

He was not pleased to see my uncle. He seemed nervous, like a man under some restraint. While my uncle talked he would take three steps straight ahead and then turn back. Abner marked it, with a query.

"Dabney," he said, "why do you turn about like that?"

The man stopped in his tracks; for a moment he seemed in a sort of frenzied terror. Then he cursed:

"Habit—damme, Abner!"

"And where did you get a habit like that?" said my uncle.

"In a ship," replied the man.

"What sort of ship?" said my uncle.

The sailor hesitated for a moment.

"Now, Abner," he cried finally, "what sort of ships are they that sail the Caribbee and rendezvous on the Dry Tortugas?" His voice took a strained, wild note. "Have they spacious cabins, or does one take three steps thus in the narrow pen of their hold?"

My uncle gathered his chin into his big fingers and looked steadily at the man.

"Strange quarters, Dabney," he said, "for a son of Thorndike Madison."

"Well, Abner!" cried the man, "what would you have? It was that or the plank. It's all very nice to be a gentleman and the son of a gentleman under the protection of Virginia; but off the Bermudas, with the muzzle of a musket pressed into your back and the sea boiling below you—what then?"

My uncle watched the man closely and with a strange expression.

"A clean death," he said, "would be better than God's vengeance to follow on one's heels."

The sailor swore a great oath.

"God's vengeance!" And he laughed. "I should not care how that followed on my heels. It's the vengeance of old Jules le Noir and the damned Britisher, Barrett, following on a man's heels, that puts ice in the blood. God's vengeance! Why, Abner, a preacher could pray that off in a meetinghouse; but can he pray the half-breed off? Or the broken-nosed Englishman?"

The man seemed caught in a current of passion that whirled him headlong into indiscretions from which a saner mood would have steered him clear.

"The Spanish Main is not Virginia!" he cried. "One does not live the life of a gentleman on it. Loot and murder are not the pastimes of a gentleman. The Spanish Main is not safe. But is Virginia safe? Is any spot safe? Eh, Abner? Show it to me if you know it!" And he plunged off into the deep broom sedge.

So it came about that an evil Frenchman with a cutlass in his teeth, and a vile old rum-soaked creature with a broken nose and a brace of pistols, got entangled in the common fancy with Dabney's legend.

Everybody in the Hills thought something was going to happen; but the wild thing that did happen came sooner than anybody thought.

One morning at sunrise a negro house boy ran in, out of breath, to say that old Clayborne had gone by at a gallop on his way to Randolph, the justice of the peace, and shouted for my uncle to come to Highfield.

Randolph had the nearer road; but Abner met him at the Madison door and the two men went into the house together.

Old Charlie was sober; but he was drinking raw liquor and doing his best to get drunk. His face was ghastly, and his hands shook so that he could keep only a few spoonfuls of the white brandy in his big tumbler. My uncle said that if ever the terror of the damned was on a human creature in this world it was on old Charlie.

It was some time before they could get at what had happened. It was of no use to bother with Charlie until the liquor should begin to steady him. His loose underlip jerked and every faculty he could muster was massed on the one labor of getting the brandy to his mouth.

Old Mariah sat in the kitchen, with her apron over her head, rocking on the four legs of a split-bottomed chair. She was worse than useless.

My uncle and Randolph had got some things out of Clayborne on the way. There had been nothing to indicate the thing that night. Dabney had gone into old Thorndike's room, as usual, with the dog. Old Clayborne had put Charlie to bed drunk, snuffed out the candles and departed to his cabin, half a mile away. That was all old Clayborne could tell of the night before. Perhaps the sailor seemed a little more in fear than usual, and perhaps Charlie was a little more in liquor; but he could not be sure on those questions of degree. The sailor lately seemed to be in constant fear and Charlie had got back at his liquor with an increased and abandoned indulgence.

What happened after that my uncle and Randolph could see for themselves better than Clayborne could tell it.

Old Thorndike's room, like the other rooms of the house, had a door that opened on a long covered porch, facing the river. This door now stood open. The ancient rusted lock plate, with its screws, was hanging to the frame. There were no marks of violence on the door. The sailor was gone. His pillow and the bedclothes were soaked with blood. All his clothes, including the red headcloth, were lying neatly folded on the arm of a chair.

The sailor's chest stood open and empty. There was a little sprinkling of blood drops from the bed to the door and into the weeds outside, but no blood anywhere else in the room. And from there, directly in a line to the river, the weeds and grass had been trampled. The ground was hard and dry, and no one could say how many persons had gone that way from the house. The dog lay just inside the door of the room, with his throat cut. It was the slash of a knife with the edge of a razor, for the dog's head was nearly severed from the neck.

It was noiseless, swift work—incredibly noiseless and swift. Dabney had not wakened, for the fowling piece stood unmoved at

the head of the bed. When the door swung open somebody had
caught the dog's muzzle and slipped the knife across his throat . . .
and then the rest.

"It must have happened that way," Randolph said.

At any rate, the unwelcome sailor was gone. He had arrived in
an abundance of mystery and he had departed in it, though where
he went was clear enough. The great river, swinging round the high
point of land, swallowed what it got. A lost swimmer in that deadly
water was sometimes found miles below, months later—or, rather,
a hideous, unrecognizable human flotsam that the Hills accepted
for the dead man.

The means, too, were not without the indication Dabney had
given in his wild talk to my uncle. Besides, the negroes had seen a
figure—or more than one—at dusk, about an abandoned tobacco
house beyond the great meadow on the landward side of Highfield.

It was a tumble-down old structure in a strip of bush between
the line of the meadow and the acres of morass beyond it—called
swamps in the South. It was ghost land—haunted, the negroes said;
and so what moved there before the tragedy, behind the great elm
at the edge of the meadow, old Clayborne had seen only at a distance, with no wish to spy on it.

Was it the inevitable irony of chance that Dabney scouted the
river with his glass while the thing he feared came in through the
swamps behind him?

By the time my uncle and Randolph had got these evidences
assembled the liquor had steadied Charlie. At first he pretended
to know nothing at all about the affair. He had not wakened, and
had heard nothing until the cries of old Mariah filled the house
with bedlam.

Randolph said he had never seen my uncle so profoundly
puzzled; he sat down in old Charlie's room, silent, with his keen,
strong-featured face as immovable as wood. But the justice saw
light in a crevice of the mystery and he drove directly at it, with no
pretension.

"Charlie," he said, "you were not pleased to see Dabney turn
up!"

The drunken creature did not lie.

"No; I didn't want to see him."

"Why not?"

"Because I thought he was dead."

"Because you did not wish to divide your father's estate with him—wasn't that it?"

"Well, it was all mine—wasn't it—if Dabney was dead?"

The justice went on:

"You tried to shoot Dabney on the night he arrived!"

"I don't know," said Charlie. "I was drunk. Ask Clabe."

The man was in terror; but he kept his head—that was clear as light.

"Dabney knew he was in danger here, didn't he?"

"Yes; he did," said Charlie.

"And he was in fear?"

"Yes," said Charlie— "damnably in fear!"

"Of you!" cried the justice with a sudden, aggressive menace.

"Me?" Old Charlie looked strangely at the man. "Why, no—not me!"

"Of what, then?" said Randolph.

Old Charlie wavered; he got another measure of the brandy in him.

"Well," he said, "it was enough to be afraid of. Look what it did to him!"

Randolph got up, then, and stood over against the man across the table.

"You Madisons are all big men. Now listen to me! It required force to break that door in, and yet there is no mark on the door; that means somebody broke it in with the pressure of his shoulder, softly. And there is another thing, Charlie, that you have got to face: Dabney was killed in his bed while asleep. The dog in the room did not make a sound. Why?"

The face of the drunken man took on a strange, perplexed expression.

"That's so, Randolph," he said; "and it's strange—it's damned strange!"

"Not so very strange," replied the justice.

"Why not?" said Charlie.

"Because the dog knew the man who did that work in your father's room!"

And again, with menace and vigor, Randolph drove at the shaken drunkard:

"Where's the knife Dabney was killed with?"

Then, against all belief, against all expectation in the men, old Charlie fumbled in a drawer beside him and laid a knife on the table. Randolph gasped at the unbelievable success of his driven query, and my uncle rose and joined him.

They looked closely at the knife. It was the common butcher knife of the countryside, made by a smith from a worn-out file and to be found in any kitchen; but it was ground to the point, and whetted to the hair-shearing edge of a razor.

"Look on the handle!" said Charlie.

They looked. And there, burned in the wood crudely, like the imitative undertaking of a child, was a skull and crossbones.

"Where did you get this knife?" said my uncle.

"It was sticking here in my table, in my room, beside my bed, when I woke up." He indicated with his finger nail the narrow hole in the mahogany board where the point of the knife had been forced down. "And this was under it."

He stooped again to the drawer and put a sheet of paper on the table before the astonished men. It was a page of foolscap, with words printed in blood by the point of the knife: "Chest empty! Put thousand in gold—elm—meadow. Or the same to you!"

And there was the puncture in the center of the sheet where the point of the knife had gone through. My uncle laid it on the table, over the narrow hole in the mahogany board, and pressed it down with the knife. The point fitted into the paper and the board.

There was blood on the knife; and the gruesome thing, thus reset, very nearly threw old Charlie back into the panic of terror out of which the brandy had helped him. His fingers twitched, and he kept puffing out his loose underlip like a child laboring to hold back his emotions.

He went at the brandy bottle. And the tale he finally got out was the wildest lie anybody ever put forward in his own defense—if it was a lie. That was the point to judge. And this was Randolph's estimate at the time.

Charlie said that, to cap all of Dabney's strange acts, about a week before this night he asked for a thousand dollars. Charlie told him to go to hell. He said Dabney did not resent either the refusal or the harsh words of it. He simply sat still and began to take on an appearance of fear that sent old Charlie, tumbler in hand, straight to his liquor bottle. Dabney kept coming in every day or two to beg for money; so Charlie got drunk to escape the thing.

"Where was I to get a thousand dollars?" he queried in the tale to my uncle and Randolph.

He said the day before the tragedy was the worst. Dabney got at him in terror for the money. He must have it to save his life, he went on desperately, Charlie said. And then he cried!

Charlie spat violently at the recollection. There was something gruesome, helpless and awful in the memory—in the way Dabney quaked; the tears, and the jingle of the earrings; all the appearance of the man so set to a part of brutal courage—and this shattering fear! The flapping of the big half-moon earrings against the man's white quivering jowls was the worst, Charlie said.

Randolph thought old Charlie colored the thing if he was lying about it. If it was the truth the delusions of liquor would account for these overdrawn impressions. At any rate, the justice promptly spoke out what he thought.

"Charlie," he said, "you're trying to stage a sea yarn by the penny writers. It won't do!"

The man reflected, looking Randolph in the face.

"Why, yes," he said; "you're right—that's what it sounds like. But it isn't that. It's the truth." And he turned to my uncle. "You know it's the truth, Abner."

Randolph said that just here, at this point in the affair, all the established landmarks of common sense and sane credibility were suddenly jumbled up. What my uncle answered was:

"I think it's all true."

Charlie took a big linen handkerchief out of his pocket and wiped his face. Then he said simply, quite simply, like a child:

"I'm afraid!"

One could doubt everything else, Randolph said; but not this. The man was in fear, beyond question.

"I've got it all figured out," Charlie continued. "They were after Dabney for something they thought he had in the chest. They offered to take a thousand dollars for their share and let him off. That's why he was so crazy to raise the money. When they found the chest empty they thought I had the thing, or knew where Dabney had concealed it; and now they are after me!"

Old Charlie stopped again and wiped his face.

"I don't want to die, Abner," he added, "like Dabney—in the bed. What shall I do?"

"There is only one thing to do," replied my uncle. "Put the money by the elm in the meadow."

"But, Abner," replied the man, "where would I get a thousand dollars, as I said to Dabney?"

"I will lend it to you," replied my uncle.

"But, Abner," said Charlie, "you haven't got a thousand dollars in gold in your pocket."

"No," replied my uncle; "but if you will give me a lien on the land I will undertake to pay the money. The estate is in ruin, but it's worth double that sum."

And Randolph said that, among the other strange, mad, ridiculous things of that memorable, extraordinary day, he wrote a deed of trust on the Madison lands to secure Charlie's note to my uncle for a thousand dollars.

So great virtue was there in my uncle's word, and such power had he to inspire the faith of men, that he rode away, leaving old Charlie at peace and confident that he had escaped from peril—whether, as Randolph wondered, it was the peril of the pirate assassins in the great swamp or the gibbet of Virginia.

Two hundred yards from the house, where the strip of bush, skirting the meadow, touched the road, my uncle got down from his horse and tied the bridle rein to a sapling.

"What now, Abner?" cried Randolph, like a man swept along in a current of crazy happenings.

"I am going in to arrange about the payment of the money," replied my uncle.

The justice swore a great oath. If my uncle was setting out to interview desperate assassins—as his acts indicated—alone and unarmed, it was the extreme of foolhardy peril. Did he think murderers would parley with him and let him come away to tell it and to lead in a posse? It was a thing beyond all sane belief!

And it is evidence of the blood in Randolph that in this conviction, with the inevitable end of the venture before his face, he got down and went in with my uncle.

The path lay along a sort of dike, thrown up in some ancient time against the swamp. Now along the sides it was grown with great reeds, water beech and the common bush of wet lands.

They came to the old tobacco house noiselessly on the damp path. The tumble-down door had been set in place.

My uncle did not pause for any consideration of finesse or safety. He went straight ahead to the door and flung it open. It was rotten and insecurely set, and it fell with a clatter into the abandoned house.

At the sound a big, gaunt figure, asleep on the floor, sprang up.

In the dim light Randolph looked about for a weapon—a piece of the broken door would do. But my uncle was undisturbed.

"Dabney," he said, "I came to arrange about the money. My agent, Mr. Gray, in Memphis, will hand it to you. There will be nothing to sign."

Randolph said he cried out, because he was astonished:

"Dabney Madison, by the living God! I thought you were dead!"

My uncle turned about.

"How could you think that, Randolph?" he said. "You yourself pointed out how the dog was killed by somebody who knew him; and you must have seen that there was no blood on the floor where the dog lay—and consequently that the dog was killed in the bed to furnish blood for the pretended murder."

"But the money, Abner!" cried Randolph. "Why do you pay Dabney Madison this money?"

"Because it is his share of his father's estate," replied my uncle.

"So you were after that!" cried Randolph; "the half of your father's estate. Damme, man, you took a lot of hell-turns on the road to that! Why didn't you sue in the courts? Your right was legal."

"Because a suit at law would have brought out his past," replied my uncle.

The man roused thus abruptly out of sleep had got now some measure of control.

"Randolph," he said, "no law of God or man runs on the sea. The trade of the sea south of the Bermudas is no business for a gentleman or to be told in the land of his father's honor. Abner knew where I'd been!"

"Yes," replied my uncle. "When I saw your bleached face; when I saw your cropped head under the pirate cloth; when I saw you take three steps in your nervous walk, and turn—I knew."

"That I had been in the Spanish Main?" said Dabney.

"That you had been in the penitentiary!" said my uncle.

6

The House of the Dead Man

We were on our way to the Smallwood place—Abner and I. It was early in the morning and I thought we were the first on the road; but at the Three Forks, where the Lost Creek turnpike trails down from the mountains, a horse had turned in before us.

It was a morning out of Paradise, crisp and bright. The spider-webs glistened on the fence rails. The timber cracked. The ragweed was dusted with silver. The sun was moving upward from behind the world. I could have whistled out of sheer joy in being alive on this October morning and the horse under me danced; but Abner rode looking down his nose. He was always silent when he had this trip to make. And he had a reason for it.

The pastureland that we were going on to did not belong to us. It had been owned by the sheriff, Asbury Smallwood. In those days the sheriff collected the county taxes. One night the sheriff's house had been entered, burned over his head and a large sum of the county revenues carried off. No one ever found a trace of those who had done this deed. The sheriff was ruined. He had given up his lands and moved to a neighboring county. His bondsmen had been forced to meet the loss. My father had been one of them; but it was not the loss to my father that bothered Abner.

"The thing does not hurt you, Rufus," he said; "but it cripples Elnathan Stone and it breaks Adam Greathouse."

Stone was a grazier with heavy debts and Greathouse was a little farmer. I remember how my father chaffed Abner when he paid his portion of this loss.

73

"'The Lord gave,'" he said, "'and the Lord hath taken away'—
eh, Abner?"

"But, Rufus," replied Abner, "did the Lord take? We must be
sure of that. There are others who take."

It was clear what Abner meant. If the Lord took he would be
resigned to it; but if another took he would follow with a weapon
in his hand and recover what had been taken. Abner's God was an
exacting Overlord and His requisitions were to be met with equanimity; but He did not go halves with thieves and He issued no
letters of marque.

When the sheriff failed Abner had put cattle on the land in an
effort to make what he could for the bondsmen. It was good grazing land, but it was watered by springs, and we had to watch them.
A beef steer does not grow fat without plenty of water. We went
every week to give the cattle salt and to watch the springs.

As we rode I presently noticed that Abner was looking down at
the horsetrack. And then I saw what I had not noticed before, that
there were three horsetracks in the road—two going our way and
one returning—but only one of the tracks was fresh. Finally Abner
pulled up his big chestnut. We were passing the old burned house.
The crumbled foundations and the blasted trees stood at the end
of a lane. There had once been a gate before the house at the end
of this lane, but it was now nailed up. The horse going before us
had entered this lane for a few steps, then turned back into the
road.

Abner did not speak. He looked at the track for a moment and
then rode on. Presently we came to the bars leading from the road
into the pasture. The horse had stopped here and its rider had got
out of the saddle and let down the bars. One could see where the
horse had gone through and the footprints of the rider were visible in the soft clay. The old horsetrack also went in and came out
at these bars.

Abner examined the man's footprints with what I thought was
an excess of interest. Travelers were always going through one's
land; and, provided they closed the bars behind them, what did it
matter? Abner seemed concerned about this traveler however.

When we had entered the field he sat for some time in the saddle; and then, instead of going to the hills where the springs were, he rode up the valley toward a piece of woods. There was a little rivulet threading this valley and he watched it as he rode.

Finally, just before the rivulet entered the woods, he stopped and got down out of his saddle. When I came up he was looking at a track on the edge of the little stream. It was the footprint of a man, still muddy where the water had run into it. Abner stood on the bank beside the rivulet, and for a good while I could not imagine what he was waiting for. Then, as he watched the track, I understood. He was waiting for the muddy water to clear so he could see the imprint of the man's foot.

"Uncle Abner," I said, "what do you care about who goes through the field?"

"Ordinarily I do not care," he said, "if the man lays up the fence behind him; but there is something out of the ordinary about this thing. The man who crossed there on foot is the same man who came in on the horse. The footprints here and at the bars show the same plate on the boot-heel. He rode a horse that had been here before today, because it remembered the lane and tried to turn in there. Moreover, the man did not wish to be seen, because he came early, hid the horse and went on foot back toward the burned house."

"How do you know that he had hidden the horse, Uncle Abner?"

For answer he beckoned to me and we rode into the woods. The leaves were damp and the horses made no sound. In a few moments Abner stopped and pointed through the beech trees, and I saw a bay horse tied to a sapling. The horse stood with his legs wide apart and his head down.

"The horse is asleep," said Abner; "it has been ridden all night. We must find the rider."

I was now alive with interest. The old story of the robbery floated before me in romantic colors. What innocent person would come here by stealth, ride his horse all night and then hide it in the woods? Moreover, as Abner said, this horse had been to the sheriff's house before today; and it had been there before the house

was burned—because it had started to enter the old lane and had
been turned back by its rider. We were all familiar with such striking examples of memory in horses. A horse, having once gone over
a road and entered at a certain gate, will follow that road on a second trip and again enter that gate.

Then I remembered the old horsetrack that had preceded this
one, and the solution of this thing appeared before me. The story
had gone about that two men had robbed the sheriff and these evidences tallied with that story. Two men had ridden into that pasture; that one track was older was because one of the men had gone
to tell the other to meet him here—had ridden back—and the other
had followed. The horse of the first robber was doubtless concealed
deeper in the wood. And why had they returned? That was clear
enough—they had concealed the booty until now and had just come
back for it.

The thrill of adventure tingled in my blood. We were on the
trail of the robbers and they could not easily escape us. The one
who had ridden this horse could not be far away, since his track in
the brook was muddy when we found it; but why had he crossed
the brook in the direction of the burned house? The way over the
hill toward the house was wholly in the open,—clean sod, not even
a tree. The man on foot could not have been out of sight of us when
we rode across the brook and round the brow of the hill—but he
was out of sight. We sat there in our saddles and searched the land,
lying smooth and open before us. There was the burned house below, bare as my hand, and the meadows, all open to the eye. A rabbit could not have hidden— where was the rider of that worn-out,
sleeping horse?

Abner sat there looking down at this clean, open land. A man
could not vanish into the air; he could not hide in a wisp of blue
grass; he could not cross three hundred acres of open country while
his track in a running brook remained muddy. He could have
reached the brow of the hill and perhaps gone down to the house,
but he could not have passed the meadows and the pasture field
beyond without wings on his shoulders.

The morning was on its way; the air was like lotus. The sun, still out of sight, was beginning to gild the hilltops. I looked up; away on the knob at the summit of the hill there was an old grave-yard—that was a curious custom, to put our dead on the highest point of land. A patch of sunlight lay on this village of the dead—and as I looked a thing caught my eye.

I turned in the saddle.

"I saw something flash up there, Uncle Abner."

"Flash," he said— "like a weapon?"

"Glitter," I said. And I caught up the bridle-rein.

But Abner put his hand on the bit.

"Quietly, Martin," he said. "We will ride slowly round the hill, as though we were looking for the cattle, and go up behind that knob; there is a ridge there and we shall not be seen until we come out on the crest of the hill beside the graveyard."

We rode idly away, stopping now and then, like persons at their leisure. But I was afire with interest. All the way to the crest of the hill the blood skipped in my veins. The horses made no sound on the carpet of green sod. And when we came out suddenly beside the ancient graveyard I fully expected to see there a brace of rob-bers—like some picture in a story;—with bloody cloths around their heads and pistols in their belts; or two bewhiskered pirates before a heap of pieces-of-eight.

On the tick of the clock I was disillusioned, however. A man who had been kneeling by a grave rose. I knew him in the twin-kling of an eye. He was the sheriff and in the twinkling of an eye I knew why he was there; and I was covered with confusion. His father was buried in this old graveyard. It was a land where men concealed their feelings as one conceals the practice of a crime; and one would have stolen his neighbor's goods before he would have intruded upon the secrecy of his emotions.

I pulled up my horse and would have turned back, pretending that I had not seen him, for I was ashamed; but Abner rode on and presently I followed in amazement. If Abner had cursed his horse or warbled a ribald song I could not have been more astonished. I was ashamed for myself and I was ashamed for Abner. How could he ride in on a man who had just got up from beside his father's grave? My mind flashed back over Abner's life to find a precedent for this conspicuous inconsiderate act; but there was nothing like it in all the history of the man.

When the sheriff saw us he wiped his face with his sleeve and went white as a sheet. And under my own shirt I felt and suffered with the man. I should have gone white like that if one had caught me thus. And in my throat I choked with bitterness at Abner. Had his heart tilted and every generous instinct been emptied out of it? Then I thought he meant to turn the thing with some word that would cover the man's confusion and save his feelings inviolate; but he shocked me out of that.

"Smallwood," said Abner, "you have come back!"

The man blinked as though the sun were in his eyes. He had not yet regained the mastery of himself.

"Yes," he said.

"And why do you come?" said Abner.

A flush of scarlet spread over the man's white face.

"And do you ask me that?" he cried. "It is the tomb of my father!"

"Your father," said Abner, "was an upright man. He lived in the fear of God. I respect his tomb."

"I thank you, Abner," replied the man. "I honor my father's grave."

"You honor it late," said Abner.

"Late!" echoed Smallwood.

"Late," said Abner.

The man spread out his hands with a gesture of resignation.

"You mean that my misfortune has dishonored my father?"

"No," said Abner, "that is not what I mean; by a misfortune no man can be dishonored—neither his father nor his father's father."

"What is it you mean, then?" said the man

"Smallwood," said Abner, "is it not before you; where you in your ownership allowed the fence around this grave to rot I have rebuilt it, and where you allowed the weeds to grow up I have cut them down?"

It was the truth. Abner had put up a fence and had cleaned the graveyard. Only the myrtle and cinquefoil covered it. I thought the sheriff would be ashamed at that, but his face brightened.

"It is disaster, Abner, that brings a man back to his duties to the dead. In prosperity we forget, but in poverty we remember."

"The Master," replied Abner, "was not very much concerned about the dead; nor am I. The dead are in God's keeping! It is our duties to the living that should move us. Do you remember, Smallwood, the story of the young man who wished to go and bury his father?"

"I do," said Smallwood, "and I have always held him in honor for it."

"And so, too, the Master would have held him, but for one thing."

"What thing?" said Smallwood.

"That the story was an excuse," replied Abner.

I saw the light go out of the man's face and his lips tremble; and then he said what I was afraid he would say.

"Abner," he said, "if you are determined to gouge this thing out of me, why here it is: I cannot bear to live in this community any longer. I am ashamed to see those upon whom I have brought misfortune—Elnathan Stone, and your brother Rufus, and Adam Greathouse. I have made up my mind to leave the country forever, but I wanted to see the place where my father was buried before I went, because I shall never see it again. You don't understand how a man can feel like that; but I tell you, when a man is in trouble he will remember his father's roof if he is living, and his father's grave if he is dead."

I was so mortified before this confession that Abner's heartless manner had forced out of the man that I reached over and caught my uncle by the sleeve. My horse stood by Abner's chestnut, and I hoped that he would yield to my importunity and ride on; but he turned in his saddle and looked first at me and then down upon the sheriff.

"Martin," he said, "thinks we ought to leave you to your filial devotions."

"It is a credit to the child's heart," replied the man, "and a rebuke to you, Abner. It is a pity that age robs us of charity."

Abner put his hands on the pommel of his saddle and regarded the sheriff.

"I have read St. Paul's epistle on charity," he said, "and, after long reflection, I am persuaded that there exists a greater thing than charity—a thing of more value to the human family. Like charity, it rejoiceth not in iniquity, but it does not bear all things or believe all things, or endure all things; and, unlike charity, it seeketh its own. . . . Do you know what thing I mean, Smallwood? I will tell you. It is Justice."

"Abner," replied the man, "I am in no humor to hear a sermon."

"Those who need a sermon," said Abner, "are rarely in the humor to hear it."

"Abner," cried the man, "you annoy me! Will you ride on?"

"Presently," replied Abner; "when we have talked together a little further. You are about to leave the country. I shall perhaps never see you again and I would have your opinion upon a certain matter."

"Well," said the man, "what is it?"

"It is this," said Abner. "You appear to entertain great filial respect, and I would ask you a question touching that regard: What ought to be done with a man who would use a weapon against his father?"

"He ought to be hanged," said Smallwood.

"And would it change the case," said Abner, "if the father held something which the son had intrusted to him and would not give it up because it belonged to another, and the son, to take it, should come against his father with an iron in his hand?"

The sheriff's face became a land of doubt, of suspicion, of uncertainty and, I thought, of fear.

"Abner," cried the man, "I do not understand; will you explain it?"

"I will explain this thing which you do not understand," replied Abner, "when you have explained a thing which I do not understand. Why was it that you came here last night and again this morning? That was two visits to your father's grave within six hours. I do not understand why you should make two trips—and one upon the heels of the other."

For a moment the man did not reply; then he spoke.

"How do you know that I was here last night? Did you see me come or did another see and tell you?"

"I did not see you," replied Abner, "nor did any one tell me that you came; but I know it in spite of that."

"And how do you know it?" said Smallwood.

"I will tell you," said Abner. "On the road this morning I observed two horse-tracks leading this way; they both turned in at the same crossroads and they both came to this place. One was fresh, the other was some hours old—it is easy to tell that on a clay road. I compared those two tracks and the third returning track, and presently I saw that they had been made by the same horse."

Abner stopped and pointed down toward the beech woods.

"Moreover," he continued, "your horse, hidden among those trees, is worn out and asleep. Now you live only some twenty miles away—that journey this morning would not have so fatigued your horse that he would sleep on his feet; but to make two trips—to go all night—to travel sixty miles—would do it."

The sheriff's head did not move, but I saw his eyes glance down. The glance did not escape Abner and he went on.

"I saw the crowbar in the grass there some time ago," he said; "but what has the crowbar to do with your two trips?"

I, too, saw now the iron bar. It was the thing that had glittered in the sun.

The man threw back his shoulders; he lifted his face and stood up. There came upon him the pose and expression of one who steps out at last desperately into the open.

"Yes," he said, "I was here last night. It was my horse that made those tracks in the road and it is my horse that is hidden in the woods now. And that is my crowbar in the grass. . . . And do you want to know why I made those two trips, and why I brought that crowbar, and why I hid my horse? . . . Well, I'll tell you, since there is no shame in you and no decent feeling, and you are determined to have it. . . . You can't understand, Abner, because you have a heart of stone; but I tell you I wanted to see my father's grave before I left the country forever. I was ashamed to meet the people over here and so I came in the night. When I got here I saw that the heavy slab over my father's grave had settled down and was wedged in against the coping. I tried to straighten it up, but I could not. . . . Well, what would you have done, Abner—gone away and left your father's tomb a ruin? . . . No matter what you would have done! I went back twenty miles and got that crowbar and came again to lift and straighten the stone over my father's grave before I left it. . . . And now, will you ride on and leave me to finish my work and go?"

"Smallwood," Abner said presently, "how do you know that your house was robbed before it was burned? Might it not be that the county revenues were burned with the house?"

"I will tell you how I know that, Abner," replied the man. "The revenues of the county were all in my deerskin saddle-pockets, under my pillow; when I awoke in the night the house was dark and filled with smoke. I jumped up, seized my clothes, which were on a chair by the bed, and ran downstairs; but, first, I felt under the pillow for my saddle-pockets—and they were gone."

"But, Smallwood," said Abner, "how can you be certain that the money was stolen out of your saddle-pockets if you did not find them?"

"I did find them," replied the sheriff; "I went back into the house and got the saddle-pockets and brought them out—and they were empty."

"That was a brave thing to do, Smallwood," said Abner— "to go back into a burning house filled with smoke and dark. You could have had only a moment."

"You speak the truth, Abner," replied the sheriff. "I had only a moment—the house was a pot of smoke. But the money was in my care, Abner. There was my duty—and what is a man's life against that!"

I saw Abner's back straighten and I heard his feet grind on the iron of his stirrups.

"And now, Smallwood," he said, and his voice was like the menace of a weapon, "will you tell me how it was possible for you to go into a house that was dark and filled with smoke, and thus quickly—in a moment—find those empty saddle pockets, unless you knew exactly where they were?"

I saw that Abner's question had impaled the man, as one pierces a fly through with a needle; and, like a fly, the man in his confusion fluttered.

"Smallwood," said Abner, "you are a thief and a hypocrite and a liar! And, like all liars, you have destroyed yourself! You not only stole this money but you tried to make your father an accomplice in that robbery. To conceal it, you hid it in this dead man's house. And, behold, the dead man has held his house against you! When you came here last night to carry away the money you found that the slab over your father's grave had fallen and wedged itself in against the limestone coping, and you could not lift it; and so you went back for that crowbar. . . . But who knows, you thief, what influence, though he be dead, a just man has with God! I came in time to help your father hold his house—and against his son, with a weapon in his hand!"

I saw the man cringe and writhe and shiver, as though he were unable to get out of his tracks; then the power came to him, and he vaulted over the fence and ran. He ran in fear down the hill and across the brook and into the wood; and a moment later he came out with his tired horse at a gallop.

Abner looked down from the hilltop on the flying thief, but he made no move to follow.

"Let him go," he said, "for his father's sake. We owe the dead man that much."

Then he got down from his horse, thrust the crowbar under the slab over the grave and lifted it up.

Beneath it were the sheriff's deerskin saddle-pockets and the stolen money!

7

A TWILIGHT ADVENTURE

It was a strange scene that we approached. Before a crossroad leading into a grove of beech trees, a man sat on his horse with a rifle across his saddle. He did not speak until we were before him in the road, and then his words were sinister.

"Ride on!" he said.

But my Uncle Abner did not ride on. He pulled up his big chestnut and looked calmly at the man. "You speak like one having authority," he said. The man answered with an oath. "Ride on, or you'll get into trouble!"

"I am accustomed to trouble," replied my uncle with great composure; "you must give me a better reason."

"I'll give you hell!" growled the man. "Ride on!"

Abner's eyes traveled over the speaker with a deliberate scrutiny.

"It is not yours to give," he said, "although possibly to receive. Are the roads of Virginia held by arms?"

"This one is," replied the man.

"I think not," replied my Uncle Abner, and, touching his horse with his heel, he turned into the crossroad.

The man seized his weapon, and I heard the hammer click under his thumb. Abner must have heard it, too, but he did not turn his broad back. He only called to me in his usual matter-of-fact voice:

"Go on, Martin; I will overtake you."

The man brought his gun up to his middle, but he did not shoot. He was like all those who undertake to command obedience without

84

having first determined precisely what they will do if their orders
are disregarded. He was prepared to threaten with desperate words,
but not to support that threat with a desperate act, and he hung
there uncertain, cursing under his breath.

I would have gone on as my uncle had told me to do, but now
the man came to a decision.

"No, by God!" he said; "if he goes in, you go in, too!"

And he seized my bridle and turned my horse into the crossroad; then he followed.

There is a long twilight in these hills. The sun departs, but the
day remains. A sort of weird, dim, elfin day, that dawns at sunset,
and envelops and possesses the world. The land is full of light, but
it is the light of no heavenly sun. It is a light equal everywhere, as
though the earth strove to illumine itself, and succeeded with that
labor.

The stars are not yet out. Now and then a pale moon rides in
the sky, but it has no power, and the light is not from it. The wind
is usually gone; the air is soft, and the fragrance of the fields fills
it like a perfume. The noises of the day and of the creatures that go
about by day cease, and the noises of the night and of the creatures that haunt the night begin. The bat swoops and circles in the
maddest action, but without a sound. The eye sees him, but the
ear hears nothing. The whippoorwill begins his plaintive cry, and
one hears, but does not see.

It is a world that we do not understand, for we are creatures of
the sun, and we are fearful lest we come upon things at work here,
of which we have no experience, and that may be able to justify
themselves against our reason. And so a man falls into silence when
he travels in this twilight, and he looks and listens with his senses
out on guard.

It was an old wagon-road that we entered, with the grass growing between the ruts. The horses traveled without a sound until
we began to enter a grove of ancient beech trees; then the dead
leaves cracked and rustled. Abner did not look behind him, and so
he did not know that I came. He knew that some one followed, but
he doubtless took it for the sentinel in the road. And I did not speak.

The man with the cocked gun rode grimly behind me. I did not know whither we went or to what end. We might be shot down from behind a tree or murdered in our saddles. It was not a land where men took desperate measures upon a triviality. And I knew that Abner rode into something that little men, lacking courage, would gladly have stayed out of.

Presently my ear caught a sound, or, rather, a confused mingling of sounds, as of men digging in the earth. It was faint, and some distance beyond us in the heart of the beech woods, but as we traveled the sound increased and I could distinguish the strokes of the mattock, and the thrust of the shovel and the clatter of the earth on the dry leaves.

These sounds seemed at first to be before us, and then, a little later, off on our right-hand. And finally, through the gray boles of the beech trees in the lowland, I saw two men at work digging a pit. They had just begun their work, for there was little earth thrown out. But there was a great heap of leaves that they had cleared away, and heavy cakes of the baked crust that the mattocks had pried up. The length of the pit lay at right angles to the road, and the men were working with their backs toward us. They were in their shirts and trousers, and the heavy mottled shadows thrown by the beech limbs hovered on their backs and shoulders like a flock of night birds. The earth was baked and hard; the mattock rang on it, and among the noises of their work they did not hear us.

I saw Abner look off at this strange labor, his head half turned, but he did not stop and we went on. The old wagon-road made a turn into the low ground. I heard the sound of horses, and a moment later we came upon a dozen men.

I shall not easily forget that scene. The beech trees had been deadened by some settler who had chopped a ring around them, and they stood gaunt with a few tattered leaves, letting the weird twilight in. Some of the men stood about, others sat on the fallen trees, and others in their saddles. But upon every man of that grim company there was the air and aspect of one who waits for something to be finished.

An old man with a heavy iron-gray beard smoked a pipe, puffing out great mouthfuls of smoke with a sort of deliberate energy; another whittled a stick, cutting a bull with horns, and shaping his work with the nicest care; and still another traced letters on the pommel of his saddle with his thumbnail.

A little to one side a great pronged beech thrust out a gray arm, and under it two men sat on their horses, their elbows strapped to their bodies and their mouths gagged with a saddle-cloth. And behind them a man in his saddle was working with a colt halter, unraveling the twine that bound the headpiece and seeking thereby to get a greater length of rope.

This was the scene when I caught it first. But a moment later, when my uncle rode into it, the thing burst into furious life. Men sprang up, caught his horse by the bit and covered him with weapons. Some one called for the sentinel who rode behind me, and he galloped up. For a moment there was confusion. Then the big man who had smoked with such deliberation called out my uncle's name, others repeated it, and the panic was gone. But a ring of stern, determined faces were around him and before his horse, and with the passing of the flash of action there passed no whit of the grim purpose upon which these men were set.

My uncle looked about him.

"Lemuel Arnold," he said; "Nicholas Vance, Hiram Ward, you here!"

As my uncle named these men I knew them. They were cattle grazers. Ward was the big man with the pipe. The men with them were their renters and drovers.

Their lands lay nearest to the mountains. The geographical position made for feudal customs and a certain independence of action. They were on the border, they were accustomed to say, and had to take care of themselves. And it ought to be written that they did take care of themselves with courage and decision, and on occasion they also took care of Virginia.

Their fathers had pushed the frontier of the dominion northward and westward and had held the land. They had fought the savage single-handed and desperately, by his own methods and with his own weapons. Ruthless and merciless, eye for eye and tooth for tooth, they returned what they were given.

They did not send to Virginia for militia when the savage came; they fought him at their doors, and followed him through the forest, and took their toll of death. They were hardier than he was, and their hands were heavier and bloodier, until the old men in the tribes of the Ohio Valley forbade these raids because they cost too much, and turned the war parties south into Kentucky.

Certain historians have written severely of these men and their ruthless methods, and prattled of humane warfare; but they wrote nursing their soft spines in the security of a civilization which these men's hands had builded, and their words are hollow.

"Abner," said Ward, "let me speak plainly. We have got an account to settle with a couple of cattle thieves and we are not going to be interfered with. Cattle stealing and murder have got to stop in these hills. We've had enough of it."

"Well," replied my uncle, "I am the last man in Virginia to interfere with that. We have all had enough of it, and we are all determined that it must cease. But how do you propose to end it?"

"With a rope," said Ward.

"It is a good way," replied Abner, "when it is done the right way."

"What do you mean by the right way?" said Ward.

"I mean," answered my uncle, "that we have all agreed to a way and we ought to stick to our agreement. Now, I want to help you to put down cattle stealing and murder, but I want also to keep my word."

"And how have you given your word?"

"In the same way that you have given yours," said Abner, "and as every man here has given his. Our fathers found out that they could not manage the assassin and the thief when every man undertook to act for himself, so they got together and agreed upon a certain way to do these things. Now, we have indorsed what they agreed to, and promised to obey it, and I for one would like to keep my promise."

The big man's face was puzzled. Now it cleared.

"Hell!" he said. "You mean the law?"

"Call it what you like," replied Abner; "it is merely the agreement of everybody to do certain things in a certain way."

The man made a decisive gesture with a jerk of his head.

"Well," he said, "we're going to do this thing our own way."

My uncle's face became thoughtful.

"Then," he said, "you will injure some innocent people."

"You mean these two blacklegs?"

And Ward indicated the prisoners with a gesture of his thumb.

My uncle lifted his face and looked at the two men some distance away beneath the great beech, as though he had but now observed them.

"I was not thinking of them," he answered. "I was thinking that if men like you and Lemuel Arnold and Nicholas Vance violate the law, lesser men will follow your example, and as you justify your act for security, they will justify theirs for revenge and plunder. And so the law will go to pieces and a lot of weak and innocent people who depend upon it for security will be left unprotected."

These were words that I have remembered, because they put the danger of lynch law in a light I had not thought of. But I saw that they would not move these determined men. Their blood was up and they received them coldly.

"Abner," said Ward, "we are not going to argue this thing with you. There are times when men have to take the law into their own hands. We live here at the foot of the mountains. Our cattle are stolen and run across the border into Maryland. We are tired of it and we intend to stop it.

"Our lives and our property are menaced by a set of reckless desperate devils that we have determined to hunt down and hang to the first tree in sight. We did not send for you. You pushed your way in here; and now, if you are afraid of breaking the law, you can ride on, because we are going to break it—if to hang a pair of murderous devils is to break it."

I was astonished at my uncle's decision.

"Well," he said, "if the law must be broken, I will stay and help you break it!"

"Very well," replied Ward; "but don't get a wrong notion in your head, Abner. If you choose to stay, you put yourself on a footing with everybody else."

"And that is precisely what I want to do," replied Abner, "but as matters stand now, every man here has an advantage over me."

"What advantage, Abner?" said Ward.

"The advantage," answered my uncle, "that he has heard all the evidence against your prisoners and is convinced that they are guilty."

"If that is all the advantage, Abner," replied Ward, "you shall not be denied it. There has been so much cattle stealing here of late that our people living on the border finally got together and determined to stop every drove going up into the mountains that wasn't accompanied by somebody that we knew was all right. This afternoon one of my men reported a little bunch of about a hundred steers on the road, and I stopped it. These two men were driving the cattle. I inquired if the cattle belonged to them and they replied that they were not the owners, but that they had been hired to take the drove over into Maryland. I did not know the men, and as they met my inquiries with oaths and imprecations, I was suspicious of them. I demanded the name of the owner who had hired them to drive the cattle. They said it was none of my damned business and went on. I raised the county. We overtook them, turned their cattle into a field, and brought them back until we could find out who the drove belonged to. On the road we met Bowers."

He turned and indicated the man who was working with the rope halter.

I knew the man. He was a cattle shipper, somewhat involved in debt, but who managed to buy and sell and somehow keep his head above water.

"He told us the truth. Yesterday evening he had gone over on the Stone-Coal to look at Daniel Coop' man's cattle. He had heard that some grazer from your county, Abner, was on the way up to buy the cattle for stockers. He wanted to get in ahead of your man, so he left home that evening and got to Coopman's place about sundown. He took a short cut on foot over the hill, and when he came out he saw a man on the opposite ridge where the road runs, ride away. The man seemed to have been sitting on his horse looking down into the little valley where Coopman's house stands. Bowers went down to the house, but Coopman was not there. The door was open, and Bowers says the house looked as though Coopman had just gone out of it and might come back any moment. There was no one about, because Coopman's wife had gone on a visit to her daughter, over the mountains, and the old man was alone.

"Bowers thought Coopman was out showing the cattle to the man whom he had just seen ride off, so he went out to the pasture field to look for him. He could not find him and he could not find the cattle. He came back to the house to wait until Coopman should come in. He sat down on the porch. As he sat there he noticed that the porch had been scrubbed and was still wet. He looked at it and saw that it had been scrubbed only at one place before the door. This seemed to him a little peculiar, and he wondered why Coopman had scrubbed his porch only in one place. He got up and as he went toward the door he saw that the jamb of the door was splintered at a point about halfway up. He examined this splintered place and presently discovered that it was a bullet hole.

"This alarmed him, and he went out into the yard. There he saw a wagon track leading away from the house toward the road. In the weeds he found Coopman's watch. He picked it up and put it into his pocket. It was a big silver watch, with Coopman's name on it, and attached to it was a buckskin string. He followed the track to the gate, where it entered the road. He discovered then that the cattle had also passed through this gate. It was now night. Bowers went back, got Coopman's saddle horse out of the stable, rode him home, and followed the track of the cattle this morning, but he saw no trace of the drove until we met him."

"What did Shifflet and Twiggs say to this story?" inquired Abner.

"They did not hear it," answered Ward; "Bowers did not talk before them. He rode aside with us when we met him."

"Did Shifflet and Twiggs know Bowers?" said Abner.

"I don't know," replied Ward; "their talk was so foul when we stopped the drove that we had to tie their mouths up."

"Is that all?" said Abner.

Ward swore a great oath.

"No!" he said. "Do you think we would hang men on that? From what Bowers told us, we thought Shifflet and Twiggs had killed Daniel Coopman and driven off his cattle; but we wanted to be certain of it, so we set out to discover what they had done with Coopman's body after they had killed him and what they had done with the wagon. We followed the trail of the drove down to the Valley River. No wagon had crossed, but on the other side we found that a wagon and a drove of cattle had turned out of the road and gone along the basin of the river for about a mile through the woods. And there in a bend of the river we found where these devils had camped.

"There had been a great fire of logs very near to the river, but none of the ashes of this fire remained. From a circular space some twelve feet in diameter the ashes had all been shoveled off, the marks of the shovel being distinct. In the center of the place where this fire had burned the ground had been scraped clean, but near the edges there were some traces of cinders and the ground was blackened. In the river at this point, just opposite the remains of the fire, was a natural washout or hole. We made a raft of logs, cut a pole with a fork on the end and dragged the river. We found most of the wagon iron, all showing the effect of fire. Then we fastened a tin bucket to a pole and fished the washout. We brought up cinders, buttons, buckles and pieces of bone."

Ward paused.

"That settled it, and we came back here to swing the devils up."

My uncle had listened very carefully, and now he spoke.

"What did the man pay Twiggs and Shifflet?" said my uncle. "Did they tell you that when you stopped the drove?"

"Now that," answered Ward, "was another piece of damning evidence. When we searched the men we found a pocketbook on Shifflet with a hundred and fifteen dollars and some odd cents. It was Daniel Coopman's pocketbook, because there was an old tax receipt in it that had slipped down between the leather and the lining.

"We asked Shifflet where he got it, and he said that the fifteen dollars and the change was his own money and that the hundred had been paid to him by the man who had hired them to drive the cattle. He explained his possession of the pocketbook by saying that this man had the money in it, and when he went to pay them he said that they might just as well take it, too."

"Who was this man?" said Abner.

"They will not tell who he was."

"Why not?"

"Now, Abner," cried Ward, "why not, indeed! Because there never was any such man. The story is a lie out of the whole cloth. Those two devils are guilty as hell. The proof is all dead against them."

"Well," replied my uncle, "what circumstantial evidence proves, depends a good deal on how you get started. It is a somewhat dangerous road to the truth, because all the sign-boards have a curious trick of pointing in the direction that you are going. Now a man will never realize this unless he turns around and starts back, then he will see, to his amazement that the signboards have also turned. But as long as his face is set one certain way, it is of no use to talk to him, he won't listen to you; and if he sees you going the other way, he will call you a fool."

"There is only one way in this case," said Ward.

"There are always two ways in every case," replied Abner, "that the suspected person is either guilty or innocent. You have started upon the theory that Shifflet and Twiggs are guilty. Now, suppose you had started the other way, what then?"

"Well," said Ward, "what then?"

"This, then," continued Abner. "You stop Shifflet and Twiggs on the road with Daniel Coopman's cattle, and they tell you that a man has hired them to drive this drove into Maryland. You believe that and start out to find the man. You find Bowers!"

Bowers went deadly white.

"For God's sake, Abner!" he said.

But my uncle was merciless and he drove in the conclusion. "What then?"

There was no answer, but the faces of the men about my uncle turned toward the man whose trembling hands fingered the rope that he was preparing for another.

"But the things we found, Abner?" said Ward.

"What do they prove," continued my uncle, "now that the signboards are turned? That somebody killed Daniel Coopman and drove off his cattle, and afterward destroyed the body and the wagon in which it was hauled away. . . . But who did that? . . . The men who were driving Daniel Coopman's cattle, or the man who was riding Daniel Coopman's horse, and carrying Daniel Coopman's watch in his pocket?"

Ward's face was a study in expression.

"Ah!" cried Abner. "Remember that the signboards have turned about. And what do they point to if we read them on the way we are going now? The man who killed Coopman was afraid to be found with the cattle, so he hired Twiggs and Shifflet to drive them into Maryland for him and follows on another road."

"But his story, Abner?" said Ward.

"And what of it?" replied my uncle. "He is taken and he must explain how he comes by the horse that he rides, and the watch that he carries, and he must find the criminal. Well, he tells you a tale to fit the facts that you will find when you go back to look, and he gives you Shifflet and Twiggs to hang."

I never saw a man in more mortal terror than Jacob Bowers. He sat in his saddle like a man bewildered.

"My God!" he said, and again he repeated it, and again.

And he had cause for that terror on him. My uncle was stern and ruthless. The pendulum had swung the other way, and the lawless monster that Bowers had allied was now turning on himself. He saw it and his joints were unhinged with fear.

A voice crashed out of the ring of desperate men, uttering the changed opinion.

"By God!" it cried, "we've got the right man now."

And one caught the rope out of Bowers' hand.

But my Uncle Abner rode in on them.

"Are you sure about that?" he said.

"Sure!" they echoed. "You have shown it yourself, Abner."

"No," replied my uncle, "I have not shown it. I have shown merely whither circumstantial evidence leads us when we go hot-foot after a theory. Bowers says that there was a man on the hill above Daniel Coopman's house, and this man will know that he did not kill Daniel Coopman and that his story is the truth."

They laughed in my uncle's face. "Do you believe that there was any such person?" My uncle seemed to increase in stature, and his voice became big and dominant.

"I do," he said, "because I am the man!" They had got their lesson, and we rode out with Shifflet and Twiggs to a legal trial.

8
The Age of Miracles

The girl was standing apart from the crowd in the great avenue of poplars that led up to the house. She seemed embarrassed and uncertain what to do, a thing of April emerging into Summer.

Abner and Randolph marked her as they entered along the gravel road.

They had left their horses at the gate, but she had brought hers inside, as though after some habit unconsciously upon her.

But half-way to the house she had remembered and got down. And she stood now against the horse's shoulder. It was a black hunter, big and old, but age marred no beauty of his lines. He was like a horse of ebony, enchanted out of the earth by some Arabian magic, but not yet by that magic awakened into life.

The girl wore a long, dark riding-skirt, after the fashion of the time, and a coat of hunter's pink. Her dark hair was in a great wrist-thick plait. Her eyes, too, were big and dark, and her body firm and lithe from the out-of-doors.

"Ah!" cried Randolph, making his characteristic gesture, "Prospero has been piping in this grovel Here is a daughter of the immortal morning! We grow old, Abner, and it is youth that the gods love."

My uncle, his hands behind him, his eyes on the gravel road, looked up at the bewitching picture.

"Poor child," he said; "the gods that love her must be gods of the valleys and not gods of the hills."

96

"Ruth amid the alien corn! Is it a better figure, Abner? Well, she has a finer inheritance than these lands; she has youth!"

"She ought to have both," replied my uncle, "It was sheer robbery to take her inheritance."

"It was a proceeding at law," replied the Justice. "It was the law that did the thing, and we can not hold the law in disrespect."

"But the man who uses the law to accomplish a wrong, we can so hold," said Abner. "He is an outlaw, as the highwayman and the pirate are."

He extended his arm toward the great house sitting at the end of the avenue.

"In spite of the sanction of the law, I hold this dead man for a robber. And I would have wrested these lands from him, if I could. But your law, Randolph, stood before him."

"Well," replied the Justice, "he takes no gain from it; he lies yonder waiting for the grave."

"But his brother takes," said Abner, "and this child loses."

The Justice, elegant in the costume of the time, turned his ebony stick in his fingers.

"One should forgive the dead," he commented in a facetious note; "it is a mandate of the Scripture."

"I am not concerned about the dead," replied Abner. "The dead are in God's hands. It is the living who concern me."

"Then," cried the Justice, "you should forgive the brother who takes."

"And I shall forgive him," replied Abner, "when he returns what he has taken."

"Returns what he has taken!" Randolph laughed. "Why, Abner, the devil could not filch a coin out of the clutches of old Benton Wolf."

"The devil," said my uncle, "is not an authority that I depend on."

"A miracle of Heaven, then," said the Justice. "But, alas, it is not the age of miracles."

"Perhaps," replied Abner, his voice descending into a deeper tone, "but I am not so certain."

They had come now to where the girl stood, her back against the black shoulder of the horse. The morning air moved the yellow leaves about her feet. She darted out to meet them, her face aglow.

"Damme!" cried Randolph. "William of Avon knew only witches of the second order! How do you do, Julia? I have hardly seen you since you were no taller than my stick, and told me that your name was 'Pete-George,' and that you were a circus-horse, and offered to do tricks for me."

A shadow crossed the girl's face.

"I remember," she said, "it was up there on the porch!"

"Egad!" cried Randolph, embarrassed. "And so it was!"

He kissed the tips of the girl's fingers and the shadow in her face fled.

For the man's heart was good, and he had the manner of a gentleman. But it was Abner that she turned to in her dilemma.

"I forgot," she said, "and almost rode into the house. Do you think I could leave the horse here? He will stand if I drop the rein."

Then she went on to make her explanation. She wanted to see the old house that had been so long her home. This was the only opportunity, to-day, when all the countryside came to the dead man's burial. She thought she might come, too, although her motive was no tribute of respect.

She put her hand through Abner's arm and he looked down upon her, grave and troubled.

"My child," he said, "leave the horse where he stands and come with me, for my motive, also, is no tribute of respect; and you go with a better right than I do."

"I suppose," the girl hesitated, "that one ought to respect the dead, but this man—these men—I can not."

"Nor can I," replied my uncle. "If I do not respect a man when he is living, I shall not pretend to when he is dead. One does not make a claim upon my honor by going out of life."

They went up the avenue among the yellow poplar leaves and the ragweed and fennel springing up along the unkept gravel.

It was a crisp and glorious morning. The frost lay on the rail fence. The spider-webs stretched here and there across the high grasses of the meadows in intricate and bewildering lace-work. The sun was clear and bright, but it carried no oppressive heat as it drew on in its course toward noon.

The countryside had gathered to see Adam Wolf buried. It was a company of tenants, the idle and worthless mostly, drawn by curiosity. For in life the two old men who had seized upon this property by virtue of a defective acknowledgment to a deed, permitted no invasion of their boundary.

Everywhere the lands were posted; no urchin fished and no schoolboy hunted. The green perch, fattened in the deep creek that threaded the rich bottom lands, no man disturbed. But the quail, the pheasant, the robin and the meadow-lark, old Adam pursued with his fowling-piece. He tramped about with it at all seasons. One would have believed that all the birds of heaven had done the creature some unending harm and in revenge he had declared a war. And so the accident by which he met his death was a jeopardy of the old man's habits, and to be looked for when one lived with a fowling-piece in one's hands and grew careless in its use.

The two men lived alone and thus all sorts of mystery sprang up around them, elaborated by the negro fancy and gaining in grim detail at every story-teller's hand. It had the charm and thrilling interest of an adventure, then, for the countryside to get this entry.

The brothers lived in striking contrast. Adam was violent, and his cries and curses, his hard and brutal manner were the terror of the negro who passed at night that way, or the urchin overtaken by darkness on his road home. But Benton got about his affairs in silence, with a certain humility of manner, and a mild concern for the opinion of his fellows. Still, somehow, the negro and the urchin. held him in a greater terror. Perhaps because he had got his coffin made and kept it in his house, together with his clothes for burial. It seemed uncanny thus to prepare against his dissolution and to bargain for the outfit, with anxiety to have his shilling's worth.

And yet, with this gruesome furniture at hand, the old man, it would seem, was in no contemplation of his death. He spoke sometimes with a marked savor and an unctuous kneading of the hands of that time when he should own the land, for he was the younger and by rule should have the expectancy of life.

There was a crowd about the door and filling the hall inside, a crowd that elbowed and jostled, taken with a quivering interest, and there to feed its maw of curiosity with every item.

The girl wished to remain on the portico, where she could see the ancient garden and the orchard and all the paths and byways that had been her wonderland of youth, but Abner asked her to go in.

Randolph turned away, but my uncle and the girl remained some time by the coffin. The rim of the dead man's forehead and his jaw were riddled with bird-shot, but his eyes and an area of his face below them, where the thin nose came down and with its lines and furrows made up the main identity of features, were not disfigured. And these preserved the hard stamp of his violent nature, untouched by the accident that had dispossessed him of his life.

He lay in the burial clothes and the coffin that Benton Wolf had provided for himself, all except the gloves upon his hands. These the old man had forgot. And now when he came to prepare his brother for a public burial, for no other had touched the man, he must needs take what he could find about the house, a pair of old, knit gloves with every rent and moth-hole carefully darned, as though the man had sat down there with pains to give his brother the best appearance that he could.

This little touch affected the girl to tears, so strange is a woman's heart. "Poor thing!" she said. And for this triviality she would forget the injury that the dead man and his brother had done to her, the loss they had inflicted, and her long distress.

She took a closer hold upon Abner's arm, and dabbed her eyes with a tiny kerchief.

"I am sorry for him," she said, "for the living brother. It is so pathetic."

And she indicated the old, coarse gloves so crudely darned and patched together.

But my uncle looked down at her, strangely, and with a cold, inexorable face.

"My child," he said "there is a curious virtue in this thing that moves you. Perhaps it will also move the man whose handiwork it is. Let us go up and see him."

Then he called the Justice.

"Randolph," he said, "come with us."

The Justice turned about. "Where do you go?" he asked.

"Why, sir," Abner answered, "this child is weeping at the sight of the dead man's gloves, and I thought, perhaps, that old Benton might weep at them too, and in the softened mood return what he has stolen."

The Justice looked upon Abner as upon one gone mad.

"And be sorry for his sins! And pluck out his eye and give it to you for a bauble! Why, Abner, where is your common sense. This thing would take a miracle of God."

My uncle was undisturbed.

"Well," he said, "come with me, Randolph, and help me to perform that miracle."

He went out into the hall, and up the wide old stairway, with the girl, in tears, upon his arm. And the Justice followed, like one who goes upon a patent and ridiculous fool's errand.

They came into an upper chamber, where a great bulk of a man sat in a padded chair looking down upon his avenue of trees. He looked with satisfaction. He turned his head about when the three came in and then his eyes widened in among the folds of fat.

"Abner and Mr. Randolph and Miss Julia Clayborne!" he gurgled. "You come to do honor to the dead!"

"No, Wolf," replied my uncle, "we come to do justice to the living."

The room was big, and empty but for chairs and an open secretary of some English make. The pictures on the wall had been turned about as though from a lack of interest in the tenant. But there hung in a frame above the secretary—with its sheets of foolscap, its iron ink-pot and quill pens—a map in detail, and the written deed for the estate that these men had taken in their lawsuit. It was not the skill of any painter that gave pleasure to this mountain of a man; not fields or groves imagined or copied for their charm, but the fields and groves that he possessed and mastered. And he would be reminded at his ease of them and of no other.

The old man's eyelids fluttered an instant as with some indecision, then he replied, "It was kind to have this thought of me. I have been long neglected. A little justice of recognition, even now, does much to soften the sorrow at my brother's death." Randolph caught at his jaw to keep in the laughter. And the huge old man, his head crouched into his billowy shoulders, his little reptilian eye shining like a crum of glass, went on with his speech.

"I am the greater moved," he said, "because you have been aloof and distant with me. You, Abner, have not visited my house, nor you, Randolph, although you live at no great distance. It is not thus that one gentleman should treat another. And especially when I and my dead brother, Adam, were from distant parts and came among you without a friend to take us by the hand and bring us to your door."

He sighed and put the fingers of his hands together.

"Ah, Abner," he went on, "it was a cruel negligence, and one from which I and my brother Adam suffered. You, who have a hand and a word at every turning, can feel no longing for this human comfort. But to the stranger, alone, and without the land of his nativity, it is a bitter lack."

He indicated the chairs about him.

"I beg you to be seated, gentlemen and Miss Clayborne. And overlook that I do not rise. I am shaken at Adam's death."

Randolph remained planted on his feet, his face now under control. But Abner put the child into a chair and stood behind it, as though he were some close and masterful familiar.

"Wolf," he said, "I am glad that your heart is softened."

"My heart—softened!" cried the man. "Why, Abner, I have the tenderest heart of any of God's creatures. I can not endure to kill a sparrow. My brother Adam was not like that. He would be for hunting the wild creatures to their death with firearms. But I took no pleasure in it."

"Well," said Randolph, "the creatures of the air got their revenge of him. It was a foolish accident to die by."

"Randolph," replied the man, "it was the very end and extreme of carelessness. To look into a fowling-piece, a finger on the hammer, a left hand holding the barrel half-way up, to see if it was empty. It was a foolish and simple habit of my brother, and one that I abhorred and begged him to forego, again and again, when I have seen him do it.

"But he had no fear of any firearms, as though by use and habit he had got their spirit tamed—as trainers, I am told, grow careless of wild beasts, and jugglers of the fangs and poison of their reptiles. He was growing old and would forget if they were loaded."

He spoke to Randolph, but he looked at Julia Clayborne and Abner behind her chair.

The girl sat straight and composed, in silence. The body of my uncle was to her a great protecting presence. He stood with his broad shoulders above her, his hands on the back of the chair, his face lifted. And he was big and dominant, as painters are accustomed to draw Michael in Satan's wars.

The pose held the old man's eye, and he moved in his chair; then he went on, speaking to the girl.

"It was kind of you, Abner, and you, Randolph, to come in to see me in my distress, but it was fine and noble in Miss Julia Clayborne. Men will understand the justice of the law and by what right it gives and takes. But a child will hardly understand that. It would be in nature for Miss Clayborne in her youth, to hold the issue of this lawsuit against me and my brother Adam, to feel that we had wronged her; had by some unfairness taken what her father bequeathed to her at his death, and always regarded as his own. A child would not see how the title had never vested, as our judges do. How possession is one thing, and the title in fee simple another and distinct. And so I am touched by this consideration."

Abner spoke then.

"Wolf," he said, "I am glad to find you in this mood, for now Randolph can write his deed, with consideration of love and affection instead of the real one I came with."

The old man's beady eye glimmered and slipped about.

"I do not understand, Abner. What deed?"

"The one Randolph came to write," replied my uncle.

"But, Abner," interrupted the Justice, "I did not come to write a deed." And he looked at my uncle in amazement.

"Oh, yes," returned Abner, "that is precisely what you came to do."

He indicated the open secretary with his hand.

"And the grantor, as it happens, has got everything ready for you. Here are foolscap and quill pens and ink. And here, exhibited for your convenience, is a map of the lands with all the metes and bounds. And here," he pointed to the wall, "in a frame, as though it were a work of art with charm, is the court's deed. Sit down, Randolph, and write." And such virtue is there in a dominant command, that the Justice sat down before the secretary and began to select a goose quill.

Then he realized the absurdity of the direction and turned about.

"What do you mean, Abner?" he cried.

"I mean precisely what I say," replied my uncle. "I want you to write a deed."

"But what sort of deed," cried the astonished Justice, "and by what grantor, and to whom, and for what lands?"

"You will draw a conveyance," replied Abner, "in form, with covenants of general warranty for the manor and lands set out in the deed before you and given in the plat. The grantor will be Benton Wolf, esquire, and the grantee Julia Clayborne, infant, and mark you, Randolph, the consideration will be love and affection, with a dollar added for the form."

The old man was amazed. His head, bedded into his huge shoulders, swung about; his pudgy features worked; his expression and his manner changed; his reptilian eyes hardened; he puffed with his breath in gusts.

"Not so fast, my fine gentleman!" he gurgled. "There will be no such deed."

"Go on, Randolph," said my uncle, as though there had been no interruption, "let us get this business over."

"But, Abner," returned the Justice, "it is fool work, the grantor will not sign."

"He will sign," said my uncle, "when you have finished, and seal and acknowledge—go on!"

"But, Abner, Abner!" the amazed Justice protested.

"Randolph," cried my uncle, "will you write, and leave this thing to me?"

And such authority was in the man to impose his will that the bewildered Justice spread out his sheet of foolscap, dipped his quill into the ink and began to draw the instrument, in form and of the parties, as my uncle said. And while he wrote, Abner turned back to the gross old man.

"Wolf," he said, "must I persuade you to sign the deed?"

"Abner," cried the man, "do you take me for a fool?"

He had got his unwieldy body up and defiant in the chair.

"I do not," replied my uncle, "and therefore I think that you will sign."

The obese old man spat violently on the floor, his face a horror of great folds.

"Sign!" he sputtered. "Fool, idiot, madman! Why should I sign away my lands?"

"There are many reasons," replied Abner calmly. "The property is not yours. You got it by a legal trick, the judge who heard you was bound by the technicalities of language. But you are old, Wolf, and the next Judge will go behind the record. He will be hard to face. He has expressed Himself on these affairs. 'If the widow and the orphan cry to me, I will surely hear their cry.' Sinister words, Wolf, for one who comes with a case like yours into the court of Final Equity."

"Abner," cried the old man, "begone with your little sermons!"

My uncle's big fingers tightened on the back of the chair.

"Then, Wolf," he said, "if this thing does not move you, let me urge the esteem of men and this child's sorrow, and our high regard."

The old man's jaw chattered and he snapped his fingers.

"I would not give that for the things you name," he cried, and he set off a tiny measure on his index-finger with the thumb.

"Why, sir, my whim, idle and ridiculous, is a greater power to move me than this drivel."

Abner did not move, but his voice took on depth and volume.

"Wolf," he said, "a whim is sometimes a great lever to move a man. Now, I am taken with a whim myself. I have a fancy, Wolf, that your brother Adam ought to go out of the world barehanded as he came into it."

The old man twisted his great head, as though he would get Abner wholly within the sweep of his reptilian eye.

"What?" he gurgled. "What is that?"

"Why, this," replied my uncle. "I have a whim— 'idle and ridiculous,' did you say, Wolf? Well, then, idle and ridiculous, if you like, that your brother ought not to be buried in his gloves."

Abner looked hard at the man and, although he did not move, the threat and menace of his presence seemed somehow to advance him. And the effect upon the huge old man was like some work of sorcery. The whole mountain of him began to quiver and the folds of his face seemed spread over with thin oil. He sat piled up in the chair and the oily sweat gathered and thickened on him. His jaw jerked and fell into a baggy gaping and the great expanse of him worked as with an ague.

Finally, out of the pudgy, undulating mass, a voice issued, thin and shaken.

"Abner," it said, "has any other man this fancy?"

"No," replied my uncle, "but I hold it, Wolf, at your decision."

"And, Abner," his thin voice trebled, "you will let my brother be buried as he is?"

"If you sign!" said my uncle.

The man reeked and grew wet in the terror on him, and one thought that his billowy body would never be again at peace. "Randolph," he quavered, "bring me the deed."

Outside, the girl sobbed in Abner's arms. She asked for no explanation. She wished to believe her fortune a miracle of God, forever—to the end of all things. But Randolph turned on my uncle when she was gone.

"Abner! Abner!" he cried. "Why in the name of the Eternal was the old creature so shaken at the gloves?"

"Because he saw the hangman behind them," replied my uncle. "Did you notice how the rim of the dead man's face was riddled by the bird-shot and the center of it clean? How could that happen, Randolph?"

"It was a curious accident of gun-fire," replied the Justice.

"It was no accident at all," said Abner. "That area of the man's face is clean because it was protected. Because the dead man put up his hands to cover his face when he saw that his brother was about to shoot him.

"The backs of old Adam's hands, hidden by the gloves, will be riddled with bird-shot like the rim of his face."

9

The Tenth Commandment

The afternoon sun was hot, and when the drove began to descend the long wooded hill we could hardly keep them out of the timber. We were bringing in our stock cattle. We had been on the road since daybreak and the cattle were tired. Abner was behind the drove and I was riding the line of the wood. The mare under me knew as much about driving cattle as I did, and between us we managed to keep the steers in the road; but finally a bullock broke away and plunged down into the deep wood. Abner called to me to turn all the cattle into the grove on the upper side of the road and let them rest in the shade while we got the runaway steer out of the underbrush: I turned the drove in among the open oak trees, left my mare to watch them and went on foot down through the underbrush. The long hill descending to the river was unfenced wood grown up with thickets. I was perhaps three hundred yards below the road when I lost sight of the steer, and got up on a stump to look. I did not see the steer, but in a thicket beyond me I saw a thing that caught my eye. The bushes had been cut out, the leaves trampled, and there was a dogwood fork driven into the ground. About fifty feet away there was a steep bank and below it a horse path ran through the wood.

The thing savored of mystery. All round was a dense tangle of thicket, and here, hidden at a point commanding the horse path, was this cleared spot with the leaves trampled and the forked limb of a dogwood driven into the ground. I was so absorbed that I did not know that Abner had ridden down the hill behind me until I

turned and saw him sitting there on his great chestnut gelding looking over the dense bushes into the thicket.

He got down out of his saddle, parted the bushes carefully and
entered the thicket. There was a hollow log lying beyond the dogwood fork. Abner put his hand into the log and drew out a gun. It
was a bright, new, one-barreled fowling-piece—a muzzleloader, for
there were no breech-loaders in that country then. Abner turned
the gun about and looked it over carefully. The gun was evidently
loaded, because I could see the cap shining under the hammer.
Abner opened the brass plate on the stock, but it contained only a
bit of new tow and the implement, like a corkscrew, which fitted to
the ramrod and held the tow when one wished to clean the gun. It
was at this moment that I caught sight of the steer moving in the
bushes and I leaped down and ran to head him off, leaving Abner
standing with the gun in his hands.

When I got the steer out and across the road into the drove
Abner had come up out of the wood. He was in the saddle, his
clenched hand lay on the pommel.

I was afraid to ask Abner questions when he looked like that,
but my curiosity overcame me.

"What did you do with the gun, Uncle Abner?"

"I put it back where it was," he said.

"Do you know who the owner is?"

"I do not know who he is," replied Abner without looking in my
direction, "but I know what he is—he is a coward!"

The afternoon drew on. The sun moved towards the far-off
chain of mountains. Silence lay on the world. Only the tiny creatures of the air moved with the hum of a distant spinner, and the
companies of yellow butterflies swarmed on the road. The cattle
rested in the shade of the oak trees and we waited. Abner's chestnut stood like a horse of bronze and I dozed in the saddle.

Shadows were entering the world through the gaps and passes
of the mountains when I heard a horse. I stood up in my stirrups
and looked.

The horse was traveling the path running through the wood
below us. I could see the rider through the trees. He was a grazer

whose lands lay westward beyond the wood. In the deep, utter silence. I could hear the creak of his saddle-leather. Then suddenly
as he rode there was the roar of a gun, and a cloud of powder smoke
blotted him out of sight.

In that portentous instant of time I realized the meaning of the
things that I had seen there in the thicket. It was an ambush to kill
this man! The fork in the ground was to hold the gun-barrel so the
assassin could not miss his mark.

And with this understanding came an appalling sense of my
Uncle Abner's negligence. He must have known all this when he
stood there in the thicket, and when he knew it, why had he left
that gun there? Why had he put it back into its hiding-place? Why
had he gone his way thus unconcernedly and left this assassin to
accomplish his murder? Moreover, this man riding there through
the wood was a man whom Abner knew. His house was the very
house at which Abner expected to stop this night. We were on our
way there!

It was in one of those vast spaces of time that a second sometimes stretches over that I put these things together and jerked
my head toward Abner, but he sat there without the tremor of a
muscle.

The next second I saw the frightened horse plunging in the path
and I looked to see its saddle empty, or the rider reeling with the
blood creeping through his coat, or some ghastly thing that
clutched and swayed. But I did not see it. The rider sat firmly in
his saddle, pulled up the horse, and, looking idly about him, rode
on. He believed the gun had been fired by some hunter shooting
squirrels.

"Oh," I cried, "he missed!"

But Abner did not reply. He was standing in his stirrups searching the wood.

"How could he miss, Uncle Abner," I said, "when he was so near
to the path and had that fork to rest his gun-barrel in? Did you see
him?"

It was some time before Abner answered, and then his reply
was to my final query.

"I did not see him," he said deliberately. "He must have slipped away somehow through the thicket."

That was all he said, and for a good while he was silent, drumming with his fingers on the pommel of his saddle and looking out over the distant treetops.

The sun was touching the mountains before Abner began to move the drove. We got the cattle out of the wood and started the line down the long hill. The road forked at the bottom of the hill—one branch of it, the main road, went on to the house of the grazer with whom we had expected to spend the night and the other turned off through the wood.

I was astonished when Abner turned the drove into this other road, but I said nothing, for I presently understood the reason for this change of plans. One could hardly accept the hospitality of a man when he had negligently stood by to see him murdered.

In half a mile the road came out into the open. There was a big new house on a bit of rising land and, below, fields and meadows. I did not know the crossroad, but I knew this place. The man, Dillworth, who lived here had been sometime the clerk of the county court. He had got this land, it was said, by taking advantage of a defective record, and he had now a suit in chancery against the neighboring grazers for the land about him. He had built this great new house, in pride boasting that it would sit in the center of the estate that he would gain. I had heard this talked about—this boasting, and how one of the grazers had sworn before the courthouse that he would kill Dillworth on the day that the decree was entered. I knew in what esteem Abner held this man and I wondered that he should choose him to stay the night with.

When we first entered the house and while we ate our supper Abner had very little to say, but after that, when we had gone with the man out on to the great porch that overlooked the country, Abner changed—I think it was when he picked up the county newspaper from the table. Something in this paper seized on his attention and he examined it with care. It was a court notice of the sale of lands for delinquent taxes, but the paper had been torn and only half of the article was there. Abner called our host's attention to it.

"Dillworth," he said, "what lands are included in this notice?"

"Are they not there?" replied the man.

"No," said Abner, "a portion of the newspaper is gone. It is torn off at a description of the Jenkins' tract"—and he put his finger on the line and showed the paper to the man— "what lands follow after that?"

"I do not remember the several tracts," Dillworth answered, "but you can easily get another copy of the newspaper. Are you interested in these lands?"

"No," said Abner, "but I am interested in this notice."

Then he laid the newspaper on the table and sat down in a chair. And then it was that his silence left him and he began to talk.

Abner looked out over the country.

"This is fine pasture land," he said.

Dillworth moved forward in his chair. He was a big man with a bushy chestnut beard, little glimmering eyes and a huge body.

"Why, Abner," he said, "it is the very best land that a beef steer ever cropped the grass on."

"It is a corner of the lands that Daniel Davisson got in a grant from George the Third," Abner continued. "I don't know what service he rendered the crown, but the pay was princely—a man would do king's work for an estate like this."

"King's work he would do," said Dillworth, "or hell's work. Why, Abner, the earth is rich for a yard down. I saw old Hezekiah Davisson buried in it, and the shovels full of earth that the negroes threw on him were as black as their faces, and the sod over that land is as clean as a woman's hair. I was a lad then, but I promised myself that I would one day possess these lands."

"It is a dangerous thing to covet the possession of another," said Abner. "King David tried it and he had to do—what did you call it, Dillworth?— 'hell's work.'"

"And why not," replied Dillworth, "if you get the things you want by it?"

"There are several reasons," said Abner, "and one is that it requires a certain courage. Hell's work is heavy work, Dillworth, and the weakling who goes about it is apt to fail."

Dillworth laughed. "King David didn't fail, did he?"

"He did not," replied Abner; "but David, the son of Jesse, was not a coward."

"Well," said Dillworth, "I shall not fail either. My hands are not trained to war like this, but they are trained to lawsuits."

"You got this wedge of land on which your house is built by a lawsuit, did you not?" said Abner.

"I did," replied Dillworth; "but if men do not exercise ordinary care they must suffer for that negligence."

"Well," said Abner, "the little farmer who lived here on this wedge suffered enough for his. When you dispossessed him he hanged himself in his stable with a halter."

"Abner," cried Dillworth, "I have heard enough about that. I did not take the man's life. I took what the law gave me. If a man will buy land and not look up the title it is his own fault."

"He bought at a judicial sale," said Abner, "and he believed the court would not sell him a defective title. He was an honest man, and he thought the world was honest."

"He thought wrong," said Dillworth.

"He did," said Abner.

"Well," cried Dillworth, "am I to blame because there is a fool the less? Will the people never learn that the court does not warrant the title to the lands that it sells in a suit in chancery? The man who buys before the courthouse door buys a pig in a poke, and it is not the court's fault if the poke is empty. The judge could not look up the title to every tract of land that comes into his court, nor could the title to every tract be judicially determined in every suit that involves it. To do that, every suit over land would have to be a suit to determine title and every claimant would have to be a party."

"What you say may be the truth," said Abner, "but the people do not always know it."

"They could know it if they would inquire," answered Dillworth; "why did not this man go before the judge?"

"Well," replied Abner, "he has gone before a greater Judge." Abner leaned back in his chair and his fingers rapped on the table.

"The law is not always justice," he said. "Is it not the law that a man may buy a tract of land and pay down the price in gold and enter into the possession of it, and yet, if by inadvertence the justice of the peace omits to write certain words into the acknowledgment of the deed, the purchaser takes no title and may be dispossessed of his lands?"

"That is the law," said Dillworth emphatically; "it is the very point in my suit against these grazers. Squire Randolph could not find his copy of Mayo's Guide on the day that the deeds were drawn and so he wrote from memory."

Abner was silent for a moment.

"It is the law," he said, "but is it justice, Dillworth?"

"Abner," replied Dillworth, "how shall we know what justice is unless the law defines it?"

"I think every man knows what it is," said Abner.

"And shall every man set up a standard of his own," said Dillworth, "and disregard the standard that the law sets up? That would be the end of justice."

"It would be the beginning of justice," said Abner, "if every man followed the standard that God gives him."

"But, Abner," replied Dillworth, "is there a court that could administer justice if there were no arbitrary standard and every man followed his own?"

"I think there is such a court," said Abner.

Dillworth laughed.

"If there is such a court it does not sit in Virginia."

Then he settled his huge body in his chair and spoke like a lawyer who sums up his case.

"I know what you have in mind, Abner, but it is a fantastic notion. You would saddle every man with the thing you call a conscience, and let that ride him. Well, I would unsaddle him from that. What is right? What is wrong? These are vexed questions. I would leave them to the law. Look what a burden is on every man if he must decide the justice of every act as it comes up. Now the law would lift that burden from his shoulders, and I would let the law bear it."

"But under the law," replied Abner, "the weak and the ignorant suffer for their weakness and for this ignorance, and the shrewd and the cunning profit by their shrewdness and by their cunning. How would you help that?"

"Now, Abner," said Dillworth, "to help that you would have to make the world over."

Again Abner was silent for a while.

"Well," he said, "perhaps it could be done if every man put his shoulder to the wheel."

"But why should it be done?" replied Dillworth. "Does Nature do it? Look with what indifference she kills off the weakling. Is there any pity in her or any of your little soft concerns? I tell you these things are not to be found anywhere in Nature—they are man-made."

"Or God-made," said Abner.

"Call it what you like," replied Dillworth, "it will be equally fantastic, and the law would be fantastic to follow after it. As for myself, Abner, I would avoid these troublesome refinements. Since the law will undertake to say what is right and what is wrong I shall leave her to say it and let myself go free. What she requires me to give I shall give, and what she permits me to take I shall take, and there shall be an end of it."

"It is an easy standard," replied Abner, "and it simplifies a thing that I have come to see you about."

"And what have you come to see me about?" said Dillworth; "I knew that it was for something you came."

And he laughed a little, dry, nervous laugh.

I had observed this laugh breaking now and then into his talk and I had observed his uneasy manner ever since we came. There was something below the surface in this man that made him nervous and it was from that under thing that this laugh broke out.

"It is about your lawsuit," said Abner.

"And what about it?"

"This," said Abner: "That your suit has reached the point where you are not the man to have charge of it."

"Abner," cried Dillworth, "what do you mean?"

"I will tell you," said Abner. "I have followed the progress of this suit, and you have won it. On any day that you call it up the judge will enter a decree, and yet for a year it has stood there on the docket and you have not called it up. Why?"

Dillworth did not reply, but again that dry, nervous laugh broke out.

"I will answer for you, Dillworth," said Abner— "you are afraid!"

Abner extended his arm and pointed out over the pasture lands, growing dimmer in the gathering twilight, across the river, across the wood to where lights moved and twinkled.

"Yonder," said Abner, "lives Lemuel Arnold; he is the only man who is a defendant in your suit, the others are women and children. I know Lemuel Arnold. I intended to stop this night with him until I thought of you. I know the stock he comes from. When Hamilton was buying scalps on the Ohio, and haggling with the Indians over the price to be paid for those of the women and the children, old Hiram Arnold walked into the conference: 'Scalp-buyer,' he said, 'buy my scalps; there are no little ones among them,' and he emptied out on to the table a bagful of scalps of the king's soldiers. That man was Lemuel Arnold's grandfather and that is the blood he has. You would call him violent and dangerous, Dillworth, and you would be right. He is violent and he is dangerous. I know what he told you before the courthouse door. And, Dillworth, you are afraid of that. And so you sit here looking out over these rich lands and coveting them in your heart—and are afraid to take them."

The night was descending, and I sat on a step of the great porch, in the shadow, forgotten by these two men. Dillworth did not move, and Abner went on.

"That is bad for you, Dillworth, to sit here and brood over a thing like this. Plans will come to you that include 'hell's work'; this is no thing for you to handle. Put it into my hands."

The man cleared his throat with that bit of nervous laugh.

"How do you mean—into your hands?" he said.

"Sell me the lawsuit," replied Abner.

Dillworth sat back in his chair at that and covered his jaw with his hand, and for a good while he was silent.

"But it is these lands I want, Abner, not the money for them."

"I know what you want," said Abner, "and I will agree to give you a proportion of all the lands that I recover in the suit."

"It ought to be a large proportion, then, for the suit is won."

"As large as you like," said Abner.

Dillworth got up at that and walked about the porch. One could tell the two things that were moving in his mind: That Abner was, in truth, the man to carry the thing through—he stood well before the courts and he was not afraid; and the other thing—How great a proportion of the lands could he demand? Finally he came back and stood before the table.

"Seven-eights then. Is it a bargain?"

"It is," said Abner. "Write out the contract."

A negro brought foolscap paper, ink, pens and a candle and set them on the table. Dillworth wrote, and when he had finished he signed the paper and made his seal with a flourish of the pen after his signature. Then he handed the contract to Abner' across the table.

Abner read it aloud, weighing each legal term and every lawyer's phrase in it. Dillworth had knowledge of such things and he wrote with skill. Abner folded the contract carefully and put it into his pocket, then he got a silver dollar out of his leather wallet and flung it on to the table, for the paper read: "In consideration of one dollar cash in hand paid, the receipt of which is hereby acknowledged." The coin struck hard and spun on the oak board. "There," he said, "is your silver. It is the money that Judas was paid in and, like that first payment to Judas, it is all you'll get."

Dillworth got on his feet. "Abner," he said, "what do you drive at now?"

"This," replied Abner: "I have bought your lawsuit; I have paid you for it, and it belongs to me. The terms of that sale are written down and signed. You are to receive a portion of what I recover; but if I recover nothing you can receive nothing."

"Nothing?" Dillworth echoed.

"Nothing!" replied Abner.

Dillworth put his big hands on the table and rested his body on them; his head drooped below his shoulders, and he looked at Abner across the table.

"You mean—you mean—"

"Yes," said Abner, "that is what I mean. I shall dismiss this suit."

"Abner," the other wailed, "this is ruin—these lands—these rich lands!" And he put out his arms, as toward something that one loves. "I have been a fool. Give me back my paper." Abner arose.

"Dillworth," he said, "you have a short memory. You said that a man ought to suffer for his lack of care, and you shall suffer for yours. You said that pity was fantastic, and I find it fantastic now. You said that you would take what the law gives you; well, so shall I.'"

The sniveling creature rocked his big body grotesquely in his chair.

"Abner," he whined, "why did you come here to ruin me?"

"I did not come to ruin you," said Abner. "I came to save you. But for me you would have done a murder."

"Abner," the man cried, "you are mad. Why should I do a murder?"

"Dillworth," replied Abner, "there is a certain commandment prohibited, not because of the evil in it, but because of the thing it leads to:—because there follows it—I use your own name, Dillworth, 'hell's work.' This afternoon you tried to kill Lemuel Arnold from an ambush."

Terror was on the man. He ceased to rock his body. He leaned forward, staring at Abner, the muscles of his face flabby.

"Did you see me?"

"No," replied Abner, "I did not."

The man's body seemed, at that, to escape from some hideous pressure. He cried out in relief, and his voice was like air wheezing from the bellows.

"It's a lie! a lie! a lie!"

I saw Abner look hard at the man, but he could not strike a thing like that.

"It's the truth," he said, "you are the man; but when I stood in the thicket with your weapon in my hand I did not know it, and when I came here I did not know it. But I knew that this ambush was the work of a coward, and you were the only coward that I could think of. No," he said, "do not delude yourself—that was no proof. But it was enough to bring me here. And the proof? I found it in this house. I will show it to you. But before I do that, Dillworth, I will return to you something that is yours."

He put his hand into his pocket, took out a score of buckshot and dropped them on the table. They clattered off and rolled away on the floor.

"And that is how I saved you from murder, Dillworth. Before I put your gun back into the hollow log I drew all the charge in it except the powder."

He advanced a step nearer to the table.

"Dillworth," he said, "a little while ago I asked you a question that you could not answer. I asked you what lands were included in the notice of sale for delinquent taxes printed in that county newspaper. Half of the newspaper had been torn off, and with it the other half of that notice. And you could not answer. Do you remember that question, Dillworth? Well, when I asked it of you I had the answer in my pocket. The missing part of that notice was the wadding over the buckshot!"

He took a crumpled piece of newspaper out of his pocket and joined it to the other half lying before Dillworth on the table.

"Look," he said, "how the edges fit!"

10

The Devil's Tools

I was about to follow my Uncle Abner into the garden when at a turn of the hedge, I stopped. A step or two beyond me in the sun, screened by a lattice of vines, was a scene that filled me full of wonder. Abner was standing quite still in the path, and a girl was clinging to his arm, with her face buried against his coat. There was no sound, but the girl's hands trembled and her shoulders were convulsed with sobs.

Whenever I think of pretty women, even now, I somehow always begin with Betty Randolph, and yet, I cannot put her before the eye, for all the memories. She remains in the fairy-land of youth, and her description is with the poets; their extravagances intrude and possess me, and I give it up.

I cannot say that a woman is an armful of apple blossoms, as they do, or as white as milk, and as playful as a kitten. These are happy collocations of words and quite descriptive of her, but they are not mine. Nor can I draw her in the language of a civilization to which she does not belong—one of wheels and spindles with its own type; superior, no doubt, but less desirable, I fancy. The age that grew its women in romance and dowered them with poetic fancies was not so impracticable as you think. It is a queer world; those who put their faith in the plow are rewarded by the plow, and those who put their faith in miracles are rewarded by miracles.

I remained in the shelter of the hedge in some considerable wonder. We had come to pay our respects to this young woman on her approaching marriage, and to be received like this was somewhat beyond our expectations. There could be nothing in this marriage on which to found a tragedy of tears. It was a love match if ever there was one.

Edward Duncan was a fine figure of a man; his lands adjoined, and he had ancestors enough for Randolph. He stood high in the hills, but I did not like him. You will smile at that, seeing what I have written of Betty Randolph, and remembering how, at ten, the human heart is desperately jealous.

The two had been mated by the county gossips from the cradle, and had lived the prophecy. The romance, too, had got its tang of denial to make it sharper. The young man had bought his lands and builded his house, but he must pay for them before he took his bride in, Randolph said, and he had stood by that condition.

There had been some years of waiting, and Randolph had been stormed. The debt had been reduced, but a mortgage remained, until now, by chance, it had been removed, and the gates of Paradise were opened. Edward Duncan had a tract of wild land in the edge of Maryland which his father had got for a song at a judicial sale. He had sold this land, he said, to a foreign purchaser, and so got the money to clear off his debt. He had written to Betty, who was in Baltimore at the time, and she had hurried back with frocks and furbelows. The day was set, we had come to see how happy she would be, and here she was clinging to my Uncle Abner's arm and crying like her heart would break.

It was sometime before the girl spoke, and Abner stood caressing her hair, as though she were a little child. When the paroxysms of tears was over she told him what distressed her, and I heard the story, for the turn of the hedge was beside them, and I could have touched the girl with my hand. She took a worn ribbon from around her neck and held it out to Abner. There was a heavy gold cross slung to it on a tiny ring. I knew this cross, as every one did; it had been her mother's, and the three big emeralds set in it were of the few fine gems in the county. They were worth five thousand dollars, and had been passed down from the divided heirlooms of an English grandmother. I knew what the matter was before Betty

Randolph said it. The emeralds were gone. The cross lying in her hand was bare.

She told the story in a dozen words. The jewels had been gone for some time, but her father had not known it until to-day. She had hoped he would never know, but by accident he had found it out. Then he had called an inquisition, and sat down to discover who had done the robbery. And here it was that Betty Randolph's greatest grief came in.

The loss of the emeralds was enough; but to have her old Mammy Liza, who had been the only mother that she could remember, singled out and interrogated for the criminal, was too much to be borne. Her father was now in his office proceeding with the outrage. Would my Uncle Abner go and see him before he broke her heart?

Abner took the cross and held it in his hand. He asked a question or two, but, on the whole, he said very little, which seemed strange to me, with the matter to clear up. How long had the emeralds been missing? And she replied that they had been in the cross before her trip to Baltimore, and missing at her return. She had not taken the cross on the journey. It had remained among her possessions in her room. She did not know when she had seen it on her return.

And she began once more to cry, and her dainty mouth to tremble, and the big tears to gather in her brown eyes.

Abner promised to go in and brave Randolph at his inquisition, and bring Mammy Liza out. He bade Betty walk in the garden until he returned, and she went away comforted.

But Abner did not at once go in. He remained for some moments standing there with the cross in his hand; then, to my surprise, he turned about and went back the way that he had come. I had barely time to get out of his way, for he walked swiftly along the path to the gate, and down to the stable. I followed, for I wondered why he went here instead of to the house, as he had promised. He crossed before the stables and entered a big shed where the plows and farm tools were kept, the scythes hung up, and the corn hoes. The shed was of huge logs, roofed with clapboards, and open at each end.

I lost a little time in making a detour around the stable, but when I looked into the shed between a crack of the logs, my Uncle Abner was sitting before the big grindstone, turning it with his foot, and very delicately holding the cross on the edge of the stone. He paused and examined his work, and then continued. I could not understand what he was at. Why had he come here, and why did he grind the cross on the stone? At any rate, he presently stopped, looked about until he found a piece of old leather, and again sat down to rub the cross, as though to polish what he had ground.

He examined his work from time to time, until at last it pleased him, and he got up. He went out of the shed and up the path toward the garden. I knew where he was going now and I took some short cuts.

Randolph's office was a wing built on to the main residence, after the fashion of the old Virginia mansion house. It was a single story with a separate entrance, so arranged that the master of the house could receive his official visitors and transact his business without disturbing his domestic household.

I was a very good Indian at that period of my life, and skilled in the acts of taking cover. I was ten years old and had lived the life of the Mohawk, with much care for accuracy of detail. True, it was a life I had now given up for larger affairs, but I retained its advantages. One does not spend whole afternoons at the bloodthirsty age of five, in stalking the turkeycock in the wooded pasture, noiselessly on his belly, with his wooden knife in his hand, and not come to the maturity of ten with the accomplishments of Uncas.

I was presently in a snowball bush, with a very good view of Randolph's inquisition, and I think that if Betty had waited to see it, she need not have gone away in so great a grief. Randolph was sitting behind his table in his pompous manner and with the dignity of kings. But for all his attitudes, he took no advantage over Mammy Liza.

The old woman sat beyond him, straight as a rod in her chair, her black silk dress smoothed into straight folds, her white cap prim and immaculate, her square-rimmed spectacles on her nose, and her hands in her lap. If there was royal blood on the Congo, she carried it in her veins, for her dignity was real. And there I think she held Randolph back from any definite accusation. He advanced with specious and sententious innuendoes and arguments, *a priori* and conclusion *post hoc ergo propter hoc* to inclose her as the guilty agent. But from the commanding position of a blameless life, she did not see it, and he could not make her see it. She regarded this conference as that of two important persons in convention assembled,—a meeting together of the heads of the House of Randolph to consider a certain matter touching its goods and its honor. And, for all his efforts, he could not dislodge her from the serenity of that position.

"Your room adjoins Betty's?" he said.

"Yes, Mars Ran," she answered. "I's always slep' next to my chile, ever since her ma handed her to me outen the bed she was borned in."

"And no one goes into her room but you?"

"No, sah, 'ceptin' when I's there to see what they's doin'."

"Then no other servant in this house could have taken anything out of Betty's room without your knowing it?"

"That's right, Mars Ran. I'd 'a' knowed it."

"Then," said Randolph, tightening the lines of his premises, "if you alone have access to the room, and no one goes in without your consent or knowledge, how could any other servant in this house have taken these jewels?"

"They didn't!" said the old woman. "I's done had all the niggers up before me, an' I's ravaged 'em an' searchified 'em."

Her mouth tightened with the savage memory.

"I knows 'em! I knows 'em all—mopin' niggers, an' mealy mouthed niggers, an' shoutin' niggers, an' cussin' niggers, an' I knows all their carryin's-on, an' all their underhan' oneryness, an' all their lowdown contraptions. An' they knows I knows it." She paused and lifted a long, black finger.

"They fools Miss Betty, an' they fools you, Mars Ran, but they don't fool Mammy Liza."

She replaced her hands together primly in the lap of her silk dress and continued in a confidential tone.

"'Course we knows niggers steals, but they steals eatables, an' nobody pays any 'tention to that. Your Grandpap never did, nor your pap, nor us. You can't be too hard on niggers, jist as you can't be too easy on 'em. If you's too hard, they gits down in the mouth, an' if you's too easy they takes the place. A down in the mouth nigger is always a wuthless nigger, an' a biggity nigger is a 'bomination!"

She paused a moment, but she had entered upon her discourse, and she continued.

"I ain't specifyin' but what there's some on this place that would b'ar watchin', an' I's had my eye on 'em; but they's like the unthinking horse, they'd slip a fril-fral outen the kitchen, or a side of bacon outen the smoke-house, but they wouldn't do none of your gran' stealin'.

"No, sah! No, sah! Mars Ran, them jules wasn't took by nobody in this house."

She paused and reflected, and her face filled with the energy of battle.

"I'd jist like to see a nigger tech a whip-stitch that belongs to my chile. I'd shore peel the hide offen 'em. Tech it! No, sah, they ain't no nigger on this place that's a-goin' to rile me."

And in her energy she told Randolph some homely truths.

"They ain't afeared of you, Mars Ran, 'cause they knows they can make up some cock an' bull story to fool you; an' they ain't afeared of Miss Betty 'cause they knows they can whip it 'roun' her with a pitiful face; but I's different. I rules 'em with the weepen of iron! They ain't none of 'em that can stand up before me with a lie, for I knows the innermost and hidden searchings of a nigger."

She extended her clenched hand with a savage gesture.

"An' I tells 'em, Mars Ran'll welt you with a withe, but I'll scarify you with a scorpeen!"

It was at this moment that my Uncle Abner entered.

Mammy Liza immediately assumed her company manners. She rose and made a little courtesy.

"'Eben', Mars Abner," she said; "is you all well?"

Abner replied, and Randolph came forward to receive him. He got my uncle a chair, and began to explain the matter with which he was engaged. Abner said that he had already got the story from Betty.

Randolph went back to his place behind the table, and to his judicial attitudes.

"There is no direct evidence bearing upon this robbery," he said, "consequently, in pursuing an investigation of it, we must follow the established and orderly formula laid down by the law writers. We must carefully scrutinize all the circumstances of time, place, motive, means, opportunity, and conduct. And, while upon a trial, a judge must assume the innocence of everybody indicated, upon an investigation, the inquisitor must assume their guilt."

He compressed his lips and continued with exalted dignity.

"No one is to be exempt from consideration, not even the oldest and most trusted servants. The wisdom of this course was strikingly shown in Lord William Russell's case, where the facts indicated suicide, but a rigid application of this rule demonstrated that my Lord Russell had been, in fact, murdered by his valet."

My uncle did not interrupt. But Mammy Liza could not restrain her enthusiasm. She was very proud of Randolph, and, like all negroes, associated ability with high sounding words. His grandiloquence and his pomposity were her delight. Her eyes beamed with admiration.

"Go on, Mars Ran," she said; "you certainly is a gran' talker."

Randolph banged the table.

"Shut up!" he roared. "A man can't open his mouth in this house without being interrupted."

But Mammy Liza only beamed serenely. She was accustomed to these outbursts of her lord, and unembarrassed by them. She sat primly in her chair with the radiance of the beloved disciple.

It is one of the excellences of vanity that it cannot be overthrown by a chance blow. However desperately rammed, it always topples back upon its pedestal. Another would have gone hope-lessly to wreckage under that, but not Randolph. He continued in his finest manner.

"Bearing this in mind," he said, "let us analyze the indicatory circumstances. It is possible, of course, that a criminal agent may plan his crime with skill, execute it without accident, and main-tain the secret with equanimity, and that all interrogation follow-ing upon his act, will be wholly futile; but this is not usually true, as was conspicuously evidenced in Sir Ashby Cooper's case."

He paused and put the tips of his extended fingers together.

"What have we here to indicate the criminal agent? No human eye has seen the robber at his work, and there are no witnesses to speak; but we are not to abandon our investigation for that. The writers on the law tell us that circumstantial evidence in the case of crimes committed in secret is the most satisfactory from which to draw conclusions of guilt, for men may be seduced to perjury from base motives, but facts, as Mr. Baron Legg so aptly puts it, 'cannot lie.'"

He made a large indicatory gesture toward his bookshelf.

"True," he said, "I would not go so far as Mr. Justice Butler in Donellan's case. I would not hold circumstantial evidence to be superior to direct evidence, nor would I take the position that it is wholly beyond the reach and compass of human abilities to invent a train of circumstances that might deceive the ordinary inexperi-enced magistrate. I would recall the Vroom case, and the lamen-table error of Sir Matthew Hale, in hanging some sailors for the murder of a shipmate who was, in fact, not dead. But even that error, sir," and he addressed my uncle directly in the heat and elo-quence of his oration, "if in the law one may ever take an illustra-tion from the poets, bore a jewel in its head. It gave us Hale's Rule."

He paused for emphasis, and my uncle spoke.

"And what was that rule?" he said.

"That rule, sir," replied Randolph, "ought not to be stated from memory. It is a nefarious practice of our judges, whereby errors creep into the sound text. It should be read as it stands, sir, in the elegant language of Sir Matthew."

"Leaving out the elegant language of Sir Matthew," replied Abner, "what does the rule mean?"

"In substance and effect," continued Randolph, "but by no means in these words, the rule directs the magistrate to be first certain that a crime has been committed before he undertakes to punish anybody for it."

"Precisely!" said my uncle; "and it is the very best sense that I ever heard of in the law."

He held the gold cross out in his big palm.

"Take this case," he said. "What is the use to speculate about who stole the emeralds, when it is certain that they have not been stolen!"

"Not stolen!" cried Randolph. "They are gone!"

"Yes," replied Abner, "they are gone, but they are not stolen. . . . I would ask you to consider this fact: If these emeralds had been stolen out of the cross, the tines of the metal which held the stones in place, would have been either broken off or pried up, and we would find either the new break in the metal, or the twisted projecting tines. . . . But, instead," he continued, "the points of the setting are all quite smooth. What does that indicate?"

Randolph took the cross and examined it with care.

"You are right, Abner," he said; "the settings are all worn away. I am not surprised; the cross is very old."

"And if the settings are worn away," continued my uncle, "what has become of the stones?"

Randolph banged the table with his clenched hand.

"They have fallen out. Lost! By gad, sir!"

My uncle leaned back in his chair, like one to whom a comment is superfluous. But Randolph delivered an oration. It was directed to Mammy Liza, and the tenor of it was felicitations upon the happy incident that turned aside suspicion from any member of his household. He grew eloquent, pictured his distress, and how his stern, impartial sense of justice had restrained it, and finally, with what seigniorial joy he now received the truth.

And the old woman sat under it in ecstatic rapture. She made little audible sighs and chirrups. Her elbows were lifted and she moved her body rhythmically to the swing of Randolph's periods. She was entranced at the eloquence, but the intent of Randolph's speech never reached her. She was beyond the acquittal, as she had been beyond the accusation.

She continued to bow radiantly after Randolph had made an end.

"Yes, sah," she said; "yes, sah, Mars Ran, I done tole you that them jules wan't took by none of our niggers."

But, as for me, I was overcome with wonder. Here was my uncle convincing Randolph by a piece of evidence which he, himself, had deliberately manufactured on the face of the grindstone.

So that was what he had been at in the shed—grinding off the tines and polishing the settings with a piece of leather, so they would give the appearance of being worn. From my point of vantage in the snowball bush, I looked upon him with a growing interest. He sat, oblivious to Randolph's vaporings, looking beyond him, through the open window at the far-off green fields. He had taken these pains to acquit Mammy Liza. But some one was guilty then! And who? I got a hint of that within the next five minutes, and I was appalled.

"Liza," said Randolph, descending to the practical, "who sweeps Miss Betty's room?"

"Laws, Mars Ran," replied the old negro, "'course I does everything fo' my chile. The house niggers don't do nothin'—that is, they don't do nothin' 'thouten I sets an' watches 'em. I sets when they washes the winders, and I sets when they sweeps, an' I sets when they makes the bed up. I's been a-settin' there all the time Miss Betty's been gone, 'ceptin', of course, when Mars Cedward was there."

She paused and tittered.

"Bless my life, how young folks does carry on! Every day heah comes Mars Cedward a-ridin' up, an' he says, 'Howdy, Mammy, I reckon if I can't see Miss Betty, I'll have to run upstairs an' look at her Ma.' An' he lights offen his horse, 'Get your key, Mammy,' he says, 'an' open the sacred po'tals.' And I gets the key outeh my pocket an' unlocks the do' an' he whippits in there to that little picture of Miss Betty's Ma, that hangs over her bureau."

The old woman paused and wiped a mist from her spectacles with an immaculate and carefully folded handkerchief.

"Yes, yes, sah, 'co'se Miss Betty does look like her Ma—she's the very spit-an'-image of her. . . . Well, I goes along back an' sets down on the stairsteps, an' waits till Mars Cedward gets done with his worshiping, an' he comes along an' says, 'Thankee, Mammy, I reckon that'll have to last me until to-morrow,' an' then I goes back an' locks the do'. I's mighty keerful to lock do's. I ain't minded to have no 'quisitive nigger ramshakin' 'roun'."

But my uncle stopped her and sent her to Betty as evidence in the flesh that she had come acquit of Randolph's inquisition. And the two men fell into a talk upon other matters.

But I no longer listened. I sat within my bush and studied the impassive face of my Uncle Abner, and tried to join these contradictory incidents into something that I could understand. Slowly the thing came to me! But I did not push on into the inevitable conclusion. Its consequences were too appalling. I saw it and let it lie.

Somebody had pried the emeralds out of that cross,—somebody having access to the room. And that person was not Mammy Liza! Abner knew that. . . . And he deliberately falsified the evidence. To acquit Mammy Liza? Something more than that, I thought. She was in no danger; even Randolph behind his judicial attitudes, had never entertained the idea for a moment. Then, this thing meant that my uncle had deliberately screened the real criminal. But why? Abner was no respecter of men. He stood for justice—clean and ruthless justice, tempered by no distinctions. Why, then, indeed?

And then I had an inspiration. Abner was thinking of some one beyond the criminal, and of the consequences to that one if the truth were known; and this thing he had done, he had done for her! And now I thought about her, too.

Her faith, her trust, the dearest illusion of her life had been imperiled, had been destroyed, but for my uncle's firm, deliberate act.

And then, another thing rose up desperately before me. How could he let this girl go on in ignorance of the truth? Must he not,

after all, tell her what he knew? And my tongue grew dry in contemplation of that ordeal. And yet again, why? Love of her had been
ultimately the motive. She need never know, and the secret might
live out everybody's life. Moreover, for all his iron ways, Abner
was a man who saw justice in its large and human aspect, and he
stood for the spirit, above the letter, of the truth.

And yet, even there under the limited horizon of a child, I
seemed to feel that he must tell her. And so when he finally got
away from Randolph, and turned into the garden, I stalked him
with desperate cunning. I was on fire to know what he would do.
Would he speak? Or would he keep the thing forever silent? I had
sat before two acts of this drama, and I would see what the cur-
tains went down on. And I did see it from the shelter of the tall
timothy-grass.

He found Betty at the foot of the garden. She ran to him in joy
at Mammy Liza's vindication, and with pretty evidences of her affection. But he took her by the hand without a word and led her to
a bench.

And when she was seated he sat down beside her. I could not
see her face, but I could hear his voice and it was wonderfully kind.

"My child," he said, "there is always one reason, if no other,
why good people must not undertake to work with a tool of the
devil, and that reason is because they handle it so badly."

He paused and took the gold cross out of his pocket.

"Now here," he continued, "I have had to help somebody out
who was the very poorest bungler with a devil's tool. I am not very
skilled myself with that sort of an implement, but, dear me, I am
not so bad a workman as this person! . . . Let me show you. . . . The
one who got the emeralds out of this cross left the twisted and broken tines to indicate a deliberate criminal act, so I had to grind
them off in order that the thing might look like an accident. . . .
That cleared everybody—Mammy Liza, who had no motive for this
act, and Edward Duncan, who had."

The girl stood straight up.

"Oh," she said, and her voice was a long shuddering whisper,
"no one could think he did it!"

"And why not?" continued my uncle. "He had the opportunity and the motive. He was in the room during your absence, and he needed the money which those emeralds would bring in order to clear his lands of debt."

The girl clenched her hands and drew them in against her heart.

"But you don't think he stole them?" And again her voice was in that shuddering whisper.

I lay trembling.

"No," replied Abner, "I do not think that Edward Duncan stole these emeralds, because I know that they were never stolen at all."

He put out his hand and drew the girl down beside him.

"My child," he continued, "we must always credit the poorest thief with some glimmering of intelligence. When I first saw this cross in your hand, I knew that this was not the work of a thief, because no thief would have painfully pried the emeralds out, in order to leave the cross behind as an evidence of his guilt. Now, there is a reason why this cross was left behind, but it is not the reason of a thief—two reasons, in fact: because some one wished to keep it, and because they were not afraid to do so.

"Now, my child," and Abner put his arm tenderly around the girl's shoulders, "who could that person be who treasured this cross and was not afraid to keep it?"

She clung to my uncle then, and I heard the confession among her sobbings. Edward Duncan was making every sacrifice for her, and she had made one for him. She had sold the emeralds in Baltimore, and through an agent bought his mountain land. But he must never know, never in this world, and my Uncle Abner must promise her that upon his honor.

And lying in the deep timothy-grass, I heard him promise.

11

The Hidden Law

We had come out to Dudley Belts' house and were standing in a bit of meadow. It was an afternoon of April; there had been a shower of rain, and now the sun was on the velvet grass and the white-headed clover blossoms. The sky was blue above and the earth green below, and swimming between them was an air like lotus. Facing the south upon this sunny field was a stand of bees, thatched with rye-straw and covered over with a clapboard roof, the house of each tribe a section of a hollow gum-tree, with a cap on the top for the tribute of honey to the human tyrant. The bees had come out after the shower was gone, and they hummed at their work with the sound of a spinner.

Randolph stopped and looked down upon the humming hive. He lifted his finger with a little circling gesture.

"'Singing masons building roofs of gold,'" he said. "Ah, Abner, William of Avon was a great poet."

My uncle turned about at that and looked at Randolph and then at the hive of bees. A girl was coming up from the brook below with a pail of water. She wore a simple butternut frock, and she was clean-limbed and straight like those first daughters of the world who wove and spun. She paused before the hive and the bees swarmed about her as about a great clover blossom, and she was at home and unafraid like a child in a company of yellow butter-flies. She went on to the spring house with her dripping wooden pail, kissing the tips of her fingers to the bees. We followed, but before the hive my uncle stopped and repeated the line that Randolph had quoted:

"'Singing masons building roofs of gold,' . . . and over a floor of gold and pillars of gold." He added, "He was a good riddle maker, your English poet, but not so good as Samson, unless I help him out."

I received the fairy fancy with all children's joy. Those little men singing as they laid their yellow floor, and raised their yellow walls, and arched their yellow roof! Singing! The word seemed to open up some sunlit fairy world.

It pleased Randolph to have thus touched my uncle.

"A great poet, Abner," he repeated, "and more than that; he drew lessons from nature valuable for doctrine. Men should hymn as they labor and fill the fields with song and so suck out the virus from the curse. He was a great philosopher, Abner—William of Avon."

"But not so great a philosopher as Saint Paul," replied Abner, and he turned from the bees toward old Dudley Betts, digging in the fields before his door. He put his hands behind him and lifted his stern bronze face.

"Those who coveted after money," he said, "have 'pierced themselves through with many sorrows.' And is it not the truth? Yonder is old Dudley Betts. He is doubled up with aches; he has lost his son; he is losing his life, and he will lose his soul—all for money—'Pierced themselves through with many sorrows,' as Saint Paul said it, and now, at the end he has lost the horde that he slaved for."

The man was a by-word in the hills; mean and narrow, with an economy past belief. He used everything about him to one end and with no thought but gain. He cultivated his fields to the very door, and set his fences out into the road, and he extracted from those about him every tithe of service. He had worked his son until the boy had finally run away across the mountains. He had driven his daughter to the makeshifts of the first patriarchal people—soap from ashes, linen from hemp, and the wheel and the loom for the frock upon her limbs.

And like every man under a single dominating passion, he grew in suspicion and in fear. He was afraid to lend out his money lest he lose it. He had given so much for this treasure that he would take no chance with it, and so kept it by him in gold.

But caution and fear are not harpies to be halted; they wing on. Betts was dragged far in their claw-feet. There is a land of dim things that these convoys can enter. Betts arrived there. We must not press the earth too hard, old, forgotten peoples believed, lest evil things are squeezed out that strip us and avenge it. And ancient crones, feeble, wrapped up by the fire, warned him: The earth suffered us to reap, but not to glean her. We must not gather up every head of wheat. The earth or dim creatures behind the earth would be offended. It was the oldest belief. The first men poured a little wine out when they drank and brought an offering of their herds and the first fruits of the fields. It was written in the Book. He could get it down and read it.

What did they know that they did this? Life was hard then; men saved all they could. There was some terrible experience behind this custom, some experience that appalled and stamped the race with a lesson!

At first Betts laughed at their warnings; then he cursed at them, and his changed manner marked how far he had got. The laugh meant disbelief, but the curse meant fear.

And now, the very strangest thing had happened: The treasure that the old man had so painfully laid up had mysteriously vanished clear away. No one knew it. Men like Betts, cautious and secretive, are dumb before disaster. They conceal the deep mortal hurt as though to hide it from themselves.

He had gone in the night and told Randolph and Abner, and now they had come to see his house.

He put down his hoe when we came up and led us in. It was a house like those of the first men, with everything in it home-made—hand-woven rag-carpets on the floor, and hand-woven coverlets on the beds; tables and shelves and benches of rude carpentry. These things spoke of the man's economy. But there were also things that spoke of his fear: The house was a primitive stockade.

The door was barred with a beam, and there were heavy shutters at the window; an ax stood by the old man's bed and an ancient dueling pistol hung by its trigger-guard to a nail.

I did not go in, for youth is cunning. I sat down on the doorstep and fell into so close a study of a certain wasp at work under a sill that I was overlooked as a creature without ears; but I had ears of the finest and I lost no word.

The old man got two splint-bottom chairs and put them by the table for his guests, and then he brought a blue earthen jar and set it before them. It was one of the old-fashioned glazed jars peddled by the hucksters, smaller but deeper than a crock, with a thick rim and two great ears. In this he kept his gold pieces until on a certain night they had vanished.

The old man's voice ran in and out of a whisper as he told the story. He knew the very night, because he looked into his jar before he slept and every morning when he got out of his bed. It had been a devil's night—streaming clouds drove across an iron sky, a thin crook of a moon sailed, and a high bitter wind scythed the earth.

Everybody remembered the night when he got out his almanac and named it. There had been noises, old Betts said, but he could not define them. Such a night is full of voices; the wind whispers in the chimney and the house frame creaks. The wind had come on in gusts at sunset, full of dust and whirling leaves, but later it had got up into a gale. The fire had gone out and the house inside was black as a pit. He did not know what went on inside or out, but he knew that the gold was gone at daylight, and he knew that no living human creature had got into his house. The bar on his door held and the shutters were bolted. Whatever entered, entered through the keyhole or through the throat of the chimney that a cat would stick in.

Abner said nothing, but Randolph sat down to an official inquiry:

"You have been robbed, Betts," he said. "Somebody entered your house that night."

"Nobody entered it," replied the old man in his hoarse, half-whispered voice, "either on that night or any other night. The door was fast, Squire."

"But the thief may have closed it behind him."

Betts shook his head. "He could not put up the bar behind him, and besides, I set it in a certain way. It was not moved. And the windows—I bolt them and turn the bolt at a certain angle. No human touched them."

It was not possible to believe that this man could be mistaken. One could see with what care he had set his little traps—the bar across the door precisely at a certain hidden line; the bolts of the window shutters turned precisely to an angle that he alone knew. It was not likely that Randolph would suggest anything that this cautious old man had not already thought of.

"Then," continued Randolph, "the thief concealed himself in your house the day before the robbery and got out of it on the day after."

But again Betts shook his head, and his eyes ran over the house and to a candle on the mantelpiece.

"I look," he said, "every night before I go to bed."

And one could see the picture of this old, fearful man, looking through his house with the smoking tallow candle, peering into every nook and corner. Could a thief hide from him in this house that he knew inch by inch? One could not believe it. The creature took no chance; he had thought of every danger, this one among them, and every night he looked! He would know, then, the very cracks in the wall. He would have found a rat.

Then, it seemed to me, Randolph entered the only road there was out of this mystery.

"Your son knew about this money?"

"Yes," replied Betts, "'Lander knew about it. He used to say that a part of it was his because he had worked for it as much as I had. But I told him," and the old man's voice cheeped in a sort of laugh, "that he was mine."

"Where was your son Philander when the money disappeared?" said Randolph.

"Over the mountains," said Betts; "he had been gone a month."
Then he paused and looked at Randolph. "It was not 'Lander. On
that day he was in the school that Mr. Jefferson set up. I had a
letter from the master asking for money. . . . I have the letter," and
he got up to get it.

But Randolph waved his hand and sat back in his chair with
the aspect of a brooding oracle.

It was then that my uncle spoke.

"Betts," he said, "how do you think the money went?"

The old man's voice got again into that big crude whisper.

"I don't know, Abner."

But my uncle pressed him.

"What do you think?"

Betts drew a little nearer to the table.

"Abner," he said, "there are a good many things going on around
a man that he don't understand. We turn out a horse to pasture,
and he comes in with hand-holts in his mane. . . . You have seen
it?"

"Yes," replied my uncle.

And I had seen it, too, many a time, when the horses were
brought up in the spring from pasture, their manes twisted and
knotted into loops, as though to furnish a hand-holt to a rider.

"Well, Abner," continued the old man in his rustling whisper,
"who rides the horse? You cannot untie or untwist those hand-
holts—you must cut them out with shears—with iron. Is it true?"

"It is true," replied my uncle.

"And why, eh, Abner? Because those hand-holts were never
knotted in by any human fingers! You know what the old folk say?"

"I know," answered my uncle. "Do you believe it, Betts?"

"Eh, Abner!" he croaked in the guttural whisper. "If there were
no witches, why did our fathers hang up iron to keep them off? My
grandmother saw one burned in the old country. She had ridden
the king's horse, and greased her hands with shoemakers' wax so
her fingers would not slip in the mane. . . . Shoemakers' wax! Mark
you that, Abner!"

"Betts," cried Randolph, "you are a fool; there are no witches!"

"There was the Witch of Endor," replied my uncle. "Go on, Betts."

"By gad, sir!" roared Randolph, "if we are to try witches, I shall have to read up James the First. That Scotch king wrote a learned work on demonology. He advised the magistrates to search on the body of the witch for the seal of the devil; that would be a spot insensible to pain, and, James said, 'Prod for it with a needle.'"

But my uncle was serious.

"Go on, Betts," he said. "I do not believe that any man entered your house and robbed you. But why do you think that a witch did?"

"Well, Abner," answered the old man, "who could have got in but such a creature? A thief cannot crawl through a keyhole, but there are things that can. My grandmother said that once in the old country a man awoke one night to see a gray wolf sitting by his fireside. He had an ax, as I have, and he fought the wolf with that and cut off its paw, whereupon it fled screaming through the keyhole. And the paw lying on the floor was a woman's hand!"

"Then, Betts," cried Randolph, "it's damned lucky that you didn't use your ax, if that is what one finds on the floor."

Randolph had spoken with pompous sarcasm, but at the words there came upon Abner's face a look of horror.

"It is," he said, "in God's name!"

Betts leaned forward in his chair.

"And what would have happened to me, Abner, do you think, if I had used my ax? Would I have died there with the ax in my hand?"

The look of horror remained upon my uncle's face.

"You would have wished for that when the light came; to die is sometimes to escape the pit."

"I would have fallen into hell, then?"

"Aye, Betts," replied my uncle, "straightway into hell!"

The old man rested his hands on the posts of the chair.

"The creatures behind the world are baleful creatures," he muttered in his big whisper.

Randolph got up at that.

"Damme!" he said. "Are we in the time of Roger Williams, and is this Massachusetts, that witches ride and men are filched of their gold by magic and threatened with hell fire? What is this cursed foolery, Abner?"

"It is no foolery, Randolph," replied my uncle, "but the living truth."

"The truth!" cried Randolph. "Do you call it the truth that creatures, not human, able to enter through the keyhole and fly away, have Betts' gold, and if he had fought against this robbery with his ax he would have put himself in torment? Damme, man! In the name of common sense, do you call this the truth?"

"Randolph," replied Abner, and his voice was slow and deep, "it is every word the truth."

Randolph moved back the chair before him and sat down. He looked at my uncle curiously.

"Abner," he raid, "you used to be a crag of common sense. The legends and theories of fools broke on you and went to pieces. Would you now testify to witches?"

"And if I did," replied my uncle, "I should have Saint Paul behind me."

"The fathers of the church fell into some errors," replied Randolph.

"The fathers of the law, then?" said Abner.

Randolph took his chin in his hand at that. "It is true," he said, "that Sir Matthew Hale held nothing to be so well established as the fact of witchcraft for three great reasons, which he gave in their order, as became the greatest judge in England: First, because it was asserted in the Scriptures; second, because all nations had made laws against it; and, third, because the human testimony in support of it was overwhelming. I believe that Sir Matthew had knowledge of some six thousand cases. . . . But Mr. Jefferson has lived since then, Abner, and this is Virginia."

"Nevertheless," replied my uncle, "after Mr. Jefferson, and in Virginia, this thing has happened."

Randolph swore a great oath.

"Then, by gad, sir, let us burn the old women in the villages until the creatures who carried Betts' treasure through the keyhole bring it back!"

Betts spoke then.

"They have brought some of it back!"

My uncle turned sharply in his chair.

"What do you mean, Betts?" he said.

"Why this, Abner," replied the old man, his voice descending into the cavernous whisper; "on three mornings I have found some of my gold pieces in the jar. And they came as they went, Abner, with every window fastened down and the bar across the door. And there is another thing about these pieces that have come back—they are mine, for I know every piece—but they have been in the hands of the creatures that ride the horses in the pasture—they have been handled by witches!" He whispered the word with a fearful glance about him. "How do I know that? Wait, I will show you!"

He went over to his bed and got out a little box from beneath his cornhusk mattress—a worn, smoke-stained box with a sliding lid. He drew the lid off with his thumb and turned the contents out on the table.

"Now look," he said; "look, there is wax on every piece! Shoemakers' wax, mark you. . . . Eh, Abner! My mother said that—the creatures grease their hands with that so their fingers will not slip when they ride the barebacked horses in the night. They have carried this gold clutched in their hands, see, and the wax has come off!"

My uncle and Randolph leaned over the table. They examined the coins.

"By the Eternal!" cried Randolph. "It is wax! But were they clean before?"

"They were clean," the old man answered. "The wax is from the creatures' fingers. Did not my mother say it?"

My uncle sat back in his chair, but Betts strained forward and put his fearful query:

"What do you think, Abner; will all the gold come back?"

My uncle did not at once reply. He sat for some time silent, looking through the open door at the sunny meadowland and the far off hills. But finally he spoke like one who has worked out a problem and got the answer.

"It will not all come back," he said.

"How much, then?" whispered Betts.

"What is left," replied Abner, "when the toll is taken out."

"You know where the gold is?"

"Yes."

"And the creatures that have it, Abner," Betts whispered, "they are not human?"

"They are not human!" replied my uncle.

Then he got up and began to walk about the house, but not to search for clews to this mysterious thing. He walked like one who examines something within himself—or something beyond the eye—and old Betts followed him with his straining face. And Randolph sat in his chair with his arms folded and his chin against his stock, as a skeptic overwhelmed by proof might sit in a house of haunted voices. He was puzzled upon every hand. The thing was out of reason at every point, both in the loss and in the return of these coins upon the table, and my uncle's comments were below the soundings of all sense. The creatures who now had Betts' gold could enter through the keyhole! Betts would have gone into the pit if he had struck out with his ax! A moiety of this treasure would be taken out and the rest returned! And the coins testified to no human handling! The thing had no face nor aspect of events in nature. Mortal thieves enjoyed no such supernal powers. These were the attributes of the familiar spirit. Nor did the human rob-ber return a per cent upon his gains!

I have said that my uncle walked about the floor. But he stopped now and looked down at the hard, miserly old man.

"Betts," he said, "this is a mysterious world. It is hedged about and steeped in mystery. Listen to me! The Patriarchs were directed to make an offering to the Lord of a portion of the increase in their herds. Why? Because the Lord had need of sheep and heifers? Surely not, for the whole earth and its increase were His. There was some other reason, Betts. I do not understand what it was, but I do understand that no man can use the earth and keep every tithe of the increase for himself. They did not try it, but you did!"

He paused and filled his big lungs.

"It was a disastrous experiment. . . . What will you do?"

"What must I do, Abner?" the old man whispered. "Make a sacrifice like the Patriarchs?"

"A sacrifice you must make, Betts," replied my uncle, "but not like the Patriarchs. What you receive from the earth you must divide into three equal parts and keep one part for yourself."

"And to whom shall I give the other two parts, Abner?"

"To whom would you wish to give them, Betts, if you had the choice?"

The old man fingered about his mouth.

"Well," he said, "a man would give to those of his own household first—if he had to give."

"Then," said Abner, "from this day keep a third of your increase for yourself and give the other two-thirds to your son and your daughter."

"And the gold, Abner? Will it come back?"

"A third part will come back. Be content with that."

"And the creatures that have my gold? Will they harm me?"

"Betts," replied my uncle, "the creatures that have your gold on this day hidden in their house will labor for you as no slaves have ever labored—without word or whip. Do you promise?"

The fearful old man promised, and we went out into the sun.

The tall straight young girl was standing before the springhouse, kneading a dish of yellow butter and singing like a blackbird. My uncle strode down to her. We could not hear the thing he said, but the singing ceased when he began to talk and burst out in a fuller note when he had finished—a big, happy, joyous note that seemed to fill the meadow.

We waited for him before the stand of bees, and Randolph turned on him when he came.

"Abner," he said, "what is the answer to this damned riddle?"

"You gave it, Randolph," he replied— "'Singing masons building roofs of gold.'" And he pointed to the bees. "When I saw that the cap on one of the gums had been moved I thought Betts' gold was there, and when I saw the wax on the coins I was certain."

"But," cried Randolph, "you spoke of creatures not human—creatures that could enter through the keyhole—creatures—"

"I spoke of the bees," replied my uncle.

"But you said Betts would have fallen into hell if he had struck out with his ax!"

"He would have killed his daughter," replied Abner. "Can you think of a more fearful hell? She took the gold and hid it in the bee cap. But she was honest with her father; whenever she sent a sum of money to her brother she returned an equal number of gold pieces to old Betts' jar."

"Then," said Randolph, with a great oath, "there is no witch here with her familiar spirits?"

"Now that," replied my uncle, "will depend upon the imagery of language. There is here a subtle maiden and a stand of bees!"

12
THE RIDDLE

I have never seen the snow fall as it fell on the night of the seventeenth of February. It had been a mild day with a soft, stagnant air. The sky seemed about to descend and enclose the earth, as though it were a thing which it had long pursued and had now got into a corner. All day it seemed thus to hover motionless above its quarry, and the earth to be apprehensive like a thing in fear. Animals were restless, and men, as they stood about and talked together, looked up at the sky.

We were in the county seat on that day. The grand jury was sitting, and Abner had been summoned to appear before it. It was the killing of old Christian Lance that the grand jury was inquiring into. He had been found one morning in his house, bound into a chair. The body sat straining forward, death on it, and terror in its face. There was no one in the house but old Christian, and it was noon before the neighbors found him. The tragedy had brought the grand jury together, and had filled the hills with talk, for it left a mystery unsolved.

This mystery that Christian sealed up in his death was one that no man could get a hint at while he was living—what had the old man done with his money? He grazed a few cattle and got a handsome profit. He spent next to nothing; he gave nothing to any one, and he did not put his money out to interest. It was known that he would take only gold in payment for his cattle. He made no secret of that. The natural inference was that he buried this coin in some spot about his garden, but idle persons had watched his house for whole nights after he had sold his cattle, and had never seen him come out with a spade. And young bloods, more curious, I think, than criminal, had gone into his house when he was absent, and searched it more than once. There was no corner that they had not looked into, and no floor board that they had not lifted, nor any loose stone about the hearth that they had not felt under.

Once, in conference on this mystery, somebody had suggested that the knobs on the andirons and the handles on the old high-boy were gold, having gotten the idea from some tale. And a little later, when the old man returned one evening from the grist-mill, he found that one of these knobs on the andirons had been broken off. But, as the thief never came back for the other, it was pretty certain that this fantastic notion was not the key to Christian's secret.

It was after one of these mischievous searchings that he put up his Delphic notice when he went away—a leaf from a day-book, scrawled in pencil, and pinned to the mantelpiece:

"Why don't you look in the cow?"

The idle gossips puzzled over that. What did it mean? Was the thing a sort of taunt? And did the old man mean that since these persons had looked into every nook and corner of his house, they ought also to have looked into the red mouth of the cow? Or did he mean that his money was invested in cattle and there was the place to look? Or was the thing a cryptic sentence—like that of some ancient oracle—in which the secret to his hoarded gold was hidden?

At any rate it was certain that old Christian was not afraid to go away and leave his door open, and the secret to guard itself. And he was justified in that confidence. The mischievous gave over their inquisitions, and the mystery became a sort of legend.

With the eyes of the curious thus on him, and that mystery for background, it was little wonder that his tragic death fired the country.

I have said there was a horror about the dead man's face as he sat straining in the chair. And the thing was in truth a horror! But that word does not tell the story. The eyes, the muscles of his jaw, the very flesh upon his bones seemed to strain with some deadly resolution, as though the indomitable spirit of the man, by sheer determination, would force the body to do its will, even after death was on it. And here there was a curious thing. It was not about the house, where his treasure might have been concealed, that the dead man strained, but toward the door, as though he would follow after some one who had gone out there.

The neighbors cut him from the chair, straightened out his limbs, and got him buried. But his features, set in that deadly resolution, they could not straighten out. Neither the placidity of death, nor the fingers of those who prepared the man for burial, could relax the muscles or get down his eyelids. He lay in the coffin with that hideous resolution on his face, and he went into the earth with it.

When the man was found, Randolph sent for Abner, and the two of them looked through the house. Nothing had been disturbed. There was a kettle on the crane, and a crock beside the hearth. The ears of seed corn hung from the rafters, trussed up by their shucks; the bean pods together in a cluster; the cakes of tallow sat on a shelf above the mantel; the festoons of dried apples and the bunches of seasoned herbs hung against the chimney. The bed and all the furniture about the house was in its order.

When they had finished with that work they did not know who it was that had killed old Christian. Abner did not talk, but he said that much, and the Justice of the Peace told all he knew to every casual visitor. True, it was nothing more than the county knew already, but his talk annoyed Abner.

"Randolph's a leaky pitcher," he said. And I think it was this comment that inspired the notion that Abner knew something that he had not told the Justice.

At any rate he was a long time before the grand jury on this February day. The grand jury sat behind closed doors. They were stern, silent men, and nothing crept out through the keyhole. But after the witnesses were heard, the impression got about that the grand jury did not know who had killed old Christian, and this conclusion was presently verified when they came in before the judge. They had no indictment to find. And when the judge inquired if they knew of anything that would justify the prosecuting attorney in taking any further action on behalf of the state, the foreman shook his head.

Night was descending when we left the county-seat. Abner sat in his saddle like a man of bronze, his face stern, as it always was when he was silent, and I rode beside him. I wish I could get my Uncle Abner before your eye. He was one of those austere, deeply religious men who might have followed Cromwell, with a big iron frame, a grizzled beard and features forged out by a smith. His god was the god of the Tishbite, who numbered his followers by the companies who drew the sword. The land had need of men like Abner. The government of Virginia was over the Alleghenies, and this great, fertile cattle country, hemmed in by the far-off mountains like a wall of the world, had its own peace to keep. And it was these iron men who kept it. The fathers had got this land in grants from the King of England; they had held it against the savage and finally against the King himself. . . . And the sons were like them.

The horses were nervous; they flung their heads about, and rattled the bit rings and traveled together like men apprehensive of some danger to be overtaken. That deadly stillness of the day remained, but the snow was now beginning to appear. It fell like no other snow that I have ever seen—not a gust of specks or a shower of tiny flakes, but now and then, out of the dirty putty-colored sky, a flake as big as a man's thumb-nail winged down and lighted on the earth like some living creature. And it clung to the thing that it lighted on as though out of the heavens it had selected that thing to destroy. And, while it clung, there came another of these soft white creatures to its aid, and settled beside it, and another and another, until the bare stem of the ragweed, or the brown leaf of the beech tree snapped under the weight of these clinging bodies.

It is a marvel how quickly this snow covered up the world, and how swiftly and silently it descended. The trees and fences were grotesque and misshapen with it. The landscape changed and was blotted out. Night was on us, and always the invading swarm of flakes increased until they seemed to crowd one another in the stagnant air.

Presently Abner stopped and looked up at the sky, but he did not speak and we went on. But now the very road began to be clogged with this wet snow; great limbs broke at the tree trunks under the weight of it; the horses began to flounder, and at last Abner stopped. It seemed to be at a sort of cross-road in a forest, but I was lost. The snow had covered every landmark that I knew. We had been traveling for an hour in a country as unfamiliar as the Tartar Steppes.

Abner turned out of the road into the forest. My horse followed. We came presently into the open, and stopped under the loom of a house. It was a great barn of hewn logs, but unused and empty. The door stood open on its broken hinges. We got down, took the horses in, removed the saddles, and filled the mangers with some old hay from the loft. I had no idea where we were. We could not go on, and I thought we would be forced to pass the night here. But this was not Abner's plan.

"Let us try to find the house, Martin," he said, "and build a fire."

We set out from the stable. Abner broke a trail through the deep snow, and I followed at his heels. He must have had some sense of direction, for we could not see. We seemed an hour laboring in that snow, but it could only have been a few minutes at the furthest. Presently we came upon broad steps, and under the big columns of a portico. And I knew the place for an old abandoned manor house, set in a corner of worn-out fields, in the edge of the forest, where the river bowed in under sheer banks a dozen fathoms down. The estate was grown up with weeds, and the house falling to decay. But now, when we came into the portico, a haze of light was shining through the fan-shaped glass over the door. It was this light that disturbed Abner. He stopped and stood there in the shelter of the columns, like a man in some perplexity.

"Now, who could that be?" he said, not to me, but to himself.

And he remained for some time, watching the blur of light, and listening for a sound. But there was no sound. The house had been abandoned. The windows were nailed up. Finally he went over to the ancient door and knocked. For answer there was the heavy report of a weapon, and a white splinter leaped out of a panel above his head. He sprang aside, and the weapon bellowed again, and I saw another splinter. And then I saw a thing that I had not noticed, that the door and the boards over the windows were riddled with these bullet holes. Abner shouted out his name and called on the man within to stop shooting and open the door.

For some time there was silence; then, finally the door did open, and a man stood there with a candle in his hand. He was a little old man with a stub of wiry beard, red grizzled hair, keen eyes like a crumb of glass, and a body knotted and tawny like a stunted oak tree. He wore a sort of cap with a broad fur collar fastened with big brass wolf-head clasps. And I knew him. He was the old country doctor, Storm, who had come into the hills, from God knows where. He lived not far away, and as a child, I feared him. I feared the flappings of his cape on some windy ridge, for he walked the country in his practice, and only rode when the distances were great. No one knew his history, and about him the negroes had conjured up every sort of fancy. These notions took a sort of form. Storm was a rival of the Devil and jousted with him for the lives of men and beasts. He would work on a horse, snapping his jaws and muttering his strange oaths, as long and as patiently as upon the body of a man. And surely, if one stood and watched him, one would presently believe that Storm contended with something for its prey. I can see him now, standing in the door with the candle held high up so he could peer into the darkness.

He cried out when he saw Abner.

"Come in," he said, "by the Eternal, you are welcome!"

"Storm!" said Abner, "you in this house!"

"And why not?" replied the man. "I walk and am overtaken by a snow; and you ride and do not escape it."

He laughed, showing his twisted, yellow teeth, and turned about in the doorway, and we followed him into the house. There was a fire burning on the hearth and another candle guttering on the table. It was a hall that the door led into—the conventional hall of the great old Southern manor house, wide mahogany doors on either side stood closed in their white frames, a white stairway going up to a broad landing, and a huge fireplace with brass andirons. The place was warm, but musty. It had long been stripped and gutted. It was hung with cobwebs and powdered down with dust. There was a small portmanteau on the table, such as one's father used to carry, of black leather with little flaps and buckles. And beside it a blue iron stone jug and a dirty tumbler.

The man set down the candle and indicated the jug and the fireplace with a queer, ironical gesture.

"I offer you the hospitality of the cup and the hearth, Abner," he said.

"We will take the hearth, Storm," replied Abner, "if you please."

And we went over to the fireplace, took off our great coats, beat out the wet snow, and sat down on the old mahogany settle by the andirons.

"Every man to the desire of his heart and the custom of his life," said Storm.

He took up the jug, turned it on end, and drained its contents into the glass. There was only a little of the liquor left. It was brewed from apples, raw and fiery, and the odor of it filled the place. Then he held up the glass, watching the firelight play in the white-blue liquor.

"You fill the mind with phantoms," he said, turning the glass about as though it held some curious drug. "We swallow you and see things that are not, and dead men from their graves."

He toyed with the glass, put it on the table, and sat down.

"Abner," he said, "I know the body of a man down to the fiber of his bones; but the mind—it is a land of mystery. We dare not trust it." He paused and rapped the table with his callous fingers.

"Against another we may be secure, but against himself what one of us is safe? A man may have no fear of your Hebrew God, Abner, or your Assyrian Devil, and yet, his own mind may turn against him and fill him full of terror. . . . A man may kill his enemy in secret and hide him, and return to his house secure—and find the dead man sitting in his chair with the wet blood on him.

And with all his philosophies he cannot eject that phantom from its seat. He will say this thing does not exist. But what avails the word when the thing is there!"

He got on his feet and leaned over the table with his crooked fingers out before him.

I was afraid and I drew closer to my uncle. This strange old man, straining over the table, peering into the shadows, held me with a gripping fascination. His wiry, faded red hair seemed to rise on his scalp, and I looked to see some horror in its grave clothes appear before him.

Abner turned his stern face upon him. It was some time before he spoke.

"Storm," he said, "what do you fear?"

"Fear!" cried the old man, his voice rising in a sharp staccato; and he made a gesture outward with his hand.

"You fear your God, Abner, and I fear myself!" But there was something in Abner's voice and in this query launched at him that changed the man as by some sorcery. He sat down, fingered the glass of liquor, and looked at Abner closely. He did not speak for some time. He appeared to be turning some problem slowly in his mind. There was a lot of mystery here to clear up. We had discovered him by chance, and surely he had received us in the strangest manner. His explanation could not be true that he had come into the house before us on this night, for the house was warm, and it could not have been heated in that time. What was the creature's secret? Why was he here, and who besieged him. These were things which he must fear to have known, and yet, he was glad to see us, glad to find us there in the snow, instead of another whom he feared to find there. And yet, we disturbed him, and he was uncertain what to do. He sat beyond the table, and I could see his eyes run over us, and wander off about the hall and return and glance at the black portmanteau.

And while he hung there between his plans, Abner spoke.

"Storm," he said, "what does all this mean?" The old man looked about him swiftly, furtively, I thought; then he spoke in a voice so low that we could hardly hear him.

"Let me put it this way, Abner," he said: "One comes here, as you come; he is met as you are met; well, what happens from all this? . . . A suspicion enters the visitor's mind. There is peril to the host in that, and he is put to an alternative. He must explain or he must shoot the guest. . . . Well, he chooses to make his explanation first, and if that fail, there is the other!

"'And,' he says, 'you have done me a service to come in; I am glad to see you.' And you say, 'What do you fear?' He answers, 'Robbers.' You say, 'What have you in this house to lose?' And he tells you this:

"Michael Dale owned this house. He was rich. When he was dying he sat here by this hearth, tapping the bricks with his cane, and peering at his worthless son. You remember that son, Abner; he looked like the Jupiter of Elis before the Devil got him. 'Wellington,' he said, 'I am leaving you a treasure here.' He had been speaking of this estate, and one thought he meant the lands, and so gave the thing no notice. But later one remembered that expression and began to think it over. One recalled where it was that Michael Dale sat and the tapping of his stick. Well, when one is going down, any straw is worth the clutching. One slips into this house and looks."

He indicated the brick hearth with a gesture.

"No, it is not there now. The gold is in that portmanteau."

He arose, opened the bag, and fumbled in it. Then he came to us with some pieces in his hand.

Abner took the gold and examined it carefully by the firelight. They were old pieces, and he rubbed them between his fingers and scraped something from their faces with his thumb-nail. Then he handed them back, and Storm cast them into the portmanteau and buckled it together. Then he sat down and drew the stone jug over beside him.

"Now, Abner," he said, "there is this evil about a treasure. It fills one full of fear. You must stand guard over it, and the thing gets on your nerves. The wind in the chimney is a voice, and every noise a footstep. At first one goes about with the weapon in his hand, and then, when he can bear it no more, he shoots at every sound."

Abner did not move, and I listened to the man as to a tale of Bagdad. Every mystery was now cleared up—his presence in this house, his fear, the bullet holes, and why he was glad to see us, and yet disturbed that we had come. And I saw what he had been turning in his mind—whether he should trust us with the truth or leave us to our own conclusions. I understood and verified in myself every detail of this story. I should have acted as he did at every step, and I could realize this fear, and how, as the thing possessed him, one might come at last to shoot up the shadows. I looked at the man with a sort of wonder.

Abner had been stroking his bronze face with his great sinewy hand, and now he spoke.

"Storm," he said, "Michael Dale's riddle is not the only one that has been read." And he told of Christian Lance's death, and the Delphic sentence that had doubtless caused it. "You knew old Christian, Storm, and his curious life?"

"I did," replied Storm, "and I knew the man who carried off the knob of the andiron. But how do you say that any man read his riddle, Abner, and how do you know that there was any riddle in it? I took the thing to be an idle taunt."

"And so did Randolph," said Abner, "but you were both wrong. The secret was in that scrawled sentence, and some one guessed it."

"How do you know that, Abner?" said Storm.

Abner did not reply directly to the point.

"Old Christian loved money," he went on. "He would have died before he told where it was hidden. And his straining toward the door, as though in death he would follow one who had gone out there, meant that his secret had been divined, and that his gold had gone that way."

"You ride to a conclusion on straws, Abner," said Storm, "if that is all the proof you have."

"Well," replied Abner, "I have also a theory."

"And what is your theory?" said Storm.

"It is this," continued Abner; "when old Christian wrote, 'Why don't you look in the cow,' he meant a certain thing. There was a row of tallow cakes on a shelf. My theory is that each year when he got the gold from his cattle, he molded it into one of these tallow cakes, turned it out of the crock, and put it on the shelf. And there, in the heart of these tallow cakes, was the old man's treasure!"

"But you tell me that the cakes were there on this shelf when you found old Christian," said Storm.

"They were," replied Abner.

"Every one of them," said Storm.

"Every one of them," answered Abner.

"Had any one of them been cut or broken?"

"Not one of them; they were smooth and perfect."

"Then your first conclusion goes to pieces, Abner. No man carried Christian's money through the door; it is there on the shelf."

"No," said Abner, "it is not there. The man who killed old Christian Lance got the gold out of those cakes of tallow."

"And, now, Abner," cried the man, "the bottom of your theory falls. How could one get the gold out of these cakes, and leave them perfect?"

"I will tell you that," replied Abner. "There was a kettle on the crane and a crock beside the hearth, and every cake of tallow on the shelf was white. . . They had been remolded! Randolph did not see that, but I did."

Storm got on his feet.

"Then you do not believe this explanation, Abner—that the gold comes from the hearth?"

"I do not," replied Abner, and his voice was deep and level. "There is tallow on these coins!"

I saw Abner glance at the iron poker and watch Storm's hand.

But the old man did not draw his weapon. He laughed noiselessly, twisting his crooked mouth.

"You are right, Abner," he said, "it is Christian's gold, and this tale a lie. But you are wrong in your conclusion. Lance was not killed by a little man like I am; he was killed by a big man like you!"

He paused and leaned over, resting his hands on the table.

"The man who killed him did not guess that riddle, Abner. . . . Put the evidences together. . . . Lance was tied into his chair before the assassin killed him. Why? That was to threaten him with death unless he told where his gold was hidden. . . . Well, Lance would not tell that, but the assassin found it out by chance. He stooped to put the poker into the fire to heat it, and torture Christian. The cakes of tallow were on a hanging shelf against the white-washed chimney; as the assassin arose, he struck this shelf with his shoulder, and one of the tallow cakes fell and burst on the hearth. Then he killed Christian with a blow of the heated poker. I know that because the hair about the wound was scorched!

"You saw a good deal in that house, Abner, but did you see a crease in the chimney where the shelf smote it, and the mark of a man's shoulder on the whitewash? And that shoulder, Abner," he raised his hand above his head, "it was as high as yours!"

There was silence.

And as the two men looked thus at each other, there was a sound as of something padding about the house outside. For a moment I did not understand these sounds, then I realized that the wind was rising, and clumps of snow falling from the trees. But to another in that house these sounds had no such explanation.

Then a thing happened. One of the mahogany doors entering the hall leaped back, and a man stood there with a pistol in his hand. And in all my life I have never seen a creature like him! There was everything fine and distinguished in his face, but the face was a ruin. It was a loathsome and hideous ruin. Made for the occupancy of a god, the man's body was the dwelling of a devil. I do not mean a clean and vicious devil, but one low and bestial, that wallowed and gorged itself with sins. And there was another thing in that face that to understand, one must have seen it. There was terror, but no fear! It was as though the man advanced against a thing that filled him full of horror, but he advanced with courage. He had a spirit in him that saw and knew the aspect and elements of danger, but it could not be stampeded into flight.

I heard Abner say, "Dale!" like one who pronounces the name of some extraordinary thing. And I heard Storm say, "Mon dieu! With a teaspoonful of laudanum in him, he walks!"

The creature did not see us; he was listening to the sounds outside, and he started for the door.

"You there," he bellowed, "again! . . . Damn you! . . . Well, I'll get you this time. . . . I'll hunt you to hell!" . . . And his drunken voice rumbled off into obscenities and oaths.

He flung the door open and went out. His weapon thundered, and by it and the drunken shouting, we could track him. He seemed to move north, as though lured that way. We stood and listened.

"He goes toward the river," said Abner. "It is God's will."

Then far off there was a last report of the weapon and a great bellowing cry that shuddered through the forest.

That night over the fire, Storm told us how he had come in from the snow and found Dale drunk and fighting the ghost of Christian Lance; how he listened to his story, and slipped the drug into his glass, and how he got him hidden, when we came, on the promise to keep his secret; and how he had fenced with Abner, seeing that Abner suspected him.

But it was the failure of his drug that vexed him.

"It would put a brigadier and his horse to sleep—that much, if it were pure. I shall take ten drops to-morrow night and see."

13
The Straw Man

It was a day of early June in Virginia. The afternoon sun lay warm on the courthouse with its great plaster pillars; on the tavern with its two-story porch; on the stretches of green fields beyond and the low wooded hill, rimmed by the far-off mountains like a wall of the world.

It was the first day of the circuit court, which all the country attended. And on this afternoon, two men crossed the one thoroughfare that lay through the county seat, and went up the wide stone steps into the courthouse.

The two men were in striking contrast. One, short of stature and beginning to take on the rotundity of age, was dressed with elaborate care, his great black stock propping up his chin, his linen and the cloth of his coat immaculate. He wore a huge carved ring and a bunch of seals attached to his watch-fob. The other was a big, broad-shouldered, deep-chested Saxon, with all those marked characteristics of a race living out of doors and hardened by wind and sun. His powerful frame carried no ounce of surplus weight. It was the frame of the empire builder on the frontier of the empire. The face reminded one of Cromwell, the craggy features in repose seemed molded over iron, but the fine gray eyes had a calm serenity, like remote spaces in the summer sky. The man's clothes were plain and somber. And he gave one the impression of things big and vast.

As the two entered between the plaster pillars, a tall old man came out from the county clerk's office. But for his face, he might have been one of a thousand Englishmen in Virginia. There was nothing in the big, spare figure or the cranial lines of the man to mark.

But the face seized you. In it was an unfathomable disgust with life, joined, one would say, with a cruel courage. The hard, bony jaw protruded; bitter lines descended along the planes of the face, and the eyes circled by red rims were expressionless and staring, as though, by some abominable negligence of nature, they were lidless.

The two approached, and the one so elaborately dressed spoke to the old man.

"How do you do, Northcote Moore?" he said. "You know Abner?"

The old man stopped instantly and stood very still. He moved the stick in his hand a trifle before him. Then he spoke in a high-pitched, irascible voice.

"Abner, eh! Well, what the devil is Abner here for?"

The little pompous man clenched his fingers in his yellow gloves, but his voice showed no annoyance.

"I asked him to have a look at Eastwood Court."

"Damn the justice of the peace of every county," cried the old man, "and you included, Randolph! You never make an end of anything."

He gave no attention to Abner, who remained unembarrassed, regarding the impolite old man as one regards some strange, new, and particularly offensive beast.

"Chuck the whole business, Randolph, that's what I say," the irascible old man continued, "and forget about it. Who the devil cares? A drooling old paralytic is snuffed out. Well, he ought to have gone five and twenty years ago! He couldn't manage his estate and he kept me out. I was like to hang about until I rotted, while the creature played at Patience, propped up against the table and the wall. A nigger, on a search for shillings, knocks him on the head. Shall I hunt the nigger down and hang him? Damme! I would rather get him a patent of state lands!"

The face of Randolph was a study in expression.

"But, sir," he said, "there are some things about this affair that are peculiar—I may say extraordinarily peculiar."

Again the old man stood still. When he spoke his voice was in a lower note.

"And so," he said, "you have nosed out a new clew and got Abner over, and we are to have another inquisition."

He reflected, moving his stick idly before him. Then he went on in a petulant, persuasive tone.

"Why can't you let sleeping dogs lie? The country is beginning to forget this affair, and you set about to stir it up. Shall I always have the thing clanking at my heels like a ball and chain?"

Then he rang the paved court with the ferrule of his stick.

"Damme, man!" he cried. "Has Virginia no mysteries, that you yap forever on old scents at Eastwood? What does it matter who did this thing? It was a public service. Virginia needs a few men on her lands with a bit of courage. This state is rotten with old timber. In youth, Duncan Moore was a fool. In age, he was better dead. Let there be an end to this, Randolph."

And he turned about and went back into the county clerk's office.

Randolph was a justice of the peace in Virginia. He looked a moment after the departing figure; then he spoke to his companion.

"He is here to have the lands of Duncan Moore transferred on the assessor's book to his own name. He takes the estate under the Life and Lives statute of Virginia, that the legislature got up to soften the rigor of Mr. Jefferson's Statute of Descents. Under it, this estate with its great English manor house was devised by the original ancestor to Duncan Moore for his life, and after him to Northcote Moore for his life, and at his death to Esdale Moore. It could have run twenty-one years farther if the scrivener had known the statute. Mr. Jefferson did not entirely decapitate the law of entail."

He paused and lifted his finger with a curious gesture.

"It is a queer family—I think the very queerest in Virginia. There is something defective about every one of them. Duncan Moore, the decedent, had no children. His two brothers died epileptics. This man, the son of the elder brother, is blind. And the son of the junior, Mr. Esdale Moore, the attorney-at-law—"

The Justice of the Peace was interrupted. A little dapper man, sunburned and bareheaded, dressed like a tailor's print, but with the smart, aggressive air of a well-bred colonial Englishman, pushed through the crowd and clapped the Justice on the shoulder.

"What luck, Randolph?" he cried. "I am sure Abner has run the assassin to cover." And he bobbed his head to Abner like one whose profession permits a certain familiarity. "Come along to the tavern; 'I would listen to your wondrous tales,' as Homer says it."

He led the way, calling out to a member of the bar, hailing an acquaintance, and hurling banter about him in the bluff, hearty fashion which he imagined to be the correct manner of a man of the people who is getting on. He was in the strength and vigor of his race at forty.

"Beastly dull, Randolph," he rattled; "nothing exciting since the dawn expect old Baron-Vitch's endless suit in chancery. But one must sit tight, rain or shine. The people must know where to find a lawyer when they want him."

He swung along with a big military stride.

"The life of a lawyer is far from jolly. I should like to cut it, Randolph, if I had a good shooting and bit of trout water. Alas, I am poor!" And he made a dramatic gesture.

One felt that under this froth the man was calling out the truth. For all his hearty interest in affairs, the law was merely a sort of game. It was nothing real. He played to win, and he had chosen his profession with care and after long reflection, as a breeder chooses a colt for the Derby, or as an English family of influence selects a crack regiment for the heir at Oxford. He cared not one penny what the laws were or the great policies of Virginia. But he did care, with an inbred and abiding interest, about the value of a partridge shooting, or the damming of a trout stream by the grist mills. These things were the realities of life, and not the actions at law or the suits in chancery.

"How does one get a fortune nowadays, Abner?" he called back across his shoulder, "for I need one like the devil. Marriage or crime, eh? Crime requires a certain courage, and they say out in the open that lawyers are decadent. With you and Randolph on the lookout, I should be afraid to go in for crime!"

He clapped a passing giant on the back, called him Harrison, accused him of having an eye on Congress, and went on across his shoulder to Abner:

"Marriage, then? Do you know a convenient orphan with a golden goose? Pleasure and a certain gain would be idyllic! The simplest men understand that. Do not the writers in Paris tell us that the French peasant on his marriage night, while embracing his bride with one arm, extends the other in order to feel the sack that contains her dowry?"

They were now on the upper floor of the tavern porch. Mr. Esdale Moore sent a negro for a dish of tea, after the English fashion.

Then he got a table at the end of the porch, somewhat apart, and the three men sat down.

"And now, Randolph," he said, "what did you find at Eastwood?"

"I am afraid," replied the Justice of the Peace, "that we found little new there. The evidence remains, with trifling additions, what it was; but Abner has arrived at some interesting opinions upon this evidence."

"I am sure Abner can clap his hand on the assassin," said the attorney. "Come, sir, let me fill your cup, and while I stand on one foot, as St. Augustine used to say, tell me who ejected my uncle, the venerable Duncan Moore, out of life."

The negro servant had returned with a great silver pot, and a tray of cups with queer kneeling purple cows on them.

Abner held out his cup.

"Sir," he said, "one must be very certain, to answer that question." His voice was deep and level, like some balanced element in nature.

He waited while the man filled the cup; then he replaced it on the table.

"And, sir," he continued slowly, "I am not yet precisely certain."

He slipped a lump of sugar slowly into the cup.

"It is the Ruler of Events who knows, sir; we can only conjecture. We cannot see the truth naked before us as He does; we must grope for it from one indication to another until we find it."

"But, reason, Abner," interrupted the lawyer, bustling in his chair; "we have that, and God has nothing better!"

"Sir," replied Abner, "I cannot think of God depending on a thing so crude as reason. If one reflects upon it, I think one will immediately see that reason is a quality exclusively peculiar to the human mind. It is a thing that God could never, by any chance, require. Reason is the method by which those who do not know the truth, step by step, finally discover it."

He paused and looked out across the table at the far-off mountains.

"And so, sir, God knows who in Virginia has a red hand from this work at Eastwood Court, without assembling the evidence and laboring to determine whither these signboards point. But Randolph and I are like children with a puzzle. We must get all the pieces first, and then sit down and laboriously fit them up."

He looked down into his cup, his face in repose and reflective.

"Ah, sir," he went on, "if one could be certain that one had always every piece, there would no longer remain such a thing as a human mystery. Every event dovetails into every other event that precedes and follows. With the pieces complete, the truth could never elude us. But, alas, sir, human intelligence is feeble and easily deludes itself, and the relations and ramifications of events are vast and intricate."

"Then, sir," said Mr. Esdale Moore, "you do not believe that the criminal can create a series of false evidences that will be at all points consistent with the truth."

"No man can do it," replied Abner. "For to do that, one must know everything that goes before and everything that follows the event which one is attempting to falsify. And this omniscience only the intelligence of God can compass. It is impossible for the human mind to manufacture a false consistency of events except to a very limited extent."

"Then, gentlemen," cried the lawyer, "you can make me no excuse for leaving this affair a mystery."

"Yes," replied my uncle, "we could make you an excuse—a valid and sound excuse: the excuse of incompetency."

Mr. Esdale Moore laughed in his big, hearty voice.

"With your reputation, Abner, and that of Squire Randolph in Virginia, I should refuse to receive it."

"Alas," continued Abner, "we are no better than other men. A certain experience, some knowledge of the habits of criminals, and a little skill in observation are the only advantages we have. If one were born among us with, let us say, a double equipment of skull space, no criminal would ever escape him."

"He would laugh at us, Abner," said the Justice.

"He would never cease to laugh," returned my uncle, "but he would laugh the loudest at the bungling criminal. To him, the most cunning crime would be a botch; fabricated events would be conspicuous patch-work, and he would see the identity of the criminal agent in a thousand evidences."

He hesitated a moment; then he added:

"Fortunately for human society, the inconsistency of false evidence is usually so glaring that any one of us is able to see it."

"As in Lord William Russell's case," said the Justice, "where the valet, having killed his master in such a manner as to create the aspect of suicide, inadvertently carried away the knife with which his victim was supposed to have cut his own throat."

"Precisely," said Abner. "And there is, I think, in every case something equally inconsistent, if we only look close enough to find it."

He turned to Mr. Esdale Moore.

"With a little observation, sir, to ascertain the evidence, and a little common sense to interpret its intent, Randolph and I manage to get on."

The lawyer put a leading question.

"What glaring inconsistency did you find at Eastwood?" he said.

Abner looked at Randolph, as though for permission to go on. The Justice nodded.

"Why, this thing, sir," he answered, "that a secretary that was not locked should be broken open."

"But, Abner," said the lawyer, "who, but myself, knew that this secretary was not locked? It was the custom to lock it, although it contained nothing but my uncle's playing cards. As I told Randolph, on the day of my uncle's death I put the key down among the litter of papers inside the secretary, after I had opened it, and could not find it again, so I merely closed the lid. But I alone knew this. Everybody else would imagine the secretary to be locked as usual."

"Not everybody," continued my uncle. "Reflect a moment: To believe the secretary locked on this night, one must have known that it was locked on every preceding night. To believe that it was locked on this night because the lid was closed, one must have known that it was always locked on every preceding night when the lid was closed. And further, sir, one must have known this custom so well—one must have been so certain of it—that one knew it was not worth while to attempt to open the secretary by pulling down the lid on the chance that it might not be locked, and so, broke it open at once.

"Now, sir," he went on, "does this not exclude the theory that Duncan Moore was killed by a common burglar who entered the house for the purpose of committing a robbery? Such a criminal agent could not have known this custom. He might have believed the secretary to be locked, or imagined it to be, but he could not have known it conclusively. He could not have been so certain that he would fail to lay hold of the lid to make sure. One must assume the lowest criminal will act with some degree of intelligence."

"By Jove!" cried the attorney, striking the table, "I had a feeling that my uncle was not killed by a common thief! I thought the authorities were not at the bottom of this thing, and that is why I kept at Randolph, why I urged him to get you out to Eastwood Court."

"Sir," replied Abner, "I am obliged to you for the compliment. But your feeling was justified, and your persistence in this case will, I think, be rewarded.

"Nevertheless, sir, if you will pardon the digression, permit me to say that your remark interests me profoundly. Whence, I wonder, came this feeling that caused you to reject the obvious explanation and to urge a further and more elaborate inquiry?"

"Now, Abner," returned Mr. Esdale Moore, "I cannot answer that question. The thing was a kind of presentiment. I had a sort of feeling, as we express it. I cannot say more than that."

"I have had occasion," continued Abner, "to examine the theory of presentiments, and I find that we are forced to one of two conclusions: Either they are of an origin exterior to the individual, of which we have no reliable proof, or they are founded upon some knowledge of which the correlation in the mind is, for the moment, obscure. That is to say, a feeling, presentiment, or premonition, may be a sort of shadow thrown by an unformed conclusion.

"An unconscious or subconscious mental process produces an impression. We take this impression to be from behind the stars, when, in fact, it merely indicates the rational conclusion at which we would have arrived if we had made a strong, conscious effort to understand the enigma before us."

He drank a little tea and put the cup back gently on the table.

"Perhaps, sir, if you had gone forward with the mental processes that produced your premonition, you would have worked out the solution of this mystery. Why, I wonder, did your deductions remain subconscious?"

"That is a question in mental science," replied the lawyer.

"Is not all science mental?" continued my uncle. "Do not men take their facts in a bag to the philosopher that he may put them together? Let us reflect a moment, sir: Are not the primitive emotions—as, for example, fear—in their initial stages always subconscious, or, as we say, instinctive? Thus, a thousand times in the day do not our bodies draw back from danger of which we are wholly unconscious? We do not go forward into these perils, and we pass on with no realization of their existence. Can we doubt, sir, that the mind also instinctively perceives danger at the end of certain mental processes and does not go forward upon them?"

The lawyer regarded my uncle in a sort of wonder.

"Abner," he said, "you forget my activities in this affair. It is I who have kept at Randolph. What instinctive fear, then, could have mentally restrained me?"

"Why, sir," replied Abner, "the same fear that instinctively restrained Randolph and myself."

Mr. Esdale Moore looked my uncle in the face.

"What fear?" he said.

"The fear," continued Abner, "of what these deductions lead to."

Abner moved his chair a little nearer to the table and went on in a lower voice.

"Now, sir, if we exclude the untenable hypothesis that this crime was committed by an unknown thief, from the motive of robbery, what explanation remains? Let us see: This secretary could have been broken open only by some one who knew that it was the custom to keep it locked. Who was certain of that custom? Obviously, sir, only those in the household of the aged Duncan Moore."

The face of the lawyer showed a profound interest. He leaned over, put his right elbow on the table, rested his chin in the trough of the thumb and finger, and with his other hand, took a box of tobacco cigarettes from his pocket and began to break it open. It was one of the elegancies of that day.

Abner went on, "Was it a servant at Eastwood Court?"

He paused, and Randolph interrupted.

"On the night of this tragedy," said the Justice of the Peace, "all the negroes in the household attended a servants' ball on a neighboring estate. They went in a body and returned in a body. The aged Duncan Moore was alive when they left the house, and dead when they returned."

"But, Randolph," Abner went on, "independent of this chance event, conclusive in itself—which I feel is an accident to which we are hardly entitled—do not our inferences legitimately indicate a criminal agent other than a servant at Eastwood Court?

"Sane men do not commit violent crimes without a motive. There was no motive to move any servant except that of gain, and there was no gain to be derived from the death of the aged Duncan Moore, except that to be got from rifling his secretary. But the one who knew so much about this secretary that he was certain it was locked, would also have known enough about it to know that it contained nothing of value."

He hesitated and moved the handle of his cup.

"Now, sir," he added, "two persons remain."

The lawyer, fingering the box of cigarettes, broke it open and presented them to my uncle and Randolph. He lighted one, and over the table looked Abner in the face.

"You mean Northcote Moore and myself," he said in a firm, even voice. "Well, sir, which one was it?"

My uncle remained undisturbed.

"Sir," he said, "there was at least a pretense of consistency in the work of the one who manufactured the evidences of a burglar. There was a window open in the north wing at the end of the long, many-cornered passage that leads through Eastwood Court to the room in the south wing where the aged Duncan Moore was killed. Now some one had gone along that passage, as you pointed out to Randolph when Eastwood Court was first inspected, because there were finger-prints on the walls at the turns and angles. These finger-prints were marked in the dust on the walls of the passage on the east side, but on the west side, beginning heaviest near Duncan Moore's room, the prints were in blood.

"These marks on the wall show that the assassin did, in fact, enter by this passage and return along it. But he did not enter by the open window. The frame of this window was cemented into the casement with dust. This dust was removed only on the inside. Moreover, violence had been used to force it open, and the marks of this violence were all plainly visible on the inside of the frame."

He stopped, remained a moment silent, and then continued:

"This corridor is the usual and customary way—in fact, the only way leading from the north wing of Eastwood Court to the south wing. Duncan Moore alone occupied the south wing. And, sir, on this night, Northcote Moore and yourself alone occupied the north wing. You were both equally familiar with this passage, since you lived in the house, and used it constantly."

Abner paused and looked at Mr. Esdale Moore.

"Shall I go on, sir?" he said.

"Pray do," replied the lawyer.

Abner continued, in his deep, level voice.

"Now, sir, you will realize why Randolph and I felt an instinctive fear of the result of these deductions, and perhaps, sir, why your subconscious conclusions went no further than a premonition."

"But the law of Virginia," put in the Justice, "is no respecter of persons. If the Governor should do a murder, his office would not save him from the gallows."

"It would not," said the lawyer. "Go on, Abner."

My uncle moved slightly in his chair.

"If the aged Duncan Moore were removed," he continued, "Northcote Moore would take the manorhouse and the lands. For Esdale Moore to take the estate, both the aged Duncan Moore and the present incumbent must be removed. Only the aged Duncan Moore was removed. Who was planning a gain, then, by this criminal act? Esdale Moore or Northcote Moore?

"Another significant thing: Mr. Esdale Moore knew this secretary was unlocked on this night; Northcote Moore did not. Who, then, was the more likely to break it open as evidence of a presumptive robbery?

"And, finally, sir, who would grope along this corridor feeling with his hands for the corners and angles of the wall, one who could see, or a blind man?"

My uncle stopped and sat back in his chair.

The lawyer leaned over and put both arms on the table.

"Gentlemen," he said, since he addressed both Randolph and Abner, "you amaze me! You accuse the most prominent man in Virginia."

"Before the law," said the Justice, "all men are equal."

The lawyer turned toward my uncle, as to one of more consideration.

"While you were making your deductions," he said, "I had to insist that you go on, for I was myself included. I was bound to hear you to the end, although you shocked me at every step. But now, I beg you to reflect. Northcote Moore belongs to an ancient and honorable family. He is old; he is blind. Surely something can be done to save him."

"Nothing," replied the Justice firmly.

Abner lifted his face, placid, unmoving, like a mask.

"Perhaps," he said.

The two men before him at the table moved with astonishment.

"Perhaps!" cried the Justice of the Peace. "This is Virginia!"

But it was the lawyer who was the more amazed. He had not moved; he did not move; but his face, as by some sorcery, became suddenly perplexed.

The tavern was now deserted; every one had gone back into the courthouse. The three men were alone. There was silence except for the noises of the village and the far-off hum of winged insects in the air. Mr. Esdale Moore sat facing north along the upper porch; Abner opposite; Randolph looking eastward toward the courthouse. My uncle did not go on at once. He reached across the table for one of the tobacco cigarettes. The lawyer mechanically took up the box with his hand nearest to the Justice of the Peace and opened the lid with his thumb and finger. Abner selected one but did not light it.

"Writers on the law," he began, "warn us against the obvious inference when dealing with the intelligent criminal agent, and for this reason: while the criminal of the lowest order seeks only to cover his identity, and the criminal of the second order to indicate another rather than himself, the criminal of the first order, sir, will sometimes undertake a subtle finesse—a double intention.

"The criminal of the lowest order gives the authorities no one to suspect. The criminal of the second order sets up a straw man before his own door, hoping to mislead the authorities. But the criminal of the first order sets it before the door of another, expecting the authorities of the state to knock it down and take the man behind it.

"Now, sir,"—my uncle paused— "looked at from this quarter, do not our obvious deductions lack a certain conclusiveness?

"If Northcote Moore were hanged for murder, Esdale Moore would take the manor-house and the landed estate. Therefore, he might wish Northcote Moore hanged, just as Northcote Moore might wish Duncan Moore murdered.

"And, if one were deliberately placing a straw man, would there be any inconsistency in breaking open a secretary obviously unlocked? The straw, sir, would be only a trifle more conspicuous!

"And the third deduction"—his gray eyes narrowed, and he spoke slowly: "If one born blind, and another, were accustomed to go along a passage day after day; in the dark, who would grope, feeling his way in the night, step by step, along the angles of the wall—the one who could see, or the blind man?"

The amazed Justice struck the table with his clenched hand.

"By the gods," he cried, "*not the blind man!* For to the blind man, the passage was always dark!"

The lawyer had not moved, but his face, in its desperate perplexity, began to sweat. The Justice swung around upon him, but Abner put out his hand.

"A moment, Randolph," he said. "The human body is a curious structure. It has two sides, as though two similar mechanisms were joined with a central trunk—the dexter side, or that which is toward the south when the man is facing the rising sun, and the sinister side, or that which is toward the north. These sides are not coequal. One of them is controlling and dominates the man, and when the task before him is difficult, it is with this more efficient controlling side that he approaches it.

"Thus, one set on murder and desperately anxious to make no sound, to make no false step, to strike no turn or angle, would instinctively follow the side of the wall that he could feel along with his controlling hand. This passage runs north and south. The bloody finger-prints are all on the west side of the wall, the prints in the dust on the east side; therefore, the assassin followed the east side of the wall when he set out on his deadly errand, and the west side when he returned with the blood on him.

"That is to say," and his voice lifted into a stronger note, "he always followed the left side of the wall.

"Why, sir?" And he got on his feet, his voice ringing, his finger pointing at the sweating, cornered man. "Because his controlling side was on the left—because he was left handed!

"And you, sir—I have been watching you—"

The pent-up energies of Mr. Esdale Moore seemed to burst asunder.

"It's a lie!" he cried.

And he lunged at Abner across the table, with his clenched *left* hand.

14

The Mystery of Chance

It was a night like the pit. The rain fell steadily. Now and then a gust of wind rattled the shutters, and the tavern sign, painted with the features of George the Third, now damaged by musket-balls and with the eyes burned out, creaked.

The tavern sat on the bank of the Ohio. Below lay the river and the long, flat island, where the ill-starred Blenner-hasset had set up his feudal tenure. Flood water covered the island and spread everywhere—a vast sea of yellow that enveloped the meadow-lands and plucked at the fringe of the forest.

The scenes in the tavern were in striking contrast. The place boomed with mirth, shouts of laughter, ribald tales and songs. The whole crew of the *Eldorado* of New Orleans banqueted in the guestroom of the tavern. This was the open room for the public. Beyond it and facing the river was the guest-room for the gentry, with its floor scrubbed with sand, its high-boy in veneered ma-hogany, its polished andirons and its various pretensions to a hostelry of substance.

At a table in this room, unmindful of the bedlam beyond him, a man sat reading a pamphlet. He leaned over on the table, between two tall brass candlesticks, his elbows on the board, his thumb marking the page. He had the dress and manner of a gentleman—excellent cloth in his coat, a rich stock and imported linen. On the table sat a top hat of the time, and in the corner by the driftwood fire was a portmanteau with silver buckles, strapped up as for a journey. The man was under forty, his features regular and clean-cut; his dark brows joined above eyes big and blue and wholly out of place in the olive skin.

Now and then he got up, went over to the window and looked out, but he was unable to see anything, for the rain continued and the puffs of wind. He seemed disturbed, and uneasy. He drummed on the sill with his fingers, and then, with a glance at his portmanteau, returned to his chair between the two big tallow candles.

From time to time the tavern-keeper looked in at the door with some servile inquiry. This interruption annoyed the guest.

"Damme, man," he said, "are you forever at the door?"

"Shall I give the crew rum, sir?" the landlord asked.

"No," replied the man; "I will not pay your extortions for imported liquor."

"They wish it, sir."

The man looked up from his pamphlet.

"They wish it, eh," he said with nice enunciation. "Well, Mr. Castoe, I do not!"

The soft voice dwelt on the "Mr. Castoe" with ironical emphasis. The mobile upper lip, shadowed with a silken mustache, lifted along the teeth with a curious feline menace.

The man was hardly over his table before the door opened again. He turned abruptly, like a panther, but when he saw who stood in the door, he arose with a formal courtesy.

"You are a day early, Abner," he said. "Are the Virginia wagons in for their salt and iron?"

"They will arrive to-morrow," replied my uncle; "the roads are washed out with the rains."

The man looked at my uncle, his hat and his greatcoat splashed with mud.

"How did you come?" he asked.

"Along the river," replied my uncle, "I thought to find you on the *Eldorado*."

"On the *Eldorado*!" cried the man. "On such a night, when the Tavern of George the Third has a log fire and kegs in the cellar!"

My uncle entered, closed the door, took off his greatcoat and hat, and sat down by the hearth.

"The boat looked deserted," he said.

"To the last nigger," said the man. "I could not take the comforts of the tavern and deny them to the crew."

My uncle warmed his hands over the snapping fire.

"A considerate heart, Byrd," he said, with some deliberation, "is a fine quality in a man. But how about the owners of your cargo, and the company that insures your boat?"

"The cargo, Abner," replied the man, "is in Benton's warehouse, unloaded for your wagons. The boat is tied up in the back-water. No log can strike it."

He paused and stroked his clean-cut, aristocratic jaw.

"The journey down from Fort Pitt was damnable," he added, "—miles of flood water, yellow and running with an accursed current. It was no pleasure voyage, believe me, Abner. There was the current running logs, and when we got in near the shore, the settlers fired on us. A careless desperado, your settler, Abner!"

"More careless, Byrd, do you think," replied my uncle, "than the river captain who overturns the half-submerged cabins with the wash of his boat?"

"The river," said the man, "is the steamboat's highway."

"And the cabin," replied my uncle, "is the settler's home."

"One would think," said Byrd, "that this home was a palace and the swamp land a garden of the Hesperides, and your settler a King of the Golden Mountains. My stacks are full of bullet holes."

My uncle was thoughtful by the fire.

"This thing will run into a river war," he said. "There will be violence and murder done."

"A war, eh!" echoed the man. "I had not thought of that, and yet, I had but now an ultimatum. When we swung in to-night, a big backwoodsman came out in a canoe and delivered an oration. I have forgotten the periods, Abner, but he would burn me at the stake, I think, and send the boat to Satan, unless I dropped down the river and came in below the settlement."

He paused and stroked his jaw again with that curious gesture.

"But for the creature's command," he added, "I would have made the detour. But when he threatened, I ran in as I liked and the creature got a ducking for his pains. His canoe went bottom upward, and if he had not been a man of oak, he would have gone himself to Satan."

"And what damage did you do?" inquired my uncle.

"Why, no damage, as it happened," said the man. "Some cabins swayed, but not one of them went over. I looked, Abner, for a skirmish in your war. There was more than one rifle at a window. If I were going to follow the river," he continued, "I would mount a six-pounder."

"You will quit the river, then," remarked my uncle.

"It is a dog's life, Abner," said the man. "To make a gain in these days of Yankee trading, the owner must travel with his boat. Captains are a trifle too susceptible to bribe. I do not mean gold-pieces, slipped into the hand, but the hospitalities of the shopkeeper. Your Yankee, Abner, sees no difference in men, or he will waive it for a sixpence in his till. The captain is banqueted at his house, and the cargo is put on short. One cannot sit in comfort at New Orleans and trade along the Ohio."

"Is one, then, so happy in New Orleans?" asked my uncle.

"In New Orleans, no," replied the man, "but New Orleans is not the world. The world is in Piccadilly, where one can live among his fellows like a gentleman, and see something of life—a Venetian dancer, ladies of fashion, and men who dice for something more than a trader's greasy shillings."

Byrd again got up and went to the window. The rain and gusts of wind continued. His anxiety seemed visibly to increase.

My uncle arose and stood with his back to the driftwood fire, his hands spread out to the flame. He glanced at Byrd and at the pamphlet on the table, and the firm muscles of his mouth hardened into an ironical smile.

"Mr. Evlyn Byrd," he said, "what do you read?"

The man came back to the table. He sat down and crossed one elegant knee over the other.

"It is an essay by the Englishman, Mill," he said, "reprinted in the press that Benjamin Franklin set up at Philadelphia. I agree with Lord Fairfax where the estimable Benjamin is concerned:

'Damn his little maxims! They smack too much of New England!'
But his press gives now and then an English thing worth while."

"And why is this English essay worth while?" asked my uncle.

"Because, Abner, in its ultimate conclusions, it is a justifica-
tion of a gentleman's most interesting vice. 'Chance,' Mr. Mill dem-
onstrates, 'is not only at the end of all our knowledge, but it is also
at the beginning of all our postulates.' We begin with it, Abner,
and we end with it. The structure of all our philosophy is laid down
on the sills of chance and roofed over with the rafters of it."

"The Providence of God, then," said my uncle, "does not come
into Mr. Mill's admirable essay."

Mr. Evlyn Byrd laughed.

"It does not, Abner," he said. "Things happen in this world by
chance, and this chance is no aide-de-camp of your God. It happens unconcernedly to all men. It has no rogue to ruin and no good
churchman, pattering his prayers, to save. A man lays his plans
according to the scope and grasp of his intelligence, and this chance
comes by to help him or to harm him, as it may happen, with no
concern about his little morals, and with no divine intent."

"And so you leave God out," said my uncle, with no comment.

"And why not, Abner?" replied the man. "Is there any place in
this scheme of nature for His intervention? Why, sir, the intelligence of man that your Scriptures so despise can easily put His
little plan of rewards and punishments out of joint. Not the good,
Abner, but the intelligent, possess the earth. The man who sees on
all sides of his plan, and hedges it about with wise precaution,
brings it to success. Every day the foresight of men outwits your
God."

My uncle lifted his chin above his wet stock. He looked at the
window with the night banked behind it, and then down at the re-
fined and elegant gentleman in the chair beside the table, and then
at the strapped-up portmanteau in the corner. His great jaw moved
out under the massive chin. From his face, from his manner, he
seemed about to approach some business of vital import. Then,
suddenly, from the room beyond there came a great boom of curses,

a cry that the dice had fallen against a platter, a blow and a gust of obscenities and oaths.

My uncle extended his arm toward the room.

"Your gentleman's vice," he said; "eh, Mr. Byrd!"

The man put out a jeweled hand and snuffed the candles.

"The vice, Abner, but not the gentlemen."

Mr. Byrd flicked a bit of soot from his immaculate sleeve. Then he made a careless gesture.

"These beasts," he said, "are the scum of New Orleans. They would bring any practice into disrepute. One cannot illustrate a theory by such creatures. Gaming, Abner, is the diversion of a gentleman; it depends on chance, even as all trading does. The Bishop of London has been unable to point out wherein it is immoral."

"Then," said Abner, "the Bishop does little credit to his intelligence."

"It has been discussed in the coffee-houses of New Orleans," replied Mr. Byrd, "and no worthy objection found."

"I think I can give you one," replied my uncle.

"And what is your objection, Abner?" asked the man.

"It has this objection, if no other," replied my uncle, "it encourages a hope of reward without labor, and it is this hope, Byrd, that fills the jail house with weak men, and sets strong ones to dangerous ventures."

He looked down at the man before him, and again his iron jaw moved.

"Byrd," he said, "under the wisdom of God, labor alone can save the world. It is everywhere before all benefits that we would enjoy. Every man must till the earth before he can eat of its fruits. He must fell the forest and let in the sun before his grain will ripen. He must spin and weave. And in his trading he must labor to carry his surplus stuff to foreign people, and to bring back what he needs from their abundance. Labor is the great condition of reward. And your gentleman's vice, Byrd, would annul it and overturn the world."

But the man was not listening to Abner's words. He was on his feet and again before the window. He had his jaw gathered into his hand. The man swore softly.

"What disturbs you, Byrd?" said my uncle.

He stood unmoving before the fire, his hands to the flame.

The man turned quickly.

"It is the night, Abner—wind and driving rain. The devil has it!"

"The weather, Byrd," replied my uncle, "happens in your philosophy by chance, so be content with what it brings you, for this chance regards, as you tell me, no man's plans; neither the wise man nor the fool hath any favor of it."

"Nor the just nor the unjust, Abner."

My uncle looked down at the floor. He locked his great bronze fingers behind his massive back.

"And so you believe, Byrd," he said. "Well, I take issue with you. I think this thing you call 'chance' is the Providence of God, and I think it favors the just."

"Abner," cried the man, now turning from the window, "if you believe that, you believe it without proof."

"Why, no," replied my uncle; "I have got the proof on this very night."

He paused a moment; then he went on.

"I was riding with the Virginia wagons," he said, "on the journey here. It was my plan to come on slowly with them, arriving on the morrow. But these rains fell; the road on this side of the Hills was heavy; and I determined to leave the wagons and ride in to-night.

"Now, call this what you like—this unforeseen condition of the road, this change of plan. Call it 'chance,' Byrd!"

Again he paused and his big jaw tightened.

"But it is no chance, sir, nor any accidental happening that Madison of Virginia, Simon Carroll of Maryland and my brother Rufus are upright men, honorable in their dealings and fair before the world.

"Now, sir, if this chance, this chance of my coming on to-night before the Virginia wagons, this accidental happening, favored

Madison, Simon Carroll and my brother Rufus as though with a
direct and obvious intent, as though with a clear and preconceived
design, you will allow it to me as a proof, or, at least, Mr. Evlyn
Byrd, as a bit of evidence, as a sort of indisputable sign, that honorable men, men who deal fairly with their fellows, have some
favor of these inscrutable events."

The man was listening now with a careful attention. He came
away from the window and stood beside the table, his clenched
fingers resting on the board.

"What do you drive at, Abner?" he asked.

My uncle lifted his chin above the big wet stock.

"A proof of my contention, Byrd," he answered.

"But your story, Abner? What happened?" My uncle looked
down at the man.

"There is no hurry, Byrd," he said; "the night is but half advanced and you will not now go forward on your journey."

"My journey!" echoed the man. "What do you mean?"

"Why, this," replied my uncle: "that you would be setting out
for Piccadilly, I imagine, and the dancing women, and the gentlemen who live by chance. But as you do not go now, we have ample
leisure for our talk."

"Abner," cried Mr. Byrd, "what is this riddle?"

My uncle moved a little in his place before the fire.

"I left the Virginia wagons at midday," he went on; "night fell
in the flat land; I could hardly get on; the mud was deep and the
rains blew. The whole world was like the pit.

"It is a common belief that a horse can see on any night, however dark, but this belief is error, like that which attributes supernatural perception to the beast. My horse went into the trees and
the fence; now and then there was a candle in a window, but it did
not lighten the world; it served only to accentuate the darkness. It
seemed impossible to go forward on a strange road, now flooded. I
thought more than once to stop in at some settler's cabin. But mark
you, Byrd, I came on. Why? I cannot say. 'Chance,' Mr. Evlyn Byrd,
if you like. I would call it otherwise. But no matter."

He paused a moment, and then continued:

"I came in by the river. It was all dark like the kingdom of Satan. Then, suddenly, I saw a light and your boat tied up. This light seemed somewhere inside, and its flame puzzled me. I got down from my horse and went onto the steamboat. I found no one, but I found the light. It was a fire just gathering under way. A carpenter had been at work; he had left some shavings and bits of candle, and in this line of rubbish the fire had started."

The man sat down in his chair beside the two tallow candles.

"Fire!" he said. "Yes, there was a carpenter at work in my office cabin to-day. He left shavings, and perhaps bits of candle, it is likely. Was it in my office cabin?"

"Along the floor there," replied my uncle, "beginning to flame up."

"Along the floor!" repeated Mr. Byrd. "Then nothing in my cabin was burned? The wall desk, Abner, with the long mahogany drawer—it was not burned?"

He spoke with an eager interest.

"It was not burned," replied my uncle. "Did it contain things of value?"

"Of great value," returned the man.

"You leave, then, things of value strangely unprotected," replied my uncle. "The door was open."

"But not the desk, Abner. It was securely locked. I had that lock from Sheffield. No key would turn it but my own."

Byrd sat for some moments unmoving, his delicate hand fingering his chin, his lips parted. Then, as with an effort, he got back his genial manner.

"I thank you, Abner," he said. "You have saved my boat. And it was a strange coincidence that brought you there to do it."

Then he flung back in his big chair with a laugh.

"But your theory, Abner? This chance event does not support it. It is not the good or Christian that this coincidence has benefited. It is I, Abner, who am neither good nor Christian."

My uncle did not reply. His face remained set and reflective.

The rain beat on the window-pane, and the drunken feast went on in the room beyond him.

"Byrd," he said, "how do you think that fire was set? A half-burned cigar dropped by a careless hand, or an enemy?"

"An enemy, Abner," replied the man. "It will be the work of these damned settlers. Did not their envoy threaten if I should come in, to the peril of their cabins? I gave them no concern then, but I was wrong in that. I should have looked out for their venom. Still, they threaten with such ease and with no hand behind it that one conies, in time, to take no notice of their words."

He paused and looked up at the big man above him.

"What do you think, Abner? Was the fire set?"

"One cannot tell from the burning rubbish," replied my uncle.

"But your opinion, Abner?" said the man. "What is your opinion?"

"The fire was set," replied my uncle.

Byrd got up at that, and his clenched hand crashed on the table.

"Then, by the kingdom of Satan, I will overturn every settler's cabin when the boat goes out to-morrow."

My uncle gave no attention to the man's violence.

"You would do wanton injury to innocent men," he said. "The settlers did not fire your boat."

"How can you know that, Abner?"

My uncle changed. Vigor and energy and an iron will got into his body and his face.

"Byrd," he said, "we had an argument just now; let me recall it to your attention. You said 'chance' happened equally to all, and I that the Providence of God directs it. If I had failed to come on tonight, the boat would have burned. The settlers would have taken blame for it. And Madison of Virginia, Simon Carroll of Maryland and my brother Rufus, whose company at Baltimore insure your boat, would have met a loss they can ill afford."

His voice was hard and level like a sheet of light.

"Not you, Byrd, who, as you tell me, are neither good nor Christian, but these men, who are, would have settled for this loss. Is it the truth—eh, Mr. Evlyn Byrd?"

The man's big blue eyes widened in his olive skin.

"I should have claimed the insurance, of course, as I had the right to do," he said coldly, for he was not in fear. "But, Abner—"

"Precisely!" replied my uncle. "And now, Mr. Evlyn Byrd, let us go on. We had a further argument. You thought a man in his intelligence could outwit God. And, sir, you undertook to do it! With your crew drunken here, the boat deserted, the settlers to bear suspicion and your portmanteau packed up for your journey overland to Baltimore, you watched at that window to see the flames burst out."

The man's blue eyes—strange, incredible eyes in that olive skin—were now hard and expressionless as glass. His lips moved, and his hand crept up toward a bulging pocket of his satin waistcoat.

Grim, hard as iron, inevitable, my uncle went on:

"But you failed, Byrd! God outwitted you! When I put that fire out in the rubbish, the cabin was dark, and in the dark, Byrd, there, I saw a gleam of light shining through the keyhole of your wall desk—the desk that you alone can open, that you keep so securely locked. Three bits of candle were burning in that empty drawer."

The man's white hand approached the bulging pocket.

And my uncle's voice rang as over a plate of steel.

"Outwit God!" he cried. "Why, Byrd, you have forgotten a thing that any schoolboy could have told you. You had forgotten that a bit of candle in a drawer, for lack of air, burns more slowly than a bit outside. Your pieces set to fire the rubbish were consumed, but your pieces set in that locked drawer to make sure—to outwit God, if, by chance, the others failed—were burning when I burst the lid off."

The man's nimble hand, lithe like a snake, whipped a derringer out of his bulging pocket.

But, quicker than that motion, quicker than light, quicker than the eye, my uncle was upon him. The derringer fell harmless to the floor. The bones of the man's slender fingers snapped in an iron palm. And my uncle's voice, big, echoing like a trumpet, rang above the storm and the drunken shouting:

"Outwit God! Why, Mr. Evlyn Byrd, you cannot outwit me, who am the feeblest of His creatures!"

15

THE CONCEALED PATH

It was night, and the first snow of October was in the air when my uncle got down from his horse before the door. The great stone house sat on a bench of the mountains. Behind it lay the forest, and below, the pasture land of the Hills.

After the disastrous failure of Prince Charles Edward Stuart to set up his kingdom in Scotland, more than one great Highland family had fled oversea into Virginia, and for a hundred years had maintained its customs. It was at the house of such a family that my uncle stopped.

There was the evidence of travel hard and long on my uncle and his horse. An old man bade him enter.

"Who is here?" said my uncle.

The servant replied with two foreign words, meaning "The Red Eagle" in the Gaelic tongue.

And he led my uncle through the hall into the dining-room. It was a scene laid back a hundred years in Skye that he came on. A big woman of middle age dined alone, in a long, beamed room, lighted with tallow candles. An ancient servant stood behind her chair.

Two features of the woman were conspicuous—her bowed nose and her coarse red hair.

She got up when she saw my uncle.

"Abner," she cried, "by the Blessed God I am glad to see you! Come in! Come in!"

My uncle entered, and she put him beyond her at the table.

"You ought to eat, Abner," she said; "for by all the tokens, you have traveled."

"A long way," replied my uncle.

"And did the ravens of Elijah send you to me?" said the woman. "For I need you."

"What need?" inquired my uncle, while he attacked the rib of beef and the baked potatoes, for the dinner, although set with some formality, was plain.

"Why, this need, Abner: For a witness whose name will stand against the world."

"A witness!" repeated my uncle.

"Aye, a witness," continued the woman. "The country holds me hard and dour, and given to impose my will. There will be a wedding in my house to-night, and I would have you see it, free of pressure. My niece, Margaret McDonald, has got her senses finally."

My uncle looked down at the cloth.

"Who is the man?" he said.

"Campbell," she answered, "and good man enough for a stupid woman."

For a moment my uncle did not move. His hands, his body, the very muscles in his eyelids, were for that moment inert as plaster. Then he went on with the potato and the rib of beef.

"Campbell is here, then?" he said.

"He came to-night," replied the woman, "and for once the creature has some spirit. He will have the girl to-night or never. He and my husband Allen Eliott, have driven their cattle out of the glades and on the way to Baltimore. Allen is with the cattle on the Cumberland road, and Campbell rode hard in here to take the girl or to leave her. And whether she goes or stays, he will not return. When the cattle are sold in Baltimore, he will take a ship out of the Chesapeake for Glasgow."

She paused and made a derisive gesture.

"The devil, Abner, or some witch trick, has made a man of Campbell. He used to be irresolute and sullen, but to-night he has the spirit of the men who lifted cattle in the lowlands. He is a Campbell of Glen Lion on this night. Believe me, Abner, the wavering beastie is now as hard as oak, and has the devil's courage. Wherefore is it that a man can change like that?"

"A man may hesitate between two masters," replied my uncle, "and be only weak, but when he finally makes his choice he will get what his master has to give him—the courage of heaven, if he go that way, or of hell, Madam, if he go that way."

"Man! Man!" she laughed. "If 'the one who is not to be named,' as we say, put his spirit into Campbell, he did a grand work. It is the wild old cattle-lifter of Glen Lion that he is the night!"

"Do you think," said my uncle, "that a McDonald of Glencoe ought to be mated with a Campbell of Glen Lion?"

The woman's face hardened.

"Did Lord Stair and the Campbells of Glen Lion massacre the McDonalds of Glencoe on yesterday at sunrise, or two hundred years back? Margaret—the fool!—said that before she got my final word."

"Is it not in an adage," said my uncle, "that the Highlander does not change?"

"But the world changes, Abner," replied the woman. "Campbell is not 'Bonnie Charlie'; he is at middle age, a dour man and silent, but he will have a sum of money from a half of the cattle, and he can take care of this girl."

Then she cried out in a sharper voice:

"And what is here in this mountain for her, will you tell me? We grow poor! The old men are to feed. Allen owes money that his half of the cattle will hardly pay. Even old MacPherson"—and she indicated the ancient man behind her chair— "has tried to tell her, in his wise-wife folderol, 'I see you in the direst peril that overtakes a lassie, and a big shouldered man to save you.' And it was no omen, Abner, but the vision of his common sense. Here are the lean years to dry out the fool's youth, and surely Campbell is big shouldered enough for any prophecy. And now, Abner, will you stay and be a witness?"

"I will be one witness," replied my uncle slowly, "if you will send for my brother Rufus to be another."

The woman looked at her guest in wonder.

"That would be twenty miles through the Hills," she said. "We could not get Rufus by the morn's morn."

"No," said Abner, "it would be three miles to Maxwell's Tavern. Rufus is there to-night."

The big-nosed, red-haired woman drummed on the cloth with the tips of her fingers, and one knew what she was thinking. Her relentless will was the common talk. What she wished she forced with no concern.

But the girl was afraid of Campbell. The man seemed evil to her. It was not evidenced in any act. It was instinct in the girl. She felt the nature of the man like some venomous thing pretending to be gentle until its hour. And this fear, dominant and compelling, gave her courage to resist the woman's will.

The long suit of Campbell for the girl was known to everybody, and the woman's favor of it and the girl's resistance. The woman foresaw what folk in the Hills would say, and she wished to forestall that gossip by the presence in her house of men whose word could not be gainsaid. If Abner and his brother Rufus were here, no report of pressure on the girl could gain belief.

She knew what reports her dominating personality set current. She, and not her husband, was the head of their affairs, and with an iron determination she held to every Highland custom, every form, every feudal detail that she could, against the detritus of democratic times and ridicule, and the gain upon her house of poverty, and lean years. She was alone at that heavy labor. Allen Eliott was a person without force. He was usually on his cattle range in the mountains, with his big partner Campbell, or in the great drive, as now, to Baltimore. And she had the world to face.

"That will be to wait," she said, "and Campbell is in haste, and the bride is being made ready by the women, and the minister is got . . . to Maxwell's Tavern!"

Then she arose.

"Well, I will make a bargain with you. I will send for Rufus, but you must gain Campbell over to the waiting. And you must gain him, Abner, by your own devices, for I will not tell him that I have sent out for a witness to the freedom of my niece in this affair. If you can make him wait, the thing shall wait until Rufus is come. But I will turn no hand to help."

"Is Campbell in the house?" said my uncle.

"Yes," she said, "and ready when the minister is come."

"Is he alone?" said Abner.

"Alone," she said, with a satirical smile, "as a bridegroom ought to be for his last reflections."

"Then," replied my uncle, "I will strike the bargain."

She laughed in a heavy chuckle, like a man.

"Hold him if you can. It will be a pretty undertaking, Abner, and practice for your wits. But by stealth it shall be. I will not have you bind the bridegroom like the strong man in the Scriptures." And the chuckle deepened. "And that, too, I think, might be no easier than the finesse you set at. He is a great man in the body, like yoursel'."

She stood up to go out, but before she went, she said another word.

"Abner," she said, "you will not blame me," and, her voice was calm. "Somebody must think a little for these pretty fools. They are like the lilies of the field in their lack of wisdom; they will always bloom, and there is no winter! Why, man, they have no more brain than a haggis! And what are their little loves against the realities of life? And their tears, Abner, are like the rains in summer, showering from every cloud. And their heads crammed with folderol—a prince will come, and they cannot take a good man for that dream!" She paused and added:

"I will go and send for Rufus. And when you have finished with your dinner, MacPherson will take you in to Campbell."

The woman was hardly gone before the old man slipped over to Abner's chair.

"Mon," he whispered, "ha'e ye a wee drop?"

"No liquor, MacPherson," said my uncle.

The old man's bleared eyes blinked like a half-blinded owl's.

"It would be gran', a wee drop, the night," he said.

"For joy at the wedding," said my uncle.

"Na, mon, na, mon!" Then he looked swiftly around.

"The eagle ha beak and talons, and what ha the dove, mon?"

"What do you mean, MacPherson?" said my uncle.

The old creature peered across the table.

"Ye ha gran' shoulders, mon," he said.

My uncle put down his fork.

"MacPherson," he said, "what do you beat about?"

"I wa horned," he replied, "wi a cowl, and I can see!"

"And what do you see?" inquired Abner.

"A vulture flying," said the old man, "but it is unco dark beneath him."

Again on this night every motion and every sign of motion disappeared from my uncle's body and his face. He remained for a moment like a figure cut in wood.

"A vulture!" he echoed.

"Aye, mon! What ha the dove to save it?"

"The vulture, it may be," said my uncle.

"The Red Eagle, and the foul vulture!" cried the old man. "Noo, mon, it is the bird of death!"

"A bird of death, but not a bird of prey." Then he got up.

"You may have a familiar spirit, MacPherson," he said coldly, "for all I know. Perhaps they live on after the Witch of Endor. It is a world of mystery. But I should not come to you to get up Samuel, and I see now why the Lord stamped out your practice. It was because you misled his people. If there is a vulture in this business, MacPherson, it is no symbol of your bridegroom. And now, will you take me in to Campbell?"

The old man flung the door open, and Abner went out into the hall. As he crossed the sill, a girl, listening at the door, fled past him. She had been crouched down against it.

She was half-dressed, all in white, as though escaped for a moment out of the hands of tiring women. But she had the chalk face of a ghost, and eyes wide with fear.

My uncle went on as though he had passed nothing, and the old Scotchman before him only wagged his head, with the whispered comment, "It wa be gran', a wee drop, the night."

They came into a big room of the house with candles on a table, and a fire of chestnut logs. A man walking about stopped on the hearth. He was a huge figure of a man in middle life.

A fierce light leaped up in his face when he saw my uncle.

"Abner!" he cried. "Why does the devil bring you here?"

"It would be strange, Campbell," replied my uncle, "if the devil were against you. The devil has been much maligned. He is very nearly equal, the Scriptures tell us, to the King of Kings. He is no fool to mislead his people and to trap his servants. I find him always zealous in their interests, Campbell, fertile in devices, and holding hard with every trick to save them. I do not admire the devil, Mr. Campbell, but I do not find his vice to be a lack of interest in his own."

"Then," cried Campbell, "it is clear that I am not one of his own. For if the devil were on my side, Abner, he would have turned you away from this door to-night."

"Why, no," replied my uncle, with a reflective air, "that does not follow. I do not grant the devil a supreme control. There is One above him, and if he cannot always manage as his people wish, they should not for that reason condemn him with a treasonable intent."

The man turned with a decisive gesture.

"Abner," he said, "let me understand this thing. Do you come here upon some idle gossip, to interfere with me in this marriage? Or by chance?"

"Neither the one nor the other," replied my uncle. "I went into the mountains to buy the cattle you and Eliott range there. I found you gone already, with the herd, toward Maryland. And so, as I returned, I rode in here to Eliott's house to rest and to feed my horse."

"Eliott is with the drove," said Campbell.

"No," replied my uncle, "Eliott is not with the drove. I overtook it on the Cheat River. The drivers said you hired them this morning, and rode away."

The man shifted his feet and looked down at my uncle.

"It is late in the season," he said. "One must go ahead to arrange for a field and for some shocks of fodder. Eliott is ahead."

"He is not on the road ahead," returned Abner. "Arnold and his drovers came that way from Maryland, and they had not seen him."

"He did not go the road," said Campbell; "he took a path through the mountains."

My uncle remained silent for some moments.

"Campbell," said my uncle, "the Scriptures tell us that there is a path which the vulture's eye hath not seen. Did Eliott take that path?"

The man changed his posture.

"Now, Abner," he said, "I cannot answer a fool thing like that."

"Well, Campbell," replied my uncle, "I can answer it for you: Eliott did not take that path."

The man took out a big silver watch and opened the case with his thumb-nail.

"The woman ought to be ready," he said.

My uncle looked up at him.

"Campbell," he said, "put off this marriage."

The man turned about.

"Why should I put it off?" he said.

"Well, for one reason, Campbell," replied my uncle, "the omens are not propitious."

"I do not believe in signs," said the man.

"The Scriptures are full of signs," returned Abner. "There was the sign to Joshua and the sign to Ahaz, and there is the sign to you."

The man turned with an oath.

"What accursed thing do you hint about, Abner?"

"Campbell," replied my uncle, "I accept the word; accursed is the word."

"Say the thing out plain! What omen? What sign?"

"Why, this sign," replied Abner: "MacPherson, who was born with a cowl, has seen a vulture flying."

"Damme, man!" cried Campbell. "Do you hang on such a piece of foolery. MacPherson sees his visions in a tin cup—raw corn liquor would set flying beasts of Patmos. Do you tell me, Abner, that you believe in what MacPherson sees?"

"I believe in what I see myself," replied my uncle.

"And what have you seen?" said the man.

"I have seen the vulture!" replied my uncle. "And I was born clean and have no taste for liquor."

"Abner," said Campbell, "you move about in the dark, and I have no time to grope after you. The woman should be ready."

"But are you ready?" said my uncle.

"Man! Man!" cried Campbell. "Will you be forever in a fog? Well, travel on to Satan in it! I am ready, and here are the women!"

But it was not the bride. It was MacPherson to inquire if the bride should come.

My uncle got up then.

"Campbell," he said, in his deep, level voice, "if the bride is ready, you are not."

The man was at the limit of forbearance.

"The devil take you!" he cried. "If you mean anything, say what it is!"

"Campbell," replied my uncle, "it is the custom to inquire if any man knows a reason why a marriage should not go on. Shall I stand up before the company and give the reason, while the marriage waits? Or shall I give it to you here while the marriage waits?"

The man divined something behind my uncle's menace.

"Bid them wait," he said to MacPherson.

Then he closed the door and turned back on my uncle—his shoulders thrown forward, his fingers clenched, his words prefaced by an oath.

"Now, sir,"—and the oath returned,— "what is it?"

My uncle got up, took something from his pocket, and put it down on the table. It was a piece of lint, twisted together, as though one had rolled it firmly between the palms of one's hands.

"Campbell," he said, "as I rode the trail on your cattle range, in the mountains, this morning, a bit of white thing caught my eye. I got down and picked up this fragment of lint on the hard ground. It puzzled me. How came it thus rolled? I began to search the ground, riding slowly in an ever-widening circle. Presently I found a second bit, and then a third, rolled hard together like the first. Then I observed a significant thing: these bits were in line and leading from your trail down the slope of the cattle range to the border of the forest. I went back to the trail, and there on the baked earth, in line with these bits of lint, I found a spot where a bucket of water had been poured out."

Campbell was standing beyond him, staring at the bit of lint. He looked up without disturbing the crouch of his shoulders.

"Go on," he said.

"It occurred to me," continued my uncle, "that perhaps these bits of lint might be found above the trail, as I had found them below it, and so I rode straight on up the hill to a rail fence. I found no fragment of twisted stuff, but I found another thing, Campbell: I found the weeds trampled on the other side of the fence. I got down and looked closely. On the upper surface of a flat rail, immediately before the trampled weeds, there was an impression as though a square bar of iron had been laid across it."

My uncle stopped. And Campbell said:

"Go on."

Abner remained a moment, his eyes on the man; then he continued:

"The impression was in a direct line toward the point on the trail where the water had been poured out. I was puzzled. I got into the saddle and rode back across the trail and down the line of the fragments of lint. At the edge of the forest I found where a log-heap had been burned. I got down again and walked back along the line of the twisted lint. I looked closely, and I saw that the fragments of dried grass, and now and then a rag-weed, had been pressed down, as though by something moving down the hillside from the trail to the burned log-heap.

"Now, Campbell," he said, "what happened on that hillside?"

Campbell stood up and looked my uncle in the face. "What do you think happened?" he said.

"I think," replied Abner, "that some one sat in the weeds behind the fence with a half-stocked, square-barreled rifle laid on the flat rail, and from that ambush shot something passing on the trail, and then dragged it down the hillside to the log-heap. I think that poured-out water was to wash away the blood where the thing fell. I do not know where the bits of lint came from, but I think they were rolled there under the weight of the heavy body. Do I think correctly, eh, Campbell?"

"You do," said the man.

My uncle was astonished, for Campbell faced him, his aspect grim, determined, like one who at any hazard will have the whole of a menace out. "Abner," he said, "you have trailed this thing with some theory behind it. In plain words, what is that theory?"

My uncle was amazed.

"Campbell," he replied, "since you wish the thing said plain, I will not obscure it. Two men own a great herd of cattle between them. The herd is to be driven over the mountains to Baltimore and sold. If one of the partners is shot out of his saddle and the crime concealed, may not the other partner sell the entire drove for his own and put the whole sum in his pocket?

"And if this surviving partner, Campbell, were a man taken with the devil's resolution, I think he might try to make one great stroke of this business. I think he might hire men to drive his cattle, giving out that his partner had gone on ahead, and then turn back for the woman he wanted, take her to Baltimore, put her on the ship, sell the cattle, and with the woman and money sail out of the Chesapeake for the Scotch Highlands he came from! Who could say what became of the missing partner, or that he did not receive his half of the money and meet robbery and murder on his way home?" My uncle stopped. And Campbell broke out into a great ironical laugh.

"Now, let this thing be a lesson to you, Abner. Your little deductions are correct, but your great conclusion is folly.

"We had a wild heifer that would not drive, so we butchered the beast. I had great trouble to shoot her, but I finally managed it from behind the fence."

"But the bits of lint," said my uncle, "and the washed spot?"

"Abner," cried the man, "do you handle cattle for a lifetime and do not know how blood disturbs them? We did not want them in commotion, so we drenched the place where the heifer fell. And your bits of lint! I will discover the mystery there. To keep the blood off we put an old quilt under the yearling and dragged her down the hill on that. The bits of lint were from the quilt, and rolled thus under the weight of the heifer."

Then he added: "That was weeks ago, but there has been no rain for a month, and these signs of crime, Abner, were providentially preserved against your coming!"

"And the log-heap," said my uncle, like one who would have the whole of an explanation, "why was it burned?"

"Now, Abner," continued the man, "after your keen deductions, would you ask me a thing like that? To get rid of the offal from the butchered beast. We would not wash out the blood-stains and leave that to set our cattle mad."

His laugh changed to a note of victory.

"And now, Abner," he cried, "will you stay and see me married, who have come hoping to see me hanged?"

My uncle had moved over to the window. While Campbell spoke, he seemed to listen, not so much to the man as to sounds outside. Now far off on a covered wooden bridge of the road there was the faint sound of horses. And with a grim smile Abner turned about.

"I will stay," he said, "and see which it is."

It was the very strangest wedding—the big, determined woman like a Fate, the tattered servants with candles in their hands, the minister, and the bride covered and hidden in her veil, like a wooden figure counterfeiting life.

The thing began. There was an atmosphere of silence. My uncle went over to the window. The snow on the road deadened the sounds of the advancing horses, until the iron shoes rang on the stones before the door. Then, suddenly, as though he waited for the sound, he cried out with a great voice against the marriage. The big-nosed, red-haired woman turned on him:

"Why do you object, who have no concern in this thing?"

"I object," said Abner, "because Campbell has sent Eliott on the wrong path!"

"The wrong path!" cried the woman.

"Aye," said Abner, "on the wrong path. There is a path which the vulture's eye hath not seen, Job tells us. But the path Campbell sent Eliott on, the vulture did see."

He advanced with great strides into the room.

"Campbell," he cried, "before I left your accursed pasture, I saw a buzzard descend into the forest beyond your log-heap. I went in, and there, shot through the heart, was the naked body of Allen Eliott. Your log-heap, Campbell, was to burn the quilt and the dead man's clothes. You trusted to the vultures, for the rest, and the vultures, Campbell, over-reached you."

My uncle's voice rose and deepened.

"I sent word to my brother Rufus to raise a *posse comitatus* and bring it to Maxwell's Tavern. Then I rode in here to rest and to feed my horse. I found you, Campbell, on the second line of your hell-planned venture!

"I got Mrs. Eliott to send for Rufus to be a witness with me to your accursed marriage. And I undertook to delay it until he came."

He raised his great arm, the clenched bronze fingers big like the coupling pins of a cart.

"I would have stopped it with my own hand," he said, "but I wanted the men of the Hills to hang you. . . . And they are here."

There was a great sound of tramping feet in the hall outside.

And while the men entered, big, grim, determined men, Abner called out their names:

"Arnold, Randolph, Stuart, Elnathan Stone and my brother Rufus!"

16

The Edge of the Shadow

It was a land of strange varieties of courage. But, even in the great hills, I never saw a man like Cyrus Mansfield. He was old and dying when this ghastly adventure happened; but, even in the extremity of life, with its terrors on him, he met the thing with his pagan notions of the public welfare, and it is for his own gods to judge him.

It was a long afternoon of autumn. The dead man lay in the whitewashed cabin staring up at the cobwebbed ceiling. His left cheek below the eye was burned with the brand of a pistol shot. The track of a bullet ran along the eyebrow, plowing into the skull above the ear. His grizzled hair stood up like a brush, and the fanaticism of his face was exaggerated by the strained postures of death.

A tall, gaunt woman sat by the door in the sun. She had a lapful of honey locust, and she worked at that, putting the pieces together in a sort of wreath. The branches were full of thorns, and the inside of the woman's hand was torn and wounded upon the balls of the fingers and the palm, but she plaited the thorns together, giving no heed to her injured hand.

She did not get up when my Uncle Abner and Squire Randolph entered. She sat over her work with imperturbable stoicism.

The man and woman were strangers in the land, preempting one of Mansfield's cabins. Their mission was a mystery for conjecture. And now the man's death was a mystery beyond it.

When Randolph inquired how the man had met his death, the woman got up, without a word, went to a cupboard in the wall, took out a dueling pistol, and handed it to him. Then, she spoke in a dreary voice:

"He was mad. 'The cause,' he said, 'must have a sacrifice of blood.'"

She looked steadily at the dead man.

"Ah, yes," she added, "he was mad!"

Then she turned about and went back to her chair in the sun before the door.

Randolph and Abner examined the weapon. It was a handsome dueling pistol, with an inlaid silver stock and a long, octagon barrel of hard, sharp-edged steel. It had been lately fired, for the exploded percussion cap was still on the nipple.

"He was a poor shot," said Randolph; "he very nearly missed."

My uncle looked closely at the dead man's wound and the burned cheek beneath it. He turned the weapon slowly in his hand, but Randolph was impatient.

"Well, Abner," he said, "did the pistol kill him, or was it the finger of God?"

"The pistol killed him," replied my uncle.

"And shall we believe the woman, eh, Abner?"

"I am willing to believe her," replied my uncle.

They looked about the cabin. There was blood on the floor and flecked against the wall, and stains on the barrel of the pistol, as though the man had staggered about, stunned by the bullet, before he died. And so the wound looked—not mortal on the instant, but one from which, after some time, a man might die.

Randolph wrote down his memorandum, and the two went out into the road.

It was an afternoon of Paradise. The road ran in a long endless ribbon westward toward the Ohio. Negroes in the wide bottom land were harvesting the corn and setting it up in great bulging shocks tied with grapevine. Beyond on a high wooded knoll, stood a mansion-house with white pillars.

My uncle took the duelling pistol out of his pocket and handed it to the Justice of the Peace.

"Randolph," he said, "these weapons were made in pairs; there should be another. And," he added, "there is a crest on the butt plate."

"Virginia is full of such folderols," replied the Justice, "and bought and sold, pledged and traded. It would not serve to identify the dead man. And besides, Abner, why do we care? He is dead by his own hand; his rights and his injuries touch no other; let him lie with his secrets."

He made a little circling gesture upward with his index finger.

"'Duncan is dead,'" he quoted. "'After life's fitful fever he sleeps well.' Shall we pay our respects to Mansfield before we ride away?"

And he indicated the house like a white cornice on the high cliff above them.

They had been standing with their backs to the cabin door. Now the woman passed them. She wore a calico sunbonnet, and carried a little bundle tied up in a cotton handkerchief. She set out westward along the road toward the Ohio. She walked slowly, like one bound on an interminable journey.

Moved by some impulse they looked in at the cabin door. The dead man lay as he had been, his face turned toward the ceiling, his hands grotesquely crossed, his body rigid. But now the sprigs of honey locust, at which the woman worked, were pressed down on his unkempt grizzled hair. The sun lay on the floor, and there was silence.

They left the cabin with no word and climbed the long path to the mansion on the hill.

Mansfield sat in a great chair on the pillared porch. It was wide and cool, paved with colored tiles carried over from England in a sailing ship.

He was the strangest man I have ever seen. He was old and dying then, but he had a spirit in him that no event could bludgeon into servility. He sat with a gray shawl pinned around his shoulders. The lights and shadows of the afternoon fell on his jaw like a plowshare, on his big, crooked, bony nose, on his hard gray eyes, bringing them into relief against the lines and furrows of his face.

"Mansfield," cried Randolph, "how do you do?"

"I still live," replied the old man, "but at any hour I may be ejected out of life."

"We all live, Mansfield," said my uncle, "as long as God wills."

"Now, Abner," cried the old man, "you repeat the jargon of the churches. The will of man is the only power in the universe, so far as we can find out, that is able to direct the movings of events. Nothing else that exists can make the most trivial thing happen or cease to happen. No imagined god or demon in all the history of the race has ever influenced the order of events as much as the feeblest human creature in an hour of life. Sit down, Abner, and let me tell you the truth before I cease to exist, as the beasts of the field cease."

He indicated the great carved oak chairs about him, and the two visitors sat down.

Randolph loved the vanities of argument, and he thrust in:

"I am afraid, Mansfield," he said, "you will never enjoy the pleasures of Paradise."

The old man made a contemptuous gesture.

"Pleasure, Randolph," he said, "is the happiness of little men; big men are after something more. They are after the satisfaction that comes from directing events. This is the only happiness: to crush out every other authority—to be the one dominating authority—to make events take the avenue one likes. This is the happiness of the god of the universe, if there is any god of the universe."

He moved in his chair, his elbows out, his fingers extended, his bony face uplifted.

"Abner," he cried, "I am willing for you to endure life as you find it and say it is the will of God, but, as for me, I will not be cowed into submission. I will not be held back from laying hold of the lever of the great engine merely because the rumble of the machinery fills other men with terror."

"Mansfield," replied my uncle, in his deep, level voice, "the fear of God is the beginning of wisdom."

The old man moved his extended arms with a powerful threshing motion, like a vulture beating the air with its great wings.

"Fear!" he cried. "Why, Abner, fear is the last clutch of the animal clinging to the intelligence of man as it emerges from the instinct of the beast. The first man thought the monsters about him were gods. Our fathers thought the elements were gods, and we think the impulse moving the machinery of the world is the will of some divine authority. And always the only thing in the universe that was superior to these things has been afraid to assert itself. The human will that can change things, that can do as it likes, has been afraid of phantasms that never yet met with anything they could turn aside."

He clenched his hands, contracted his elbows, and brought them down with an abrupt derisive gesture.

"I do not understand," he said, "but I am not afraid. I will not be beaten into submission by vague, inherited terrors. I will not be subservient to things that have a lesser power than I have. I will not yield the control of events to elements that are dead, to laws that are unthinking, or to an influence that cannot change.

"Not all the gods that man has ever worshiped can make things happen to-morrow, but I can make them happen; therefore, I am a god above them. And how shall a god that is greater than these gods give over the dominion of events into their hands?"

"And so, Mansfield," said Abner, "you have been acting just now upon this belief?"

The old man turned his bony face sharply on my uncle.

"Now, Abner," he said, "what do you mean by this Delphic sentence?"

For reply, my uncle extended his arms toward the whitewashed cabin.

"Who is the dead man down there?"

"Randolph can tell you that," said Mansfield.

"I never saw the man until to-day," replied the Justice.

"Eh, Randolph," cried the old man, "do you administer the law and have a memory like that? In midsummer the justices sat at the county seat. Have you forgot that inquisition?"

"I have not," said the Justice. "It was a fool's inquiry. One of Nixon's negro women reported a slave plot to poison the wells and

attack the people with a curious weapon. She got the description
of the weapon out of some preacher's sermon—a kind of spear. If
she had named some implement of modern warfare, we could have
better credited her story."

"Well, Randolph," cried the old man, "for all the wisdom of your
justices, she spoke the truth. They were pikes the woman saw, and
not the spears of the horsemen of Israel. Did you notice a stranger
who remained in a corner of the courtroom while the justices were
sitting? He disappeared after the trial. But did you mark him,
Randolph? He lies dead down yonder in my negro cabin."

A light came into the face of the Justice.

"By the Eternal," he cried, "an abolitionist!"

He flipped the gold seals on his watch fob; then he added, with
that little circling gesture of his finger:

"Well, he has taken himself away with his own hands."

"He is dead," said Mansfield, thrusting out his plowshare jaw,
"as all such vermin ought to be. We are too careless in the South of
these vicious reptiles. We ought to stamp them out of life whenever we find them. They are a menace to the peace of the land.
They incite the slaves to arson and to murder. They are beyond the
law, as the panther and the wolf are. We ought to have the courage
to destroy the creatures.

"The destiny of this republic," he added, "is in our hands."

My uncle Abner spoke then:

"It is in God's hands," he said.

"God!" cried Mansfield. "I would not give house room to such a
god! When we dawdle, Abner, the Yankees always beat us. Why,
man, if this thing runs on, it will wind up in a lawsuit. We shall be
stripped of our property by a court's writ. And instead of imposing
our will on this republic, we shall be answering a little New England lawyer with rejoinders and rebuttals."

"Would the bayonet be a better answer?" said my uncle.

"Now, Abner," said Mansfield, "you amuse me. These Yankees
have no stomach for the bayonet. They are traders, Abner; they
handle the shears and the steel-yard."

My uncle looked steadily at the man.

"Virginia held that opinion of New England when the King's troops landed," he said. "It was a common belief. Why, sir, even Washington riding north to the command of the Colonial army, when he heard of the battle of Bunker Hill, did not ask who had won; his only inquiry was, 'Did the militia of Massachusetts fight?' It did fight, Mansfield, with immortal courage."

My uncle Abner lifted his face and looked out over the great valley, mellow with its ripened corn. His voice fell into a reflective note.

"The situation in this republic," he said, "is grave, and I am full of fear. In God's hands the thing would finally adjust itself. In God's slow, devious way it would finally come out all right. But neither you, Mansfield, nor the abolitionist, will leave the thing to God. You will rush in and settle it with violence. You will find a short cut of your own through God's deliberate way, and I tremble before the horror of blood that you would plunge us into."

He paused again, and his big, bronzed features had the serenity of some vast belief.

"To be fair," he said, "everywhere in this republic, to enforce the law everywhere, to put down violence, to try every man who takes the law in his own hand, fairly in the courts, and, if he is guilty, punish him without fear or favor, according to the letter of the statute, to keep everywhere a public sentiment of fair dealing, by an administration of justice above all public clamor—in this time of heat, this is our only hope of peace!"

He spoke in his deep, level voice, and the words seemed to be concrete things having dimensions and weight.

"Shall a fanatic who stirs up our slaves to murder," said Mansfield, "be tried like a gentleman before a jury?"

"Aye, Mansfield," replied my uncle, "like a gentleman, and before a jury! If the fanatic murders the citizen, I would hang him, and if the citizen murders the fanatic, I would hang him too, without one finger's weight of difference in the method of procedure. I would show New England that the justice of Virginia is even-eyed. And she would emulate that fairness, and all over the land the law would hold against the unrestraint that is gathering."

"Abner," cried Mansfield, "you are a dawdler like your god. I know a swifter way."

"I am ready to believe it," replied my uncle. "Who killed the mad abolitionist down yonder?"

"Who cares," said the old man, "since the beast is dead?"

"I care," replied Abner.

"Then, find it out, Abner, if you care," said the old man, snapping his jaws.

"I have found it out," said my uncle, "and it has happened in so strange a way, and with so curious an intervention, that I cannot save the State from shame."

"It happened in the simplest way imaginable," said Randolph: "The fool killed himself."

It was not an unthinkable conclusion. The whole land was wrought up to the highest tension. Men were beginning to hold their properties and their lives as of little account in this tremendous issue. The country was ready to flare up in a war, and to fire it the life of one man would be nothing. A thousand madmen were ready to make that sacrifice of life. That a fanatic would shoot himself in Virginia with the idea that the slave owners would be charged by the country with his murder and so the war brought on, was not a thing improbable in that day's extremity of passion. To the madman it would be only the slight sacrifice of his life for the immortal gain of a holy war.

My uncle looked at the Justice with a curious smile.

"I think Mansfield will hardly believe that," he said.

The old man laughed.

"It is a pretty explanation, Randolph," he said, "and I commend it to all men, but I do not believe it."

"Not believe it!" cried the Justice, looking first at my uncle and then at the old man. "Why, Abner, you said the woman spoke the truth!"

"She did speak it," replied my uncle.

"Damme, man!" cried the Justice. "Why do you beat about? If you believe the woman, why do you gentlemen disbelieve my conclusion on her words?"

"I disbelieve it, Randolph," replied my uncle, "for the convincing reason that I know who killed him."

"And I," cried Mansfield, "disbelieve it for an equally convincing reason—for the most convincing reason in the world, Randolph,"—and his big voice laughed in among the pillars and rafters of his porch — "because I killed him myself!"

Abner sat unmoving, and Randolph like a man past belief. The Justice fumbled with the pistol in his pocket, got it out, and laid it on the flat arm on his chair, but he did not speak. The confession overwhelmed him.

The old man stood up, and the voice in his time-shaken body was Homeric:

"Ho! Ho!" he cried. "And so you thought I would be afraid, Randolph, and dodge about like your little men, shaken and overcome by fear." And he huddled in his shawl with a dramatic gesture.

"Fear!" And his laugh burst out again in a high staccato. "Even the devils in Abner's Christian hell lack that! I shot the creature, Randolph! Do you hear the awful words? And do you tremble for me, lest I hang and go to Abner's hell?"

The mock terror in the old man's voice and manner was compelling drama. He indicated the pistol on the chair arm.

"Yes," he said, "it is mine. Abner should have known it by the Mansfield arms."

"I did know it," replied my uncle.

The old man looked at the Justice with a queer ironical smile; then he went into the house.

"Await me, Randolph," he said. "I would produce the evidence and make out your case."

And prodded by the words, Randolph cursed bitterly.

"By the Eternal," he cried, "I am as little afraid as any of God's creatures, but the man confounds me!"

And he spoke the truth. He was a justice of the peace in Virginia when only gentlemen could hold that office. He lacked the balance and the ability of his pioneer ancestors, and he was given over to the vanity and the extravagance of words, but fear and all the manifestations of fear were alien to him.

He turned when the old man came out with a rosewood box in his hand, and faced him calmly.

"Mansfield," he said, "I warn you. I represent the law, and if you have done a murder, I will get you hanged."

The old man paused, and looked at Randolph with his maddening ironical smile.

"Fear again, eh, Randolph!" he said. "Is it by fear that you would always restrain me? Shall I be plucked back from the gibbet and Abner's hell only by this fear? It is a menace I have too long disregarded. You must give me a better reason."

Mansfield opened the rosewood box and took out a pistol like the one on the arm of Randolph's chair. He held the weapon lightly in his hand.

"The creature came here to harangue me," he said, "and like the genie in the copper pot, I gave him his choice of deaths."

He laughed, for the fancy pleased him.

"In the swirl of his heroics, Abner, I carried him the pistol yonder, to the steps of my portico where he stood, and with this other and my father's watch, I sat down here. 'After three minutes, sir,' I said, 'I shall shoot you down. It is my price for hearing your oration. Fire before that time is up. I shall call out the minutes for your convenience.'

"And so, I sat here, Abner, with my father's watch, while the creature ranted with my pistol in his hand.

"I called out the time, and he harangued me: 'The black of the negro shall be washed white with blood!' And I answered him: 'One minute, sir!'

"'The Lord will make Virginia a possession for the bittern!' was his second climax, and I replied, 'Two minutes of your time are up!'

"'The South is one great brothel,' he shouted, and I answered, 'Three minutes, my fine fellow,' and shot him as I had promised! He leaped off into the darkness with my unfired pistol and fled to the cabin where you found him."

There was a moment's silence, and my uncle put out his arm and pointed down across the long meadow to a grim outline traveling far off on the road.

"Mansfield," he said, "you have lighted the powder train that God, at His leisure, would have dampened. You have broken the faith of the world in our sincerity. Virginia will be credited with this man's death, and we cannot hang you for it!"

"And why not?" cried Randolph, standing up. He had been prodded into unmanageable anger. "The Commonwealth has granted no letters of marque; it has proclaimed no outlawry. Neither Mansfield nor any other has a patent to do murder. I shall get him hanged!"

My uncle shook his head.

"No, Randolph," he said, "you cannot hang him."

"And why not?" cried the Justice of the Peace, aroused now, and defiant. "Is Mansfield above the law? If he kills this madman, shall he have a writ of exemption for it?"

"But he did not kill him!" replied my uncle.

Randolph was amazed. And Mansfield shook his head slowly, his face retaining its ironical smile.

"No, Abner," he said, "let Randolph have his case. I shot him."

Then he put out his hand, as though in courtesy, to my uncle. "Be at peace," he said. "If I were moved by fear, there is a greater near me than Randolph's gibbet. I shall be dead and buried before his grand jury can hold its inquisition."

"Mansfield," replied my uncle, "be yourself at peace, for you did not kill him."

"Not kill him!" cried the man. "I shot him thus!"

He sat down in his chair and taking the pistol out of the rosewood box, leveled it at an imaginary figure across the portico. The man's hand was steady and the sun glinted on the steel barrel.

"And because you shot thus," said Abner, "you did not kill him. Listen, Mansfield: the pistol that killed the Abolitionist was held upside down and close. The brand on the dead man's face is under the bullet hole. If the pistol had been held as usual, the brand would have been above it. It is a law of pistol wounds: as you turn the weapon, so will the brand follow. Held upside down, the brand was below the wound."

A deepening wonder came into the old man's ironical face.

"How did the creature die, then, if I missed him?"

Abner took up the weapon on the arm of Randolph's chair.

"The dead man did not shoot in Mansfield's fantastic duel," he said. "Nevertheless this pistol has been fired. And observe there is a smeared bloodstain on the sharp edges of the barrel. I think I know what happened.

"The madman with his pistol, overwrought, struggled in the cabin yonder to make himself a 'sacrifice of blood' and so bring on this war. Someone resisted his mad act—some one who seized the barrel of the pistol and in the struggle also got a wounded hand. Who in that cabin had a wounded hand, Randolph?"

"By the living God!" cried the Justice of the Peace. "The woman who plaited thorns! It was a blind to cover her injured hand!"

Abner looked out across the great meadows at a tiny figure far off, fading into the twilight of the distant road that led toward the Ohio.

"To cover her injured hand," he echoed, "and also, perhaps, who knows, to symbolize the dead man's mission, as she knew he saw it! The heart of a woman is the deepest of all God's riddles!"

17
The Adopted Daughter

"Isn't she a beauty—eh, Randolph?" Vespatian Flornoy had a tumbler of French brandy. He sucked in a mouthful. Then he put it on the table.

The house was the strangest in Virginia. It was of some foreign model. The whole second floor on the side lying toward the east was in two spacious chambers lighted with great casement windows to the ceiling. Outside, on this brilliant morning, the world was yellow and dried-up, sere and baked. But the sun was thin and the autumn air hard and vital.

My uncle, Squire Randolph, the old country doctor, Storm, and the host, Vespatian Flornoy, were in one of these enormous rooms. They sat about a table, a long mahogany piece made in England and brought over in a sailing ship. There were a squat bottle of French brandy and some tumblers. Flornoy drank and recovered his spirit of abandon.

Now he leered at Randolph, and at the girl that he had just called in.

He was a man one would have traveled far to see—yesterday or the day ahead of that. He had a figure out of Athens, a face cast in some forgotten foundry by the Arno, thick-curled mahogany-colored hair, and eyes like the velvet hull of an Italian chestnut. These excellencies the heavenly workman had turned out, and now by some sorcery of the pit they were changed into abominations.

Hell-charms, one thought of, when one looked the creature in the face. Drops of some potent liquor, and devil-words had done it, on yesterday or the day ahead of yesterday. Surely not the things that really had done it—time and the iniquities of Gomorrah. His stock and his fine ruffled shirt were soiled. His satin waistcoat was stained with liquor.

"A daughter of a French marquis, eh!" he went on. "Sold into slavery by a jest of the gods—stolen out of the garden of a convent! It's the fabled history of every octoroon in New Orleans!"

Fabled or not, the girl might have been the thing he said. The contour of the face came to a point at the chin, and the skin was a soft Oriental olive. She was the perfect expression of a type. One never could wish to change a line of her figure or a feature of her face. She stood now in the room before the door in the morning sun, in the quaint, alluring costume of a young girl of the time—a young girl of degree, stolen out of the garden of a convent! She had entered at Flornoy's drunken call, and there was the aspect of terror on her.

The man went on in his thick, abominable voice:

"My brother Sheppard, coming north to an inspection of our joint estate, presents her as his adopted daughter. But when he dropped dead in this room last night and I went about the preparation of his body for your inquisition—eh, what, my gentlemen! I find a bill of sale running back ten years, for the dainty baggage!

"French, and noble, stolen from the garden of a convent, perhaps! Perhaps! but not by my brother Sheppard. His adopted daughter—sentimentally, perhaps! Perhaps! But legally a piece of property, I think, descending to his heirs. Eh, Randolph!"

And he thrust a folded yellow paper across the table.

The Justice put down his glass with the almost untasted liquor in it, and examined the bill of sale.

"It is in form!" he said. "And you interpret it correctly, Flornoy, by the law's letter. But you will not wish to enforce it, I imagine!"

"And why not, Randolph?" cried the man.

The Justice looked him firmly in the face.

"You take enough by chance, sir. You and your brother Sheppard held the estate jointly at your father's death, and now at your brother's death you hold it as sole heir. You will not wish, also, to hold his adopted daughter."

Then he added:

"This bill of sale would hold in the courts against any unindentured purpose, not accompanied by an intention expressed in some overt act. It would also fix the status of the girl against any pretended or legendary exemption of birth. The judges might believe that your brother Sheppard was convinced of this pretension when he rescued the child by purchase, and made his informal adoption at a tender age. But they would hold the paper, like a deed, irrevocable, and not to be disturbed by this conjecture."

"It will hold," cried the man, "and I will hold! You make an easy disclaimer of the rights of other men."

Then his face took on the aspect of a satyr's.

"Give her up, eh! to be a lady! Why Randolph, I would have given Sheppard five hundred golden eagles for this little beauty—five hundred golden eagles in his hand! Look at her, Randolph. You are not too old to forget the points—the trim ankle, the slender body, the snap of a thoroughbred. There's the blood of the French marquis, on my honor! A drop of black won't curdle it."

And he laughed, snapping his fingers at his wit.

"It only makes the noble lady merchandise! And perhaps, as you say, perhaps it isn't there, in fact. Egad! old man, I would have bid a thousand eagles if Sheppard had put her up. A thousand eagles! and I get her for nothing! He falls dead in my house, and I take her by inheritance."

It was the living truth. The two men, Vespatian Flornoy and his brother Sheppard, took their father's estate jointly at his death. They were unmarried, and now at the death of Sheppard, the surviving brother Vespatian was sole heir, under the law, to the dead man's properties: houses and lands and slaves. The bill of sale put the girl an item in the inventory of the dead man's estate, to descend with the manor-house and lands.

The thing had happened, as fortune is predisposed to change, in a moment, as by the turning of dice.

At daybreak on this morning Vespatian Flornoy had sent a negro at a gallop, to summon the old country doctor, Storm, Squire Randolph and my uncle Abner. At midnight, in this chamber where they now sat, Sheppard as he got on his feet, with his candle, fell and died, Vespatian said, before he could reach his body. He lay now shaven and clothed for burial in the great chamber that adjoined.

Old Storm had stripped the body and found no mark. The man was dead with no scratch or bruise.

He could not say what vital organ had suddenly played out—perhaps a string of the heart had snapped. At any rate, the dead man had not gone out by any sort of violence, nor by any poison. Every drug or herb that killed left its stamp and superscription, old Storm said, and one could see it, if one had the eye, as one could see the slash of a knife or the bruise of an assassin's fingers.

It was plain death "by the Providence of God," was Randolph's verdict. So the Justice and old Storm summed up the thing and they represented the inquiry and the requirements of the law.

My uncle Abner made no comment on this conclusion. He came and looked and was silent. He demurred to the 'Providence of God' in Randolph's verdict, with a great gesture of rejection. He disliked this term in any human horror. "By the abandonment of God," he said, these verdicts ought rather to be written. But he gave no sign that his objection was of any special tenor. He seemed profoundly puzzled.

When the girl came in, at Vespatian's command, to this appraisal, he continued silent. At the man's speech, and evident intent, his features and his great jaw hardened, as though under the sunburned skin the bony structure of the face were metal.

He sat in his chair, a little way out beyond the table, as he sat on a Sunday before the pulpit, on a bench, motionless, in some deep concern.

Randolph and Vespatian Flornoy were in this dialogue. Old Storm sat with his arms folded across his chest, his head down. His interest in the matter had departed with his inspection of the dead man, or remained in the adjoining chamber where the body lay, the eyelids closed forever on the land of living men, shut up tight like the shutters of a window in a house of mystery. He only glanced at the girl with no interest, as at a bauble.

And now while the dialogue went on and Storm looked down his nose, the girl, silent and in terror, appealed to my uncle in a furtive glance, swift, charged with horror, and like a flash of shadow. The great table had a broad board connecting the carved legs beneath, a sort of shelf raised a little from the floor. In her glance, swift and fearful, she directed my uncle's attention to this board.

It was a long piece of veneered mahogany, making a shelf down the whole length of the table. On it my uncle saw a big folded cloth of squares white and black, and a set of huge ivory chess-men. The cloth was made to spread across the top of the table, and the chess-men were of unusual size in proportion to the squares; the round knobs on the heads of the pawns were as big as marbles. Beside these things was a rosewood box for dueling-pistols, after the fashion of the time.

My uncle stooped over, took up these articles and set them on the table.

"And so, Flornoy," he said, "you played at chess with your brother Sheppard."

The man turned swiftly; then he paused and drank his glass of liquor.

"I entertained my brother," he said, "as I could; there is no coffee-house to enter, nor any dancing women to please the eye, in the mountains of Virginia."

"For what stake?" said my uncle.

"I have forgotten, Abner," replied the man, "—some trifle."

"And who won?" said my uncle.

"I won," replied the man. He spoke promptly.

"You won," said my uncle, "and you remember that; but what you won, you have forgotten! Reflect a little on it, Flornoy."

The man cursed, his face in anger.

"Does it matter, Abner, a thing great or small? It is all mine to-day!"

"But it was not all yours last night," said my uncle.

"What I won was mine," replied the man.

"Now, there," replied my uncle, "lies a point that I would amplify. One might win, but might not receive the thing one played for. One might claim it for one's own, and the loser might deny it. If the stake were great, the loser might undertake to repudiate the bargain. And how would one enforce it?"

The man put down his glass, leaned over and looked steadily at my uncle.

Abner slipped the silver hooks on the rosewood box, slowly, with his thumb and finger.

"I think," he said, "that if the gentleman you have in mind won, and were met with a refusal, he would undertake to enforce his claim, not in the courts or by any legal writ, but by the methods which gentlemen such as you have in mind are accustomed to invoke."

He opened the box and took out two pistols of the time. Then his faced clouded with perplexity. Both weapons were clean and loaded.

The man, propping his wonderful face in the hollow of his hand, laughed. He had the face and the laughter of the angels cast out with Satan, when in a moment of some gain over the hosts of Michael they forgot the pit.

"Abner," he cried, "you are hag-ridden by a habit, and it leads you into the wildest fancies!"

His laughter chuckled and gurgled in his throat.

"Let me put your theory together. It is a very pretty theory, lacking in some trifles, but spirited and packed with dramatic tension. Let me sketch it out as it stands before your eye. . . . Have no fear, I shall not mar it by any delicate concern for the cunning villain, or any suppression of his evil nature. I shall uncover the base creature amid his deeds of darkness!"

He paused, and mocked the tragedy of actors.

"It is the hour of yawning graveyards—midnight in this house. Vespatian Flornoy sits at this table with his good brother Sheppard. He has the covetousness of David the son of Jesse, in his evil heart.

He would possess the noble daughter of the Latin marquis, by a sardonic fate sold at childhood into slavery, but by the ever watchful Providence of God, for such cases made and provided, purchased by the good brother Sheppard and adopted for his daughter!

"Mark, Abner, how beautifully it falls into the formula of the tragic poets!

"The wicked Vespatian Flornoy, foiled in every scheme of purchase, moved by the instigation of the Devil, and with no fear of God before his eyes, plays at chess with his good brother Sheppard, wins his interest in the manor-house and lands, and his last gold-piece—taunts and seduces him into a final game with everything staked against this Iphigenia. The evil one rises invisible but sulphurous to Vespatian's aid. He wins. In terror, appalled, aghast at the realization of his folly, the good brother Sheppard repudiates the bargain. They duel across the table, and Vespatian, being the better shot, kills his good brother Sheppard!

"Why, Abner, it is the plan of the 'Poetics.' It lacks no element of completeness. It is joined and fitted for the diction of Euripides!"

The man declaimed, his wonderful fouled face, his Adonis head with its thick curled hair, virile and spirited with the liquor and the momentum of his words. Old Storm gave no attention. Randolph listened as to the periods of an oration. And my uncle sat, puzzled, before the articles on the table. The girl now and then, when the speaker's eyes were on my uncle, by slight indicatory signs affirmed the speech, and continued strongly to indicate the chessmen.

My uncle began to turn the pieces over under the protection of his hand, idly, like one who fingers about a table in abstraction. Presently he stopped and covered one of the pieces with his hand. It was a pawn, large, like the other chess-men, but the round ivory knob at the top of it was gone. It had been sawed off!

The man Flornoy, consumed with his idea, failed to mark the incident, and moved by the tenor of his speech, went on:

"This is the Greek plan for a tragedy. It is the plan of Athens in the fifth century. It is the plan of Sophocles and Æschylus. Mark how it turns upon the Hellenic idea of a dominating Fate: a Fate in control over the affairs of men, pagan and not good. The innocent and virtuous have no gain above the shrewd and wicked. The good Sheppard dies, and the evil Vespatian takes his daughter, his goods and lands to enjoy in a gilded life, long and happy!"

He thought the deep reflection in my uncle's face was confusion at his wit.

"That ending would not please you, Abner. Luther and Calvin and John Wesley have lived after Aristotle assembled this formula in his 'Poetics.' And they will have the evil punished—a dagger in the wicked Vespatian's heart, and the virgin slave, by the interposition of the will of Heaven, preserved in her virginity. And so you come, like the Providence of God, to set the thing in order!"

My uncle looked up at the man, his hand covering the mutilated pawn, his face calm in its profound reflection.

"You quote the tragic poets, with much pedantry," he said. "Well, I will quote them too: 'Ofttimes, to win us to our harm, the instruments of darkness tell us truth!' How much truth, in all this discourse, have you told us?"

"Now, Abner," cried the man, "if it is truth you seek, and not the imaginations of a theory, how much could there be in it? If it were not for the granite ledges of reality, one might blow iris-colored bubbles of the fancy and watch them, in their beauty, journey to the stars! But alas, they collide with the hard edges of a fact and puff out.

"To begin with, the pistols have not been fired!"

"One could reload a pistol," replied my uncle.

"But one could not shoot a man, Abner, and leave no mark of the bullet on his body!"

He paused and addressed the old doctor.

"I sent for Storm, when I sent for Randolph, to rid me of every innuendo of a gossip. Ask him if there is a mark of violence on my brother's body."

The old man lifted his lined, withered face.

"There is no mark on him!" he said.

Vespatian Flornoy leaned across the table.

"Are you sure?" he said. "Perhaps you might be mistaken."

The words were in the taunting note of Elijah to the priests of Baal.

The old man made a decisive gesture. "*Voilà!*" he said, "I have handled a thousand dead men! I am not mistaken!"

Vespatian Flornoy put up his hands as in a great, hopeless gesture.

"Alas, Abner," he said, "we must give up this pretty theory. It does honor to your creative instinct, and save for this trifle, we might commend it to all men. But you see, Abner, Storm and the world will unreasonably insist that a bullet leaves a mark. I do not think we can persuade them against their experience in that belief. I am sorry for you, Abner. You have a reputation in Virginia to keep up. Let us think; perhaps there is a way around this disconcerting fact."

And he put his extended palm across his forehead, in mock reflection.

It was at this moment, when for an instant the man's face was covered, that the girl standing before the door made a strange indicatory signal to my uncle Abner.

Vespatian Flornoy, removing his hand, caught a glimpse of the girl's after-expression. And he burst out in a great laugh, striking the table with his clenched hand.

"Egad!" he cried. "By the soul of Satan! the coy little baggage is winking at Abner!"

He saw only the final composition of the girl's face. He did not see the stress and vigor of the indicatory sign. He roared in a pretension of jealous anger.

"I will not have my property ogle another in my house. You shall answer for this, Abner, on the field of honor. And I warn you, sir: I have the surest eye and the steadiest hand in the mountains of Virginia."

It was the truth. The man was the wonder of the countryside. He could cut a string with a pistol at ten paces; he could drive in a carpet-tack with his bullet, across a room. With the weapon of the time, the creature was sure, accurate to a hair, and deadly.

"No man," he cried, "shall carry off this dainty baggage. Select your weapon, Abner; let us duel over this seduction!"

He spoke in the flippancies of jest. But my uncle's face was now alight with some great comprehensive purpose. It was like the face of one who begins to see the bulk and outlines of a thing that before this hour, in spite of every scrutiny, was formless.

And to Flornoy's surprise and wonder, my uncle put out his hand, took up one of the pistols and suddenly fired it into the wood of the mantelpiece beyond the table. He got up and looked at the mark. The bullet was hardly bedded in the veneer.

"You use a light charge of powder, Flornoy," said my uncle.

The man was puzzled at this act, but he answered at once.

"Abner," he said, "that is a secret I have learned. A pistol pivots on the grip. In firing, there are two things to avoid: a jerk on the trigger, and the tendency of the muzzle to jump up, caused by the recoil of the charge. No man can control his weapon with a heavy charge of powder behind the bullet. If one would shoot true to a hair, one must load light."

It seemed a considerable explanation. And not one of the men who heard it ever knew whether it was, in fact, the controlling cause, or whether another and more subtle thing inspired it.

"But, Flornoy," said my uncle, "if to kill were the object of a duelist, such a charge of powder might defeat the purpose."

"You are mistaken, Abner," he said. "The body of a man is soft. If one avoids the bony structure, a trifling charge of powder will carry one's bullet into a vital organ. There is no gain in shooting through a man as though one were going to string him on a thread. Powder enough to lodge the bullet in the vital organ is sufficient."

"There might be a point in not shooting through him," said Abner.

The man looked calmly at my uncle; then he made an irrelevant gesture.

"No object, Abner, but no use. The whole point is to shoot to a hair, to lodge the bullet precisely in the point selected. Look how a light charge of powder does it."

And taking up the other pistol, he steadied it a moment in his hand, and fired at Abner's bullet-hole. No mark appeared on the mantel board. One would have believed that the bullet, if the barrel held one, had wholly vanished. But when they looked closely, it was seen that my uncle's bullet, struck precisely, was driven a little deeper into the wood. It was amazing accuracy. No wonder the man's skill was a byword in the land.

My uncle made a single comment.

"You shoot like the slingers of Benjamin!" he said.

Then he came back to the table and stood looking down at the man. He held the mutilated ivory pawn in his closed left hand. The girl, like an appraised article, was in the doorway; Storm and Randolph looked on, like men before the blind moving of events.

"Flornoy," said Abner, "you have told us more truth than you intended us to believe. How did your brother Sheppard die?"

The man's face changed. His fingers tightened on the pistol. His eyes became determined and alert.

"Damme, man," he cried, "do you return to that! Sheppard fell and died, where you stand, beside the table in this room. I am no surgeon to say what disorder killed him. I sent for Storm to determine that."

My uncle turned to the old eccentric doctor.

"Storm," he said, "how did Sheppard Flornoy die?"

The old man shrugged his shoulders and put out his nervous hands.

"I do not know," he said, "the heart, maybe. There is no mark on him."

And here Randolph interrupted.

"Abner," he said, "you put a question that no man can answer: something snaps within the body, and we die. We have no hint at the cause of Sheppard's death."

"Why yes," replied my uncle, "I think we have."

"What hint?" said Randolph.

"The hint," said Abner, "that the eloquent Vespatian gave us just now in his discourse. I think he set out the cause in his apt recollection from the Book of Samuel."

He paused and looked down at the man.

Vespatian Flornoy got on his feet. His face and manner changed. There was now decision and menace in his voice.

"Abner," he said, "there shall be an end to this. I have turned your ugly hint with pleasantry, and met it squarely with indisputable facts. I shall not go any further on this way. I shall clear myself now, after the manner of a gentleman."

My uncle looked steadily at the man.

"Flornoy," he said, "if you would test your innocence by a device of the Middle Ages, I would suggest a simpler and swifter method of that time. Wager of battle is outlawed in Virginia. It is prohibited by statute, and we cannot use it. But the test I offer in its place is equally medieval. It is based on the same belief, old and persistent, that the Providence of God will indicate the guilty. And it is not against the law."

He paused.

"The same generation of men who believed in Wager of Battle, in the Morsel of Execration, in the red-hot plowshares, as a test of the guilt of murder, also believed that if the assassin touched his victim, the body of the murdered man would bleed!

"Flornoy," he said, "if you would have recourse to one of those medieval devices, let it be the last. Go in with me and touch the body of your brother Sheppard, and I give you my word of honor that I will accept the decision of the test."

It was impossible to believe that my uncle Abner trifled, and yet the thing was beyond the soundings of all sense.

Storm and Randolph, and even the girl standing in the door, regarded him in wonder.

Vespatian Flornoy was amazed.

"Damme, man!" he cried, "superstitions have unhinged your mind. Would you believe in a thing like that?"

"I would rather believe it," replied my uncle, "than to believe that in a duel God would direct the assassin's bullet."

Then he added, with weight and decision in his voice:

"If you would be clear of my suspicion, if you would be free to take and enjoy the lands and properties that you inherit, go in before these witnesses and touch the dead body of your brother Sheppard. There is no mark appearing on him. Storm has found no wound to bleed. You are innocent of any measure in his death, you tell us. There's no peril to you, and I shall ride away to assure every man that Sheppard Flornoy died, as Randolph has written, by the 'Providence of God.'"

He extended his arm toward the adjacent chamber, and across the table he looked Flornoy in the face.

"Go in before us and touch the dead man."

"By the soul of Satan!" cried the man, "if you hang on such a piece of foolery, you shall have it. The curse of superstition sticks in your fleece, Abner, like a burr."

He turned and flung open the door behind him and went in. The others followed—Storm and Randolph behind the man, the girl, shaken and fearful, and my uncle Abner.

Sheppard Flornoy lay prepared for burial in the center of the room. The morning sun entering through the long windows flooded him with light; his features were sharply outlined in the mask of death, his eyelids closed.

They stood about the dead man, at peace in this glorious shroud of sun, and the living brother was about to touch him when my uncle put out his hand.

"Flornoy," he said, "the dead man ought to see who comes to touch him. I will open his eyes."

And at the words, for no cause or reason conceivable to the two men looking on, Vespatian Flornoy shouted with an oath, and ran in on my uncle.

He was big and mad with terror. But even in his youth and fury he was not a match for my Uncle Abner. Liquor and excess failed before wind and sun and the clean life of the hills. The man went down under my uncle's clenched hand, like an ox polled with a hammer.

It was Randolph who cried out, while the others crowded around the dead man and his brother unconscious on the floor.

"Abner, Abner," he said, "what is the answer to this ghastly riddle?"

For reply my uncle drew back the eyelids of the dead man. And stooping over, Randolph and old Storm saw that Sheppard Flornoy had been shot through the eye, and that the head of the ivory pawn had been forced into the bullet-hole to round out the damaged eyeball under the closed lid.

The girl sobbed, clinging to my uncle's arm. Randolph tore the bill of sale into indistinguishable bits. And the old doctor Storm made a great gesture with his hands extended and crooked.

"*Mon Dieu!*" he cried, in a consuming revulsion of disgust. "My father was surgeon in the field for Napoleon, I was raised with dead men, and a drunken assassin fools me in the mountains of Virginia!"

18
Naboth's Vineyard

One hears a good deal about the sovereignty of the people in this republic; and many persons imagine it a sort of fiction, and wonder where it lies, who are the guardians of it, and how they would exercise it if the forms and agents of the law were removed. I am not one of those who speculate upon this mystery, for I have seen this primal ultimate authority naked at its work. And, having seen it, I know how mighty and how dread a thing it is. And I know where it lies, and who are the guardians of it, and how they exercise it when the need arises.

There was a great crowd, for the whole country was in the courtroom. It was a notorious trial.

Elihu Marsh had been shot down in his house. He had been found lying in a room, with a hole through his body that one could put his thumb in. He was an irascible old man, the last of his family, and so, lived alone. He had rich lands, but only a life estate in them, the remainder was to some foreign heirs. A girl from a neighboring farm came now and then to bake and put his house in order, and he kept a farm hand about the premises.

Nothing had been disturbed in the house when the neighbors found Marsh; no robbery had been attempted, for the man's money, a considerable sum, remained on him.

There was not much mystery about the thing, because the farm hand had disappeared. This man was a stranger in the hills. He had come from over the mountains some months before, and gone to work for Marsh. He was a big blond man, young and good looking;

of better blood, one would say, than the average laborer. He gave his name as Taylor, but he was not communicative, and little else about him was known.

The country was raised, and this man was overtaken in the foothills of the mountains. He had his clothes tied into a bundle, and a long-barreled fowling-piece on his shoulder. The story he told was that he and Marsh had settled that morning, and he had left the house at noon, but that he had forgotten his gun and had gone back for it; had reached the house about four o'clock, gone into the kitchen, got his gun down from the dogwood forks over the chimney, and at once left the house. He had not seen Marsh, and did not know where he was.

He admitted that this gun had been loaded with a single huge lead bullet. He had so loaded it to kill a dog that sometimes approached the house, but not close enough to be reached with a load of shot. He affected surprise when it was pointed out that the gun had been discharged. He said that he had not fired it, and had not, until then, noticed that it was empty. When asked why he had so suddenly determined to leave the country, he was silent.

He was carried back and confined in the county jail, and now, he was on trial at the September term of the circuit court.

The court sat early. Although the judge, Simon Kilrail, was a landowner and lived on his estate in the country some half dozen miles away, he rode to the courthouse in the morning, and home at night, with his legal papers in his saddle-pockets. It was only when the court sat that he was a lawyer. At other times he harvested his hay and grazed his cattle, and tried to add to his lands like any other man in the hills, and he was as hard in a trade and as hungry for an acre as any.

It was the sign and insignia of distinction in Virginia to own land. Mr. Jefferson had annulled the titles that George the Third had granted, and the land alone remained as a patent of nobility. The Judge wished to be one of these landed gentry, and he had gone a good way to accomplish it. But when the court convened he became a lawyer and sat upon the bench with no heart in him, and a cruel tongue like the English judges.

I think everybody was at this trial. My Uncle Abner and the strange old doctor, Storm, sat on a bench near the center aisle of the court-room, and I sat behind them, for I was a half-grown lad, and permitted to witness the terrors and severities of the law.

The prisoner was the center of interest. He sat with a stolid countenance like a man careless of the issues of life. But not everybody was concerned with him, for my Uncle Abner and Storm watched the girl who had been accustomed to bake for Marsh and red up his house.

She was a beauty of her type; dark haired and dark eyed like a gypsy, and with an April nature of storm and sun. She sat among the witnesses with a little handkerchief clutched in her hands. She was nervous to the point of hysteria, and I thought that was the reason the old doctor watched her. She would be taken with a gust of tears, and then throw up her head with a fine defiance; and she kneaded and knotted and worked the handkerchief in her fingers. It was a time of stress and many witnesses were unnerved, and I think I should not have noticed this girl but for the whispering of Storm and my Uncle Abner.

The trial went forward, and it became certain that the prisoner would hang. His stubborn refusal to give any reason for his hurried departure had but one meaning, and the circumstantial evidence was conclusive. The motive, only, remained in doubt, and the Judge had charged on this with so many cases in point, and with so heavy a hand, that any virtue in it was removed. The Judge was hard against this man, and indeed there was little sympathy anywhere, for it was a foul killing—the victim an old man and no hot blood to excuse it.

In all trials of great public interest, where the evidences of guilt overwhelmingly assemble against a prisoner, there comes a moment when all the people in the court-room, as one man, and without a sign of the common purpose, agree upon a verdict; there is no outward or visible evidence of this decision, but one feels it, and it is a moment of the tensest stress.

The trial of Taylor had reached this point, and there lay a moment of deep silence, when this girl sitting among the witnesses suddenly burst into a very hysteria of tears. She stood up shaking with sobs, her voice choking in her throat, and the tears gushing through her fingers.

What she said was not heard at the time by the audience in the court-room, but it brought the Judge to his feet and the jury crowding about her, and it broke down the silence of the prisoner, and threw him into a perfect fury of denials. We could hear his voice rise above the confusion, and we could see him struggling to get to the girl and stop her. But what she said was presently known to everybody, for it was taken down and signed; and it put the case against Taylor, to use a lawyer's term, out of court.

The girl had killed Marsh herself. And this was the manner and the reason of it: She and Taylor were sweethearts and were to be married. But they had quarreled the night before Marsh's death and the following morning Taylor had left the country. The point of the quarrel was some remark that Marsh had made to Taylor touching the girl's reputation. She had come to the house in the afternoon, and finding her lover gone, and maddened at the sight of the one who had robbed her of him, had taken the gun down from the chimney and killed Marsh. She had then put the gun back into its place and left the house. This was about two o'clock in the afternoon, and about an hour before Taylor returned for his gun.

There was a great veer of public feeling with a profound sense of having come at last upon the truth, for the story not only fitted to the circumstantial evidence against Taylor, but it fitted also to his story and it disclosed the motive for the killing. It explained, too, why he had refused to give the reason for his disappearance. That Taylor denied what the girl said and tried to stop her in her declaration, meant nothing except that the prisoner was a man, and would not have the woman he loved make such a sacrifice for him.

I cannot give all the forms of legal procedure with which the closing hours of the court were taken up, but nothing happened to shake the girl's confession. Whatever the law required was speedily got ready, and she was remanded to the care of the sheriff in order that she might come before the court in the morning.

Taylor was not released, but was also held in custody, although the case against him seemed utterly broken down. The Judge refused to permit the prisoner's counsel to take a verdict. He said that he would withdraw a juror and continue the case. But he seemed unwilling to release any clutch of the law until some one was punished for this crime.

It was on our way, and we rode out with the Judge that night. He talked with Abner and Storm about the pastures and the price of cattle, but not about the trial, as I hoped he would do, except once only, and then it was to inquire why the prosecuting attorney had not called either of them as witnesses, since they were the first to find Marsh, and Storm had been among the doctors who examined him. And Storm had explained how he had mortally offended the prosecutor in his canvass, by his remark that only a gentleman should hold office. He did but quote Mr. Hamilton, Storm said, but the man had received it as a deadly insult, and thereby proved the truth of Mr. Hamilton's expression, Storm added. And Abner said that as no circumstance about Marsh's death was questioned, and others arriving about the same time had been called, the prosecutor doubtless considered further testimony unnecessary.

The Judge nodded, and the conversation turned to other questions. At the gate, after the common formal courtesy of the country, the Judge asked us to ride in, and, to my astonishment, Abner and Storm accepted his invitation. I could see that the man was surprised, and I thought annoyed, but he took us into his library.

I could not understand why Abner and Storm had stopped here, until I remembered how from the first they had been considering the girl, and it occurred to me that they thus sought the Judge in the hope of getting some word to him in her favor. A great sentiment had leaped up for this girl. She had made a staggering sacrifice, and with a headlong courage, and it was like these men to help her if they could.

And it was to speak of the woman that they came, but not in her favor. And while Simon Kilrail listened, they told this extraordinary story: They had been of the opinion that Taylor was not guilty when the trial began, but they had suffered it to proceed in order to see what might develop. The reason was that there were certain circumstantial evidences, overlooked by the prosecutor, indicating the guilt of the woman and the innocence of Taylor. When Storm examined the body of Marsh he discovered that the man had been killed by poison, and was dead when the bullet was fired into his body. This meant that the shooting was a fabricated evidence to direct suspicion against Taylor. The woman had baked for Marsh on this morning, and the poison was in the bread which he had eaten at noon.

Abner was going on to explain something further, when a servant entered and asked the Judge what time it was. The man had been greatly impressed, and he now sat in a profound reflection. He took his watch out of his pocket and held it in his hand, then he seemed to realize the question and replied that his watch had run down. Abner gave the hour, and said that perhaps his key would wind the watch. The Judge gave it to him, and he wound it and laid it on the table. Storm observed my Uncle with, what I thought, a curious interest, but the Judge paid no attention. He was deep in his reflection and oblivious to everything. Finally he roused himself and made his comment.

"This clears the matter up," he said. "The woman killed Marsh from the motive which she gave in her confession, and she created this false evidence against Taylor because he had abandoned her. She thereby avenged herself desperately in two directions. . . . It would be like a woman to do this, and then regret it and confess."

He then asked my Uncle if he had anything further to tell him, and although I was sure that Abner was going on to say something further when the servant entered, he replied now that he had not, and asked for the horses. The Judge went out to have the horses brought, and we remained in silence. My Uncle was calm, as with some consuming idea, but Storm was as nervous as a cat. He was out of his chair when the door was closed, and hopping about the room looking at the law books standing on the shelves in their leather covers. Suddenly he stopped and plucked out a little volume. He whipped through it with his forefinger, smothered a great oath, and shot it into his pocket, then he crooked his finger to my

Uncle, and they talked together in a recess of the window until the Judge returned.

We rode away. I was sure that they intended to say something to the Judge in the woman's favor, for, guilty or not, it was a fine thing she had done to stand up and confess. But something in the interview had changed their purpose. Perhaps when they had heard the Judge's comment they saw it would be of no use. They talked closely together as they rode, but they kept before me and I could not hear. It was of the woman they spoke, however, for I caught a fragment.

"But where is the motive?" said Storm.

And my Uncle answered, "In the twenty-first chapter of the Book of Kings."

We were early at the county seat, and it was a good thing for us, because the court-room was crowded to the doors. My Uncle had got a big record book out of the county clerk's office as he came in, and I was glad of it, for he gave it to me to sit on, and it raised me up so I could see. Storm was there, too, and, in fact, every man of any standing in the county.

The sheriff opened the court, the prisoners were brought in, and the Judge took his seat on the bench. He looked haggard like a man who had not slept, as, in fact, one could hardly have done who had so cruel a duty before him. Here was every human feeling pressing to save a woman, and the law to hang her. But for all his hag-ridden face, when he came to act, the man was adamant.

He ordered the confession read, and directed the girl to stand up. Taylor tried again to protest, but he was forced down into his chair. The girl stood up bravely, but she was white as plaster, and her eyes dilated. She was asked if she still adhered to the confession and understood the consequences of it, and, although she trembled from head to toe, she spoke out distinctly. There was a moment of silence and the Judge was about to speak, when another voice filled the court-room. I turned about on my book to find my head against my Uncle Abner's legs.

"I challenge the confession!" he said.

The whole court-room moved. Every eye was on the two tragic figures standing up: the slim, pale girl and the big, somber figure of my Uncle. The Judge was astounded.

"On what ground?" he said.

"On the ground," replied my Uncle, "that the confession is a lie!"

One could have heard a pin fall anywhere in the whole room. The girl caught her breath in a little gasp, and the prisoner, Taylor, half rose and then sat down as though his knees were too weak to bear him. The Judge's mouth opened, but for a moment or two he did not speak, and I could understand his amazement. Here was Abner assailing a confession which he himself had supported before the Judge, and speaking for the innocence of a woman whom he himself had shown to be guilty and taking one position privately, and another publicly. What did the man mean? And I was not surprised that the Judge's voice was stern when he spoke.

"This is irregular," he said. "It may be that this woman killed Marsh, or it may be that Taylor killed him, and there is some collusion between these persons, as you appear to suggest. And you may know something to throw light on the matter, or you may not. However that may be, this is not the time for me to hear you. You will have ample opportunity to speak when I come to try the case."

"But you will never try this case!" said Abner.

I cannot undertake to describe the desperate interest that lay on the people in the courtroom. They were breathlessly silent; one could hear the voices from the village outside, and the sounds of men and horses that came up through the open windows. No one knew what hidden thing Abner drove at. But he was a man who meant what he said, and the people knew it.

The Judge turned on him with a terrible face.

"What do you mean?" he said.

"I mean," replied Abner, and it was in his deep, hard voice, "that you must come down from the bench."

The Judge was in a heat of fury.

"You are in contempt," he roared. "I order your arrest. Sheriff!" he called.

But Abner did not move. He looked the man calmly in the face.

"You threaten me," he said, "but God Almighty threatens you." And he turned about to the audience. "The authority of the law," he said, "is in the hands of the electors of this county. Will they stand up?"

I shall never forget what happened then, for I have never in my life seen anything so deliberate and impressive. Slowly, in silence, and without passion, as though they were in a church of God, men began to get up in the courtroom.

Randolph was the first. He was a justice of the peace, vain and pompous, proud of the abilities of an ancestry that he did not inherit. And his superficialities were the annoyance of my Uncle Abner's life. But whatever I may have to say of him hereafter I want to say this thing of him here, that his bigotry and his vanities were builded on the foundations of a man. He stood up as though he stood alone, with no glance about him to see what other men would do, and he faced the Judge calmly above his great black stock. And I learned then that a man may be a blusterer and a lion.

Hiram Arnold got up, and Rockford, and Armstrong, and Alkire, and Coopman, and Monroe, and Elnathan Stone, and my father, Lewis, and Dayton and Ward, and Madison from beyond the mountains. And it seemed to me that the very hills and valleys were standing up.

It was a strange and instructive thing to see. The loud-mouthed and the reckless were in that courtroom, men who would have shouted in a political convention, or run howling with a mob, but they were not the persons who stood up when Abner called upon the authority of the people to appear. Men rose whom one would not have looked to see—the blacksmith, the saddler, and old Asa Divers. And I saw that law and order and all the structure that civilization had builded up, rested on the sense of justice that certain men carried in their breasts, and that those who possessed it not, in the crisis of necessity, did not count.

Father Donovan stood up; he had a little flock beyond the valley river, and he was as poor, and almost as humble as his Master, but he was not afraid; and Bronson, who preached Calvin, and

Adam Rider, who traveled a Methodist circuit. No one of them believed in what the other taught; but they all believed in justice, and when the line was drawn, there was but one side for them all.

The last man up was Nathaniel Davisson, but the reason was that he was very old, and he had to wait for his sons to help him. He had been time and again in the Assembly of Virginia, at a time when only a gentleman and landowner could sit there. He was a just man, and honorable and unafraid.

The Judge, his face purple, made a desperate effort to enforce his authority. He pounded on his desk and ordered the sheriff to clear the courtroom. But the sheriff remained standing apart. He did not lack for courage, and I think he would have faced the people if his duty had been that way. His attitude was firm, and one could mark no uncertainty upon him, but he took no step to obey what the Judge commanded.

The Judge cried out at him in a terrible voice.

"I am the representative of the law here. Go on!"

The sheriff was a plain man, and unacquainted with the nice expressions of Mr. Jefferson, but his answer could not have been better if that gentleman had written it out for him.

"I would obey the representative of the law," he said, "if I were not in the presence of the law itself!"

The Judge rose. "This is revolution," he said; "I will send to the Governor for the militia."

It was Nathaniel Davisson who spoke then. He was very old and the tremors of dissolution were on him, but his voice was steady.

"Sit down, your Honor," he said, "there is no revolution here, and you do not require troops to support your authority. We are here to support it if it ought to be lawfully enforced. But the people have elevated you to the Bench because they believed in your integrity, and if they have been mistaken they would know it." He paused, as though to collect his strength, and then went on. "The presumptions of right are all with your Honor. You administer the law upon our authority and we stand behind you. Be assured that we will not suffer our authority to be insulted in your person." His voice grew deep and resolute. "It is a grave thing to call us up against you, and not lightly, nor for a trivial reason shall any man dare to do it." Then he turned about. "Now, Abner," he said, "what is this thing?"

Young as I was, I felt that the old man spoke for the people standing in the courtroom, with their voice and their authority, and I began to fear that the measure which my Uncle had taken was high handed. But he stood there like the shadow of a great rock.

"I charge him," he said, "with the murder of Elihu Marsh! And I call upon him to vacate the Bench."

When I think about this extraordinary event now, I wonder at the calmness with which Simon Kilrail met this blow, until I reflect that he had seen it on its way, and had got ready to meet it. But even with that preparation, it took a man of iron nerve to face an assault like that and keep every muscle in its place. He had tried violence and had failed with it, and he had recourse now to the attitudes and mannerisms of a judicial dignity. He sat with his elbows on the table, and his clenched fingers propping up his jaw. He looked coldly at Abner, but he did not speak, and there was silence until Nathaniel Davisson spoke for him. His face and his voice were like iron.

"No, Abner," he said, "he shall not vacate the Bench for that, nor upon the accusation of any man. We will have your proofs, if you please."

The Judge turned his cold face from Abner to Nathaniel Davisson, and then he looked over the men standing in the courtroom.

"I am not going to remain here," he said, "to be tried by a mob, upon the *viva voce* indictment of a bystander. You may nullify your court, if you like, and suspend the forms of law for yourselves, but you cannot nullify the constitution of Virginia, nor suspend my right as a citizen of that commonwealth."

"And now," he said, rising, "if you will kindly make way, I will vacate this courtroom, which your violence has converted into a chamber of sedition."

The man spoke in a cold, even voice, and I thought he had presented a difficulty that could not be met. How could these men before him undertake to keep the peace of this frontier, and force its lawless elements to submit to the forms of law for trial, and deny any letter of those formalities to this man? Was the grand jury, and the formal indictment, and all the right and privilege of an orderly procedure for one, and not for another?

It was Nathaniel Davisson who met this dangerous problem.

"We are not concerned," he said, "at this moment with your rights as a citizen; the rights of private citizenship are inviolate, and they remain to you, when you return to it. But you are not a private citizen. You are our agent. We have selected you to administer the law for us, and your right to act has been challenged. Well, as the authority behind you, we appear and would know the reason."

The Judge retained his imperturbable calm.

"Do you hold me a prisoner here?" he said.

"We hold you an official in your office," replied Davisson, "not only do we refuse to permit you to leave the courtroom, but we refuse to permit you to leave the Bench. This court shall remain as we have set it up until it is our will to readjust it. And it shall not be changed at the pleasure or demand of any man but by us only, and for a sufficient cause shown to us."

And again I was anxious for my Uncle, for I saw how grave a thing it was to interfere with the authority of the people as manifested in the forms and agencies of the law. Abner must be very sure of the ground under him.

And he was sure. He spoke now, with no introductory expressions, but directly and in the simplest words.

"These two persons," he said, indicating Taylor and the girl, "have each been willing to die in order to save the other. Neither is guilty of this crime. Taylor has kept silent, and the girl has lied, to the same end. This is the truth: There was a lovers' quarrel, and Taylor left the country precisely as he told us, except the motive, which he would not tell lest the girl be involved. And the woman, to save him, confesses to a crime that she did not commit.

"Who did commit it?" He paused and included Storm with a gesture. "We suspected this woman because Marsh had been killed by poison in his bread, and afterwards mutilated with a shot. Yesterday we rode out with the Judge to put those facts before him." Again he paused. "An incident occurring in that interview indicated that we were wrong; a second incident assured us, and still later, a third convinced us. These incidents were, first, that the Judge's watch had run down; second, that we found in his library a book with all the leaves in it uncut, except at one certain page; and, third, that we found in the county clerk's office an unindexed record in an old deed book." There was deep quiet and he went on:

"In addition to the theory of Taylor's guilt or this woman's, there was still a third; but it had only a single incident to support it, and we feared to suggest it until the others had been explained. This theory was that some one, to benefit by Marsh's death, had planned to kill him in such a manner as to throw suspicion on this woman who baked his bread, and finding Taylor gone, and the gun above the mantel, yielded to an afterthought to create a further false evidence. It was overdone!

"The trigger guard of the gun in the recoil caught in the chain of the assassin's watch and jerked it out of his pocket; he replaced the watch, but not the key which fell to the floor, and which I picked up beside the body of the dead man."

Abner turned toward the judge.

"And so," he said, "I charge Simon Kilrail with this murder; because the key winds his watch; because the record in the old deed book is a conveyance by the heirs of Marsh's lands to him at the life tenant's death; and because the book we found in his library is a book on poisons with the leaves uncut, except at the very page describing that identical poison with which Elihu Marsh was murdered."

The strained silence that followed Abner's words was broken by a voice that thundered in the courtroom. It was Randolph's.

"Come down!" he said.

And this time Nathaniel Davisson was silent.

The Judge got slowly on his feet, a resolution was forming in his face, and it advanced swiftly.

"I will give you my answer in a moment," he said.

Then he turned about and went into his room behind the Bench. There was but one door, and that opening into the court, and the people waited.

The windows were open and we could see the green fields, and the sun, and the far-off mountains, and the peace and quiet and serenity of autumn entered. The Judge did not appear. Presently there was the sound of a shot from behind the closed door. The sheriff threw it open, and upon the floor, sprawling in a smear of blood, lay Simon Kilrail, with a dueling pistol in his hand.

19

THE DEVIL'S TRACK

It was a trivial matter that took my Uncle Abner onto the Dillworth lands.

He could not have had an inkling of the tragedy that he rode into.

He used to illustrate this mystery in events with example cases from the Scriptures. One never knew what lay ahead. If he rose up early to his task about the fields he might come upon the Ancient Enemy with his bag of tares sowing the land that he was going down to till.

We could not foresee the activities of the Evil One.

In peace about the duties of the commonplace, a man might come at any moment on the evidences of his tragic work. Under the quiet of his roof and in the serenity of the fields one forgot the inexplicable free hand of the Devil.

It was written in the second chapter of the Book of Job:

> *From whence comest thou?*
> *And Satan answered the Lord, and said,*
> *From going to and fro in the earth, and from walk-*
> *ing up and down in it.*

He did go to and fro in the earth, and sometimes one came on his track and the appalling evidences of destruction where he had walked. One always found some human wreckage about the place.

Abner never undertook to explain this mysterious freedom. But it was clear to him that the dominion of the King of Kings did not exclude the ravages of this marauder. The Devil was no cowardly spirit slipping in covertly in the dark and lying-by hidden in the day, and by insidious indirection pulling down what God built up. He destroyed and ruined, swaggering in his stride across the earth.

And in that work he was open and unafraid.

Had he not with a brazen effrontery unequaled gone in with the sons of God when they came to present themselves before the Lord . . . to present himself? And he had answered in that High Presence with an ironic impudence that staggered the human mind.

He took his freedom with this new world that the Lord had created for His pleasure.

He walked, as he liked, up and down in it.

And it was on this morning of early April that my Uncle Abner came upon his track.

It was the matter of a line fence that took my uncle to the Dillworth lands. A portion of the old rail fence that made the line would no longer turn the cattle. The chestnut rails had rotted, the fence had been repaired on occasion, but the time had arrived when it must be rebuilt.

My uncle had spoken more than once with Dillworth, but he could not be brought to help rebuild the fence.

He said that the fence was not on the line; he had discovered the position of the ancient corners; the fence should be moved back some distance on my uncle's side.

This was a common pretension where one wished to contend with his neighbor about a line.

The fact was that no line of a survey in this western portion of Virginia could be accurately established. The early surveys, at best, had been carelessly run. The hickory and the oak marked for corners, with three chips taken out with an ax, had been felled by the pioneer or rotted down, or been uprooted by the wind. And the county surveyors that followed had completed the confusion.

It was one of these uncertain lines that had now come into dispute between Dillworth and my Uncle Abner.

It was a morning, as I have said, of early April.

The rail fences glistened in the frost. The roads were hard and dry, the fields green as with a close-napped velvet cloth tacked smoothly over them.

Abner entered the Dillworth lands where they extended to the highway.

There was no gate, but the split-rail fence could be anywhere laid down for a horse to cross. He had no hope of bringing Dillworth to an agreement on the matter; and so he intended to go on to Randolph to give Dillworth a legal notice.

Randolph was the justice of the peace and his lands adjoined.

It was a country of little hills and narrow well-sodded valleys, lying westward from the great slope of the Alleghenies, toward the Ohio. It was an old cattle country, long cleared and fenced; held for the most part in great tracts that passed down in families and did not change. The wooded ridges were not cut out and the sodded valleys were rarely broken by the plow.

My uncle Abner ascended the first hill, crossed its summit, and disappeared into the valley beyond.

It was an hour before he came out onto the second hilltop beyond this valley.

The summit of the farther hill had a fringe of wood along its ridge. My uncle stopped behind the screen of this wood, got down from his horse and moved carefully forward among the trees. The whole aspect and bearing of the man had changed. He had ridden into the Dillworth lands at his leisure and with no concern. In ten minutes his great chestnut horse should have covered the distance from the first hilltop to the second.

And yet that journey had occupied an hour.

And Abner had passed from unconcern at the trivialities of life to the tension of its tragedies.

That tension was everywhere in the features and actions of the man.

He moved with caution into the line of timber, leaving the great horse a little below the summit, covered, out of view. The horse remained, unmoving, a cast in bronze, flooded with the morning sun as though it were a pagan idol at the approaches to a sacred grove.

Within an hour, in the crossing of a valley, from one hilltop to another, the purpose, the activities, the whole aspect of the man had changed.

In the seclusion of that hidden valley my Uncle Abner had come on the Devil's track!

He entered the wood and stood for some time searching the second valley beyond the ridge, while he remained himself hidden. Then he returned to his horse and, keeping under cover of the hilltop, made a long detour to the east entirely along the whole range of the hill.

He descended with its slope and entered the second valley as though he had come into the Dillworth lands directly from the Randolph estate on one of the cattle paths winding through the hollows.

He came out of a grove of beech trees into this second valley.

He found Dillworth here separating some bullocks, his horse tied to an oak tree.

The man, overcome with greed, had built his pens and set up his cattle scales in this valley, precisely between the two great grazing boundaries that he possessed. It was a precaution out of avarice. With his cattle scales built here he could weigh the bullock out of its bed and so avoid the loss from drift that other men suffered from driving their cattle out to weigh them on the road. He was now in his cattle pens, on foot, with a club in his hand, picking out some bullocks and forcing them through a gate into another pen.

He was a big man with a heavy face, little shifty eyes and a stolid countenance.

One looking up at him as he passed would have read him incorrectly. He was far from stupid. He was a good judge of cattle. He had a gambler's instinct, a brutal courage that could not be turned aside, and, in the intricacies of a financial matter, he found always some way to his own advantage.

He had, too, a pagan worship of the land.

He would have gone to crucifixion to extend his acres.

He was in debt for the great boundary where he now stood, extending south to my uncle's line, and he had taken a gambler's chance to pay it. As it happened, the running of events was agreeable to his hazard. He had bought up herds of cattle in the hills and now the market had advanced.

He had a silent partner in these transactions, but even with a division of gain he would by this stroke of fortune split his debt in two.

If he had struck out for himself he would have cleared the land. But he was not altogether trusted and his contracts required the buttress of a better name. He was close-mouthed in these affairs and few persons knew the extent of his partner's interest; and those like Abner were not certain.

My uncle got down by the oak and looked over Dillworth's horse, its head, shape of its limbs and its feet.

"You ride a horse taken up from pasture," he said.

The man in the cattle pens went on with his work; he knew the mission on which Abner came, and it did not please him.

"Yes, and before he goes on the road he must be taken to the shop."

That term in the hills meant always the shop of a blacksmith. It had no other meaning.

"It's a good young horse," continued my uncle, "but it is nervous. It has been badly broken."

Dillworth paused a moment in the cattle pens.

"I break them to my will," he said. "When I take an animal in hand I put it in fear of me. It is my way, Abner."

"It is one way," replied my uncle, "but it is not the best way. An animal can be controlled by fear. But it is the last measure to be taken with it. We forget their kindly instinct. A horse, in nearly every instance, will try to do the very best that he can understand. If we take a little patience with him he will invariably reward that patience."

He walked slowly from the oak over the carpet of green sod in the direction of the cattle pens, his hands behind him, his face lifted.

"And there is another reason, Dillworth," he went on. "You will find it written in the Scriptures. 'A righteous man regardeth the life of his beast.'"

Dillworth struck the bullock before him with the club.

"I waste no time on the Scriptures," he muttered.

"But would it have been wasted, Dillworth?" replied my uncle. "I think you would have made a gain of something more than time if you had read the fourth chapter of the Book of Genesis. . . . Do you know that chapter?"

"I do not," replied the man. "But I know the thing that brings you to me, Abner. And it is an idle mission. I will not lay down a rail until the line is set back to the corners."

My uncle stopped sharp in his stride.

"I had forgotten about the fence," he said.

Dillworth closed the gate after the steer; then he turned to Abner.

"Forgotten about the fence!" he echoed. "Then what is the damned business that you are on?"

My uncle made a strange gesture.

"Why, sir," he said, "you have got the very word. 'Damned,' Dillworth, is the word."

The man did not reply. He went on with his work. He was selecting a few thin cattle to take up and feed a little grain. The beef steer in this land were not corn fattened. The herds were turned out to pasture in the early spring. The rich blue grass put on weight. The sod was fed with lime leached out by the rain from the thick stratum that lay along the summit of the hills.

The bullock turned out on such pasture would wax fat, as though he were grain fed.

It would take about five acres to the steer, but with that range in these sodded fields he would put on 300 pounds and be fat for market at the middle of the summer.

But sometimes in the spring, as here with Dillworth, a few thin steers that had not come well through the winter would be taken out of the herd and fed a little grain.

There was not much substance in the first grasses.

And it was a custom to help the thin steer over these first weeks of turning out to grass. Corn on the cob was crushed and fed, a gallon to the bullock, poured out in heap for him on some dry spot of the pasture. But for this additional feeding the thin cattle had to be taken out and kept in some small field apart from the herd.

It was a common custom that Dillworth was concerned with on this April morning.

But he was handling his cattle in a brutal manner, the club in his hand and his harsh voice cursing at the natural effort of the bullock to resist a separation from his fellows. He tramped about his pens while Abner remained standing in the field outside.

My uncle's face was grave and he was fallen into some deep reflection, but he seemed now to come to a conclusion, a plan to follow.

"Dillworth," he said, "the rod of land along a disputed line is no thing to kill for or to burn a roof. I would avoid a quarrel with you. But this fence will no longer separate our cattle, and something must be done."

Dillworth closed the gate on his last bullock and came out of the pens.

He set his club down against the plank fence, tested the iron hook in the staple and came on toward my uncle. These acts, primitive and of no consequence in themselves, seemed to restore the man's composure.

"Now, Abner," he said, "you talk in reason, and I can understand you. But when you come at me in the dark with big threatening words I can only answer you in kind.

"I wish to settle this line matter with you, but I will not be robbed in the transaction. I have discovered the correct position of the corners."

"And how have you discovered them?"

The man did not reply directly. He began at a distant angle.

"Well, Abner," he said, "you know how the line of the present fence between us was determined. Old Haymond laid it out. Stewart, from whom I bought, and Monroe, from whom your father bought, could not agree, and so they sent for this county surveyor to run the line. The deeds they held called for a poplar at the north and chestnut oak at the south. But these trees were no longer standing.

"Stewart said that Monroe's negroes had cut the poplar in the night to get a coon out, and that bee hunters had felled the chestnut oak, and to establish the line they must find the stumps. Monroe held in reply that the whole survey of the region had been pushed west and that to make the line conformable to the plats at Richmond it must be moved back on Stewart. The thing was leading to bad blood, and so they sent for old Haymond with his compass. But what could old Haymond, or for that, the best surveyor to the Crown, do in such a case without the corners?

"And he did the worst thing. He prayed and read the Bible and talked sanctimoniously of goodwill, and kindly feeling, and the love of God, and so got Monroe and Stewart to agree and build the fence.

"That settled nothing, Abner. It only served to send the disputed question on to us."

He stopped and, bending over, wiped his hands on the sod to remove the sweat. And in that posture, his head down near the earth, my uncle suddenly cried out to him:

"Do you hear a voice, Dillworth?"

The man stood up and looked about him.

"Why, no, Abner," he said. "What voice?"

My uncle repeated a strange gesture.

"I had forgotten, Dillworth," he said, "that you do not read the Scriptures. It is all written in that fourth chapter of the Book of Genesis."

Then he turned about.

"But here is your man Twiggs come to help you drive your cattle. If you please, I would like to send him with a note to Randolph. If we are to settle this thing between us there should be a witness and the agreement should be written out in legal form and acknowledged before a justice."

Twiggs, riding a farm horse, had come in from the direction of Dillworth's house and he was now approaching.

Dillworth turned toward him. He did not understand what Abner meant and imagined his Scriptural imagery of language related to the approach of Twiggs. He took also Abner's suggestion to indicate that he would agree to some modification of the line.

This was the gain he sought.

He held out only for some sort of compromise that would add a little to his lands. He was quite willing to send Twiggs on such a mission.

Randolph's house was distant no farther than a mile through the fields, and the cattle in the pens could profitably wait if by that brief delay he could gain a rod of land, made legal by an agreement that could be entered of record in the office of the clerk of the county court.

He called Twiggs in and directed him to carry my uncle's message. Abner tore a page out of a notebook, wrote a few lines on it in pencil and folded it. He handed it up to Twiggs, charging him to give it only into Randolph's hand, and so sent the man riding on his journey.

Twiggs could not read, and for that reason Abner knew that the contents of the note was safe from him. If he could have read it he would have been appalled. For my uncle had written:

> I have found the Devil's track in Dillworth's hollow. Come in with your men.

But in the serenity of his ignorance he rode away, a little man in big jean breeches rolled up to his boot tops and a jacket of the same material buttoned around his middle. He trotted down the valley, through the grove of beech trees, on his way to Randolph . . . on his way to the fatality that bears the name of a god!

There was the dry butt of a locust lying near where Abner stood. It had been intended for a gatepost, but it was hollow when cut into and so had been abandoned. Dillworth came over and sat down on this log. His temper had returned to its stolid equanimity. There is this essential quality in every dull-witted man—a dread of what he does not understand. The alarm about him is more fearful than

in other men when an object moves toward him out of some ob-
scurity. He draws back from it and, when he must, he approaches
it with a greater caution.

Abner had thus thrown him into fear by expressions that he
could not follow and his grave concern had put his temper up. He
understood now the whole drift of the affair and in the relief of it
he turned genial. He bade my uncle sit down beside him, got out
his pocketbook and searched for something in it.

He opened one or two folded papers in his search.

My uncle watched him sharply out of the corner of his eye, and
one of these folded papers that Dillworth quickly hid behind another he particularly noticed. It was only for a moment, for the
fraction of a moment, that the paper opened in Dillworth's fingers, but in that fated instant Abner saw the writing and the name
set on it.

It was a piece of foolscap, ruled with blue lines and folded together. It was soiled and the edges along the folds were worn as
though it had been carried a long time among the papers of the
pocketbook, either by Dillworth or another.

Then he came upon the thing he sought—a little plat made in
red ink on a piece of parchment such as the old land warrants
issued by the governors of Virginia were accustomed to be inscribed
on.

"Here, Abner," he said, "is the survey of my lands, as I bought
from Stewart. You will see that the line between us is a straight
line. But the present corners are two rods east. That is to say, two
rods over on my land. The fool compromise that old Haymond ran
robbed Stewart of two rods along the whole length of that line. It
must have been that in this frolic of good will Stewart was drunk
with liquor. No man in the calm possession of his mind would have
agreed to a thing like that."

He paused and leaned a little toward my uncle. His voice descended into a lower note.

"And I will tell you, Abner, a further circumstance that you do
not know. Before he died old Stewart told me that the agreed line
was a fraud. And he told me where to find the corners."

My uncle spoke then, looking out before him.

"A dead man!" he said.

Dillworth turned a little.

"Why, yes," he said, "Stewart is a dead man. But is that any reason that the information he gave me is a lie?" He put the fingers of his hands together and added with a sanctimonious air:

"The dead do not lie."

"They do not," replied my uncle. "It is the living who lie."

"Then, Abner," continued Dillworth, as if his end was accomplished, "we will set back the line when Randolph rides in to write the paper."

And my uncle answered him, looking out across the fields.

"There may be, then," he said, "the evidence of another dead man to consider."

Dillworth turned sharply toward him. In his concern about his acres he took these words to mean that my Uncle would counter with some equal story attributed to the deceased Monroe.

"What dead man, Abner? Have you also some testimony of a dead man?"

"I have," replied my uncle. "And I know now that this information is correct. You have said it, Dillworth—the dead do not lie!"

The cunning in Dillworth moved him to edge out of this corner.

"It's just an old saying," he muttered. "Old sayings are not always true."

And the reply surprised him.

"You are right, Dillworth," said my uncle. "The old sayings are not always true. Sometimes they are made up out of the very stuff of error. Take for example the old saying: 'Dead men tell no tales.' It is old, Dillworth, but it is wholly and profoundly false. They tell!"

He struck his big knee with his clenched hand.

"And there is no way to stop them. The mouth of the living can be closed by fear or the hope of gain. We can reach the living, but how can we reach the dead?

"Men fancy that there is security in silence. But in silence there is no security. Men may lie, but circumstances cannot."

"Well," said Dillworth, "I know Stewart did not lie about this line. I don't know what Monroe told you."

"Monroe told me nothing," Abner replied. "I was thinking of another dead man."

"Was it Haymond, then? He was gone to the grave before you were old enough to remember."

My uncle answered in his deep, level voice:

"It was no dead man from his grave!"

He arose and walked over to the cattle pens.

"The price of cattle has advanced," he said.

Dillworth caught at that, for it was on ground he knew.

"A dollar a hundred, Abner."

"You have contracted for a thousand cattle," continued my uncle. "You should make a good deal of money, Dillworth, if you do not have to divide it with a partner."

The man remained seated on the log.

"Well," he said, "as it happens I won't have to divide it with a partner."

My uncle turned sharply on his heels.

"As what happens?"

Dillworth shifted his position.

"It was this way, Abner. I took Marsh in when I went out last fall to buy these cattle. I thought they would make some money. We had been partners once in a while in trades, and I thought it was only fair to give him the chance to come in with me. He was mealy-mouthed about it. And I went ahead with the understanding that he could have an interest if he wanted it. A little later, when the market got uncertain, he told me that he didn't want an interest in the cattle I had contracted. That ended it. I went ahead on my own hook.

"But this spring, when the market went up, he wanted me to take him in again. He was here the other day and said he would come back to see me about it. But I told him it was no use to come back. A man can't blow hot and cold with me, Abner. He stays in or he goes out."

He stood up then, as though his slow-moving mind had come to a decision.

"I look for him to come in here today."

And he jerked his head in a sort of gesture toward the hill from which my uncle had first looked down at him.

Abner extended his arm toward the hill and the valley beyond it.

"Over there," he said. "Why would Marsh expect to find you over there?"

The gesture of the head in Dillworth had been unconscious.

"Well," he said, "I don't mean any particular place. I told Marsh that I was coming into this boundary today to get out these thin steers. He might ride anywhere over it to look for me."

Then he added:

"As it happened, the cattle were all on this end of the boundary and I have not crossed the hill. I found them in this valley in their beds about the scales here. I have been here all morning."

Abner did not reply.

He walked around the pens and through the cattle and about the valley, as though he idled, waiting until Randolph should arrive. He had taken up the club that Dillworth had set down beside the gate. It was a section of a dogwood sapling some four feet in length and whittled round at one end as though intended to fit into a hole—the hole of a two-inch auger.

When he spoke he went back to the matter of the partnership which Dillworth had explained.

"If there was no writing between you and Marsh," he said, "there is no legal evidence of any partnership. It would be merely then the question of whose word is taken . . . if Marsh should go before a judge."

"Marsh will not go before a judge," said Dillworth.

My uncle looked out at the hills. Again he spoke in his level voice:

"Perhaps he has already gone before a Judge."

My uncle did not look toward Dillworth. He walked about. He came now to the tree by Dillworth's horse. He stopped by the limb to which the animal was tied and suddenly spoke to Dillworth, extending his arm up the valley.

"Is that far steer lame?" he asked. "Or is it only the roll in his walk?"

Dillworth turned to look in the direction of the bullock, and in the moment that his head was turned Abner made a gesture as though to strike the young horse.

The startled horse went back on his haunches, doubling the limb.

Dillworth turned at the sound.

"This is a dangerous horse," said Abner.

"He's a tame horse," replied Dillworth. "You must have scared him."

"Is there any tame horse?" continued Abner as in reflection. "Do not the Scriptures tell us that a horse is a vain thing for safety? And is it not the common experience of man that a horse may be quiet under him for years and then, with no warning, at some inconsequential thing rear and throw him?"

Dillworth stopped. The words seemed to suggest something to him.

"Why, yes, Abner," he said, "that's the truth. I used to tell Marsh that. You know the horse he rides. It seems tame enough. But I have seen that horse shy at a shadow or a wisp of ragweed in a field, and whirl like a whiplash.

"I told Marsh that his horse would kill him some day. And he will kill him, Abner. As you have said, is there any tame horse?

"Take your own horse, Abner. You think you know him, but how can you tell what he might do if he were startled?"

The horse was a friend and a brother to my uncle. He would go without his dinner, but this horse was fed. He would go without a cup of water, but this horse drank, and wherever he might be this horse was bedded before he slept. It was a greater wonder then that he made this hostile gesture at Dillworth's horse.

"Let us ride out," he said. "Perhaps we shall find Randolph coming in."

He got into the saddle, and the two of them rode east. As they rode my uncle talked.

By the indirectness of this talk he came to Dillworth's form of contract with the graziers. There would be no writing, for such purchases were verbal, and one's word held.

Once given, it was sacred. No cattleman in these hills went back on his word if he were a person of any substance.

What Abner drove at was to find if Dillworth had brought Marsh's name into these transactions. And under the subtleties of Abner's indirections the facts came out. Dillworth had made the contracts in the autumn in his own name, but with the assurance added that Marsh was a partner in the purchase.

"You see, Abner," he said, "Marsh fooled me. I thought he was going in with me, so I told everybody that he was a partner, and so I considered him at the time. Then when he backed out on me I took the contracts over myself."

They came out of the little wood into a larger open valley that led eastward to the highway. The contour of the land formed here the apex of an angle. The first valley which my uncle had entered along on this April morning also came out here. The little rivulets from the two valleys joining at the point made the larger stream that flowed eastward toward the river.

Abner turned his horse into this farther valley. "Randolph has not yet come," he said. "Let us ride in and look at this line fence."

"We had better wait for Randolph," Dillworth said.

My uncle did not pull up his horse. He rode on.

"Why wait?" he said. "Randolph will come in, and if Marsh is looking for you through the boundary we may find him."

There came, for a moment, a dreadful indecision into Dillworth's face.

Then he made his resolution and rode in.

They rode over the carpet of beech leaves, silent. My uncle carried the club that he had picked up at the cattle pen where Dillworth had set it down. They came out into the pasture land beyond the wood and my uncle stopped beside a sled under a tree at the border of the wood.

"You are not careful of your implements, Dillworth," he said. "This sled will rot in the wet summer months."

"It's an old sled," replied Dillworth. "The runners are worn out."

But my uncle remained a moment by the sled, and behind the man as though to verify his theory. Three dogwood standards only were on the sled. The fourth auger hole of the sled frame was empty.

He overtook Dillworth in the next moment.

Suddenly the man beside Abner stopped and pointed toward the rise of the hill.

"There's Marsh's horse," he said. "Now I wonder what has happened."

My uncle looked in the direction at the big gray horse, cropping the grass, the rein under its feet, the saddle empty.

"What could have happened?" replied my uncle. "Marsh has got down to await your coming, Dillworth, and turned loose the horse."

The man swung about in his saddle.

"No," he said, "the thing I have feared for Marsh has happened. That horse has thrown him and he is dead."

The prediction was too true.

They came presently to Marsh lying on the earth, his arm doubled under him. They got down and hurried to the body, but it was clear that the man was dead.

Dillworth made a great gesture, flinging out his hands.

"Good God!" he cried. "What an awful accident!"

My uncle stood looking down at Marsh. He made no exclamation of surprise.

"Accident!" he echoed.

"Why, yes, Abner," Dillworth hurried on, "the very accident against which I have so often warned him."

Dillworth went on as though emotion overcame him.

"Damn the horse," he cried. "If I had a rifle I would shoot it."

"Shoot the horse?"

"Yes!" Dillworth roared. "Shoot the horse! He has killed Marsh and he should not live on to kill another!"

"Well, Dillworth," Uncle Abner said, "the horse cannot speak to deny your charge of murder, and someone ought to speak for him. Let us see what defense the horse could make.

"You will notice, Dillworth, that the injury from which Marsh died is on the top of his head—across the top of his head—and there is a deep, ragged incision in the skull at this point. It is not a general crushing fracture of the skull. It is a sharp narrow fracture, breaking through the bone. The sod could not make that fracture."

"It was a stone!" said Dillworth. "Marsh's head struck on a stone."

"I thought of that," replied my uncle. "But if you will look closely about this portion of the pasture you will see it is free of stones. There is not a stone to be found anywhere around Marsh."

It was true.

My uncle went on in his level voice:

"And in addition to this, if the horse could speak he could present further evidence. He could point out that there has been another horse here."

"How?" said Dillworth. "There is no track."

"Not here," replied my uncle, "but walk with me." And he went with Dillworth to the rivulet. "There," he said, pointing to the stream, "is a clear footprint stamped in the wet earth."

Dillworth stooped over.

"And what of this, Abner?" he said. "Marsh's horse has perhaps crossed here at this grazing."

"Why, no," replied my uncle. "The horse would also clear himself of this if he could speak before the judge. He would say, 'Your Honor, when I was in that pasture I had an iron shoe on every foot, and it was a barefoot horse that has made this print.' And he would speak the truth, Dillworth; you can see that the horse that made that print was barefoot, and you can look at Marsh's horse and you will find him shod all around."

Dillworth remained, looking at the print.

"If it is not the track of Marsh's horse," he muttered, "then it may be the track of the Devil, for all I know."

Abner answered him in his even voice:

"You name the authority correctly," he said. "The Devil has walked here.

"But he was not alone here. There was another with the Devil to do his work for him . . . and I know the man!"

Dillworth stood up at that and faced my uncle with a sullen countenance.

"Then, Abner," he said, "you know more than I know. I was not here."

"Dillworth," replied my uncle, "if you find a man falsifying the details of a thing, will you believe his conclusion on it? Four times this morning I have taken you in a lie. You said Marsh's horse was vicious, and it is the tamest horse in the hills. You said that you found your cattle sleeping by the scales. I looked closely and there was not a bed about them. You said there was no written contract between you and Marsh, and yet when you opened your pocket-book to find the land plat, I saw the paper with your names. You said you were not in this valley, and here is the track of your horse, for I examined his feet by the oak tree and he is barefoot."

His voice became big and dominant.

"Dillworth," he said, "you are a thief and an assassin and a liar!

"There was a profit in this partnership and you wanted the whole gain for yourself . . . so you killed Marsh and stole away the paper that would be evidence against you.

"And, sir," his voice rang as over metal, "you carried the very implement of this murder in your hand. Look at it, Dillworth. It is a standard from that sled yonder. Like the three others, it is a piece of dogwood. The whittled end of it fits the auger hole in the frame."

He cast the dogwood standard of the sled down on the sod before the man.

And at the gesture the primordial brute in Dillworth overcame him. He darted forward with a sort of bellow and seized the club.

". . . and I will kill you too!"

But the sound of horses stopped him in his murderous intent. Randolph and his men were entering the valley.

From whence comest thou?
And Satan answered the Lord, and said,
From going to and fro in the earth, and from walk-
    ing up and down in it.

20
THE GOD OF THE HILLS

Abner used to say that one riding on a journey was in God's hand.

He never knew what lay before him; death standing in the road, invisible, as before the prophet; or a kingdom as in the case of Saul. One set out with his little intention, and found himself a factor in some large affair.

It is certain that my uncle had no idea of what he would come into when he rode on this early summer morning to Judge Bensen's house. It was some distance through the hills and he traveled early, with the dawn. He wished an hour with Bensen before the judge rode in to the county seat; for it was in the court term, and Bensen was the circuit judge.

It was a custom remaining in Virginia after the dominion of King George had passed.

The circuit judges were persons of property and distinction. They traveled on their circuits, holding their courts here and there about the country. There would be a group of counties in a circuit. And the county seat would take its name, not infrequently, from the fact that it was the domicile of these circuit courts. One finds the name remaining—Culpepper Court House, and the like.

Land was the evidence and insignia of distinction in Virginia.

One's importance was measured by his acres.

Every man who would command the attention of his fellows stood on an estate in lands. Judge Bensen lived some miles from the county seat. He had got a thousand acres from his father, and added to it. He had never married. He lived alone, with negro servants, in their white-washed quarters, at some distance from his ancient house. His earnings and his salary from the state went to the purchase of new lands.

He had introduced the Hereford, and turning aside from the customs of the men about him, he bred young cattle, instead of fattening the beef bullock for the market. It happened then that Bensen's young cattle were not easily to be equaled. If one bought from him one got a drove of bullocks of one type, with no mongrel to be sold off to the little trader. Bensen had 200 young cattle—stockers, as they were called—for sale. And my uncle went, early, on this summer morning to see the drove; and to buy the cattle if he could, before Bensen set out for his court—on his horse with his legal papers in his saddle bags.

It was scarcely daylight when Abner descended into the long valley that extended north to the county seat, and in which lay the Bensen lands. At the foot of the hill where the road entered the valley he came on a man sitting his horse in the road. It was early, an hour before the sun, and there was a vague mist in this lowland.

The man and the horse looked gigantic.

Beyond them through an avenue of trees was the heavy outline of a house, still dark, from which the life within it had not yet awakened to the new day.

The whole earth was dry and the road bedded down with dust. My uncle was almost on the man before he knew him. It was Adam Bird, a traveling preacher of the hills, on his gray mare. The big old man was sitting motionless in his saddle looking up through the avenue of maples toward the shadowy house. He did not hear my uncle's horse in the soft dust until it was nearly on him. His hands lay on the pommel of his saddle and his face was lifted like one in some deep reflection.

He called out when he saw my uncle.

"Abner," he said, "do you see that house."

He did not pause for a reply from Abner nor for any formality of salutation. He went on, and directly, as though he merely uttered now aloud the thing that was passing in his mind.

"Caleb Greyhouse lived there until the devil took him. He married Virginia Lewis—for a woman when she is young will be a fool. She is long dead but she left a daughter that is a Lewis too. Not a Greyhouse, by the mercy of God! And now Abner," and he brought one of his big hands, clenched, down on the pommel of the saddle, "these accursed judges are going to dispossess her of her inheritance!"

My uncle knew what the man meant. It was common knowledge. Caleb Greyhouse had left a will written some years before, when the girl was young, leaving his estate, houses and lands, to his daughter, with a bequest to his brother who was to be the guardian and administrator of it. It had been written by Coleman Northcote, one of the best lawyers in Virginia, and so remained, until the girl had grown up. Then, when she had fallen in love, and wished to marry the son of a neighbor with whom Greyhouse had quarreled over a few acres of ridge land, the irascible old man had added a codicil to the will giving the whole estate to his brother, and no dollar and no acre to the girl.

The case was before the circuit court, now sitting, for the girl had got a sort of lawyer, and brought a suit. But she had no money and no case.

Northcote had written the will only too accurately, with precise care for every technical detail. The codicil added by Greyhouse followed the form in Mayo's Guide. It was written and signed by the testator and contained no legal flaw. There seemed nothing that any court could do. Nevertheless, Bensen had called in a judge from a neighboring circuit to sit with him and decide the case. The case was before the judges. And it was the act of these judges and the case before them that moved the traveling preacher of the hills.

"Did Bensen decide the case?" replied my uncle.

"He did not," said Bird, "but the judge with him clamored to decide it and have it done, for he wished to go back to his circuit. Bensen delayed a little for he had a plan of his own about this thing.

He said he would write an opinion and they would decide today. But it was an abominable pretension, Abner. They will dispossess the girl . . . unless the Lord God Almighty moves somewhere in this thing."

Again his big hand descended on the pommel of his saddle, as though he pounded the timber of a pulpit.

"And He will move in it! It is so written in The Book. If the widow and the orphan cry to me I will surely hear their cry."

He brought his big hand up and over his face and his voice descended into a lower note.

"She came to me and said, 'Uncle Adam, will you pray for me to win my case.' And I said I will not pray; for I will not supplicate the Lord God Almighty to do justice. I will call His attention to this wrong. . . . And I stood up and cried to Him! And the word of the Lord came to me. And I saddled my horse, and rode down here and called Bensen out. He came shuffling with his little lawyer talk. It was the law. He had no discretion. He could not help the wrong of it. And besides I was in contempt of his court to talk with him about the case.

"In contempt of his court, Abner!"

And again the old man made his powerful dramatic gesture.

"I, the servant of God, in contempt of his court when I protested against a wrong! . . . I told Bensen that he was in contempt of God's court, and that if he went forward with this injustice Jehovah would include him in the damnation that followed after it."

He paused and looked my uncle in the face.

"For Bensen, Abner, is not guiltless in this thing. He will profit by it. He has coveted these lands as we all know and tried to purchase them. Old Caleb Greyhouse would not sell. But this brother will sell. And Bensen will get the lands he covets."

And again the old man returned to his dramatic vigor.

"And he shall not escape the damnation that followed Ahab the King of Samaria; because he takes the land he covets through the act of another.

"The writing of clerks and seals of courts shall not bring it to him guiltless, even as the writing of Jezebel and the sealing thereof

did not bring the lands that he coveted to Ahab guiltless. . . . I go
now, Abner, as Elijah went to the King of Samaria! And if he say
like that other, 'Hast thou found me, O mine enemy?' I will answer, I have found thee!"

He made a great sweeping gesture and turned his horse north
in the valley. He rode as though he rode alone in the vague mist
that lifted from the lowland and hung above the fields; a thin gray
smoke screen spreading like a blanket.

The old man had not asked whither my uncle rode nor to what
end.

He went like one on some tremendous mission, alone.

Abner followed. The circuit rider had brought a new element
into this affair. A gain to Bensen at the end of it that my uncle had
not considered. But now that the point was touched on he remembered. It was common knowledge that it was a covetous intent with
Bensen to extend his lands; to add a field. He had endeavored to
buy the Greyhouse tract. And it was the truth that while Caleb
Greyhouse would not sell, this brother who took the estate under
the written codicil would sell it to the last acre. He had sold all
that he had received from his father as an inheritance except a few
acres and a house on the highway near the Bensen residence.

There was a dissolute, a reckless strain in the man that was not
in Caleb Greyhouse.

He wished to be a factor in political affairs, and lacking the
confidence of the people he attached his fortunes to other men;
and so he had got to be a sort of deputy about the courthouse, and
a chimney-corner lawyer, with knowledge enough to thumb
through the deed books searching for some defect in a title upon
which he could bring a suit, or extort a blackmail.

He had a marked pride in this pretension.

In the suit before the judges, on the will, he appeared with much
visible ostentation for himself. There was, as it happened, little
peril to his case, for the girl, with no money to hire a competent
attorney, had only a chimney-corner lawyer like himself. And so
the case was one for judges to decide as it appeared, on its face,
before them. . . . Bensen would get the land. This Barnes Greyhouse,

in funds, would try for the Assembly of Virginia. And with money he might win. There was here, as in every land, an element of the electorate that could be persuaded by a demagogue and a little money in the hand.

My uncle rode on after the old preacher, his big chestnut horse moving noiselessly in the deep dust. But his heart was troubled.

The girl came up sharply outlined in his memory: fair-haired and slender, with the hope and the charm of the immortal morning. There was no reason why she should not go, in joy, to the youth that she loved.

He was of a better family and a better blood than Greyhouse.

Because that irascible old man had quarreled with the boy's father about some acres of stony land along a ridge line, everyone of the blood was damned. All were enemies, and endowed by that enmity with every vice.

Old Greyhouse would have no marriage with his enemy.

He fell into a fury of wild talk at the mere mention of it. And on a certain night, heated in that fury, he had written out the codicil that divested his daughter of his estate. It was not certain that at the bottom of the man he, in fact, wished to make that alienation.

In anger, affection is sometimes overridden.

Perhaps if he had had time, in illness, for reflection, he would have canceled it. Blood, as the old adage said, was thicker than water when death approached and one came to pass on the material things that one had gathered together in one's life.

But he had no such time.

Death came on him in the fields.

He had fallen, in harvest, at a stroke of sun. The farm hands carried him in. But he was already out of life. He lay for some hours in a coma, in his daughter's arms. Once, as the field hands told, he tried to stroke her hair and make known to her something that moved vaguely in his mind.

But he had had his hour, and he was granted no extension.

What he had written, he had written.

Death would not release his hand to cancel it.

It was the old eternal story.

Men acted in their anger to do wrong, as though they had a privilege of life; as though at their wish or need, in extremity, they would be granted a stay of execution until they could set their affairs in order and adjust any wrong they had accomplished.

The day was breaking.

The fog, extended through the valley, was lifting and parting into long streamers of white mist. The hills in the distance were sharp and clear in the morning light. In a short time the sun would appear. Already in the fields the cattle were at pasture.

My uncle had come up with the circuit rider.

And at once when the big chestnut emerged from the mist by his gray mare, the old man began to talk. He began, as before, with no introductory sentence.

"Abner," he said, "your father lived long in this land, and he did good in the sight of the Lord and not evil. And I can name a hundred men like him who have stood for righteousness. But in that company there is no Greyhouse. Old Caleb was the best. He was hard and mean but he was not a liar nor a thief. But this other, this Barnes Greyhouse, is the worst of an evil generation. His hands are full of evil. Did not little Benny Wilmoth, in despair, shoot himself in his house because this creature searching through the deed books found a defect in his title and brought a suit to dispossess him of his farm. It was a sort of murder, Abner!"

He thrust his clenched hand out.

"There was no law to hale Barnes Greyhouse into the court and hang him. But was he any less guilty for that lack? The hand of Virginia could not reach him. But, Abner, is he beyond God's hand? By little twists and turns a nimble man may slip away from the law. But he will not slip away from the vengeance of God."

His clenched hand made a great sweeping curve, as though it cleared a swathe before him.

"Abner," he said, "I will not be silent before this outrage. I will call Bensen to his door and warn him. I have seen it in a dream. He is a party to this wrong, and the Lord will make his house like the house of Jeroboam, the son of Nebat . . . and this Barnes Greyhouse!" He spread out the fingers of his extended arm as in the pronouncement of a curse. "As the dogs licked up the blood of Ahab in the pool of Samaria, shall the dogs lick up his blood! . . . for in shame, and in blackness, and in violence shall he go out of life!"

My uncle did not reply. This old man of the hills who stood for righteousness, like all who give themselves wholly to some principle of honor, had the dignity of the thing behind him. And he was not afraid. Neither courts nor judges could overawe him.

My uncle was in a deep reflection. He knew of this matter what was current gossip in the hills. But he did not know, until this morning, the sweeping terms in which Caleb Greyhouse, in his anger, had written out the codicil to this will. It would be, he had imagined, a sort of guardianship in the brother over the girl's estate until she came to a legal age, or some manner of trust. With such a writing there would be hope. But with a direct bequest in terms there would be no hope.

He was in a great perplexity and his mind turned from the mission on which he came.

It was broad day now with the sun beginning to appear. They drew near to Bensen's house.

In the pasture by the road strolling down to water at the brook were the drove of young Hereford cattle. They were unequaled; as like in form and coloring as though they were all born of one mother, by some miracle of maternity on the same day of the year, and so reared and suckled. No cattleman of the hills could have passed that drove and not pulled up his horse to look it over, for in his mind's eye, after that, he would have carried the model for all other young cattle in the world.

And yet my uncle did not pull up his horse.

The two men passed in silence and, making a sharp turn in the road beside some oak trees, came to Bensen's house. They stopped in wonder. The house was open; the negroes were hovering about as in a panic. Randolph's gig was before the door. He came out when they appeared.

"Abner," he said, "you are come, and I was about to send a negro for you. Bensen is dead!

"You arrive also, Adam," he said, "as at a direction of God. It is the house of death that you have come to, and it is one of the duties of the preacher of the Gospels to minister to the dead. Come in."

"I will not come in," replied the old man. "But I will get down and sit before the door, for I did not come in peace."

But my uncle cried out astonished.

"Dead!" he echoed. "Bensen dead! What killed him?"

"Now, that," replied Randolph, "is the mystery that I was about sending after you to solve. Bensen was killed in the night as he sat here in his library at work among his books."

On the way in with Abner, Randolph explained the details of what had happened.

The circuit court was sitting.

The case over the will of Caleb Greyhouse was on the docket.

For some reason Bensen wished another judge to sit with him to decide the case and so had called in West from a neighboring circuit. There was no reason for this, Randolph said, for there was no ground on which to contest the will. Coleman Northcote had written it some years before. Northcote was the best chancery lawyer in Virginia, and he made no errors in a legal paper. The will was correctly drawn, signed by the testator, and witnessed as the law required.

Later, Caleb Greyhouse had added a codicil in his own handwriting, on the blank sheet of the will. The codicil followed the form in Mayo's Guide and was signed, dated, and sealed in every feature, also as the law required.

Of course this attack on the will broke down at once. There was no technical error in it.

The codicil added below the will on the same sheet of foolscap was also unassailable. It followed the legal form, was written by the testator in his own hand and signed by him.

It became thus, under the law of Virginia, a holograph will and required no witnesses.

West wanted to decide the case at once from the bench, so he could get back to his circuit. But Bensen said they would take it under advisement until morning.

That night all the negroes about the place went to a frolic at the county seat.

They left the judge at work in his library, when they went out at dark.

In court time it was the custom of the judge to work late over his legal papers and so they had put new candles in the sticks on his table and lighted them before they left the house. They had been delayed in setting out, and as they left the house the judge had come to the door and directed them to stop on the way and ask Barnes Greyhouse to come and see him.

The man lived not farther than a quarter of a mile along the road.

They gave the message and saw him take his hat and cane and set out.

The frolic ran late. It was well toward dawn when the servants returned.

There was no light in Bensen's library or about the house and they naturally assumed that the judge had put out the lights and gone to bed.

In the morning when they came into the house they found the tragedy, and in terror sent for Randolph.

He found the library as the assassin had left it, for the negroes had not gone in.

The judge had been killed as he sat before his table. He had been struck down from behind, apparently without warning. The assassin had used the poker from the fireplace. It was a terrific blow for it had crushed in the skull. The man had fallen sidewise under the table, for a second blow aimed at him had struck the table itself, leaving an indentation in the walnut wood.

The iron fire-poker lay on the floor behind the chair in which the judge had been sitting.

The deed had been done late, for the candles had burned down almost to the cup of the sticks before they had been extinguished. They had been snuffed out.

Randolph pointed out the iron poker, the mark on the walnut table, and the blood smear on the hardwood floor where the judge had fallen. Abner looked carefully about the room. And while he thus studied the situs of the crime, Randolph gave his opinion.

"This, Abner," he said, "will be the work of some vindictive convict. Our circuit judges are always in peril from these creatures when they come back from the penitentiary. I have seen them, when they were sentenced, scowl hard at the judges and mutter what they would do in revenge, when they should at length go free.

"This will be the work of such a creature. Bensen, in the counties of his circuit, will have sentenced all sorts of men for all sorts of felonies.

"But it is a peril of honor, Abner. And the one who dies from it dies in the service of his country, as though he died in battle before her enemies."

My uncle did not reply.

But there came a voice through the open door in answer.

The voice of the old circuit rider sitting in the sun. "He did not die in honor, Randolph. Bensen died as a dog dieth!"

Randolph made a gesture as of one who dismisses the extravagances of a child with whom he will not contend. He got out some sheets of paper and sat down at a corner of the table to make a note of the details of the tragedy, accurately as he had found them on this morning.

Abner remained standing by the table, his big hand gathered about his chin, looking at the two tall candlesticks, with their bits of candles burned down to the cups.

New tallow candles had been put in on this night. These candles would burn long, almost from the dark till morning. They had been put in new on this night, and there was only a fragment left when the assassin had snuffed them out.

It was some time before my uncle moved, then he took up the snuffers and with the sharp point lifted the bits of candle out of the cups of the candlesticks.

But he did not otherwise disturb them.

He replaced them as they had been, put down the snuffers at their place, and went over to the far corner of the room.

There lying in the corner was a thing that he had noticed but upon which he had made no comment. It was a small fragment of wood.

At first he had thought it a chip from the table broken off by the impact of the blow that had been directed at Bensen as he fell forward under it. But the table was walnut, and this fragment was some dark wood of a close texture. He did not take it up, nor disturb it where it lay in the corner, but he stooped over and studied it intently.

He arose, went over to the fireplace.

He took up the iron poker and turned it about in his hand.

There was a coating of ashes on the poker, extending from the point halfway to the handle, and over this toward the point was the blood of the man who had been murdered.

Abner put the poker down and remained for some moments by the hearth.

No fire had been lighted in it on this night. But there was a heap of wood ashes where former fires had burned. Abner looked about him.

Randolph wrote sitting at a corner of the table with his back toward him. The old circuit rider was invisible beyond the open door; the negroes had withdrawn in frightened groups beyond the house.

There was no one to question the thing he did—for he was not yet ready to be questioned—and kneeling down on the brick hearth he put his hand into the heap of ashes.

Then he withdrew his hand, smoothed the surface of the heap as it had been, dusted the ashes from his hand, and rose.

He went around Randolph to the door and stepped out.

It was early in the morning.

No one had arrived, for the servants when they had found Bensen dead had sent word only to Randolph, through the hills. And Abner and old Adam had come by chance.

Abner did not pause.

He went on across the grassplot to the road. He stopped there and looked carefully about.

Then he walked north in the dust of the road, in the direction of the county seat. He went slowly, pausing now and then, and retracing now and then a step. Finally he stopped, advanced, returned, and stood still.

There was a little wood of scrub oak on his right hand, and a rail fence. He crossed the fence and began to look about in this tangle of scrub oak.

It was some time, perhaps half an hour, before he got back to the house.

There was a haircloth sofa, facing toward a bookcase in a far corner of the room. Abner went past Randolph to the sofa and leaning over the back put down on it something that he had brought with him, concealed under his long coat.

He returned to the table where Randolph sat before his sheets of paper.

The man had been so taken up with what he wrote that he had not marked my uncle's absence.

Abner put out his hand and took up, from beyond Randolph, a law book with a cracked back. It was a volume of early legal reports.

The book fell open midway of the volume where the back was cracked.

And when my uncle saw the page before him his face changed.

He read and his features hardened.

He was about to speak when the voice of a man entering from the road stopped him.

It was Barnes Greyhouse.

He was a big man with a heavy brutal face laid over with a sort of fawning geniality. He walked with a slight limp, for in some drunken brawl, at an earlier time, he had been injured.

Randolph rose as the man came in; and my uncle turned about toward the door.

But he did not move.

The man blurted out a jumble of greeting and amazed expletives at the tragedy.

"Good God!" he said. "Bensen murdered. Who could have killed him?"

My uncle did not reply.

But Randolph made a little gesture as of one who has penetrated to a meaning hidden from other men.

"It is the work of some convict that Bensen has sent to the penitentiary. Such creatures hold always a vindictive resentment against the judge; as though their punishment were his work."

"You are right, Randolph," said Greyhouse. "That's the explanation."

He uttered the words as though the conclusion could not be gainsaid, and was a pronouncement in finality. But there was a sort of eagerness in the voice and manner of the man.

My uncle spoke then.

"Greyhouse," he said, "you were here last night."

The man turned with a gesture of assent.

"Yes," he said, "early in the night. The negroes passing said Bensen wished to see me, and I walked down. But I was here for a few moments only. The judge had sent for me to say that he and West would decide the case at once when they convened in the morning, and that I should come early into the court. I left the judge as I found him, sitting at his table there, and walked home. It was early; about dark."

"Were the candles lighted on Bensen's table?" inquired my uncle.

"Yes," replied the man, "just lighted, I think, as I came in; it was about dark."

"And the candles, Greyhouse; were they new tall candles, as the negroes say?"

"Yes, Abner," he replied, "I can answer that. They were new tall candles for I noticed the flicker of the wick where the pointed ends had not yet caught up with the tallow."

Abner leaned over the table and took up Randolph's pencil.

"That is an important fact," he said, "for fragments only of these candles were burning in the sticks when the assassin snuffed them out after the murder. I think a note should be made of your observation to confirm what the negroes say."

He put out his hand with the pencil in his fingers to write a line on Randolph's memorandum. But he bore too heavily and the point of the pencil broke. He turned toward Greyhouse with the pencil in his hand.

"Lend me your knife," he said.

The man took a penknife from his breeches and handed it to my uncle. Abner opened the knife and turned back to the table. But he did not sharpen the pencil. He put down the knife and pencil on the table and stood up.

My uncle looked hard at Greyhouse.

"You think Bensen was killed, late in the night, by some vindictive assassin who slipped in behind him. Is that our belief, Greyhouse?"

"Why, yes," he said, "that is the obvious conclusion. Here are the candles burned down to the cups and the bloody poker. It is indicated in these evidences. Bensen was murdered by some released convict who had a grudge against him, and slipping in behind killed him with the poker."

He was interrupted by a voice; a voice big and dominant that seemed to envelop and fill up the room. "Bensen was not killed with the poker."

The three men turned as with a single motion of their bodies.

The old circuit rider was standing in the door. Greyhouse cried out at the words.

"How do you know that?"

The old circuit rider looked hard at the man.

"I know it," he answered, "as God knows it."

Then he closed his mouth and was silent.

It was my Uncle Abner that broke the silence.

"Adam is right," he said, "Bensen was not killed with the poker, nor in the time or manner that these evidences would indicate, for they are false and set up to mislead. There is blood on this poker. But there was no blood from the fracture of the skull that killed the judge and therefore there would be no blood on the implement with which the blow was dealt. There was hemorrhage only from the dead man's face where he lay under the table. But this poker

was not there. It lay on the floor behind the chair. And consequently, it was made bloody by design."

He paused and turned toward the table.

"But this," he said, "was not the first thing that puzzled me.
The first thing was the aspect of these candlesticks. If new tallow
candles had burned down in them to the cups, the shafts of the
sticks would have been fouled over with dripping grease. They were
not so fouled. The shafts of the candlesticks were clean as you see
them. How could that happen? The wicks of the bits of candles
had been snuffed out. That was clear. But how could the candles
have burned down to these bits, and there follow no drip of tallow?

"There was a reason. And I found that reason."

He took up the iron snuffers and with their sharp point lifted
the bits of candles out of the cups of the sticks. The explanation
was apparent. The candles had been cut off with a knife.

There was silence and he continued:

"What had become of the candles? I searched the room here. I
found a certain thing but not the candles."

He made a gesture toward a distant corner, and went on.

"I looked again at the poker. It had a coating of wood ashes on
it, as though it had been thrust into the heap yonder in the fireplace. Thrust in before it had been dipped into Bensen's blood, for
the coating of ashes was underneath the blood. . . . Then I found
the candles."

He crossed the room with long strides, seized the poker, thrust
it into the heap of ashes in the fireplace, and raked out the two
long candles, cut off at their tips.

He put down the poker and stood up.

"The whole thing was clear now. Bensen had been killed early
in the night when the candles were hardly lighted, and with some
implement other than this poker; by one who had acted on a sudden determination to thus kill; and after the act endeavored to falsify events. He cut off the candles and snuffed them out. He made
a hole in the ashes with the poker and concealed them and then,
remembering that an implement must be found, had thought of

the poker in his hand, and dipping it in the man's blood laid it on the floor behind the chair."

My uncle turned toward Greyhouse.

"Greyhouse," he said, "you are the one who came here early in the evening!"

The features of the man sagged and sweated. But there was a certain courage in him.

"Abner," he cried, "you go mad with your neat little conclusions. Why should I wish Bensen's death? I of all persons would wish his life; for today he and West would decide this will case in my favor."

Again the room reverberated with a voice that filled it. Again the old circuit rider spoke.

"Greyhouse," he said, "you are a liar! . . . I saw this thing in a dream; not all, but a fragment of it. I saw you and Bensen in this room, in anger. He beat a book, opened on the table, with his clenched hand and, from behind, you advanced on him, with something in your hand . . . not the poker, for it was setting against the chimney. You are a liar!"

The big accused creature wavered.

And Abner spoke, when the old man had ended.

"Yes, Greyhouse," he said, "you are a liar. I understand the whole thing to the end, although I have had no part in Adam's vision. That which was confused and hidden is now disclosed and clear. Bensen coveted these lands and he undertook to force you to a sale; a sale that would be a sort of dividing of the loot."

He crossed to the table and opened the volume of Virginia reports at the page where it fell apart from the broken back.

"Look!" he said. "Look, Randolph. Here on this page is the syllabus of a decision of the Supreme Court of Virginia, holding that a will and its codicil must be uniform to be valid. It cannot be half in one form and half in another. If the body of the will is written by someone other than the decedent and signed and witnessed, then the codicil must be so written and signed and witnessed.

"I understand it. I understand it clearly to the end. Bensen found this case last night and he sent for Barnes Greyhouse and held the case over him like a club to force a sale of these lands to him at some little price. He must take the price or Bensen would bring in the case today. And so they quarreled, and Bensen beat the book for emphasis, breaking the back under his clenched hand. . . . And so Barnes Greyhouse killed him, knowing that West had no knowledge of this case and would decide in favor of the will, and the girl, with no money, could not take it to a higher court!"

There was utter silence. Then my uncle went on. "Where is your cane, Greyhouse?"

The man did not reply, but his baggy face began to tremble.

"I will answer for you," continued Abner. "Listen, Greyhouse. I went over your track in the dust of the road. It was a clear track and beside it, also in the dust, was the round imprint of the ferrule of your cane. It was all along beside your tracks as you came here from your house, but on your return it was only to be seen beside your tracks for a certain distance. At the field of scrub oaks, on the right of the road, I could no longer find it. What did that mean, Greyhouse? It meant that at this point you had thrown the cane away. . . . And why did you throw it away? Because you discovered, there, on your way from this murder, that the cane with which you had killed Bensen had suffered an injury that you might be called on to explain. Look, I will show you, for I found it in the scrub-oak wood by the roadside." He took up the cane from where it was hidden by the sofa and presented it to the man. It was a big heavy crook-handled cane of black wood like teak, and a split-off fragment at the turn of the crook was missing.

"Look at it, Greyhouse," he cried. "Look at it! A piece at the turn of the crook is missing, split off when the cane struck the table, under the powerful blow that you aimed at Bensen when he went down out of the chair. And that piece of it is yonder in the corner of the room."

He crossed with great strides, picked up the fragment of wood, and placed it on the crook of the cane. "Look, Greyhouse, how the piece fits!"

He made a great gesture.

"There is other evidence against you. Why, sir, it cries like the blood of Abel . . . your knife, there on the table, has tallow on the blade where you cut the candles!"

Panic was on the trapped man and he bolted past my uncle through the open door.

But his foot tripped at the sill and he fell headlong outside, on the flag-paved path. His head struck a fragment of sharp curb and a thin trickle of blood flowed out. Then he got staggeringly to his feet to escape. But my uncle overtook him and the negroes hurried up to help pin him down.

In the confusion as they drew near, the two hounds hovering about them paused and began to lick the blood where it had trickled on the curb.

The old circuit rider—sitting motionless in the sun, his white head uncovered, his big body, clothed in its rusty-colored homespun, filling up the chair—put out his hand and pointed to the thing.

It was the fulfilling of the prophecy.

As the dogs licked up the blood of Ahab in the pool of Samaria, so shall the dogs lick up his blood.

21

The Dark Night

It was night. The dark had fallen swiftly.

The heavens had been overcast all day, with a shower of rain in the afternoon. There had been no twilight. The dark had descended like a black cup put down over the world. There was a threat of rain in the autumn night, and of the chill of the approaching winter.

The road, narrow and wooded on either side, went slowly up. There was no fence and occasionally the horse, missing his way, went into the bushes. It was incredibly dark; a thick palpable dark. Abner could not see the road. He could not see the big chestnut horse under him.

But both my uncle and the horse knew the country and the road they traveled.

My uncle rode with the bridle slack in his hand. He was in a deep reflection, for he had come, without warning, on one of those mysterious complications of events that sometimes await us at a crossroads or beyond a turn of the way.

Randolph, when he could not understand these things, used to write down as an explanation of his verdict that they had occurred by an act of God. But it was a term that my uncle vigorously rejected. God had no part in these affairs. Randolph would quote the English judges and Mr. Blackstone. But my uncle was sternly against the term. They were acts of the devil, and if Randolph wished to set down the truth, not by the act of God, but by the abandonment of God, his verdict should be written.

He had by chance turned aside one of these misleading verdicts.

But for him on this autumn evening, the plan not of God but of the devil would have gone forward, darkening the affair into a mystery that could not be solved, and must be dismissed with Randolph's verdict. But he had come on it, by chance, in time.

He rejected, also, that word "chance." It was a fool's word like so many others in our tongue. There was a purpose in every moving of events. Because the understanding of that purpose was denied us, we disclaimed the purpose. It was a way writ large in the affairs of men.

It was wisdom in my uncle to leave the horse to his devices. He knew the road, and whither his master journeyed. And he had the instincts of his race and his own experience to guide him. When my uncle's stirrup touched the bushes he corrected his direction, and so with care kept to the middle of the road. Perhaps, also, in the dark he could see better than the man, for his people carried no lights about the fields and had only their eyes to aid them. Doubtless in the old time, when the early man accepted the light the sky gave, he had as good an eye; when he ran in the dark by the wolf's muzzle, or fled from the trumpeting mastodon in the flat land, he was the equal in his parts of any other creature—his ear was as keen and his eye as able to manage in the dark. But when he got him lamps and candles and devious devices to help him out he became a lesser creature in himself.

And my uncle always remembered what we usually forget, that within the field of his activities, and according to his experience of life, the animal does not make mistakes. Errors are too deadly dangerous to him. A single one may result instantly in death. He used to point out to the careless urchin that if the little animal he pursued forgot a single thing that he had learned or made a single error in his judgment, he would not live a day. The human lout could blunder on and live, but not so the rabbit in the meadow or the gray squirrel in the tree top.

What the horse has learned he knows. You can trust him to remember. He will not forget. And on this night in early autumn my uncle trusted to his horse. It had its base, I think, in the fact that my uncle never deceived the horse: He acted always with him as one would with a man of honor. He kept always the word and the gesture of his promise to him, with a strict accounting that was never permitted to relax.

The road ascended to a hilltop, winding in and out among the trees.

The horse with care followed it, although no detail of the way was visible. The threat of rain in the chill air became manifest in a patter on the leaves and the splash of a vagrant drop on Abner and the horse. But before it gathered into a steady downfall a light appeared, and presently, as though he had come out onto the level of a hilltop, the horse stopped.

The light was the gleam of a lantern in a stable, and presently at my uncle's call the bulk of a man appeared.

He was a big man with stooped shoulders so marked that it gave him the aspect of a hump. He stood in the doorway with the lantern thrust out before him so he could see who it was that sat the horse yonder in the dark. The strained posture in the man was that of fear. And for the moment, with the fear on him, he was silent. Then, when he knew who came, the aspect of fear fell from him like a garment. For a moment there were immobility and uncertainty on the man; then, as on the instant, an idea, vaguely at the back of his mind, advanced and seized him. He stood up like one who, fearing a menace, finds a blessing at his hand.

"Abner!" he cried. "Light off, and let me put away your horse. I am glad to see you."

"Brant," replied my uncle, "you may not be glad to see me, for I do not come in peace."

My uncle's words sounded distant and detached in the dark. But the man took only a casual notice of them. He was ridden by the idea in his mind.

"I know, Abner," he answered with a laugh. "I owe you a little money. But we will not quarrel over it. Light off."

It was a term in the hills taken from the Scriptures. And it was a common form of greeting when one rode in and the host came out in welcome.

My uncle did not reply. The rain was beginning to fall. He got down and led the horse into the stable, removed the saddle, bedded him down and fed him. And as he went out he passed his hand over him, as in a manner of caress.

He did also a further thing; as he passed the bin from which he had taken out the corn for the horse, he put down a piece of silver on the lid. In the dark Brant would not find it. But it would be there for him when the light came. Then he went out with the man to the house.

Brant went before with the lantern.

It swung with the man's stride, and my uncle following looked carefully at the earth, lighted at Brant's feet. The rain was falling and the clay of the road was wet.

They came to the long portico before the old house and went in. There was no light anywhere about the house, for the man's wife had gone back to her people and was dead; and by the mercy of God, as the country said it, there were no children. No negro would live here and the farm hands could be hired only for the day.

The man was impecunious and mean; a hard master and one not to be endured; and with that larger vice, a courage to take where a value could be taken and not count the cost, if his cunning could find a way. And yet withal he did not prosper. He was in debt, and among his creditors he owed my uncle.

Brant stopped a moment on the portico and looked out toward the west.

He was motionless and the light now unmoving lay about his feet. Then he turned with an intake of the breath that in the silence was clearly audible. It was like the act of one in some anxiety or of one who waited on an event that might make or mar him.

Then he lifted the latch and went in.

He carried a lantern of that old type that the peddlers used to sell, made of tin and punched with holes, with a candle in it. He took out the candle and lighted some others about the room. They were the tallow candles of the time, in the flat tin candlestick that the peddler carried also in his pack. They were cheap, and here in Brant's house they were uncleaned and coated over with old grease.

He placed them on a table and went over to the fireplace. There was a blackened log in it and some half-burned embers. He raked them together, added some bark from a wood box on the hearth and lighted them with the candle. Then he stood up.

"Abner," he said, "you will have some supper?"

"No," replied my uncle. "But while you eat I will stand here by the fire."

He came over to the chimney and spread out his hands to the flame. It was cold, as I have written, and he was damp from the rain.

It was late for the evening meal in the hills, for men got up with the dawn and lay down with the dark, as, from all evidence, Nature intended them to do. Brant took my uncle's answer to mean that he had eaten, but this was not the fact. The meaning behind Abner's negative had a larger purpose. It was an old, deep-seated feeling in our fathers that they would not eat in a house to which they did not go in friendship as a guest, unless it was a public house in which they could pay down for the service.

The man went out to the kitchen with his candle and my uncle remained standing before the fire. It caught, crackled and flamed up, and with the two candles on the table the room was in a manner lighted.

It was a big old room of an ancient house, with windows of small panes looking toward the west; the direction from which my uncle had ridden up; the direction toward which Brant had turned about for that tense moment on the portico. It was a low room with the long poplar rafters visible. They had been whitewashed in an earlier time and the flakes of lime had scaled off and fallen. There was a worn rag carpet on the floor, some ancient chairs and a table. The table stood midway of the room before the fire, and among the litter on it was a German Bible.

It was an old and notorious ornament; a piece of ancient furniture, well known in the neighborhood. It had been brought in by the first Brant on a pack horse when he crossed the mountains from the east, and carried out of Europe in a sailing ship. It was a massive book with a brass clasp and a lock.

It was, as I have written, a piece of furniture, for it had remained, locked, there on the table for all time that any one in the
neighborhood could remember. It was a gibe at Brant that he never
opened it, and it was a common gossip. A comment on it did not
escape old Adam Bird in his direct and drastic sermons: "As Brant
kept the Word of God shut in with a lock in this world, so would
Satan keep Brant shut in with a lock in the world to come."

There were no indirections in the sermons of old Adam Bird.

"Do you hint at me?" one had said to him. And he replied, "I do
not hint at you, sir; I name you by your name!"

And so he had named Brant by his name when he spoke of his
locked Bible. But the Bible was sometimes opened, for the key had
come down with the book; at his wife's death, when they had
brought her back for burial, Brant had unlocked it for the preacher.

Two things about the room drew my uncle's attention as he
stood before the fire. This ancient Bible on the table was one of
them and the other was a long-barreled deer rifle on two dogwood
forks above the fireplace.

Abner looked up at the rifle and moved closer to it. His face
became grave. The deep lines came out. In the gleam of the fire it
was a face of bronze. He reached up and took the rifle down, turned
it over, fingered it a moment about the hammer and replaced it on
the dogwood forks. He turned then toward the Bible on the table;
an aspect of it caught his eye. He went over to it with a definite
purpose. It was locked, but nevertheless he was able with some
difficulty to accomplish the thing he had in mind.

He returned now to the fire.

But the aspect and the manner of the man were changed. He
was no longer in that deep reflection, detached, puzzled, as when
in the dark, he had trusted for the highway to his horse. He stood
now before the fire, his hands behind him, his face lifted, his lined
features firm and resolute.

He was hardly back in this posture before the fire when Brant
entered. He came in with his candle from the kitchen, snuffed it
out between his fingers, replaced it in the tin lantern on the hearth

and went over to the window that looked out across the portico to the west. He peered out; his big body doubled over.

"What do you look for, Brant?" said my uncle. The man started and stood up.

"Why, nothing, Abner," he replied. "I would see if the rain comes."

"If you look only for the rain," said Abner, "you will find it. It comes. It is here."

It was in fact come with an increasing vigor. It pattered on the roof and ran off into the gutters. And my uncle added to his words:

"But sometimes, Brant, a man will look for a thing that does not come. Chance, as men say, thrusts in, or the providence of God prevents it. . . . Do you believe in the providence of God, Brant?"

For a moment the man looked quietly at my uncle before the fire at the end of the half-lighted room. Then there came a gleam of some resolution in his face.

"I don't know, Abner," he said. "But if it sent you to my house tonight I am ready to believe in it."

"Believe in it, then," replied my uncle, "for it surely sent me to your house."

Brant turned back into the room. He made a gesture as of one who dismisses a thing of no importance.

"And I am glad to see you, Abner. I live alone and the neighbors are not friendly. I am glad to see you, even if you come to collect a debt. It is an honest debt, for I bought the heifer of you and gave my due bill for the price. And I will pay it if you will wait a little. Not long, Abner—not long. I shall have the money for you soon. Times are hard. The meadows have been dwarfed by drought. There is only half a crop of hay, and the pasture is light. It will be a hard winter we go into. But you hurt me, Abner, when you say like old Adam Bird that you do not come in peace. A debt is no matter for a quarrel. One may overlook the tirades of old Adam, stamping about his pulpit, for there is no one of us exempt from his indictments. He has included me on more than one occasion; damned me, Abner, and set apart a place in hell for me. But he cannot send me to that selected place."

"He cannot. But there is one who can."

"What one?" said Brant.

"Yourself," said Abner.

Brant laughed. But it was the sort of laughter that did not reach within him. He glanced over his shoulder toward the window. But there was only the dark outside and the rain. If he looked for something through that window it did not arrive.

The thing did not escape my uncle. But he was silent, and Brant went on. He put out his arm and struck his clenched hand on the table.

"Old Adam is an intolerable nuisance. Why should we put up with his vitriol tongue? If he were a younger man he would be called to account. His hymn book would not save him. There is no license in a preacher to villify a citizen. One could have the law on him for this abuse."

The man ran on as though he talked to gain time in which to consider some vital thing. And at his words there came a grim smile over my uncle's features. There came as in a picture the old circuit rider haled into the circuit court for slander. It would be a scene worth traveling far to see, and it would crowd the court room and the road outside; from every quarter the people would travel in. They would come early in their wagons, as to the county fair. There would be miles of horses. It would be an event without a parallel. And with one like Brant to bring the action, it would be an event incomparably dramatic. And a debacle in its issue.

No judge in Virginia could control old Adam before that audience. He would turn the court into a meetinghouse, the bench into a pulpit. No earthly power could stop him. He would be, in his conception, in such a case, the prophet of the Lord and above all temporal authority. The judge could not lock him up. He could with dignity do one thing only, withdraw and leave the old man to preach his sermon. And if Brant had been flecked with a whip before, he would now be scourged with a scorpion.

But the words of the man were idle, and to cover another purpose. He talked to give himself time for a decision. And he approached it with what he now came to say.

"Where is Randolph; at his house or on a journey?" It was a query that my uncle did not expect.

He looked down at Brant, for there was something in the man's face that puzzled him. Did he wish that Randolph might be absent? Did he fear him? Did he on the contrary hope for something from him? With all that Abner knew on this tragic night, this inquiry seemed a strange one to make. He gave the answer with his eye on Brant.

"Randolph will be at his house tomorrow."

My uncle was astonished at the answer.

"Tomorrow," said Brant, "we will both go to him."

There was a sudden gust of rain against the window, and Brant turned, looking over his shoulder. But there was nothing to be seen through the window.

"Why should I go with you?" Abner said.

"Because you are here," replied Brant. "And I am glad you came to see me, Abner," he added.

And he was pleased. There could be no doubt about it.

"Abner," he said, "from which direction did you come?"

"From the west," my uncle said.

"You would pass, then, near Nathan Arnold's house?"

"Yes."

"It is time he should be back with the money for the cattle that he drove overland to Baltimore. He would owe you, Abner, as he owes me and the others."

He hesitated before he added his final sentence. "Did you by chance meet him on the way?"

"No.

"Was there anyone in his house?"

"There was no one in his house," replied my uncle, "and I came on here."

Brant leaned back in the chair, like one escaping from a pressure. He took a deep breath, filling his lungs far down. He passed his big hand over his face.

My uncle observed him closely. The relief in the man at his reply was clearly obvious.

But he gave no sign that he had observed the change, and he added:

"The house seemed empty. Arnold's wife, I believe, is on a visit to her father over the mountains."

"Yes," said Brant. "It is a long journey, but he should be back, Abner, with the money."

He referred to a custom in the hills. A cattleman would make up a drove to go overland to Baltimore, purchasing his bullocks from the graziers, and he would pay with the money he brought back from his sale. There was no adequate way to transport money by drafts and checks, and so the cattleman carried back the money with him.

Brant rose. He walked about the room. And as he walked he looked out through the windows toward the west.

Abner knew what was moving in his mind.

"Do you look for a light, Brant?"

The man pulled up with a jerk; his face startled.

"A light?" he said. "Why should I look for a light?"

"Well," replied my uncle, "you might be looking for a light in Arnold's house. It is time, as you have said, for him to be home from Baltimore, with the money for the cattle. If he arrived in the night he would set a candle burning."

Brant's face cleared.

"I was not looking for a light in Arnold's house."

Then my uncle said:

"Arnold will not be in his house tonight."

"Not in it tonight!"

Brant repeated the words as one puts out his hand in the dark.

"No," replied Abner, "he will not be in it tonight. He was in the house this evening, but he has gone away"

"Were you at the house?"

It was a sharp, incisive query.

"Yes," continued Abner, "I stopped there to see if Arnold had returned, and if so to get the money for the cattle I had sold him. He was not in the house. But he had been in it."

"How did you know that?"

"I knew it for several reasons," Abner went on. "The window to the sitting room was pushed up and open, where he had forced an entrance, for the house had been closed in his wife's absence, and Arnold likely had no key to it; there were some dishes on a table in the room, and some fragments of food where he had eaten, and a kettle on the hearth."

"You were in the house then?" said Brant.

"The door was not fastened," replied my uncle. "I called when I rode up before the house. There was no reply, although I could see that someone had come in. Then I noticed the open window and some tracks in the flower bed before it. I got down and went into the house. Arnold had been there, from the evidence that I have mentioned. But he was not now in the house; and from a certain other thing I thought he would not be back in it."

"What thing?" said Brant.

"A thing," continued Abner, "that had a marked significance. The tin box in which Arnold kept his notes and deeds and which used to sit on a shelf above the mantelpiece had been taken down and the contents sorted over for any note or other evidence of value. Clearly he did not intend to return."

He paused and looked Brant steadily in the face.

"Where did he go?"

"How should I know, Abner?"

"Well," replied my uncle, "you were at Arnold's house before I was."

"How do you know that?"

"There was a shower of rain late this afternoon. Your footprints were clearly visible in the wet dust. You arrived at Arnold's house after that shower of rain. But Arnold was before you. He was in the house when the rain fell. There were his footprints in the soft earth of a flower bed, under the window that he had to force up before he could get into the house. Those footprints had been made in the dry earth, and therefore before the rain shower. I know Arnold's footprints, as anyone would know them, for he has a club-foot like his father."

"But how did you know my footprints?"

"I did not know them," continued Abner, "until I walked behind you from the stable here, in the rain, tonight. But there was a track of a horse leading from Arnold's house this way, and I followed that. You were only a little way before me, Brant, and it was nearly night."

My uncle was watching carefully for the effect of this speech on Brant.

And now to his amazement the man laughed.

"Abner," he said, "you are correct in your conclusions. But you have unearthed no mare's nest, and you have discovered nothing that I did not intend to tell you. I was at Arnold's house this evening. I saw him, and I came home. Let me go back a little. Did I not say that I was glad to see you when you came; and did I not say that we would go together in the morning to see Randolph? There was a reason for that, Abner; a deep and moving reason."

He sat down now, behind the table where he had been standing.

"You were right, Abner," he went on, "to conclude that Arnold had gone away and would not return. He has done that very thing; and he has left us all in a lot of trouble. . . . I will tell you what I know, and tomorrow we will go to Randolph. Arnold owed me for a few steers, as he owed you and other men for his drove. I needed this money to pay you and I was looking out for Arnold to come back, and so, today, as I was near his place, I rode in. I found Arnold in his house. He was sorting out some papers from his tin box and he was terribly disturbed. He made no mystery about it. He said that on his way home over the mountain he had been robbed.

"The money for the cattle had been taken from him. He did not know what to do. He had come on home to talk the matter over with his wife. But as she had not returned, he had made up his mind to go to her at her father's place in Maryland. He had no money with which to pay us for the cattle. But he would take what securities he had that could be used to raise money; and as his wife's people were persons of property and influence, they might be able to help him find the money to pay for the cattle.

"He begged me to say nothing. He would slip out over the mountains to his wife's people. No one would know he had been here, and he would return just as soon as he could raise the money."

Abner did not move.

"And so," he said, "Arnold has disappeared."

"That was his intention, Abner, to slip out of the county. You were there after I came away. If you did not find him he has disappeared."

"Then," replied my uncle, "he has disappeared more mysteriously than any man that I have ever heard of, for he was not in the house and there was no track of either the man or his horse outside."

"That might be, Abner," Brant said. "In his panic and with such a resolution, it is possible that Arnold tied his horse out somewhere, and came across the fields to his house. He would keep out of the roads. There was no track of a horse when I came to the house. In fact, I came, as one might say, by chance. I was after a pronged buck that had been foraging in my corn, and I followed it through the woods. Then when I came in sight of Arnold's house I rode in."

"Did you get a shot at the buck?"

"No," said Brant. Then as though something had occurred to him too late, he brought his hand swiftly across his mouth.

My uncle seemed to take no notice of the gesture.

"Did you see Arnold's horse?"

"No."

"It was not in the stable, then, when you went there to look?"

"How did you know I went to the stable?"

"There was your track," said Abner, "leading from Arnold's gate to the stable and back again to where your horse stood."

"That is right, Abner," he said. "I did not see anyone about when I rode in, and so I walked over to the stable when I got down. But the door was closed."

My uncle turned a little and was looking up at the rifle on the forks above the fireplace.

"And so you missed the buck," he said.

"Yes. It was a long shot." Then he corrected the reply, brought up by a memory. "That is to say, Abner, I did not get a shot at the buck, as I told you. But I did shoot to turn him out from the gap to the mountains. It was a long shot at the butt of a shagbark hickory to make a racket to the east of the gap."

My uncle's thoughts were evidently in another quarter, for he took his wallet out of his pocket and began searching through the papers in it.

Brant watched him, and also covertly he watched the windows toward the west.

Abner presently found the thing he sought, replacing the wallet in his pocket. Then he came over to the table and put it down.

"Here is your due bill, Brant, for three hundred dollars," he said. "I would like you to take it up."

"I can't take it up," replied the man.

But my uncle was obdurate. He was hard now and determined in his manner, and he insisted on the payment of the note. Brant made every form of apology, but it did not move him. If Brant had no money then he must give him something else of value for it. And finally as though driven into a corner the man made the offer that my uncle seemed to wish.

"I have no money," he said, "but I will give you anything else I have."

"I am determined to have it," replied my uncle, and his voice was hard and cold as a piece of metal. "And I accept your offer, Brant. I will take something for my note."

His eyes rested on the table.

"I will take this Bible."

At the words Brant burst out with an oath and darted forward.

"Not that, Abner," he cried, "not that, in God's name!"

"And why not?" replied my uncle, his voice still cold and hard. "It is of no value to you."

"But it is!" cried Brant. "It is! It is! You can take anything else, Abner, but not that."

The shaken man was in a very panic of concern. But my uncle remained cold and hard.

"It is a locked Bible," Abner went on, "the locked Bible that has brought you into criticism. The locked Bible on which old Adam Bird preached his sermon. You never open it—at least you never open it except at a time of death—as when your wife was buried. At a time of death, Brant. Why are you concerned about it?"

The man strove to get some measure of control.

"Why, Abner," he said, "it belonged to my father and his father's father. I could not part with it. It is all they have left me out of death."

My uncle repeated the word in his cold, even voice. "Death!"

He was standing before the fireplace on the big flagstone hearth, his hands behind him.

"And so, Brant," he said, "it is death that gives that book a value to you."

For a moment he was silent. Then he went on in that strange level voice.

"There was One born in a manger. Candles are sometimes used in His service and this Book is the record of Him. Think of it, Brant, the candle and the Book and the manger!"

"What do you mean, Abner?" he said, and his voice seemed thin and far down in his big body.

"I mean," replied my uncle, "that these things, the candle and the Book and the manger, are symbols used in the service of God, and you have used them, Brant, in the service of the devil!"

He went on, his words, slow and even, like a pronouncement of doom.

"They are symbols of life, Brant, and you have made them symbols of death! Listen to me: I rode into Arnold's house. It was nearly dark. I knew Arnold had been there from the evidences I have told you and I knew that someone else had been there and had ridden away a few minutes before I arrived, for there were the tracks in the wet earth leading from the house to the stable and returning to where the horse had been hitched.

"There was something peculiar about these tracks. The footprints going toward the stable from the house were deeply imprinted in the wet earth of the road, and parallel, while the ones returning were one before the other and less deeply imprinted. This meant that the one going to the stable had been carrying something heavy, which he had not carried back. I went into the house.

"I could not find Arnold although he had surely entered. There were the dishes and his tin box and the scattered papers. But the man was gone. There was also another thing: The oval rag-carpet by the table where Arnold had been sitting was also gone—the outline of it on the dust of the floor was clearly visible.

"Why had Arnold vanished, and this carpet rug, and what was the heavy burden that had been carried to the stable? I went to the stable. It was closed, as I have told you. But, as I did not tell you, I unfastened the door and went in. I found Arnold's horse tied in a stall, and still farther on, set deep in a manger where no current of air would disturb it I found a long tallow candle burning. It was set in the hay and had just been lighted. The end of the manger beyond it was packed and tramped down with hay, although there was no animal in that stall to be fed. I took out the hay, and under it at the bottom of the manger was Arnold's dead body, shot through the heart and wrapped in the carpet rug.

"The thing was clear now; Arnold had come home with the money for the cattle, someone had come along the row of bushes before the house, observed him through the open window, shot him from this ambush—for here was the mark of a rifle butt in the wet earth beside the footprints—robbed him, rifled his tin box, hidden the body and the bloody carpet in the stable, and set a lighted candle to fire the building later on, when the assassin should be safely in his house."

My uncle's voice went on, without accent, without emotion, like a Fate.

"I did not know who this assassin was, but the track of the horse led toward your house, and, as you owed me for the heifers on your due bill, I came on here. I watched your footprints, as we came in the rain from the stable, and it was the same footprint that I had seen at Arnold's house. I found your rifle lately fired and with the stock wet. I found you watching for the light from the burning barn—the light through the windows to the west—that would never

appear, for I had extinguished the candle. And I found you glad to
see me; glad, Brant, not for the reason you have given, but because
you would have a witness to your alibi."

My uncle's voice went up in a higher, harder note. "But you
had invoked too many symbols, Brant! What had you done with
the money? There was the manger and the candle. Then I noticed
the Bible on the table. The locked Bible. The Bible you open only
at death. It had been opened, for there were fresh key scratches
about the brass lock, and the covers were bulged as though it had
been closed with difficulty. I examined it while you went out to
eat."

Abner moved away from the fireplace to the table.

"And so I found where you had hidden the money! As though,
Brant—as though one symbol had led on to another. The manger,
the candle and the Book!"

There was a moment of utter silence, then Brant slipped around
the table to the hearth and, whipping down the rifle from the forks
above the fireplace, struck at my uncle, a swift terrific blow, club-
bing the rifle, his hands around the muzzle.

It was all done in an instant of time.

And it was a miracle that my uncle could evade it. But perhaps
he had divined what the man was at, for he did evade it by a snap
of his body backward. And as Brant passed in the momentum of
his murderous intent, Abner struck him with a short drive upward
of his clenched left hand. There was the whole weight of my uncle's
body in it. It caught Brant squarely on the angle of the jaw and he
went down in a heap on the floor.

The blow of the clubbed rifle missed my uncle. But it struck
the Bible on the table. It was a terrific blow, for it burst the brass
clasp and broke the covers and the lock. The book leaped open,
and the money and the notes and papers of the murdered Arnold,
concealed between the pages, fluttered out.

22

THE MYSTERY AT HILLHOUSE

I.

Abner pulled up his horse and looked down at the sweep of country that fell away from the range of the Alleghenies westward toward the Ohio.

It descended in the vast arc of a circle.

The rim of the mountains bowed around it; a bench of the range making a sort of elevated plateau, wide, and with but a slight descent. From this bench, falling sharply away, the country sloped over long, steep, sodded fields to the river and meadow beyond.

It is the oldest cattle country in America.

For a hundred years it has been fenced and pastured.

The pioneer cleared it when the continent was young; when the territories west were a crown colony; when Virginia, in its indefinite vast boundaries, was an empire; when the Allegheny range was a sort of Chinese Wall against the red hordes of the West.

But it was no unclaimed land spotted with the squatter's patch.

It was held from the earliest time, in large tracts under grants from George. True, that Hanoverian king had only a paper title. It was the painted kings in their villages along the Ohio who had possession. And they were not to be ejected by any parchment warrant. Neither were the determined men who crossed the mountains from Maryland and Virginia to be dispossessed.

Thus for a decade a barbarous war went on. It was a war unwritten and unremembered except in the brief memorial of some pioneer setting down what his father could recall, at the end of life, wrapped up by the fire.

The Hanoverian king gave his grant and went his way. And the men who held his warrants depended on themselves. No redcoat crossed the ridge of the mountains to help them when the savage raided. They cleaned the forests and sodded down their fields and made the land. And when the time came, they rode north with George of Virginia against this English king. But they rode like feudal barons with their retainers, and their independent spirit in them. These were the fathers, and the sons who came after them were not of weaker stuff.

One must carry this history in his memory if he is to understand the land that lay before Abner on this October afternoon. And by that word I mean the men who held it; their sturdy independence; their direct methods; their impatience with the dilatory government of Virginia, that was distant and hedged about with forms.

The law was all well enough when there was time.

But when there was no time, they acted swiftly and for themselves. They were not always right, but for that matter neither is the law court. The judge's writ has taken away the orphan's inheritance and hanged its man, by error, and by perjury, and by both, when every safeguard of human ingenuity has been thrown about it.

And so we must not hurry to condemn our fathers.

They had to deal swiftly with the thief and the assassin. Nevertheless, at the time I write of, there were men here who saw a better way. I do not mean a dreamer or a weakling, I mean men like my Uncle Abner.

You cannot understand this unless you understand the man. He was a crag of common sense, Randolph used to say, on which the opinions and theories of fools broke and went to pieces. He was big, with a face that might have been forged out by a smith.

A grim, deeply religious man—like those who followed Cromwell.

But he did not practice either sufferance or nonresistance to a wrong. Abner belonged to the Church Militant and he was in the service of a War Lord.

It was a grazing country.

The fat cattle were driven overland to Baltimore, for market, across the mountain range of the Alleghenies into Maryland.

Abner was returning from one of these long drives on this October afternoon. His men who had traveled with the cattle were scattered on the trails back and he rode alone. His big chestnut horse was tired, and either that reason, or something impressive in the vast sweep of the land suddenly uncovered before him, caused the man to pull up in the road.

Far below, where the road trailed out into the lowlands by the river, there was a whitewashed tavern; a spot in the sun. And beyond it, farther down the narrow valley, was Hillhouse, the manor that old Thorndyke Patterson had builded at the foot of the long slope above the river.

Abner was motionless and silent.

The horse, resting in the sun, was like a bronze, dyed with a dye.

There was a thicket above the road, and now suddenly with no warning sound a man slipped out of this wood, crossed the rail fence and stepped down into the road. The man, moving thus covertly as in some fear, did not see Abner until he was almost on the horse.

He was a little lank man of the hills, with a narrow face.

He carried a bundle in a grist sack. Abner knew the man. He was a sort of tenant farmer, renting a bit of the Patterson land at its highest point on the bench of the mountains, a little meadow and a field. But he was in fact a trapper, and in no good repute. His dogs disturbed the cattle; and the holes in the sodded hills that he dug out he did not refill. It was a source of constant quarrel with old Webster Patterson. The holes washed into gullies. And the two threatened one another.

Abner's horse brought the man up shortly.

"Jefferson," he said, "you travel blind like Baalam."

The man was startled in his stride, and hung a moment before he got his balance. Fear in the background of his face came out.

"I am in a hurry, Abner," he replied, "I did not see you."

"And why do you hurry?" said my uncle. "Have you so far to go?"

"A long way," replied the man, "over the mountains into Maryland."

"Into Maryland," repeated my uncle. "What takes you into Maryland?"

The man did not at once reply.

He looked about him, at the empty road, at the long range of the mountains, at the fields below. His face lengthened and there came a sort of whine into his voice.

"What keeps me here, Abner?" he said. "The grazers do not like me, and if a thing happens it is straightway laid down at my door. I am charged with every petty misdemeanor. If lightning strikes a haystack, I have burned it; if a passing tramp sleeps in an empty barn loft and knocks out the ashes of his pipe, it is I who have sent the building up in smoke. I alone in this whole country am supposed to travel in the night. All others are abed—honest men asleep!

"I am hounded, Abner, and I can no longer bear it. I have some feeling like other men. And in every direction there is only a scowling face. To every cattleman I am a creature of the devil; my dogs disturb the cattle. I am a trespasser laying down their fences and leaving the gates to bang off their hinges in the wind."

The man went on as though enamored of his words.

"The landowner does not consider the good I do. I destroy the mink and the weasel that forage on his hen roosts, the polecat that eats the quail eggs and the varmints that burrow in his pasture. . . . But these benefits that I give are not regarded."

He paused.

"Tell me, Abner, how does the deadfall, set along the ridges, interfere with pasture? It cannot trap a steer. There is no wizardry in these hills that changes a bullock to a mink when the moon comes up. And yet if a steer is dead, it is I who have killed him. He eats the poisonous buckeye and he dies, and I in some manner have brought about his death; fed him some deadly herbage or sprinkled the grass before his nose with arsenic. And if a horse goes lame from a twisted leg in a bog crossing, it is I who have ridden it in the night."

My uncle looked steadily at the man. There was about his face the shadow of an ironical smile.

"You forget, Jefferson," he said, "that the fat bullock is a gentleman, accustomed to his leisure, and not to be disturbed when he is sleeping in the night. No man regards your traps. But we will not have the pasture land dug up in holes; and we will not have the cattle maddened by a pack of dogs. On these counts the complaint against you is established. But not on the arson; and not on any poisoner charge. Why should you flee away as though you had done a murder?"

The final sentence was an idle addendum to my uncle's words. But on the instant at them the man went white. His mouth sagged, and moisture came out on his face.

"Murder, Abner," he faltered, "what do you know about murder?"

My uncle laughed.

"The raccoon, Jefferson," he replied, "is not a citizen of Virginia and no writ runs against his premeditated killing. You cannot be haled into the circuit court on that. But your explanation of your exodus does not convince me."

He extended his arm and pointed toward the little farm on the narrow plateau above the Patterson lands.

"You have a house there, some goods, some utensils, a cow perhaps and some farm equipment, and I find you here with clothing in a sack. A householder does not emigrate into Maryland in this fashion. What is the truth about this matter?"

The man covered his weak mouth with his hand. His face took on a sort of childish simplicity.

"Abner," he said, moving his hand upward over his face, "all men trust you, and I trust you too. A thing has happened and I am afraid!"

Anyone could see that the creature had come finally to his real motive.

My uncle brought his clenched hand down on the pommel of his saddle. His voice hardened, sharpened and lifted out of its casual note.

"My friend," he said, "that is the worst reason in the world! A man cannot flee from fear. From any other thing he may flee away if it seems expedient, but on fear, under no conditions can he turn his back. He must face fear! Fear is the challenge to our courage. And courage, Jefferson, is the greatest thing we have—when it goes there is nothing left worth the distinguishing definition of a man. Honor, justice, even righteousness itself are all based on courage. If you are on your way from fear you must go back and face it!"

"But, Abner," the man whined, "how can I face it?"

"How can you not face it," replied my uncle, "even be it murder? Guilty or innocent there is no other way. If we face up to the things we fear, even to the gallows, we have somehow the respect of men. But every human creature loathes a coward. And there is no solution in a flight. It is the abandonment of one's manhood to the pit!"

"But, Abner," the man's voice was in a whisper, "you do not know the dreadful thing behind me."

"No matter," replied my uncle. "The thing before you is a worse thing. A man can be hanged and bear it, but he cannot be crucified by his own contempt. No matter what you fear you cannot be worse off than Saul. Abandoned by God and doomed by Samuel, he put his armor on and went up, with his trumpets blowing, to a battle that he could not win!"

The man standing in the road looked up, something dawned vaguely in his face.

"Will you stand behind me, Abner, if I go back?" he said.

"And if I do not," replied my uncle, "you will have the greater gain of standing behind yourself."

The man hesitated a moment, searching my uncle's face. Then he turned away.

Abner watched the man climb the ancient rail fence, matted with yellow vines, and return, as he had come, along the bench of the mountains toward his house. It sat in a field and a bit of meadow above the Patterson lands. He had rented the few poor acres from old Webster Patterson some years before. And by reason of indefinite words written in the lease, Patterson could not now eject him, for all their bitter quarrels.

Abner spoke to his horse and rode slowly on.

But he rode now in a deep reflection.

To what end did the tireless energies of God concern themselves? And of what moment were the tragedies of men? They came and passed, were born and stepped into Eternity. Few and evil—as the third Patriarch said it—usually, were the days of a life. And they vanished clear away! The dim record of their succession was even here, in this land comparatively new. What trace remained of the pioneer's cabin and the pioneer? A little heap of stones where the chimney had finally fallen. And before the pioneer the red man, already a legend. And before that painted nomad, another race of which not even a legend remained; only their burial mounds on this high plateau of the range, paved with flat stones, under which their bones had disintegrated.

They also in this scriptural language had vanished clear away, leaving only these mounds of sepulcher and some fanciful wild tales imagined by their successors.

Apt and descriptive was the Book of Job! Like a song, like a shadow on a wall were the whole race of men. Of what moment were their little tragedies! How they came and how they passed. Whether one went swiftly and in violence, or slowly in one's bed, did it matter? The thing that mattered was what the soul of man took with him on his way. And the only thing he could take was the form into which this inexplicable environment shaped his soul.

He rode on.

Below, the long highway wound down like a yellow ribbon.

The world lay peaceful in the sun, as in the silence of a benediction. The great red horse, stained with sweat, moved slowly under his master, who sat with his big plowshare jaw bedded into his collar. They descended into a ravine of the mountain and came out into a drove of cattle.

The first bullock appeared on a little rise of the road, regarded them with a sort of peaceful intent, and was joined by another.

Abner pulled up by the roadside for the drove to pass.

He knew the cattle. They belonged to old Webster Patterson! Sixty young steers that the eccentric old man had held to autumn, refusing to sell them to the traders who bought in the field and drove overland to Baltimore.

A dog, with a great air of competence, kept a few bullocks moving in the front of the drove. And by reason of the dog, Abner knew that the purchaser came from beyond the mountains. A dog was not a cattle driver in this westward portion of Virginia. The fat steer in this land was like the sacred bulls of Egypt, to be moved gently and at his leisure. A dog was too impatient of delay, and would not always regard the rule; the Median rule that suffered no amendment—too slowly the fat steer cannot be driven!

The cattle sauntered past, and the purchaser with another dog appeared.

He was on foot and white with dust.

He was a stranger to my uncle, but he was a stranger that one regarded. He was a big black-bearded man, with the shoulders of an ox, a barrel chest, and fingers like the coupling pins of a cart. Builded to pull down pillars or to grind blinded at a Philistine mill, was the fancy that my uncle got. Abner spoke to the man, with the usual salutation to the stranger on a road.

The man nodded and trudged on. But my uncle stopped him.

"You have bought the Patterson cattle," he said.

"I have," replied the man.

He stopped now and faced Abner squarely, his heavy shoulders forward as in a sort of menace, as though he held the road and held his position in it. Held it as with a challenge. The manner, too, of the man was surly; as though he would not be questioned and would not be stopped. There was no courteous aspect about the man.

"They are well-shaped young cattle; kept over for another year they will average fifteen hundred; but they are light for Baltimore. Are you from Maryland?"

"I am," replied the man, but in no pleasant humor.

My uncle did not regard this manner. He spoke as to the usual stranger on the road.

"You travel alone," he said.

"I do," replied the man. "I came over the mountain alone, I go back alone. And at no man's permission."

"You took some chance then," said Abner. "Webster Patterson would sell only for the money in his hand, and you must have carried the money. Were you not afraid?"

The big man lifted his shoulders. He squared his body in the road.

"Afraid," he echoed. "Of what should I be afraid?"

"A fine thing, courage," was Abner's comment. "I put it near the top of all earthly excellence. But there are some forms of courage that take a higher merit than other forms." He paused. "A moral courage, for example, that takes one back to face a thing of danger from which one has well escaped, would be, I think, the highest form."

The man's eyes shifted a bit as though uncertain of my uncle's meaning.

"What are you driving at?" he said, chopping the words off under his thick beard.

"This only," continued my uncle, "that as a man of courage and unafraid would you return of your own will into danger from which you could escape by flight, if no man compelled you, and you could do as you pleased about it?"

The man did not at once reply. He looked at the far-off valley from which he had come up, at the cattle moving forward before the dog, and then up at my uncle. And his surly manner advanced into a menace.

"I would do as I pleased about it," he said. "And as for you, sir"—and although he did not move, he seemed to advance against my uncle— "you can ride on to the devil. I will not be stopped and questioned."

He strode after the drove of cattle, swaggering in the road as though it were a king's highway that his prowess had preempted.

Abner watched him disappear into the ravine that obscured the road.

Evening was on the way.

It would be dark before the cattle traveled halfway to the summit of the mountain.

One must carry in the mind the long distance from the ridge of the range to the valley. It was well into the afternoon when my uncle came out on the summit of the mountain at the gap where it crossed toward Maryland. And now half on the way down, the sun was moving into the west and long shadows were beginning to appear.

The horse traveled slowly, and seemed by this leisure gait to regain the reserve of strength that it had expended on the journey.

Abner seemed again lost in a deep reflection, and the horse had its idle way.

There was time aplenty. Night would bring them to the tavern in the valley. One could see it, a splotch of white in the shadows.

The road was not always clear to the eye except at certain turns and angles of it. It would be hidden over long distances by the shoulders of the hills. They went on. The afternoon lengthened and drew on to evening. The temperature of the air began to change, the shadows to crowd in.

There had been no sound in the world but the hum of the autumn insect, the chatter of the squirrel or the far-off hammering of a woodpecker on a dead chestnut limb. But now, below, some distance on the road, there was the sound of horses; and emerging from one of the long hollows into which the road wound, Abner saw a company of men coming from the valley.

The thing brought my uncle up sharply in the saddle.

He became on the instant alert and vital. His introspection slipped off like a garment. He pulled up the horse and stopped. But it was not beside the road, as with the cattle, that he stopped.

It was squarely in the middle of the road, as though he held it.

And there in the middle of the road he waited. He had changed. He was now a resolute, determined figure, grim-faced and silent.

Abner knew the men. They were cattle graziers of the hills and he divined the mission they were on.

But he was puzzled at the leader.

He was not a man that such a company would select to lead—a little trader of no particular standing in the county, and with a decidedly doubtful past. He bought and sold the cattle refuse of the hills, cows and heifers. Sylvester Dix had been concerned with more than one questionable venture.

He pulled up in the road before my uncle.

"Abner," said Dix, "did you pass a drove of cattle?"

"I did," replied my uncle, but he was looking beyond Dix to the men behind him.

Dix drove his heel into his horse. "Come on," he said, "there is time to get our man before the night falls."

But my uncle turned his horse across the road.

"Dix," he said, "what is this venture that you are on?"

"This, Abner," he said, "if you do not know it: Webster Patterson has been killed and robbed and we have raised the country to overtake his assassin and bring him back."

"This is grave news," replied my uncle. "Do you know who this assassin is?"

"We do," said Dix. "It's the man from Maryland with the cattle."

"And how do you know it?" said Abner.

"I will tell you," replied the man, "and you will see precisely how we know. We found Webster Patterson dead in the orchard by his house, his pocketbook rifled and his cattle gone. This is what happened: A stranger with two dogs came in from Maryland—a big surly creature. He inquired for a drove of good light steers and was sent on to Patterson. He trades with Patterson for cattle by the head, pays Patterson down in cash, turns the cattle into the road with the dogs to hold them, comes back to the house, kills Patterson, retakes the money he has paid and hurries the cattle over the mountains before he is apprehended."

Abner's face was grave.

"Who saw all this?" he said.

"I saw it," continued Dix. "I was on the road with a bunch of heifers. From a rise in the road I saw the cattle, the stranger and his dogs. And I saw old Webster Patterson going into the orchard from his house. I came on. The Fairfax Wood shut out the view from me. But some half hour later, when I came up to the house, I saw old Webster lying in the orchard. I got off and went to him. He was dead. There was a maul near him. The whole back of his head had been crushed in with the maul. I carried him into the house; on the way, as his coat was open, his pocketbook dropped out. There was no money in it. Here it is. You can see for yourself."

He produced the pocketbook and opened it on the pommel of his saddle.

My uncle looked hard at the man.

"Dix," he said, "you make a case against yourself. Webster Patterson is killed and you come here with his empty pocketbook."

The man's face changed.

"A case against myself!" he echoed.

"That is it," continued Abner, "a case against yourself! You know of this cattle sale, you see the cattle in the road and you know the money has been paid down in cash, for it is the custom with a stranger. You come on, you find old Webster Patterson in the orchard, you engage him in talk and, while he is not looking, strike him from behind.

"You rob the body and then raise a *posse comitatus* on your own authority to arrest a stranger for the murder."

Abner lifted his great body in the saddle.

"Dix," he said, "you have gone too far. This empty pocketbook would hang you. Why did you bring this pocketbook to prove, sir, that you had robbed the body of your victim?"

The man's slack face went white. "It fell out of the dead man's pocket," he stuttered. "It fell out; there was no money in it."

"No money in it!" repeated Abner. "And why, sir, should we believe that on your word? Is your word so good? Have you taken such care to stand behind it? Is there a man here who would sell you a bullock on your word, or trust you for a dollar on it?"

Abner laughed. There was a dry, hard irony in the laugh.

"Dix," he cried, "you are riding toward the gallows, and you are carrying a rope to hang you!"

And at the drive of the words the appalled creature went to pieces.

Fear overcame him.

He lashed his horse and dashed past my uncle in mortal terror.

Abner turned. His horse was swifter and he overtook the man. He caught the rein of the bridle and pulled him up.

"Dix," he said, "you are a fool, will you also be a coward! Do you want the world to believe you guilty? Flight is confession; don't you see that? If you run away there is no jury in the hills will believe you."

He held the horse firmly with his big hand and pulled the shaken man together.

"You do not believe me, Abner," the creature stuttered, "and who will believe me?"

"And what of that," replied my uncle. "If you have the courage for a crime have also the courage to face what follows after it. If you are innocent of murder why should you convict yourself by fear? There is no gain in fear! Get your courage in your teeth, Dix, and ride back."

The others had come on.

The motive in the little company had turned about like a weathervane. They would now take Dix into custody for the murder. But they had cooled off.

They had excuse for these swift reprisals.

The law was slow and, along this range, cattle were stolen and run over the border into Maryland. The thing had become an intolerable outrage and no longer to be borne. The land was on its feet against it. This murder had been a flame to hemp. From one point of view the case against the stranger was conclusive. But here from Abner's words was a view from another quarter. They were no longer certain, and in this changed mood my uncle had his will with them.

They should return and leave this thing to him.

The man with the Patterson cattle could not get over the state line for a day; Dix should wait a legal inquiry. And so for all their tragic purpose they turned out into the crossroads and my uncle went on toward the tavern, dimly outlined in the twilight.

But before he continued on his journey, my uncle called Dix back and gave him a verbal message to take on to the stranger with the cattle. Dix should ride alone and say only the precise words in the message that my uncle sent. It seemed a curious thing to send Dix of all the company on such a mission. But on the other hand was he not more certain than any other, in his present changed mood, to do precisely what Abner told him? At any rate it pleased my uncle to select him; since he rode so hard to overtake this stranger, he should ride to a proper purpose.

Abner went on. His meeting with the trapper on the mountain and the big cattle driver took now a different aspect. Their words, their incidental acts had now an indicatory significance. Or they were, in the light of what he now knew, capable of that construction. Looked at by a grand jury in an inquisitorial sitting, these acts were signboards conspicuous with meaning. The hurried flight of the fur trapper, his fear, his significant sentence on the dreadful thing behind him, emerged into a broader field.

Abner had now a higher feeling for the courage of the man.

It was then from no verbal quarrel with old Webster Patterson that the creature fled. But in what manner was he complicated in this tragedy? And what of the big surly stranger? Surely his manner was against him; and he had the physical structure for the deed as Dix had so vividly described it. With a maul for a weapon this man could fell an ox.

Was he in fact the assassin and the robber?

It would be the simple elements of crime to pay down his money and recover it with a blow. And yet his arrow at a venture against Dix might have reached the bull's-eye!

He had loosed that arrow with another purpose.

The law and the orderly procedure of the law must be strengthened. The land was running into violence. The direct action of angered persons would presently supersede the law. Men would be judged and punished in hot blood and all the orderly procedure of government would go to pieces.

It were better for the guilty to go free than to put the land in chaos.

And so my uncle had set his face against it. And so he had driven the implications of the crime on Dix with all the force he could; to confound the posse and lay the guilt on the leader of it. He had gone about that work with no gentle hand, and to his wonder he had succeeded beyond all conjecture.

Panic had enveloped Dix.

It had taken all the persuasion he could manage to get the shaken creature to await the orderly procedure of the law. Was the man in fact guilty? Had the count of his verbal indictment set out the truth? His influence on the illegal *posse comitatus* was no great wonder. Men taking the law into their hands fall into confusion at a doubt.

And Abner's word in this land was taken always for a thing accomplished.

At his word they had left this thing to him! The obligations of it were now on him. He must consider the items of that obligation. He must clear the mystery of this crime; and he must find the man who did it.

Two acts were indicated—he must stop the stranger with the cattle before noon tomorrow and he must send for Randolph.

In this latter need chance favored him.

When he came out from a bend of the road before the tavern he saw Randolph's gig. The negro driver was standing beside the horse.

Abner got down before the door, gave his own horse into the care of Randolph's driver and went in. The little tavern sat fronting on the highway; a covered porch extended its full length. It was neat and whitewashed; even the fences running on either side were white. The tavern keeper was an invalid, bedridden in an upper room, but the energy of his eccentric wife was enough for two.

She was a conspicuous figure in the hills.

Her tongue ran, and she knew every variety of gossip. But for all her words, in the remote recesses of her she was a person of sound common sense. Her comment on events was shrewd except when those events could be garnished with some supernatural fancy.

Signs concerned her.

She tapped on wood to appease the witches. She nailed up a horseshoe for good luck; and she crossed her fingers and made the usual sign when the salt spilled on her table. All the fancies attendant on the dead disturbed her; what the dying said and the prophetic words of those in the senility of age. The woman half believed that the paralytic condition of her husband had been effected by an evil eye, or the sorcery of some enemy's incantation.

There was a fire burning on the hearth when my uncle entered; for there is a chill in this land at autumn, when the sun goes down beyond the great wall of the hills.

Randolph stood before this fire, his hands spread out to the flame. He was the justice of the peace, a neighbor to Abner and a gentleman.

You are not to think of him as a justice of our modern time.

The office of justice of the peace in that day, in Virginia, followed the English manner. The idea of it was inherited from the English law. The king, to keep his peace, selected the most influential men in his counties for this office. Virginia, with some like vague intent, continued to select such men.

And under this large conception it was an office of no little honor. At this time, and even beyond the mountains to the west, it was so regarded; only a landowner and a gentleman would hold it. We have traveled far since then.

I have said that Randolph was a neighbor and a friend to Abner. Their lands adjoined; and my uncle held him, for his qualities of a man, in high regard.

But his mannerisms were the annoyance of my uncle's life.

He was vain and pompous and enamored with the extravagance of words. But he was a gentleman beneath it, and the impulses from which he acted were those of a man of honor.

He turned as my uncle entered.

"Abner!" he cried. "By the eternal, I am glad to see you. Did you by any chance come on a *posse comitatus?*"

"I did," replied my uncle, "and I turned it back."

"You did right," said Randolph. "It had no authority to act, it came together at no call from me. It rode outside the law. It was a mob. Its arrests would have been illegal; any citizen apprehended by it could have resisted with a weapon in his hand. Who led it?"

"It had the very strangest leader," replied my uncle. "Sylvester Dix."

Randolph swore, snapping his finger above the fire. "A pretty gentleman to enforce the law. Sylvester Dix—a crooked trader and a drunken lout!"

He fingered the bunch of seals attached to the big watch in his pocket.

"When the people rush in before the law, it is always such vermin who go first—loud-mouthed and blatant and swaggering in their saddles. I drove hard, Abner, to get here before him, and if I had arrived on time I would have flayed his hide. Sylvester Dix to usurp the legal procedure of Virginia!"

And in his disgust he stamped the hearthstones.

"It was not this stranger from Maryland who killed and robbed old Webster Patterson. It is clear to any legal mind who did it. But if this cattle buyer from the East were the guilty one, it is not for a mob to bring him back. Virginia is not yet so feeble that she requires the aid of Dix or that she must send a company on horse to take up a man without a warrant."

He ran on, stimulating himself into a fury.

He was dressed with some elegance after the manner of the time. He had been educated beyond the mountains. He had a great estate in lands. He lived like the gentry of a somewhat earlier day and on the westward side of the Alleghenies he had come to consider himself as a sort of ambassadorial figure, representing in his person the sovereign dignity of Virginia.

"I will sit tomorrow," he said when he had gotten back his judicial calm, "determine this assassin and hold him for the circuit court. The case is clear."

Abner came over to the fire and sat down in one of the high-backed splint-bottom chairs.

He made no comment on this speech and Randolph continued with his discourse.

"This will be the doing of old Calhoun Patterson."

My uncle looked up at that.

"Calhoun Patterson!" he said. "Was he with Webster at the time?"

This was another light on the complicated mystery.

"He was," said Randolph. "He had ridden over in the morning, and he was there all day. There is no mystery about it; Calhoun Patterson did this murder."

He paused and fingered the gold seals about his waistcoat.

"I should not make so definite a pronouncement," he went on, "if I were to sit tomorrow as a court of final determination.

"But I sit only as a court of inquiry to send the whole case on to the inquisitorial investigation of the grand jury, and to the circuit court. I do not determine guilt. I hold only on probable cause and my finding entails no penal sentence. I therefore speak with a larger liberty than a circuit judge in the same position."

My uncle was in deep reflection.

If Calhoun Patterson had been present on this day, then the whole tragic mystery shifted to another angle. How could the man from Maryland or Dix or the trapper from the mountain dare to go about a murder with this witness in the environs of the place?

This added information deepened the puzzle.

Abner knew Calhoun Patterson, the details of his life and all about his relations with his brother. It was the story of a bitter hatred—that blood hatred in some family quarrels.

The father, old Thorndyke Patterson, after the death of Calhoun's mother, had taken a second wife. It was a marriage out of his class. The new wife was from the far South and not to be definitely placed; an octoroon woman from New Orleans, the county gossips said.

From this marriage Webster Patterson was born.

There was only a year or two of difference between the sons, for the first wife died at Calhoun's birth, and the second was brought in within the year. But while the difference in age was slight, the difference in feeling between the two men was widely variant. Calhoun considered himself outside the social status of his brother; of a different and more elevated class. The first wife had been of a good Virginia family and the second tainted. A Creole, Thorndyke said when he brought the new wife in; an octoroon the county dubbed her.

There was a difference too in the inherent natures of the men.

Calhoun was outspoken and above-board with what he had to say. There was little circumlocution in the man. Where he stood was never at any time in doubt. Webster was the reverse of this, crafty and diplomatic, with an eye to gain, and out of these motives he courted the favor of his father.

As age weakened the old man, Webster's influence controlled him.

He made a will leaving his estate to Webster for his life and after that son's death to Calhoun. Webster had given this disposition a sort of honorable intent; there was his mother to take care of and the manor house and lands should remain together in one hand, while the woman lived, and not be split up and divided, with no home for her to sit in when the feebleness of age grew on her.

For himself he did not care.

After this, as he pretended, Calhoun could have the whole estate. He wished it only for his life, that was to say for the term only of his mother's comfort. But the county was not convinced, and Calhoun condemned the pious pretension in the plainest language. He went to live, at some little distance, on a bit of property from his own mother's family. But he came back to the Patterson mansion when he pleased, and loitered about it as he liked with the freedom of a sharer in it.

To this habit in Calhoun, Webster gave no concern.

He ignored the man and went about his own affairs. He had gotten what he wanted, and if the price were this annoyance he would not disturb himself about it.

Nor was he to be disturbed at what Calhoun gossiped and threatened in his drunken talk. With a certain vision he saw that the very extravagance and persistence of this talk would finally denude it of any influence. He was right in this conception.

The habits of Calhoun aided to this end.

As the man grew older he took to the common vice, and now, at the approach of his age, he was rarely sober. But for all this the county respected Calhoun above his brother. The man did not lie, he was honorable in his small affairs and he said out frankly what he thought. Webster, as I have written, was the reverse of this. There was always some covert intent, to his own advantage, in what he did. He was penurious and hard-handed in his trades; his manner and his words were always a pretension.

And he respected and regarded nothing.

The county knew Webster Patterson for what he was.

Sometimes, perhaps, they did him an injustice. For example, when the manor burned there was not lacking one to say that Webster lighted it and put it out when the damage to the portico and front would not exceed the insurance to replace it. And the source of some of the materials for that repair remained in the public memory as a sort of practical looting of the dead.

Thus the history of the family ran.

The old octoroon woman entered into age and died, Webster lived on in his pretensions, and Calhoun drunken and more voluble in his threats against him.

All this passed through my uncle's memory while the justice talked.

Was Randolph by chance right in his conjecture? Had old Calhoun finally come to the point of acting on his threat?

The conclusion was not outside of one's experience. A threat to do a deed, long weakened by idle repetition, was sometimes, in the heat of sudden provocation, carried out. But the theory had certain phases that were not convincing. The robbery of the body was the main point.

That fact stood out.

It was the prime indicatory fact pointing to the others in this affair. It would be the moving motive in this man from Maryland and Dix if either were in fact the criminal agent. It would not be the motive in the trapper—if he were behind the thing. This tenant farmer on the bench of the mountain above the Patterson lands would have a cause, rather, in his verbal clashes with old Webster. The ill will between the two of them was known. Abner required no confession, out of the trapper's conversation, to establish this.

It was the common knowledge of the countryside.

Webster had been white-heated into an evil humor when he found that the words of limitation in his lease would not permit him to eject the tenant from the house, the little meadow and the field, where his estate extending over the bench of the mountain ran to the line. He would not pay for a legal paper, so he wrote the lease himself.

And, from ignorance of the legal construction of his terms, he gave the man an extended freehold that he could not revoke. This discovery put him in a fury. And the two, violent in their language, did not meet without a fishwives' quarrel. It was the comedy of the countryside.

There was motive here.

But the main fact, pronounced by Randolph, stood in the way. If Calhoun Patterson had been present on the day of Webster's murder, did not that fact put a conjectural case against these other persons out of court?

Who could go about such an assassination before a witness?

It would be the extremity of folly to take such a chance even if the witness were not, for the actual moment, visible. He could not be far away. He might appear out of the house or from some quarter at any time. It was a hazard too dangerous to be taken by anyone in reason. This would exclude Dix and the man from Maryland.

But would it necessarily exclude the trapper?

He would be acting in hot blood if he were the guilty agent; and hot blood did not act in reason. But if so, how could old Calhoun fail to have knowledge of the thing if he were idling about the place?

Randolph was in the swing of his speech while my uncle was in this reflection. And his next sentence tumbled the fabric of these probabilities into chaos.

"Calhoun was drunk when he arrived, and he got more liquor in him as the day advanced. He had come by Ephram Dillworth's still, so his supply was ample. He was more in liquor, then, than was customary with him, and therefore more determined in his purpose. He was on his way to kill Webster Patterson, he told Dillworth, when he stopped for a supply of liquor. But as the threat was in the usual tenor of his talk Dillworth gave it no attention. In this conclusion Dillworth was in error. Calhoun meant precisely what he said."

Randolph went on.

"I hold the early English judges in a high regard, and it was their belief that if a man contemplated a criminal act over a great length of time, finally in the end he was pretty certain to accomplish it. Therefore, in their criminal trials, they admitted evidence of threats and a longstanding hostile intent against the victim."

He paused and assumed a judicial air.

"I do not maintain, as one having some knowledge of the law, that such evidence is in any sense conclusive, or attains to that degree of certainty that would justify a verdict of guilty on it. I would consider it merely as persuasive. I would, of course, require further evidence: Proof of the *corpus delicti*—that is to say, in fact, the crime; and some evidence, direct or strongly circumstantial, connecting the accused with the criminal act. This would make up the case if I were sitting on our circuit bench."

He made a little gesture as of one who dismissed a pleasing fancy.

"But before me on probable cause, as in my court tomorrow, I would consider the motive, the opportunity, and this hostile intent, as evidenced by the accused's threats, over a long period of time, as making a conclusive case."

But my uncle was not listening to this discourse.

If Calhoun Patterson was drunk, the whole affair swung back to its early status. There was no menace to the assassin in a drunken man stretched out on a bed or heaped up in a corner. There might in fact be some gain in it.

The assassin could make the argument which he had just considered, and at the worst, sober or drunken, a third person was a straw man for the defense; a device to split up suspicion.

The tragic mystery stood precisely where it was!

On an autumn morning, in his orchard, in plain view of anyone who might happen to appear, with his brother about the house, Webster Patterson had been killed and robbed. Some three thousand dollars received from the sale of his cattle had been taken. He had been struck down by a blow that crushed in the skull.

The weapon, evidently used for that murderous assault, lay near him, an ordinary hickory maul. There was no eyewitness to the deed for all the open space in which the things had been accomplished. Or at least there was no eyewitness that would admit such knowledge.

There was circumstantial evidence.

But these evidential signs took their virtue from the drift of the theory in which they were considered. As one believed so were these signs capable of interpretation. The great crushing blow would indicate the ox-shouldered stranger; the empty pocketbook in question would fix the crime on Dix. And robbery as motive would fit either one. Quarrels and bad blood made up a case against the trapper. And here was old Calhoun with every motive, come, as he declared, to do the thing himself!

As one got deeper in contemplation of this mystery one got more confused. The thing turned backward on itself like intriguing and vicious circles that fell one into the other, with no point of beginning and no end. A Janus with a different face toward every observer that approached it!

The tavern keeper's wife came in to lay the table and put on the supper.

And while she was about that work she talked.

"I knew something awful would happen to old Webster," she began.

"Why?" said Randolph.

"Well," the woman continued, "you can't rob the dead and get away with it. I suppose old Webster thought dead men could not hurt him. . . . That's a fool thing to think. You know what a live man can do. You are in the dark with a dead man. Nobody can protect himself from a dead man."

"What are you talking about?" said Randolph.

"I mean the ancient people on the mountain," the woman went on. "Old Webster was crazy to violate their grave. Nobody with any sense would have dug into the burial mound of the ancient people and carted off the flat stones over their graves to pave his portico."

Randolph understood then what the woman meant. It was a half-forgotten scandal, kept in memory by the superstitions of the time.

When Webster Patterson came to rebuild the front of Hillhouse after the fire, he had brought down the flat stones, from a burial mound of the ancient race that had inhabited this land in prehistoric times. The floors of these mounds, within, were laid over with flat stones. Webster had opened the great one on the bench of the mountain above his land and used the flat stones to replace the tiles of the portico cracked in the fire.

Randolph made a quick, deprecatory gesture.

"You talk like a fool," he said. "The dead had nothing to do with ejecting Webster Patterson out of life."

"Maybe so, squire," continued the woman, "and maybe not. How does anybody know what the dead can do? It's terrible business to make the dead mad at you. I wouldn't like to rile the dead. You can see a living man coming to kill you, but you can't see a dead one coming. I don't know anything about how old Webster was killed. I don't know what happened. But I know what his old mother said would happen!"

"What did she say would happen?" said Randolph, in the mock solemnity of one speaking to a child.

"She went on terrible when Webster brought down the flagstones; cried and wrung her hands. She said something awful would happen to Webster. She didn't know what it was then. But when

she was dying she knew what it was—the dying can see what is going to happen; an' she saw it. The doctor said it was the delirium
of death. But a doctor don't know everything!"

The woman was warming to the memory and her tongue ran.

"Of course you never can get the straight of a thing like that.
Everybody puts something to it. I wasn't there. There was nobody
there but Webster, the doctor and Calhoun, but the thing leaked
out. Such things always leak out. . . . The old octoroon woman was
wrapped up in a chair by the fire—you're always cold when you're
dyin'—and she kept screaming out about what she saw about the
awful thing that would happen to Webster. The doctor couldn't stop
her. They had to hold her in the chair."

But Randolph's patience had reached the end.

"Shut up," he said. "It's an old housewife's tale, empty and idle."

The woman turned about to my uncle, silent by the fire.

"You know the Scriptures, Abner," she said. "There are lots of
stranger things written in the Scriptures."

"Yes, Matilda," he replied, in his even level voice. "There are
stranger things written in the Scriptures."

He looked through the windowpane.

It was dark. The heavens were overcast. No star was out.

But four lights were visible: a candle at a window in the trapper's house; a gleam in the manor in the valley; another to the west
where the trader lived; and a fire, halfway up the mountain road,
where the man from Maryland camped out with his cattle.

Four lights, burning in a darkened world!

By which one of these did the murderer sit, fearful of the morning?

II.

The day broke with the hard clear sun of autumn in these hills,
on a thin veneer of frost. The air was crisp and vital.

The leaves on the oaks in the woods were red, the hickories
yellow, and the sweep of grasses in the meadow was like a drift of
purple smoke. The corn in the cultivated fields stood like lined up

warriors, in their even rows; shocks bound with grapevines, for the day of wire was yet long into the future. The split-rail fences bound in the pastures, with now and then a gate or a bar of poles.

There was little other fence.

The cut nail was used, but it came overland from the Ohio, brought in by the wagons when they made their biennial journey for salt and iron.

For the most part the chestnut timber was felled and split.

There was art or what the natives called a "sleight" in this, as there was art in laying the worm for the fence— the first line of rails, each corner on a stone, upon which the structure of the fence was to be erected; after which it was finished with a stake and rider. The great pastures running to the crest of the mountains were all enclosed with this fence. The haystacks standing in the meadows had a foundation of these rails for a base. They were enclosed by a like fence with a high rider to hold out the bullock, until the heavy snows came.

Abner was out early on his horse. He was profoundly puzzled and he wished to find out what he could before Randolph set about his inquisition. The sun had not appeared when he left the tavern. It was gray dawn, with a white haze in the valley.

He took a cattle path along the face of the mountain toward the house of the trapper sitting on the bench above the Patterson lands. That path trailed leisurely in its ascent. The fat steer does not make his highway steep. Practically, the natives used to say, he was a better surveyor than the townsman with his compass, for he ran no arbitrary line, and when a ledge of stone or a slip in the hill opposed his route he found an easy grade around it.

There was no hill too steep for this surveyor.

If the fields were turned into pasture there would be a path laid out for the owner and his horse, with no fee to pay and no townsman quartered on the household.

The path lay, a great slant, across the rise of the Patterson lands to the trapper's house.

Below in the narrow valley was the river, not wide but running at some points deep, as though, in fury at the banks that bound it,

it had digged a pit. Fords crossed it in the shallows. But here, below where Abner rode, it was deep even in this time of drought.
The Patterson lands that he ascended on the path lay in two narrow benches above this river. On the lowest level sat the mansion
house that old Webster Patterson had rebuilt in his life after the
fire had damaged it.

It stood white in the dawn, with its fluted columns, and its portico paved with flat stones. The highway ran between the mansion
and the river. To the east was the orchard, paralleled with the house
and like it separated from the river by the road. To the west were
the barns and outhouses of the place. The highway, as I have written, paralleled the whole length of the place, and edging to its border was the deep channel of the river.

The pasture land, with no fence to break it, rose a steep slope
to the narrow bench that lay almost at the summit of the mountain. Here was the trapper's house, on the few acres that old
Webster had so unwittingly conveyed for a term of life to the man
that he had ever after endeavored to get rid of.

And here below the house was the great mound of the ancient
people.

The mound that Webster had cut into and ravished, and thereby
set idle gossips to all sorts of fanciful conjecture: predictions of a
doom, woven out of fragments from the Book of Kings and the folk-
lore legends of old baleful ghosts, jealous of the ground above their
bones and moving to a vengeance that no human precaution could
turn aside.

It gave the gossips in the hills, like the tavern keeper's wife,
embroidered material for prediction, and a great thrill at this tragedy accomplished. They would have no rational explanation—an
assassin with a weapon in his hand, or human motive. Reason and
common sense and the usual practical experience of man, in such
affairs, were not to be considered.

The thing had been predicted and it had come about!

It was of no concern that their most ingenious fancy could not
picture the tragic act. And the absurdities about such an explanation did not disturb them.

In the visibility of daylight, on this October morning, old
Webster Patterson had been violently dispossessed of life, in the
most open place one could imagine—the orchard by the house. If
Dix were to be believed—and this portion of his story was evidently,
in its prime essentials, true—the period of time about the tragedy
was contracted to some thirty minutes. Dix had seen him from a
rise in the road going into the orchard from the house, and later
when he came out from the obscuring hollow of the road before
the place he found him dead. Webster had been killed swiftly within
those thirty minutes—and evidently with the implement found near
the body, the hickory maul.

Someone coming up from behind had killed him. It was the
work of someone whom he did not suspect of that design or someone who had come in stealth without his knowledge. The man had
evidently no warning or any apprehension in his mind of danger.

There was no evidence of struggle.

The dead man's features were undisturbed by terror.

On the instant and without warning he had died. In a moment
of time he had gone down under the impact of that powerful blow.
He lay pitched forward on the earth, his arm extended, the maul
behind him.

This was not a tragedy of vengeance agreeable to the methods
of a ghost.

It was not the procedure of the baleful dead men in old housewife tales. They came gibbering in the darkness, and in terror their
victim went to his account, his face distorted and a fear stamped
in it that the relaxation of death could not decompose. These were
treasured and persisting details, indicatory and conclusive evidence, by which a supernatural agency could be distinguished.

Nor had any dead man in all the history of such supernal raids
ever looted the body of his victim!

His life they looted, but no one of them had ever gone into his
pocket. This fact, not to be omitted, should have given the tavern
keeper's wife some pause in her supernatural explanation of the
tragedy. But one has seen a judge with a trained legal mind do no
better when he was summing up the evidence on some theory of

guilt that had got into his head when the trial opened. And so the greatest writers on the law have warned us that circumstantial evidence has a way of pointing in the direction that one's mind has already taken; and to measure its values from that point of view. It was afternoon before Squire Randolph got at his hearing.

It pleased him to move always with due legal forms. The law was not to be hurried in his person. The dignity of Virginia was to be maintained. And he took a greater leisure by reason of that usurpation which the hasty *posse comitatus* had assumed.

He came smartly from the tavern in his gig.

The negro driver had enjoyed no idle morning. The horse glistened in a shiny coat that had been cleaned and rubbed down with a cloth; the gig washed and every buckle in the harness polished.

In his care for elegance Randolph was still a justice of the crown and must maintain its dignity of trappings.

It was an irreparable regret that he could not sit on his inquisitions in a powdered wig. He came briskly up the steps and through the crowd of people to the portico.

The whole county was assembled.

The puzzling mystery about the tragic event intrigued the world. The lawn before the manor house was crowded and men stood about the portico. The country had come in as it came in to the county seat on the first day of the circuit court.

It was a stage set as Randolph wished and he could not resist it. He opened his proceeding with a speech.

And but for the mannerisms of the man the speech would have been effective. It was on the danger of mob activities in a criminal matter. In such affairs the Commonwealth of Virginia alone could act. All violence was against the state. It was the state's concern.

No individual could assume that right.

If he usurped it, he thereby violated the very law that he was undertaking to maintain, and became a criminal like the man he hunted. A *posse comitatus* could not assemble at its pleasure, nor at the will of any private citizen. It must be called together by some officer of the law. It must have the state behind it.

And in this district he was that authority of the state. A crime was no private matter. It was no outrage that any individual could adjust or avenge, or any community of individuals. It was a violation of the law, and to be handled by the instrumentalities that the law set up.

This great basic fact was vital.

Whenever men took the law into their own hands all orderly government was ended. Respect for the peace and dignity of Virginia was a greater thing than the arrest of any fugitive. It were better for every criminal to escape than to break down the forms of law.

And in that tenor he roared and threatened.

He would appear before the judges, he would memorialize the governor. And he stamped the portico and gesticulated with his clenched hand.

And his speech, for all its extravagance of manner, had its effect.

He was verbose and pompous, with the vanity of birth about him. And his judicial functions were on him like a royal garment. He had got a smattering of law somewhere in his youth and he paraded the gleaning of those years. But he was a man of principle under this veneer of manner. He stood-for what he believed was justice with no care for what other men might think about it. And for his sincerity and courage he commanded every man's respect.

There was no doubt about this courage.

He would have barred the way against all the riders in the hills, with no thought of safety to himself.

The inquiry then got under way.

A table had been placed on the portico and Randolph sat down behind it. He sat like a king's governor as though on this autumn afternoon, before him, alone the whole matter of this mysterious murder was to be heard and ended. All the persons concerned in the affair were before him on the portico: Dix, the stranger from Maryland, the trapper, and my uncle Abner.

It was late when Abner had come in.

He had ridden down from the ridge of the mountains on one of the descending cattle paths and he had gone carefully over the orchard where the deed of violence had been accomplished. He stood now in the crowd, his hands behind him, his face inscrutable, looking down at Randolph. Calhoun Patterson sagged beyond the justice in a big split-bottomed chair, blear-eyed and shaken, disappearing now and then into the house to brace his nerves with liquor.

Randolph had no belief in the guilt of any other in this tragic affair except Calhoun. But he opened his inquiry with the heifer trader. He called him up, administered the oath— "the truth, the whole truth and nothing but the truth so help you God"—and began with Dix. He was in no pleasant humor with the man.

"Dix," he said, "you are in contempt of my authority. You raised a hue and cry in this affair, and for the price of a bastard farthing I would send you on to the circuit court."

He struck the table with his clenched hand.

"Your grandfather was a gentleman but you have crawled a long way down from him. I have little regard for your word even on oath, but I will hear you.

"Did you kill old Webster Patterson?"

"No," said Dix. "Why should I wish to kill him?"

Randolph roared at the reply.

"The devil take you!" he cried. "Do you turn about to question me! Well, sir, since you ask it, I will answer your infernal impudence. You might wish to kill him for the money in his pocket."

"I didn't know he had any money!" said Dix.

"What?" ejaculated Randolph. "You saw his cattle in the road and you know as well as any man in the hills that Webster Patterson's cattle do not go out of the pasture until he gets the money in his hand."

"I did not think about that," replied the witness.

"Eh!" said Randolph. "You didn't think about it! You are a scoundrel, Dix, if we are to believe the gossip, but you are not a fool; of course you thought about it."

There was a ripple of laughter in the crowd.

"Did you see anybody about the place when you came up?"

"No," said Dix. "I saw old Webster lying in the orchard. He looked like he was dead, and I got off my horse and carried him into the house. I didn't see anybody about. The cattle and the man who had bought them had gone on, they were out of sight over the rise of the road beyond the house."

Randolph was surprised at this reply for it put some of his conclusions out of joint.

"Did you see Calhoun?"

"No, I didn't see him. I didn't know he was about the place until after I carried old Webster into the house."

"When did you find Calhoun was there?"

"I saw him when I was carrying Webster up the steps. He was lying here on the portico, on the bench against the wall. I could not see him from the road or the orchard."

"And you thought Webster was alone when you came up."

"That's right," replied the witness. "I thought old Webster was alone. You see he lives here by himself."

Randolph shot his head forward at the reply. "Ah!" he said. "That puts another face on the thing! Let us look at this thing for a moment. You ride up. You find old Webster Patterson alone in the orchard. You know he has just sold his cattle for you have seen them being driven off by this purchaser from Maryland. You know Webster has the money from this sale. You see no other person about the place . . . these are evidential facts with a new importance."

He paused and sat back in his chair, as with a judicial gesture.

"In all our trials in the circuit courts one charged with a crime is presumed to be innocent, and the procedure cannot go forward upon an assumed hypothesis of guilt. But upon a preliminary hearing before a justice of the peace, such a hypothesis of guilt may be considered if it is agreeable to the facts.

"This is permissible upon the theory that the finding of the justice is not conclusive, and undertakes to fix neither the guilt nor the innocence of the accused.

"Now," and he turned suddenly on Dix. "Where, sir, did you get this pocketbook?"

The sudden drive disconcerted the witness and his face went white.

"It fell out of Webster's pocket when I picked him up."

"It fell out!" repeated Randolph. "Was it not in the inside pocket of the man's waistcoat? The waistcoat would be buttoned around it."

The witness hesitated. He saw the end toward which Randolph drove and he was disturbed.

"I unbuttoned his waistcoat," he answered. "I wanted to find out if he was dead, if his heart had stopped."

Randolph turned about in a decisive manner.

"Now, Dix," he said, "you might as well realize how this thing looks. A person, with no enviable reputation in the community, knows that an old man has just received a considerable sum of money. He finds him alone. He has every reason to believe that there is no one else about. He stops, ties up his horse to the fence, goes to the old man in the orchard, and there while engaging him in conversations manages to slip up behind him and strike him dead. Now what would be the next step? Obviously to search the body for money, and after he had got the money to carry the dead man into the house, on the pretension that he had found him murdered."

Randolph suddenly paused in this discourse, for a new idea seemed to strike him. He shot it like an arrow into Dix.

"Why didn't the assassin kill Calhoun when he found him on the portico?"

"He was drunk," replied Dix. "They didn't have to kill him."

"They!" roared Randolph. "You mean I."

Panic seized Dix. He turned toward Abner. My uncle did not speak and he made no gesture, but he looked Dix steadily in the face and something of his ebbing courage flowed back and steadied the shaken man.

"I mean," he said, "that whoever killed Webster was in no danger from Calhoun. He was sprawled out on the bench against the wall. I had a lot of trouble to rouse him, and then what he said to me showed that the man was maudlin drunk."

"What did he say?"

"Well," the witness continued, "he cursed when I tried to rouse him, and muttered and went on. I had a lot of trouble to make him understand what had happened, and when the thing did seem finally to filter into his mind he only cursed the more. He didn't give a fiddler's dam for Webster, he said. If Webster was dead it was the best news that he had ever heard. Let the devil keep him. And then he asked me if I had a bottle with me. He wanted another drink of liquor."

Abner had turned about and his steady gaze held Dix together. The man went on with some measure of control.

"I shook him and tried to get him up, but he only cursed on at me. He had always intended to kill Webster, he said. He had ridden over this day to kill him. If Webster was dead what more did anybody want? Webster had robbed him of his father's lands by a trick of words in the will. Did I know about the trick? He made some drunken gestures. He said that Webster was the damnedest scoundrel in the world. He robbed everybody. He even robbed the dead. The flat stones of the portico where we stood had been stolen from the grave mound of the ancient people on the mountain . . . did I know about the violation of that sepulcher, and how Webster's dying mother had warned him? And then he began to cry."

"To cry?" said Randolph.

"Yes," replied Dix, "he began to cry."

"From distress at his brother's death?"

"No," said Dix, "it was because I troubled him about it. It was because I came in to disturb him."

"So you found old Calhoun maudlin drunk?"

"Well, squire," Dix answered, "he was either awful drunk or he was shamming it."

Randolph received that reply with his former ejaculation.

"Ah!" he said. "Drunk or pretending to be drunk!"

But he reserved the point, as a lawyer takes an exception in a trial, and turned back to the salient feature of his inquiry.

"What did you do then?"

Dix was looking at my uncle, as though to keep his courage up.

"Abner knows what I did. I spread the news of the murder, picked up all the people I could find at hand and started after the stranger who had bought the cattle. You see if the man once crossed the line into Maryland, we could not bring him back. The law of Virginia don't run over the line."

"And it doesn't seem to run here either," thundered Randolph. "Why didn't you send for me?"

The witness' voice became apologetic.

"There was no time, squire," he continued. "We had to get the man back before he crossed the line. We were after him when Abner stopped us."

Randolph shot in a comment with a gesture of his clenched hand to make it vivid.

"And it was a piece of blessed luck for you," he snapped. "If you had gone on, I would have carted the whole bevy of you to the penitentiary. It was God's providence that you met up with Abner."

The man's head went down and his voice stuttered a little in his sentence.

"We didn't think about that until Abner explained it to us. You see, squire, everything pointed toward this man. That's the way it looked to me, and that's the way it looked to everybody else."

"Except Abner," said Randolph.

The man wavered.

"I don't know about Abner. He stopped us, and he turned the thing on me with the twist of a word; and it scared me. I own up to it. I don't know what Abner thinks."

"But you know what he said?"

"Yes, he said that courage was the greatest thing in the world, and to come back and face the law . . . and here I am."

The crowd about the portico turned toward my uncle. But he remained silent and Randolph went on with his interrogation.

"So Abner broke up your little party, eh?"

"Well, squire," continued Dix, "he made the thing look first one way and then the other, and he promised the men to bring this stranger back himself."

He stopped and looked over the crowd, and some steps behind my uncle he marked the big-shouldered man from Maryland.

"There he is!" he said.

Everybody turned to look. But the stranger was not disturbed by the scrutiny. He stood with his great shoulders thrown forward and his arms folded across his chest as though he disregarded and defied the world. But like my uncle he was silent and for the moment Randolph did not address him. He returned to Dix.

"How was Abner to bring him back? He had no more authority than your illegal posse to send out a warrant."

"He sent me on with a message."

"What sort of message?"

"Well, squire," said Dix, "it didn't seem like much of a message. He said to tell the man what had happened, and to ask him to come back to your hearing, and to add that he didn't seem to be a coward."

Randolph moved the papers before him, idly on the table. He saw what a man like Dix could never see: the virtue in the last words of that message; the challenge to one's manhood in it; the compelling force of it beyond any mere legal writ. No man of courage could go on after such a message to him.

And the consideration moved Randolph's suspicion closer up to Dix.

He put it into his question.

"What made you so certain that this stranger had killed Webster Patterson?"

Dix shifted his body from one foot to the other.

"Everything looked that way, as I told you a while ago," he began in a low uneven voice. "I had seen the cattle in the road, and the old man going into the orchard, and then when I finally came up, I found him murdered and robbed. It must have been done while I was coming up. There wasn't much time, not more than half an hour at the furthest. Nobody else could have come in, or I would have seen him.

"Besides, it looked like the work of a big man. Webster was killed with the maul, for it lay there behind him, a big hickory maul with an iron band around it. The whole back of his head was crushed in. It was a terrific blow. And besides the body was robbed. That would be the man's motive, of course. I thought he had paid Webster for the cattle and then followed him out into the orchard, killed him and taken the money back."

"That made a case against the stranger?" said Randolph.

"Yes."

Randolph struck the table suddenly with his open hand.

"Well," he said, "does it not make a better case against you?"

He drove on after his manner with the thing he had in mind.

"Listen to me, if you please. You knew that the cattle had been sold for you saw them being driven away. You knew that Webster Patterson had received the money for you knew the rigid rule from which he never departed, to get the cash in his hand. You knew he lived alone, and so there would be no servants and no farm hands about. And you had further a weighty and significant advantage over the cattle buyer. You would have at hand, convenient and designated, another person who could be accused of the crime. Here in time, place, opportunity, conduct and motive was another upon whom the onus of the murder could be placed. Does it not—"

And he thundered the concluding words at Dix. "Does it not, sir, make a better case for the grand jury against you?"

The man's face went slack. Panic seized him. He saw again what he had seen when Abner stopped him in the road. He did not reply and Randolph continued.

"And what does the looting of the body prove? Does your explanation exclude this hypothesis? Is it not equally agreeable to a theory of your guilt? The money for the cattle was in old Webster's pocket when he went into the orchard and it was gone when you carried the body back."

It was at this point that the big stranger from Maryland suddenly interrupted the proceeding.

"You are mistaken, sir," he said, addressing Randolph. "The money was not in Webster Patterson's pocket when he went into the orchard."

The words were like an explosive cartridge dropped onto the portico among the people. Everybody turned in amazement toward the speaker.

Randolph turned on him, but he remained undisturbed.

The first query of the justice was not the one that had occurred to anybody else.

"Why are you concerned to clear Dix?"

"The devil can take Dix," replied the man. "It's the truth I'm after."

"And it's the truth I am after," continued Randolph. "But if Dix goes free the suspicion for this murder moves up to you."

"Let it move where it pleases," replied the man, for he was undisturbed. "That's the truth about it."

The defiance in the stranger hardened Randolph. "Then you didn't, in fact, pay Webster Patterson for the cattle."

"Yes, I paid him."

"In money?"

"Yes."

"How much money?"

"I bought the cattle by the head," the man replied. "There were sixty steers; I paid him three thousand dollars."

"Where was Webster Patterson when you paid him?"

"He was in the kitchen. I looked at the cattle early. Patterson was with me. He rode over the pasture and I walked. After I bought the cattle we turned them into the road. I left my dogs to hold them and came around by the barn to the kitchen to give the man his money."

Randolph interrupted with a collateral question.

"Did you see Calhoun Patterson or anyone else about the place?"

"No," replied the man, "there was nobody around that I saw. But I didn't go to the front of the house. I was not on this portico."

Randolph came then to the vital point. "Do you know where
the money is?"

"No," replied the man, "I don't know where it is."

There was a common movement of surprise about the crowd.

"What!" cried Randolph. "You don't know where it is after all
this talk?"

But the stranger was not to be jostled out of his equanimity.

"How could I know where the money is?" he went on. "This
man here"—and he turned toward Abner— "sent me word last night
that Webster Patterson had been killed and robbed, and asked me
to come back to the hearing and tell what I knew about it. I didn't
kill him and rob him and so I don't know where the money is. But
I know where it was."

Randolph executed a derisive gesture, flinging out his fingers.

"You make a nice distinction in your grammar."

"I make the distinction of the truth in it," replied the stranger.
"And I intend to stick to that. This man Patterson went out of the
kitchen when I went out, and closed the door. He went on toward
the orchard while I returned past the stable to the cattle, and so I
know he did not have the money in his pocket."

"Where was it then?" cried Randolph.

"Now I can answer that," said the witness. "I can tell you where
it was. I counted out the money, to Patterson, on the kitchen table.
He thumbed it over to see that it was right and to make sure that
every bill was the issue of a solvent bank. Then he folded it up and
put it into the bottom of the clock. The clock was on the mantelpiece over the kitchen fireplace. It had a little door at the bottom.
He unlocked this door with a key that he took out of his pocketbook—you have it before you on the table—then he locked the door,
put the key in the pocketbook, put the pocketbook back into the
inside pocket of his waistcoat, and went out with me."

The mystery was reaching its solution.

If Webster Patterson had been paid for the cattle and the money
had not been taken, then robbery was not the motive for the murder and this man, with Dix, was plainly clear of suspicion of it.
The case against them turned on this vital point. Evidently this

stranger could be moved to murder only with the intent to take back what he had paid.

And Dix could have no motive but gain if he were the criminal agent.

The people waited, almost without a sound, until Randolph got the key, and then they went with him through the house into the kitchen, leaving old Calhoun Patterson in his chair alone on the portico.

The crowd of people moved with Randolph, as I have said. My uncle went in with him and stood before the mantelpiece while the justice fitted the key into the lock. Abner looked carefully at the door and the lock.

It was a tense moment, for on the truth or falsehood of this stranger's statement the whole case against the two men turned.

It was a dramatic moment, as I have written, and Randolph in it made as large a dramatic gesture as he could.

He moved with a ponderous deliberation; put up his hand and paused, before he turned the key. Then he gave the key a twist and flung the door back open.

The clock was empty!

He stood an instant, unmoving, while the tense interest ebbed. And then he turned away with an oath.

"By the eternal!" he cried, "there is some tomfoolery about all this!"

He strode through the crowd and sat down at his table.

Was there, perhaps, some understanding between these two suspected men? Had they perhaps acted together in it on some common plan?

It was possible to imagine.

Dix traded, in his small way, over the mountains to Maryland. Who could say what questionable persons he had come to know about the taverns, or what sort of plot to rob old Webster Patterson he might conjure up? And this cattle buyer with his dogs might be any sort of creature, good or evil, except that it was evident to all, as it had been evident to Abner, that he was not a coward.

These reflections were evident to the people in attendance on the hearing as they were evident to Randolph.

But one thing disturbed him.

Why should this stranger break into his inquisition in order merely, in its effect, to direct a conclusive suspicion against himself? Why should he speak out here, compelled by no interrogation, in order to clear Dix and set his own feet in the dock?

Randolph turned on the man, with a bitter face.

"I understand now," he said. "Your nice discrimination is the *is* and *was*. You knew where the money was, but you have no idea where it is. Well, sir, I am beginning to have a very definite idea where it is. This thing begins to look like your work. Dix may be right. His illegal posse may have been on the right track."

He glared over the people at the man.

"I have a notion," he roared, "to close this hearing, release Dix and hold you for the grand jury. . . . You killed old Webster Patterson!"

He shot his accusing finger at the man like a threatening weapon.

He did not believe what he said. He had another theory.

The people took it for his judicial sentence.

And one among these people, who looked on, was troubled and overcome by it. He stood beside Abner as in the shadow of a great rock. Courage was not a gift from God in him, and it was with a great effort that he spoke. But he did speak, and his words brought every man on the portico facing about to hear him.

"He didn't kill him!" he said.

Randolph turned heavily in the chair.

"What!" The menace in his voice seemed to swing like a moved weapon toward the speaker.

But the little trapper near my uncle did not go on. He stood with a white face, his finger pointed toward the stranger, as though those words exhausted in him the conquest of his fear. He had come down from the summit of the mountain, after Abner, and he had stood about silent while the inquiry advanced; always near my uncle, as though that dominant figure kept up the spirit in him.

Randolph sat back in his chair and looked steadily at the man. "How do you know that?"

The little trapper did not reply. He seemed confused and troubled.

Randolph went on:

"Did you know this man?" and he indicated the big stranger who stood apparently at his ease and unconcerned.

The trapper moved a little closer to my uncle's elbow. "No," he said.

"Did you ever see him before?"

"No.

"Were you here about this place when old Webster Patterson was killed?"

"No.

Randolph's temper was getting on its feet and out of hand.

"By the eternal," he cried, "you are well fitted out with negatives for a gentleman who breaks in to decide a case. The whole kit of you seem to travel in a fog. I begin to believe that you are all tarred with the same stick, and that there is not a word of truth among you."

And again he pounded on the table.

"I will have no more of these accursed interruptions by you. I am going to begin this hearing at the point where I think its solution lies."

He turned toward old Calhoun Patterson. That creature sat, as I have written, in a great split-bottomed chair beyond the table. He was in liquor, and apparently without concern about what happened.

Randolph smoothed out his waistcoat, arranged the articles on his table and assumed his imperial calm. His manner now was that of a judge who began anew with a judicial hearing. He rapped for order. And then he put old Calhoun under oath.

"You were in this house with the decedent, Webster Patterson, on the day of his death?"

"Yes," replied Calhoun.

"You were alone here with your brother?"

"He was only my half brother," said Calhoun. "My mother was a lady!"

"That has nothing to do with it," interrupted Randolph.

"Yes, it has," said Calhoun.

The liquor in him stimulated the witness to a stubborn unconcern.

"It's got everything to do with it. If my father had not married, for his second wife, that octoroon woman from Louisiana, Webster wouldn't have been here. The courts could have annulled the marriage, but there was Webster and, after my father died, Webster rebuilt his house and brought the old mulatto in. He was a third black himself—Webster was—inside and outside. . . . He got my inheritance by a trick. Do you know about the trick?"

Randolph raised his hand and made an impatient gesture.

"I am not concerned about that," he said.

"Well, I'm concerned about it," continued Calhoun. "I've always been concerned about it. When my father was dying Webster got him to make a will and leave all his property to him first, and then to me. The courts said that meant Webster took everything as long as he lived. Do you see the trick in it?"

"I see the motive in it," replied Randolph, "for you to kill your brother."

"My half brother," corrected Calhoun. "My mother was a lady!"

"Well, your half brother, then," said Randolph. "You wanted to kill him, didn't you?"

"Of course I wanted to kill him," replied Calhoun. "Everybody knows that. And I would have killed him long ago, if the prophecy of that old octoroon woman hadn't fooled me. I wanted to see if it was going to turn out the way she said it would."

"It's more likely," said the justice, "that Webster made it up to toil you along. Was he afraid of you?"

"Yes, he was," replied Calhoun. "He was damnably afraid of me . . . except when I was drunk."

"And you were drunk on the day Webster was killed?"

"Of course I was drunk," replied Calhoun. "Drunk as a lord. Didn't I tell you that?"

"And so Webster wasn't afraid of you on that day, and you were able to slip up behind him with the maul."

Old Calhoun did not reply. He got up unsteadily and went into the house for a drink of liquor.

It was at this moment, while the man was about in the house, that the third of these inexplicable interruptions was injected into the hearing.

It was the stranger from Maryland who spoke:

"He couldn't have slipped up behind him with the maul, because this man Patterson had the maul on his shoulder when he went into the orchard. He said that he had set out a lot of young apple trees with a stake to hold them. There had been a season of wind, and he was going into the orchard to tighten the stakes."

Randolph turned in the chair. I think he would have exploded at this point if Abner had not come into the thing.

He stooped over the table and called the attention of the justice to the key with which the clock door had been unlocked.

"Randolph," he said, "this is not the key to the clock. This is a larger key filed down. It has been made to fit the lock, but it is not the original key to it. You can see the marks of the file."

The thing as Abner put it was clearly true. One could see how the larger key had been shaped down with a file. And this fact brought in a further probability. If the original key was in the possession of some unknown person, then the money might have been taken by someone other than these suspected men.

Randolph seized on this new clue until he could get his wits together.

"Calhoun," he said when the witness came out from his liquor, "is there another key to the clock?"

"Yes," replied the man, "there's another key. Webster made that key you have on your table. But the clock belonged to my mother, and I have the right key."

He fumbled in his pocket and produced the key; then he went over and sat down in his chair.

And once again on this afternoon Randolph launched a criminal charge against his witness—and for once he reached the mark.

"It was you, then, who took the money out of the clock."

"Well, Randolph," replied the man, "it was my money, wasn't it? I didn't steal it. I took it out of the clock last night after Webster was dead. And after Webster was dead, according to my father's will, everything came to me."

The very success of Randolph's question, at a venture, put him for a moment out of balance.

"Why didn't you tell me this?"

"You didn't ask me," replied Calhoun.

"Well," said the justice, "I am going to ask you some things now. You rode here on this day of Webster Patterson's death with the premeditated intent to kill him?"

"Yes, I did," said Calhoun.

"And you did kill him!"

"Well," replied Calhoun, "you see I got drunk."

"Then you killed him when you were drunk?"

"Now, Randolph," replied Calhoun, "how do I know what I did when I was drunk?"

There was a bit of smothered laughter in the crowd outside. But Randolph drove straight on with his query. "A man may do a thing when he's drunk and not remember it when he is sober; isn't that true?"

"Of course it's true," said Calhoun. "I've done all kinds of things when I was drunk, that I didn't remember. I went out one night and shot a dog when I was drunk and the next day when I saw the dead dog in the yard I wondered who had killed it. . . . But you see," he added, "I had intended all along to kill that dog."

"Precisely," said Randolph, "and all along—as you put it—you had intended to kill Webster."

Old Calhoun looked about in a sort of perplexity.

"If I hadn't got drunk I would know what happened."

"I know what happened," said Randolph. "The intent to kill Webster was stamped on your subconscious mind and you acted on that intent when you were drunk. It could have been you only. There was nothing else to kill Webster."

Abner spoke then.

"There was something else to kill him!"

Randolph turned sharply behind his table.

"What do you mean, Abner?"

"I was thinking," replied my uncle, "about what Calhoun said a while ago. He indicated in that answer that although he had formed the purpose to kill Webster Patterson and the fixed intent, he nevertheless waited for another agency to kill him. What was that agency? May I inquire a moment of the witness?"

"Certainly," said Randolph. "We are here to arrive at the truth."

And he sat back in his chair, in a large judicial calm, as though it embraced the world.

"Calhoun," said Abner, "you intended to kill Webster Patterson years ago. Why did you wait?"

"I told you," replied the witness. "I waited to see what was going to happen to him."

"Was he in danger?"

"I don't know," said Calhoun. "The old octoroon woman said he was."

"And you believed he was?"

"I hoped he was," replied the witness. "I hoped something would kill him."

Abner made no comment on that reply. He turned from Calhoun and addressed Randolph as though he were the highest dignitary in Virginia.

"Our justices," he said, "in these inquisitions are allowed a latitude of inquiry not permitted to the circuit courts. They are not to be hampered by the narrow rules of evidence. They may search in every direction for the truth. It is a wise and complimentary provision of our law, for it will permit us here to go into a collateral matter that a more technical tribunal, concerned with the limitations of procedure, might deny us."

The vague irony in the manner and the stilted language were lost on Randolph. He saw only the tribute to the patriarchal conception of his office, and he visibly expanded with the subtle praise.

Abner turned back to the witness, and with a deft query drew out the substance of the thing upon which Calhoun Patterson had depended. It was, in brief, the legend on which the tavern keeper's wife had based her story.

When Webster Patterson came to repair the manor which he had taken by the deed, after the fire, he found it necessary to replace the tile on the portico. The tile had crumbled and he wished to lay the floor with flags. The best available flat stone paved the tomb of the ancient dead people on the mountains.

He cut away into the mound and brought down the stone.

His mother, the old octoroon woman, when she knew what he was about, cried out from her chair beside the fire.

Webster was mad to violate this sepulcher!

The burial places of these ancient people were always sealed up with a curse. One broke into them at the hazard of that curse. A doom would follow—death, unforeseen, awful and violent would overtake him. . . . He was as good as dead!

And she kneaded her thin yellow hands, and wailed in her padded chair beside the fire.

She was old, paralytic, at the end of life, and no persuasive argument could silence her. Her mother, her grandmother could see far when they were dying and she could see!

But Webster went on disregarding what he called a superstition. And the old woman finally fell silent. A little later she went out of life.

And as she died she cried out that she saw a huge devil issue from the violated tomb, leap down in great bounds as on an iron hoof, slay Webster with a single blow, and disappear out of sight and hearing under the water of the river!

The legend was vaguely known to the crowd about the portico, and with time it had been colored and confused. But it accurately remained in the memory of Calhoun Patterson.

It was clear how the half-drunken witness depended on the thing, as an agency of vengeance in his behalf, for he repeated it precisely to the word.

The justice of the peace interrupted.

He ignored the witness and addressed my uncle.

"I'm afraid, Abner," he said, "that a theory of defense, here, cannot be built up around old wives' tales. A curse cannot call down a destroying agency out of the supernatural."

My uncle seemed to regard the justice as a man in wonder.

"Randolph," he said in his deep level voice, "you are a deacon in the church and say things like that! The Scriptures are crowded with examples. . . . Have your forgotten the fire from heaven that destroyed the priests of Baal?"

"But the miracle," said Randolph, "was at the invocation of a prophet. Destroying demons do not issue out of tombs."

"And again," replied my uncle, "you forget the Scriptures. The demon in the country of the Gadarenes, according to Saint Mark, not only came out of the tombs, but he was so terrible that no chain could bind him."

His voice moved into a firmer note.

"The blow that killed Webster Patterson was terrific. The crushing power of it was beyond any human hand, utterly beyond the liquor-enfeebled strength of old Calhoun Patterson. Only a demon from a tomb . . . only a demon like that one in the Gospel of Saint Mark with the Samson strength to pluck chains asunder could have dealt it. . . . Come with me, Randolph, and I will show you the evidence of that destroying agency. I will show you the very marks in the baked earth where this avenging thing from the tomb of the ancient people on the mountain landed as with an iron hoof as it leaped down on old Webster Patterson."

There was a commanding dignity in my uncle's voice.

And a sort of vague fear fell on the folk about the portico.

They went into the orchard—the justice, my uncle Abner and the crowd of people from the countryside.

A stake indicated the point at which the body had been found.

There was no mark about the vicinity of this stake. But some dozen paces farther up in a direct line toward the mountain the baked earth was ripped as with the horn of an anvil; and on a line with this, ten paces below the dead man where the orchard touched the road above the river, it was thus ripped again.

"Look, Randolph," cried my uncle, "how this avenging agency from the violated tomb landed on its awful hoof, smote Webster Patterson from the air as it winged over him, landed again at this point below, and with a final leap, that no human creature could have equaled, passed out of sight and hearing into the great bosom of the river. Shall you say—shall you say, sir, that the old octoroon woman dying by the fire did not foresee in every detail the mysterious avenging agency that ejected Webster Patterson out of life!"

And for once the awe of something beyond all human knowledge put the imperious manner of Randolph out of court.

In the presence of it he was simple and direct.

He dismissed his wits, exonerated the suspected persons and arose.

He made no comment.

But on the way to his gig he took my uncle by the arm and walked apart with him.

"Abner," he said, "what is the meaning of this mysterious thing?"

"I will tell you the facts," replied my uncle, "and you can interpret the meaning as you please.

"When old Webster Patterson ravaged the burial mount he left one of the flat stones set up over the opening to the tomb. The little trapper on the morning of the tragedy moved it, from curiosity, in order to look in. The stone slipped out of his hands, rolled down the slope of the meadow, gaining momentum on the way. It passed over the bench of the mountain, down the long steep incline of the pasture, behind the orchard, struck Webster Patterson, and plunged into the river."

Randolph made a great gesture.

"An accident!" he cried. "It was an accident!"

"Now that," replied my uncle Abner, "will depend on how you are willing to regard it. . . . It is a world of mystery!"

And so it came about that because the land possessed one man of sound common sense, with the ability to put courage into wavering persons, and the force to compel them to face the thing they feared, four men, innocent of murder, were set free, and the mystery of an inexplicable death was cleared up.

COACHWHIP PUBLICATIONS

COACHWHIPBOOKS.COM

ALSO AVAILABLE

COACHWHIPBOOKS.COM

NOVEMBER JOE

DETECTIVE OF THE WOODS

H. HESKETH-PRICHARD

NOVEMBER JOE

ISBN 1-61646-013-X

ALSO AVAILABLE

CoachwhipBooks.com

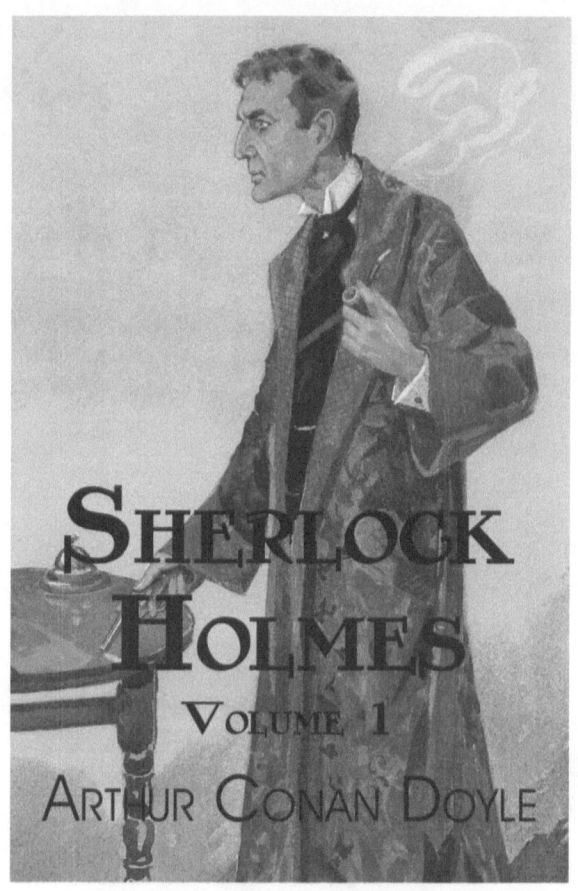

SHERLOCK HOLMES

Volume 1: ISBN 1-61646-006-7

Volume 2: ISBN 1-61646-007-5

Volume 3: ISBN 1-61646-008-3

ALSO AVAILABLE

COACHWHIPBOOKS.COM

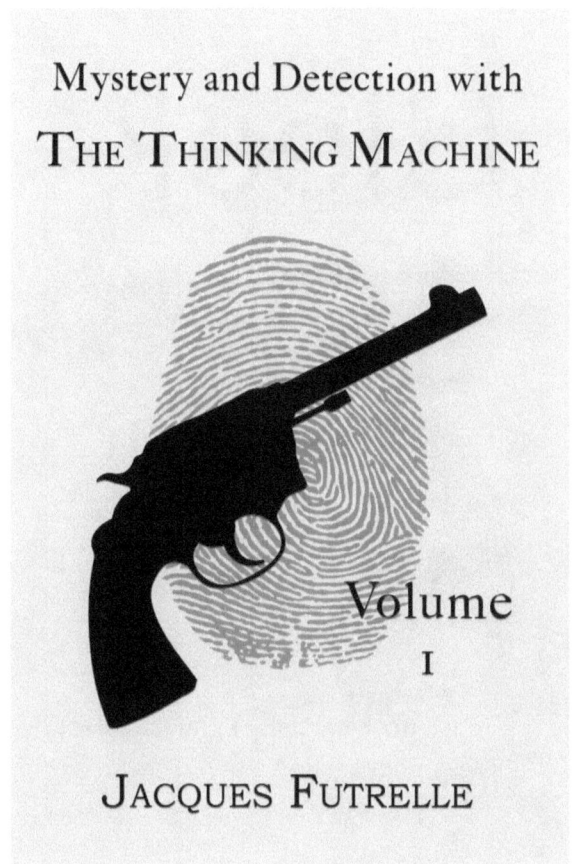

Mystery and Detection with

THE THINKING MACHINE

Volume

I

JACQUES FUTRELLE

THE THINKING MACHINE

Volume 1: ISBN 1-930585-70-5

Volume 2: ISBN 1-930585-71-3

ALSO AVAILABLE

COACHWHIPBOOKS.COM

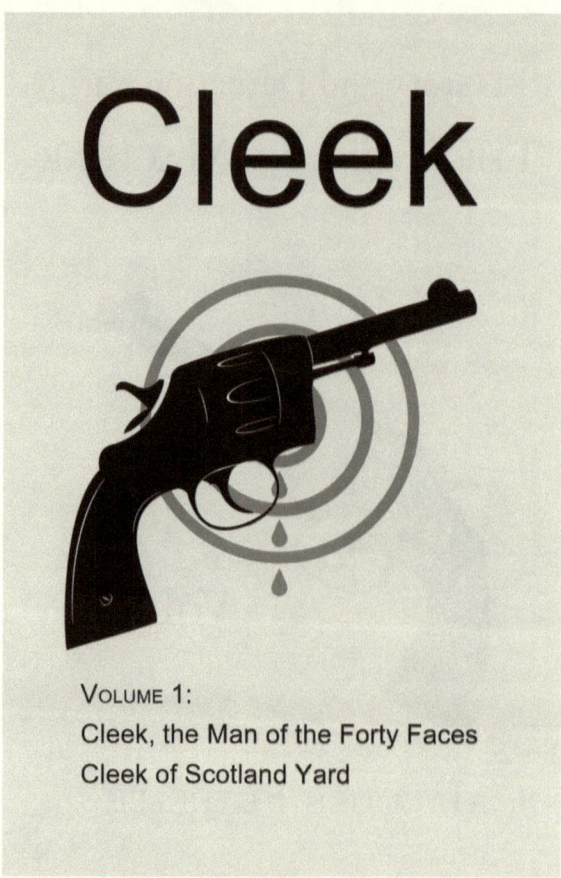

Cleek

VOLUME 1:
Cleek, the Man of the Forty Faces
Cleek of Scotland Yard

CLEEK

Volume 1: ISBN 1-930585-97-7
Volume 2: ISBN 1-930585-98-5
Volume 3: ISBN 1-930585-99-3

ALSO AVAILABLE

COACHWHIPBOOKS.COM

Crime and Adventure

with

A. J. Raffles,

Gentleman Thief

ERNEST WILLIAM HORNUNG

A. J. RAFFLES,
GENTLEMAN THIEF

ISBN 1-930585-68-3

ALSO AVAILABLE
COACHWHIPBOOKS.COM

The
Dupin Mysteries
and Other Tales of Ratiocination

EDGAR ALLAN POE

EDGAR ALLAN POE`S
THE DUPIN MYSTERIES

ISBN 1-930585-69-1

Also Available

CoachwhipBooks.com

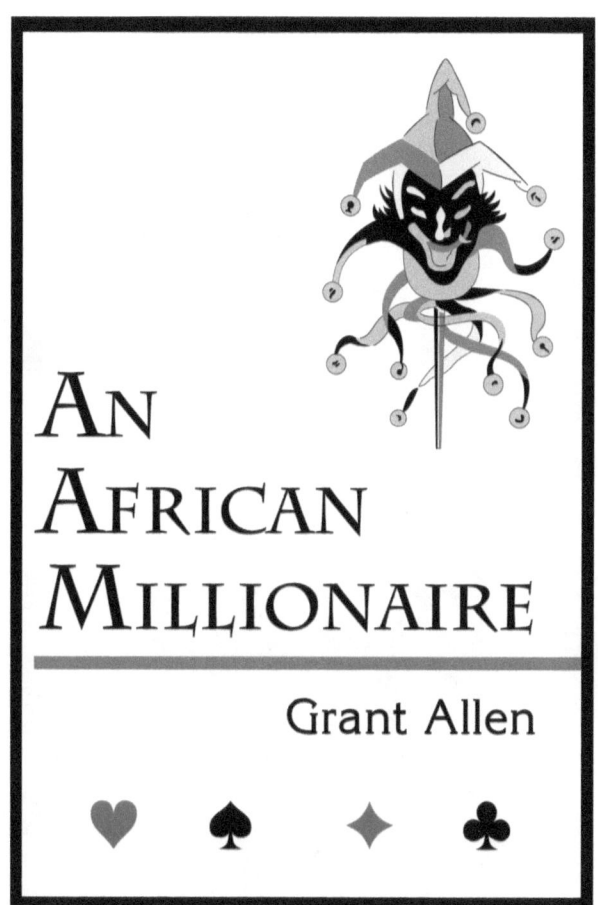

An African Millionaire

Grant Allen

An African Millionaire

ISBN 1-61646-014-8

ALSO AVAILABLE

COACHWHIPBOOKS.COM

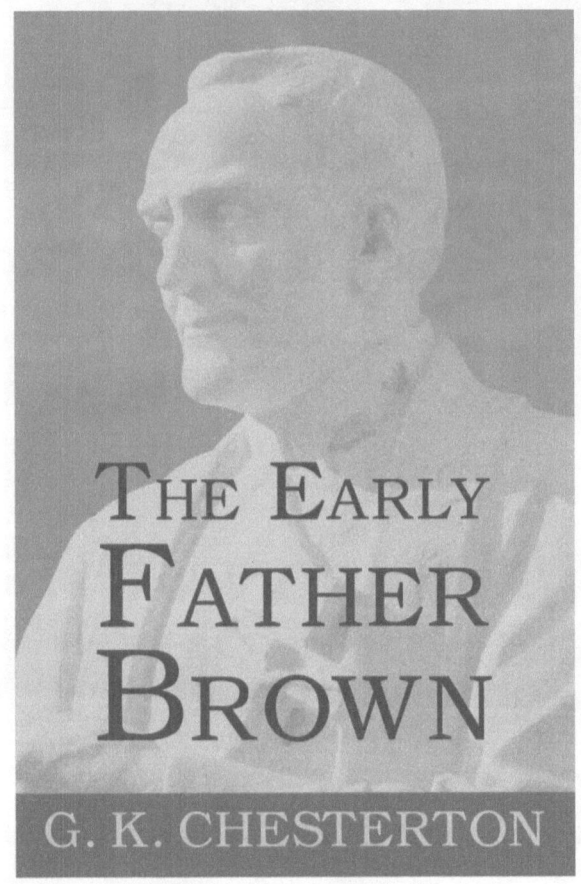

THE EARLY FATHER BROWN

ISBN 1-61646-012-1

ALSO AVAILABLE

COACHWHIPBOOKS.COM

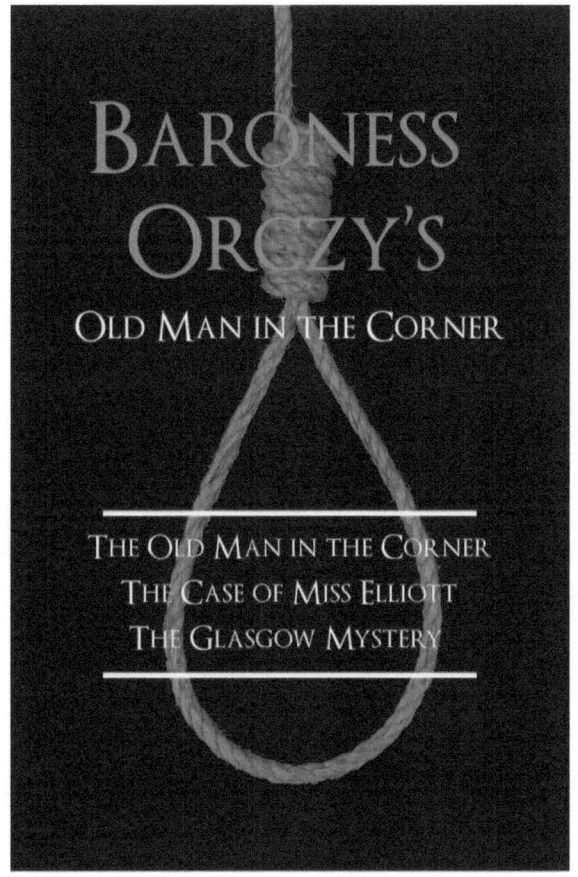

BARONESS ORCZY`S OLD MAN IN THE CORNER

ISBN 1-61646-015-6

www.ingramcontent.com/pod-product-compliance
Lightning Source LLC
Chambersburg PA
CBHW032233010726
47494CB00002B/480